DESPERATE MEMORIES

STELLA MACLEAN

Cataloguing and Publication information is available from The Canadian ISBN Service System, Library and Archives Canada.

Title: Desperate Memories

Identifiers:

ISBN: Print 13-978-0-9878295-4-2.

Digital 978-0-9878295-7-3

Formatting Services: Sweet' N Spicy Designs

Cover Design: https://www.hellhagproductions.com

PROLOGUE

The snap of gunfire cut the air. Robyn McGill leapt back, slamming her shoulder into the stern rail of the sailboat. Fear choked the breath from her lungs as she slid into the safety of the cockpit.

Her movements were slowed by a sense of disbelief as she edged along the roughened, fiberglass decking. With the light of the companionway guiding her, she crawled toward the safety of the cabin until her fingers bumped against cold metal. She gripped the rounded, deadly shape of a gun.

Panic pulsed through her, as if driven by a giant bellows, penetrating every part of her being. This couldn't be happening to her. Not here. Not now.

She sensed a sudden movement near the bow of the boat.

"Nathan? Peter?" Robyn's words joined the gray mist floating around her as she grabbed the boat's wheel and pulled herself to her feet.

Her eyes scanned the forward deck. The only sound was the lap, lap, lap of the frigid Atlantic water against the hull, and the occasional slap of a sail in the fog-shrouded stillness. Silence, like a malevolent force, clung to everything.

She needed to talk to Nathan, to feel her fiancé's arms around her, to be reassured she had only dreamed——

There! *Another movement beyond the cabin door near the foresail.* "Nathan," *she cried, her breath leaving a trail of mist in the cool night air.*

Silence.

Terror stiffened her shoulders, making her heart smash into her ribs.

Robyn slid down the companionway to the cabin below. Her gaze swept the space. Gleaming teak and the smooth, rounded surfaces of the cabin's interior were awash in the muted light offered by brass sconces.

In the comfort of the luxurious quarters below deck, Robyn could almost believe that nothing was wrong. She walked toward the bow of the boat, checking each space as she went: the head, silent and immaculate; the mirrored hanging locker, displaying a full-length image of a woman whose eyes radiated fear as they peered back at her. And finally, the forward cabin with its rich, burgundy duvet and shimmering brass lamps.

A silver framed photo of her brother, Peter, holding a prized racing trophy was displayed in a stationary frame attached to the table. His insulated storm jacket lay on the bed next to his wallet and keys. Everything was just as it should be. Robyn sobbed in relief.

She knew where the men in her life were and what they were doing: playing cards in the cabin at the stern of the boat. She raced back, through the main cabin, and flung open the door to the aft suite. "You guys had me scared to death!"

Her hands clutched the door. The graphic violence of the room yanked the air from her lungs. Pictures dangled crookedly from the walls. The locker door clung to the wall by a single hinge. The mattress of the queen-sized bed lay disemboweled, bleeding white foam through huge tears in the quilted fabric.

"Oh, My God!" Robyn sobbed as she covered her mouth to block a scream, her fingers cold and sticky against her lips.

Slowly, she lifted her hands from her face. Half-dried blood covered her palms and traced bizarre patterns up the length of her quivering fingers.

A bloodcurdling scream tore from her lips.

The ringing of a phone filled the air, wrenching her awake and away from the painful nightmare. Force of habit had Robyn clutching the phone before it stopped ringing. "Yes."

"Dr. McGill?"

"Yes."

"It's the Emergency Room calling. There's been a six-car pileup, and we need all the help we can get."

Robyn groped in the darkness for the bedside lamp and turned it on, flooding the room with light. "I'll be right there," she muttered while a ghostlike dream faded into the night.

Dropping the phone back into its cradle, she slumped against the pillows. Try as she might, she couldn't bring the dream back from its hiding place. All that remained was an overwhelming sense of guilt that she was somehow responsible for what happened. A guilt that years of therapy could not erase.

What had she done that was so awful as to cause this recurring nightmare? It had to have some basis in reality. She'd awakened the same way for the past two nights, to the same nightmare that had plagued her for three years.

Was it only a disturbing nightmare? Born of her imagination and all her unanswered questions? A terrible dream of no real importance, with no basis in reality?

Robyn hoped so, but didn't know anymore.

She threw back the bedclothes and scuffed down the hall to the bathroom. Not wanting to wake her ten-year-old nephew, Jason, who slept soundly in his room, Robyn eased the door closed and turned on the light.

Her eyes ached as light flooded over her. Squinting into the mirror, she rubbed a damp facecloth over her heated skin. Worry lines marred her expression, making the anxiety in her eyes stand out against her pallid skin.

Once again she was gripped by an unsettling sense of foreboding. While she waited for the confusing feelings to fade away as they always did, she shoved her tear-matted hair from her forehead and wished with all her heart that the nightmare would just go away. And stay away.

Her fingers trembled against her pale lips. Her throat ached, her head pounded in rhythm with her heart. More than anything in the world, Robyn prayed she'd feel safe again.

Maybe it was too late.

Maybe it had always been too late....

CHAPTER ONE

The smell of salt water clung to her nostrils as Doctor Robyn McGill climbed the passenger ramp onto the ferry. After last night in the Emergency Room, she welcomed the pin pricks of chilled air that told her she was awake and alive.

Last night a little boy had died despite all she'd done to save him. She could still feel the way his little sister had wrapped her arms around Robyn's neck, her sobs mingling with Robyn's distress at the senseless loss of life.

Yet, as much as last night had been horribly difficult, helping people who needed her was why she'd chosen her career. Being able to save lives made her life complete. She'd had never – not for one moment – regretted her career choice.

But the past three years and the demands of her medical practice, as well as adjustments and loss in her personal life had reduced her social life to the occasional dinner out with colleagues. She was aware of her hermit tendencies and as her mother said, she knew she needed to start moving her life forward from the deadly accident that had taken her brother and her fiancé from her.

She stared out across the open deck of the ferry toward the motley collection of bird-watchers, and wondered what in heaven's name had ever made her think that getting on a ferry today was a good idea.

Her psychiatrist had thought that facing her fear of water would help her, but she wasn't convinced. Despite her trepidation, she was headed toward Grand Island, off the coast of Maine, to go bird watching as a way to honor the memory of her brother, Peter. She was traveling with a group of friends she hadn't had a lot of time for lately.

She liked her creature comforts and wasn't sure she wanted to shiver away the hours on some fog-soaked patch of shoreline while waiting for a stray owl to appear. But she agreed with her shrink that she needed to reconnect to her friends, to the people she used to enjoy spending time with and who had been there for her when she needed them.

Though she was surrounded by familiar people once they'd arrived at the ferry terminal Robyn couldn't shake the feeling that someone was watching her. She scanned the faces of the passengers moving about the deck, chatting in small groups.

No one met her assessing gaze.

Exhaustion was playing tricks on her mind. She rubbed her forehead trying to push away a grinding headache behind her eyes that made her neck tight.

The shudder, created by the powerful surge of the ferry easing away from the dock, vibrated through Robyn with the jarring intensity of a tuning fork. Her fear of open water assailed her and foreboding ran cold and shapeless along her shoulders.

"I'm glad you decided to come with us," Lisa Wade said,

against the force of the cold breeze that had them both wrapping their down-filled vests closer to their bodies.

Still fearful of the ferry ride, she hadn't made up her mind to go until late last night. "Me too." As much as she might dread the thought of a ferry ride, she was glad to have a chance to spend time with her best friend. She and Lisa had a lot of catching up to do.

Robyn smiled at Lisa as she moved into an area free of the breeze from the bow of the ferry. She tucked her chin into her collar.

Lisa Wade, with her model-perfect body and pencil-straight blond hair, attracted the admiring glances of every man she passed. In contrast, Robyn looked like a Panda bear with her less-than-perfect body beneath a vest she'd bought in a rushed trip to the Portland Mall.

Robyn was the complete opposite of Lisa in all the female ways that counted. Lisa collected men like credit cards, to be maxed out and discarded, while Robyn had only ever loved one man, Nathan Green, who had died in a sailboat accident along with her brother. There had been a time in their relationship when Robyn and Lisa's friendship had been put to the testall – over Nathan. But that was a long time ago, and they were different people now.

"I'm freezing. Let's get a cup of coffee. At least our fingers will be warm," Robyn suggested, glancing around the empty deck as passengers decided it was too chilly for them. All that remained was a small group of stoic bird-watchers who huddled together, their binoculars pointed toward a fog-shrouded rocky outcropping off the starboard side of the vessel.

"There's probably some poor misguided tern sitting on the shore over there, totally unaware of all the attention," Lisa said, closing the steel door to the interior of the ship as she followed Robyn into the inviting warmth of the tiny canteen. The air had a stuffy sweetness with the aroma of coffee competing with the smell of damp wool jackets.

They managed to nab the last two stools at the counter and sank gratefully into the black vinyl-covered seats. The undulating movement of the ferry jostled the occupants of the stools against one another as the deck rose with each swell of the incoming tide.

"Wish I'd brought my mitts." Robyn blew on her fingers to warm them as she glanced around the crowded space.

Lisa was scanning the donut case. That was another thing about Lisa that Robyn grudgingly admired. Lisa never gained an ounce, no matter how much food she consumed, while Robyn had been forced to join the salad brigade just to prevent extra pounds. But she didn't have to worry about her weight today. Her appetite had abandoned her the minute her feet hit the boarding ramp.

"What are you having?" Lisa asked without taking her gaze from the glass case with a dwindling selection of goodies.

"Nothing, just coffee."

"You're sure?" Lisa's raised eyebrows said it all. "This isn't like you. Are you all right?"

"Thanks. I'm fine. I just want this ferry ride to be over."

"I know what you mean," Lisa said around a hearty bite of her chocolate-glazed donut as she fished a napkin out of the overstuffed dispenser.

Robyn braced against the sway of the ferry. "I don't know why I'm torturing myself this way. What ever made me believe that being on open water would be therapeutic?"

"You wanted to get away," Lisa reminded her, wiping the paper napkin across her lips.

Robyn gripped the edge of the scarred Formica countertop and willed her stomach to settle. "The next time I decide I want to go out on the water, remind me of this trip, will you?"

"You got it," Lisa said as her gaze wandered around the room.

Robyn reached for the steaming cup of coffee the kid behind the counter had placed in front of her. "I hope we don't run into rough weather."

Lisa's gaze swung back to Robyn. "Not to worry." She did a *rat-a-tat-tat* on her chest. "Your favorite man is aboard," Lisa said, sarcasm dripping off her words.

"*Are you kidding?* Where?" Robyn demanded.

"Over there." Lisa nodded in the general direction of the door.

They'd just learned that Brad Allen, was replacing the man who was supposed to lead the bird-watching tour. And there he was, just inside the door. "I signed on for this adventure because I thought Brad wasn't going to be here. I see enough of him at work. Damn! I really don't want to make a scene...."

"You? Make a scene? Now, *that* I'd like to see. It's more likely the sky would fall," Lisa said, winking at the young man behind the counter, whose cheeks immediately flamed pink.

"Keep it up. We'll see how you feel when he starts hovering around you."

"Won't happen. It's you Tarzan wants; it's you he'll have, Jane," Lisa teased.

"*Shh!* He'll hear you."

"So what?"

"So, I don't need him fussing around me now."

"Is he still trying to weasel his way into your life?"

"Every chance he gets. Last night I had to call Respiratory Therapy, and guess who appeared?"

"What are you going to do about him?"

"There isn't much I can do. He's totally kind and considerate, always wants to help, and he's even offered to take Jason to a ball game, or to soccer practice. Mom thinks Brad is just trying to be kind and supportive, trying in his own way to get over what happened to Peter and Nathan."

"What do you think?"

Robyn shrugged. "Who knows? Maybe that's it."

"Just as well we got the last two stools, or we'd have company," Lisa said, eyeing Brad as he pushed the hood of his jacket off his head and searched the room.

Robyn smiled as she watched the guy that just served them. Lisa was unaware of the young man trying to look cool behind the counter. His gaze was locked on Lisa while he waited for a chance to get her attention. The color had died down in his cheeks, but the eager expression on his face gave him away.

Out of the corner of her eye, Robyn saw Sandy Fowler coming toward her, her uneven gait made even more so by the gentle rolling movement of the boat. Today her mouse-brown hair was tied back in a severe knot. "I wonder what they've found?" Robyn asked.

"What who's found?" Lisa stopped eating and followed Robyn's gaze.

Sandy, her face alight with excitement, gave them a thumbs up before grabbing the counter for support. "The fog's starting to lift. There's a Bald Eagle off the port bow," she called out over the ringing of the video lottery terminals.

Lisa and Robyn exchanged glances and zipped up their vests. "I knew it was too good to last. Lead on," Lisa called out with a hint of resignation.

Robyn got up to follow the two women from the canteen when she remembered something. "I'll have to meet you out there."

Lisa stopped. "Oh, no you don't. No sneaking away on this one. If I go, you go."

Robyn rolled her eyes. "I'll be there in a couple of minutes. I left my binoculars in the van. You go ahead."

"You'll have to get the keys from Brad," Lisa said, her eyebrows lifting.

"No. Dr. McGill, I have the keys," Sandy said. "I had to go down to get a warmer sweater for under my jacket. Be careful on those stairs – they're pretty difficult when the boat's moving," Sandy cautioned as Robyn started toward the door leading down to the vehicle decks.

Robyn's hiking boots made a hollow clanging sound on the metal steps as she descended onto the lower deck. The steel walls of the open car deck were coated in a sheen of dampness, giving the space a glacial quality. The sound of water rushing along the hull competed with the dull roar of the ferry's diesel engines.

The pungent odor of diesel fuel surrounded Robyn as she stopped at the bottom of the steps to get her bearings. There was no one in sight, but that wasn't unusual. All passengers were required to go up on deck when the ferry left the dock. Seeing the white van parked on the waterside of the deck, she eased between the empty cars near the stairs.

A sudden queasiness took hold of Robyn as she made her way toward the parked van.

Not now! Taking a fortifying breath, she wove her way toward the van, the keys making a putty imprint in the palm of her hand. Robyn reached the van and unlocked the side door. Relieved to see her binoculars resting on the seat, she reached in.

Her hands began to shake, the air in her lungs refused to move. She couldn't breathe!

Recognizing the panic attack for what it was, Robyn

struggled to remain calm. She gripped the edge of the seat, closed her eyes and thought of Peter's son, Jason. Jason needed her. She and her mother were all the family he had left in the world.

Pushing back her fear, Robyn grabbed her binoculars, then slammed the door shut and stumbled to the side of the deck. Her knees wobbled as she braced them against the steel guardrail.

She gulped life-giving air, and felt her panic ease. She could do this. She could stop the panic. Relief trickled through her as she focused her gaze on the rippling expanse of water kicked up by the speed of the ferry. As if in response to her need, the sun cracked through the fog and seemed to warm the air around her. Robyn squinted into the bright, welcoming light and leaned back to take full advantage of the reprieve.

"Watch it!" A coarse male voice – as unyielding as the steel around her – startled her.

"Sorry," she muttered, clutching the rail as she moved out of the man's way. Robyn looked up into his face. Large silver-framed aviator sunglasses hid most of his face, while a blinding shaft of sunlight coming from behind his shoulder obscured the man's features.

Without another word the stranger moved off.

Robyn didn't bother to look his way as she heard his boots clomping across the steel deck. She skirted the vehicles and hurried to the bottom of the steps.

The dimly lit, narrow stairwell loomed menacingly above her, but the safety afforded by friends waiting up on deck drove her forward. Robyn made it to the massive steel door and shoved it open.

"Whoa! What's this?" A rich baritone voice, with just the hint of a French accent, rolled over her as she fell headlong into the man's arms.

Robyn clutched his navy jacket as she steadied herself. The neat gold lettering, denoting an officer of the law, caught Robyn's attention first. The man holding her, with his deep brown eyes with very appealing squint lines, was a police officer.

Robyn fought back her deep-seated distrust at the sight of anybody in law enforcement. *Ignore him. Keep moving.* "Excuse me," she said, trying to get by him.

The officer nodded toward the closed door behind her. "What were you doing down there?"

His quizzical expression was set off by a twinkle in his eyes that suggested he was making fun of her.

But it didn't matter whether the handsome officer holding her so gently had a sense of humor or not. She didn't owe him any explanation about her activities. Not now. Not ever again. She eased out of his grip. "I forgot something."

"I'd be more careful the next time. Roaming around the open decks of a ferry can be dangerous." He smiled again, and this time Robyn was aware of a feeling other than distrust. Some sort of odd appeal, she thought but ignored the sensation.

What it was she didn't know. Didn't care.

Luke Carlisle prided himself on being good at hiding his feelings when the situation called for it – thanks to years of undercover work. Yet, as he locked gazes with the woman standing in front of him, his heart did a rebellious jump and bump in his chest.

With her dark curls, and high cheekbones, the stranger resembled his ex-wife--more than he liked. He had spent many desperate hours trying to salvage a woman who couldn't escape her own demons long enough to be his wife.

He wanted to ignore the woman standing in front of him,

13

but he couldn't. There was something compelling about her, something unlike many of the women he knew...yet he couldn't put his finger on exactly what it was.

She was a refreshing change from the skimpily clad tourists who roamed the many passenger decks of the ferry. Many people crossing over to the island didn't realize that the ferry ride would be cold by mid-September. They ended up huddled inside the ferry's lounge just to keep warm. Not that he didn't enjoy the view provided by some of the young women dressed as if they were going for a walk on a sun-drenched beach. He did. But it was also nice to see a woman who had the good sense to dress for the weather.

And from what he could see, there wasn't the usual collection of pierced body parts. Nice, he mused as he waited for her gaze to meet his.

Her demeanor was a different story. He noted the hurried rise and fall of the woman's chest under her quilted vest, and the haunted uncertainty in her gaze. There was a sallow quality to her skin, and tiny beads of perspiration clung to her upper lip. Maybe she was seasick...

"Are you feeling okay?"

Her glance never made it to his face. "Yes, of course."

Why would a beautiful woman come running up the stairs from the car deck with the fear of God in her eyes? And why, when asked a simple question, did she avoid eye contact?

"You're sure?"

She lowered her head, and a sweep of curls cascaded over her face, hiding her expression. "Yes. Is there a problem, officer?"

Luke picked up on the hint of defiance in her voice. "You tell me."

"I'm not aware of any problem." This time she met his stare, her eyes challenging him.

The fear he'd seen earlier was gone, or had been carefully hidden. Just a hint of pink along the crest of her cheekbones was the only sign that something had disturbed her. He had to admit – except for the lingering anxiety in her eyes – she looked like a woman who could take care of herself. Still, she was almost too calm, her air of self-assurance running counter to the way she'd behaved only minutes earlier.

As if aware that she was being assessed, the woman met his inquiring gaze, her mocking half-smile now lighting her eyes. Suddenly he felt like an over anxious kid.

She lifted her shoulders in a slight shrug. "I'm fine. You don't have to worry about me."

"Glad to hear it," he said, knowing he sounded like a Boy Scout on patrol.

The wall of fog that had clung to the ferry during the hour-long crossing moved off to form a scowling mass against the horizon. The breeze had backed off toward the west, leaving the air fresh, with just a hint of warmth from the sun. Grand Island, with its archipelago of tiny, rock-strewn islands, had been a bird haven for centuries. Thousands of tourists appeared every spring and fall to take part in bird-watching expeditions.

Lisa and Robyn stood on the deck near the bow enjoying the hesitant warmth of the sun as the ferry eased past the end of the pier.

"There are so many good memories here," Robyn said, thankful to have made the crossing without being ill. The trip might turn out okay after all.

"I know. I know," Lisa said, giving her a hug. "And there will be more good times here, you'll see. How's Jason making out?"

She already missed the freckle-faced menace, especially

his disarming smile. She had come to love her brother's son as if he were her own. When she'd first adopted Jason, she hadn't been convinced she'd make a good parent. Yet, as time passed and her parenting fears began to subside, she came to appreciate how much happiness they brought to each other's lives. "He's better. School is so much better this year, and he's taken up baseball. And horses. He's crazy about horses."

"And how are you doing?"

Robyn's throat ached with unshed tears. "About the same. Hardly a day goes by that I don't think about Peter and Nathan, and that night on the boat. If only I could remember…. I woke up the other night after another dream…. I couldn't remember any of it but I was terrified."

"Don't do this to yourself."

"I know, but—"

"If this trip is going to be too difficult for you, we can always go back to the mainland tonight on the return ferry," Lisa said, her voice warm and sympathetic.

"Peter used to love leading the fall trip to Grand Island to look for migrating warblers. I want to make this trip. I want to remember happier times. I have to move on. I can't expect Jason to get over the loss of his father if I can't."

Lisa smiled encouragingly. "Let's change the subject. You don't need any more stress today. What did you and the handsome police officer talk about?" she asked, glancing around at the restless passengers waiting for the ferry to swing into its docking area.

"Nothing. He wanted to know what I was doing on the car deck." Robyn tucked her chin into her collar, trying to ignore the look in Lisa's eyes. She knew what her friend was up to, besides just trying to change the topic – Lisa, the matchmaker, was on full alert.

"Well, he's one handsome man. He reminded me of someone...." Lisa muttered, then brightened. "I love that staunch officer look; the eyes forward, strong chin, clean-cut stuff."

"Since when did you become such a connoisseur of police officers?"

"Since I started working on my new feature story. Did you know that a few police officers and a handful of coast guard officers are pretty well all that stand between us and tons of drugs waiting to be sent ashore from Columbia?"

"Where did you hear that?"

"I've been interviewing some of the people involved. My producer agreed to do a series of documentaries. I'm excited about it. It's not a very happy story, for sure. To start with, I'm focusing on the two teenagers who mysteriously disappeared in Portsmouth, and how that led to accusations against a police officer's wife..." Lisa's voice lowered.

"Why can't I remember that officer's name? Not much was said at the time in the media as the cop was totally innocent of any wrongdoing. He actually had the unpleasant job of turning his wife in," Lisa muttered, deep in thought.

"What an awful thing to do! Imagine being married to someone who was willing to turn you in," Robyn said, indignantly.

"I understand he had no choice, but I don't remember the details."

Robyn lowered her voice. "Isn't poking around the lives of drug lords dangerous?"

"It could be, I suppose."

Robyn glanced around, and was relieved to see that most of the passengers had moved to the side of the ferry where the ramps were being put in place for their debarkation. "Whatever made you decide to work on that particular story?"

"A friend of mine is a cousin of one of the girls. It's a story that's never been told. Few people consider an isolated island like this one as the ideal place for drug distribution. With its picturesque villages and tiny ports filled with charming shops and artists colonies, no one thinks such ugliness could go on there." Lisa smiled, her enthusiasm evident in the lilt of her voice. "That's my lead in, actually. The whole contrast thing."

"You don't mean this island?"

"No solid information on this one, but I wanted to come and see for myself. Get a little of the context for my reporting."

"You're giving me goose bumps," Robyn said as quietly as she could. "I want you to be careful, Lisa. Please."

"I will. You don't have to worry about me," Lisa said, rocking back on her heels as the ferry lurched before sliding up against the docking ramp.

"Good," Robyn said, raising her face to the warm sun and closing her eyes for a few seconds.

Lisa glanced around the deck. "I was hoping for one last glimpse of your officer friend."

"Never mind. I can live without meeting him again. Let's go." Robyn moved toward the ramp.

Lisa grabbed her arm. "Look up." She pointed. "Up on the upper deck, near the bridge. Isn't that him?"

"The things I do for my match-making friend," Robyn muttered, glancing toward the upper deck. "Yes, it––"

And standing just a few feet from the officer was a man who looked vaguely like the man from the car deck. His silver framed sunglasses glinted in the bright light. He tanned skin and carefully trimmed beard were partially hidden by the hood of his gray jacket.

The man turned his mirrored gaze her way.

"Let's go," Robyn said, putting all thoughts of both men from her mind.

. . .

A large navy blue van sat in a vacant lot across from the ferry terminal. A gentle breeze stirred the fir boughs overhead, creating a sighing sound that added to the sense of peace and tranquility afforded by the first rays of warm sun.

The van's occupant sucked on a cigarette as he watched an eighteen-wheeler lumber up the ferry ramp, blocking his view. "Damned truck," Leo Lord muttered to himself as he adjusted his binoculars and studied the area. The man sat waiting to spot a particular van among the vehicles driving off the ferry.

He'd received a hurried call from someone he hadn't heard from in years. Someone he owed his life to. The friend from his past was calling in a favor. The description of a particular woman and the van had been pretty clear. All he had to do was check the plate number then follow the white van and see where it went. Easy actually.

The bleep of his cell phone broke the silence. He crushed the cigarette butt out in the ashtray and lifted his cell to his ear, keeping his eyes on the traffic. He held the binoculars steady with the other hand. "Yeah."

He listened, and the longer he listened, the more surprised he became.

Leo Lord didn't like surprises. "Sounds like you have a problem, my friend. How can I help?"

"I need an end date to cover the business we discussed."

So, something had changed for his friend in the past few hours… Now, instead of just following her and passing along information, his friend wanted a hit. But Leo didn't care. It was the money he was after.

"Sure. I'll need to work out the details with you." *Damned right.* To come out of retirement and do this job would cost his friend money. Lots of money.

"No problem. Just let me know," the voice on the other end of the line said.

So his long lost friend was willing to pay the full price. Leo would love to know why the man wanted this particular hit. A woman wasn't usually the target. But hell, who cared? His money did the talking. He felt the familiar whirl of adrenaline in his gut at the thought of what he would do. "Leave it with me."

But his friend didn't seem satisfied with that and went on to explain the parameters.

Leo waited, listening and wishing he could just click off. It wasn't safe to stay on the air. His friend knew that better than anyone. This hit, and its urgency, definitely had his friend upset.

"Thanks, I owe you one," the voice offered, back now to its normal smooth tone.

"No. When this is over, consider us even, my friend," Leo said as he lowered his binoculars. Talking on the phone always made him nervous. Besides, a change in plans meant that Leo had things to do – things that couldn't wait. "We'll talk later," Leo said, his finger hovering over the 'end' button.

"I appreciate all you've done for me." The phone clicked off.

What in hell just happened?

He got out of the van and packed up the photographic equipment he'd set up earlier. Outdoor photography was his best cover, and one that had turned into a real hobby in his retirement. With infinite care, he placed the expensive equipment in the back of the van while surreptitiously scanning the vehicles coming off the ferry.

Closing the rear door, he climbed back into the driver's seat and watched as the parade of cars continued to roll off the ramp. A white van bobbed into view and eased up to the stop sign a few hundred yards in front of him. Bolting upright, he focused the binoculars on the license plate.

Bingo!

He cranked the van to life.

This was it. His whole body flushed with enjoyment, confident his rifle with the high-powered scope lay within reach, nestled in the back. In his prime he had been the best in the business.

This particular contract would be easy. No one suspected what would happen. This lonely island, with its handful of full-time residents, would never know who did the deed. He'd do what he was paid to do and then slip back into the anonymity of his retirement.

And if he were spotted, no one would give a thought to the fact that he was out and about. They'd assume he'd felt the urge to shoot a few pictures.

Urge to shoot, all right! But not pictures. In a matter of hours, he'd get a chance to curl his finger over the trigger and feel the thrill of power when the bullet hit its target.

Nothing could come close to that feeling. Nothing. He eased out onto the road – several vehicles behind the van – right behind a car with two kids staring out the back window at him. He settled for the sedate pace set by the lead vehicle as they moved down the only road leading from the ferry terminal. He drove carefully, his mind racing over the possibilities. And for the first time in a long time, Leo felt really alive.

Adrenaline kicked his pulse into overdrive as the van signaled a turn into the lane leading toward Raven's Nest Inn. What had his friend said? *'Bird watchers'?* He laughed out loud, considering the open spaces the group would visit. Places for him to hide while he waited for the perfect shot. What more could he ask for?

The whole killing thing was usually a bigger challenge for

him. More of a chase. But who cared? Killing had been in his blood ever since he shot his first deer at fifteen.

He grinned to himself. It wasn't quite the same. After all, a deer was a bigger challenge. Hell, one time he'd nearly missed a deer because it spooked and ran.

This particular quarry wouldn't get the chance to run....

CHAPTER TWO

WELCOME TO RAVEN'S NEST INN: read a gold-lettered black sign resting on an easel just inside the pine doors of the Inn. The large lobby, with its ceiling-high stone fireplace and over-sized and over-stuffed pine sofas, beckoned them.

"Would you look at this?" Robyn pointed to another sign dangling from the corner of the easel. "It says they're having a murder mystery weekend this weekend."

Lisa gazed over Robyn's shoulder at the black-and-white sign depicting Sherlock Holmes with his trusty magnifying glass. "What better place to have a mystery weekend than on an island where nothing happens? We should sign up. It beats birding any day of the week, as far as I'm concerned."

"After a week of wall-to-wall patients, I don't need any more mayhem in my life. I'll stick to birds." Robyn smiled at her friend.

"Have it your way. But it could be fun."

Their hiking boots clunked on the hardwood floors as they crossed the lobby.

"May I help you ladies?" the man behind the huge pine desk asked.

"We're here with the bird-watching group," Lisa said, giving him the benefit of her perfect smile, along with their names.

"Wonderful!" he effused. I have your room ready on the second floor in the main part of the Inn," he said. As he spoke directly to Lisa, he perked up, like a bird preening its feathers.

Robyn chuckled to herself. *Was there a male in the world immune to Lisa's charm?* She followed her friend across the lobby to the bottom of the steps leading to the upper levels.

Sunshine spilled across the gold-and-blue rag rug resting at their feet. A large watercolor painting of a right whale rising out of the water greeted them as they reached the top of the stairs. Two doors down the hallway, at the back of the inn, facing the herb garden they found their room.

"We'd better get a move on," Lisa said as she arranged her clothes neatly in the drawers, and placed her duffel bag in the bottom of the closet.

"Yeah, I suppose we don't want to be late." Robyn tossed her collection of sweats, underwear and socks into one of the drawers.

"What are you going to do about Brad?"

Robyn rolled her eyes. "Why are we talking about him?"

"Just concerned about you, that's all."

"Thanks, but you don't have to worry about me. I'm going to avoid Brad as much as possible." Robyn tossed her bag beside Lisa's in the bottom of the closet.

Entering the bathroom, Robyn admired the shining gold and cream color scheme, and wondered if the person who'd done such a nice job could be hired to put a touch of pizzazz in her house.

"Now I know how you stay so gorgeous," Robyn said

over her shoulder, moving one of Lisa's many cosmetic bags to make room on the bathroom counter for her one small bag.

"Are you changing the subject?"

"What?" Robyn asked, adjusting two of the bags on the narrow counter space. Lisa's bag tipped, spilling several items out on the floor. *"Drat!"* she muttered, bending down. She picked up a prescription bottle half-full of a highly addictive painkiller and wondered why Lisa was taking such a powerful medication? Robyn stuffed the pill bottle back in Lisa's case. Perhaps Lisa was still having bouts of pain from her pelvis that had been fractured over a year ago.... But as Lisa's doctor, she hadn't prescribed the pills.

She wondered about the quality of her friendship if she hadn't taken the time to know what's going on in Lisa's life.

"Are you listening?" Lisa asked.

"Yeah. Sorry." Robyn placed Lisa's prescription and the other contents back in the bag.

"I said, Brad sounds a little obsessive to me."

"Me too." Robyn wanted this to be the last conversation about Brad, but knew how persistent her friend could be when it came to trolling for information on a subject.

"What can I do to help?" Lisa asked. "Maybe we can find him a girlfriend. What about Sandy? Would she be interested in Brad?"

"Sandy's hooked on somebody else. I've never seen her as happy as she's been the past few months. No one seems to know the details," Robyn said absently.

"A secret lover! Fantastic! How do you know so much about Sandy?"

"I shouldn't have said anything. She's my patient, but I know you'll keep this private. Ever since her mother's illness last fall. She's been pretty lonely so it's nice she's found someone."

"Half the people in the world can claim to be your patient, Robyn. You're going to burn out," Lisa warned.

"I hear you," Robyn replied as she debated whether or not to bring up the pill issue.

"What does your father think of you working so hard? Is he still after you to take a plastic surgery specialty?"

"The great Dr. Geoffrey McGill is living in Florida with yet another woman half his age. I've been moved down his list of concerns."

"Don't you just love families?"

"No kidding!" Robyn muttered as she stood in the doorway to the bathroom.

Lisa slid into a large, overstuffed chair and tucked her legs under her. "What you need is someone new in your life, a distraction from your workload and family responsibilities. Someone who cares only for you. He also needs to be sexy and smart," Lisa mused.

"Well, the sexy qualification takes all the birders off the list, and this is a small island. Guess you'll have to do your matchmaking another time."

"You never know who might be just around the corner," Lisa said, wagging her finger.

Robyn gave a long pent-up sigh. "Can we move on to something more interesting?"

"If you say so." Lisa glanced casually at her watch and jumped up. "Hey! We were supposed to be downstairs ten minutes ago."

They grabbed their binoculars and jackets and headed for the stairs.

Brad Allen stood waiting at the bottom of the steps, issuing instructions to each member of the group as they passed.

"We're going to Bear Harbor first, and then over to Simmons Marsh to check for herons."

When Robyn reached the bottom step, he put his hand over hers where it rested on the railing. With startling blue eyes and reddish hair, Brad had a boyish quality to him that made him seem perfectly harmless.

"Are you all right?" A deep furrow traced a line between his brows.

"I'm fine."

"Robyn, if there's anything I can do for you...." He sandwiched her hand between his and squeezed affectionately.

"There isn't." Robyn pulled her hand slowly but firmly from under his fingers.

Brad moved closer and whispered in her ear. "There's so much going on you don't know about. I had a call from a friend. You and I need to talk."

Annoyed, Robyn cleared her throat and squared her shoulders. "About what?"

"We can't always have what we want," Brad said, a strange glint in his eyes.

"What do you mean? How would you know what I want?"

He lowered his voice. His gaze swept past her. "Trust me. I know. So don't be too quick to brush me off."

The navy blue van sat in a vacant driveway behind the inn, sheltered from sight by a row of pine trees and an azalea hedge. A cigarette dangled precariously from Leo Lord's lips as he watched the inn. "Damned apple tree," he whispered to himself as he adjusted his binoculars to get a better look.

Searching for any sign of his target, he swung the binoculars from the herb garden where guests were gathered, to the parking lot at the side door of the inn. The doors of the white van were open and people were climbing in.

Suddenly she was there, big as life and ready to board the van.

He couldn't believe how easy this was. He started the engine, ready to move into position when the van left the inn parking lot. He didn't know how much time he would have when they stopped to bird watch and he didn't care. This would be the easiest money he'd ever made...

While he followed the white van at a discreet distance he mentally ticked off the photographic equipment he'd buy with the money.

Two hours later, and Leo Lord's patience was wearing thin. The only sound that played along Simmons Marsh was the soft sigh of a dying breeze in the pines along the edge of the grass-lined creek. Dusk lurked in the trees across the spit of sand leading out to open water. The tall grass along the shore offered a sanctuary for Leo, who crouched low in its depths.

When the woman came back into his sights back in Bear Harbor she'd been surrounded by people. He'd followed the lumbering van filled with bird watchers from Bear Harbor to the marsh. This location gave him the perfect shot – this was classic; one he'd remember for a long time after the job was done.

Adjusting his camera with its high-powered lens, Leo watched the scene across from him. The birders moved back and forth between the van and the sandy knoll a mere two hundred yards from him. He saw his quarry move with another woman to set up a tripod with a scope on it. He couldn't help but grin to himself. Scope to scope; what a laugh!

His mind wrapped around the fantasy. *What if she looked right at him through her scope as he used his scope to sight her?*

The thought of pulling the trigger with her staring at him through her birding scope gave him a rush.

His victims seldom saw him before he fired. But this time, for one energizing instant, she would know his power over her. Leo grinned at the thought. Music to his senses.

There! He watched her put her eye to the scope as he tucked his camera away and reached for his rifle.

"There's a night heron over there." Brad pointed across to a tall pine on the other side of the creek. "He's up against the trunk of the tallest pine, about halfway down. It's immature, so his brown feathers blend in with the tree trunk making him hard to spot. Best to use a scope."

He turned to the group. "Does everyone see where I'm pointing?"

Fog-dampened air brushed against Robyn's cheek as she moved her scope in the direction Brad indicated. Excitement washed through her as she searched for the bird. She hadn't done any bird watching since Peter's death, and it felt good to be back at it, out in the fresh air.

"Lisa, I can hardly believe it. We're going to see a night heron."

"If you say so," Lisa said, standing next to Robyn.

Robyn scanned the tall grasses in front of a clump of pines. "I've found the base of the pine Brad's pointing at."

Shivering, Lisa zippered her jacket up under her chin and hunched her shoulders against the cold. "All this for a bird," she mumbled.

"Seriously. I see something...not a bird though." Robyn's breath caught in her throat as she spotted someone low in the grass across from her – just in front of the pine trees. It was probably another birder. She adjusted the resolution of her scope and zeroed in on the spot. A man faced her, his image filling her field of vision.

Leo could see the logo on the front of her jacket, crisp and clear. It was the exact spot where he wanted the bullet to enter her body. He moved the rifle slightly and saw another woman standing beside her. Blood roared in his ears. Maybe, he could bag both of them.

One for his friend and one for him.

Spreading his weight evenly on his legs, he readied himself to fire. The soft sand and hard roots of the marsh grasses hampered his movement, but only momentarily. He felt the muscles in his thighs flex to his command as he braced himself and took careful aim.

Nothing could stop him, not now. The course was set, the trajectory known. He could see his quarry clearly through the rifle scope and he took pleasure in the fact that the smile she was smiling would be her last.

He centered the cross hairs of his rifle over the crest on her red jacket and took a steadying breath.

"Oh! My God!" Robyn choked out the words.

"What is it?" Lisa moved closer.

"He's got a gun!"

With hypnotic slowness, Robyn scrambled sideways. Her boots caught in the sand, and she pitched forward. A cracking sound filled the air as a razor sharp pain burned through her arm.

Near her someone wailed in agony.

Forcing her eyes open, she stared around her. Lisa's now limp form came into focus where she lay sprawled on the sand a few feet away, a dark red smudge widening over her chest. "Lisa!"

Lisa faced her and opened her eyes, trying to focus. "Oh Robyn, I'm so sorry..."

"I need help here. Lisa's hurt!" Robyn screamed as she edged forward on her hands and knees, earning her a sickening flood of pain in her arm. Looking down, she saw a tear in the sleeve of her jacket. Blood trickled though the opening.

Heedless of the pain, Robyn reached Lisa in doctor mode and pressed her shaking fingers over the oozing chest wound. "Lisa, hang on. You're going to be okay. Just hang on," she said, willing her voice to stay strong and reassuring. *Where was everybody?* Lisa could go into shock any moment and precious seconds crept by as people wove in and out of Robyn's line of vision.

"Robyn, I have to t-t-tell you s-something before--" Lisa stuttered, pain contorting her face.

"Not now. Just stay still," Robyn pleaded, holding her hand against the wound with as much strength as she could muster.

Anxious voices filled the air, but Robyn couldn't concentrate on them. She felt herself sway dangerously and her head began to spin. She shifted to maintain pressure on Lisa's wound.

"Lisa! Someone, help Lisa." Robyn heard her voice through a cavern-like space.

"It's all right. Help's on the way." It was Brad's voice, his familiar reassurance offering comfort.

As if watching from a distant point, Robyn saw people move toward Lisa and place a jacket over her still form.

Brad placed his hand over Robyn's. "I'll take over from here. You're hurt. Sit down."

"No. I can't." She eased the words out over the pounding

in her chest as she turned to her best friend. "Stay with me. Please stay with me, Lisa."

Lisa's pulse fluttered beneath Robyn's fingers as she pressed on the soft skin over Lisa's carotid artery. "Her pulse is rapid and thready. Respiration's shallow. Call 911 and get the first aid kit from the back of the van," Robyn ordered just before her eyes closed and she crumpled onto the sand.

CHAPTER THREE

L uke Carlisle loosened the neck of his shirt as he glanced around the crime scene. Two women shot, one seriously, by a sniper's bullet. No apparent motive, but Luke was a long way from labeling it a random incident. On an island where no one had ever fired a gun at another human being, a random attack on two people, visitors to the island, didn't make any sense.

The crime scene looked much the same as it had last night. And this morning, there still wasn't much to go on. According to Brad Allen, the group leader, the victims – Lisa Wade and Dr. Robyn McGill – were best friends.

Did the motive for the attack involve both of them?

And why did the shooter pick an isolated island at sunset? None of it added up, but Luke had no doubt the pieces would fall into place before too long. Some of the locals had to have seen something, and in a place where everyone knew everyone else's business, someone would likely come forward with information.

"Luke, we've found the spot where the gun was fired. No spent shells, and the shooter brushed all boot prints and marks from the area. All we have to go on is flattened grass that lined up with the spot where the women stood. This was a professional hit," Andrew Webb offered. Andrew, the officer in charge of the Crime Unit from the mainland, had been on the scene since the night before.

Remorse mixed with the excess caffeine floating in Luke's stomach. "He would have followed the van, or had someone arrange to bring him here to get a clear shot."

"Makes sense," Andrew muttered, his gaze scanning the shoreline beyond the crime scene. A professional hit meant that someone wanted one or both of the women dead.

Resigned to what lay ahead, Luke adjusted his mirrored sunglasses in the glaring morning light and scanned the area cordoned off by the yellow tape. "Any idea why?"

"Too soon to tell. Anything at this point is pure speculation, but if we're speculating.., I'd say there's always the possibility this was drug related." Andrew shrugged his jacket on over his shoulders as he prepared to leave.

Not another drug problem. Anything but that. Luke watched Andrew complete his work, methodically putting everything in their proper places in the back of the van.

"It's been a long night for you," Luke offered

"That's the way it goes in this business." Andrew gave him a half smile. "How are things going for you?"

Luke saw Andrew's question for what it was – a friend's concern. He was really asking how Luke was coping with life on a small island after being accustomed to handling high profile drug cases on the mainland. Luke didn't have an answer. It had been one day at a time for so long he'd grown accustomed to thinking of his life in isolated parts, rather than as a whole.

"Fine. Getting to know a few of the locals."

The Drug Unit had been a part of Luke's life and leaving it had been difficult – something he worked hard to forget.

He still heard from some team members, but had no desire to go back to a life that held so many bad memories.

Andrew closed the back doors of the van. "Glad to hear you're doing okay. A local mentioned there are lots of fish in the rivers here. We'll have to go trout fishing one of these days."

"I'll hold you to it," Luke said, walking with Andrew to the driver's door.

"Damn right." Andrew gave Luke a friendly punch on the shoulder.

"Thanks for your help, Andrew. Call me as soon as you have anything. In the meantime, I'll interview all the members of the birding group and any other witnesses. I'm headed for the hospital now."

"We'll be in touch." Andrew closed the door and started the engine.

As Luke stepped back and watched the van pull away, he was thankful for his good fortune that his days of investigating drug busts were over. His life on Grand Island might not be exciting, or particularly stimulating, but it was all his.

After surviving the grumbling of the ferry operator over delays created by the investigation, Luke arrived at the local hospital on the island. He'd asked they delay the departure of the morning ferry an hour on the off chance that interviewing the doctor who'd been involved in the shooting would give him some sort of description he could check against the passengers boarding the ferry. There wasn't a hope in hell that the shooter would be on the ferry, even if the witness could give him a physical description. A professional hit man would have a fail proof exit strategy, but Luke still had to cover all the bases.

· · ·

"I'm sorry, Isabel; I have to talk to Dr. McGill now. It can't wait."

Isabel, the nurse in charge of the twenty-bed hospital in Pier Point, put her hands on her hips and planted her feet on the tile floor. The gesture stopped less determined souls from pushing their point, but not him and certainly not today. "If Lisa Wade dies, this will be a murder investigation, Isabel, and Robyn McGill is a witness."

Isabel dropped her shoulders just slightly, an indication that she accepted his right to talk to her patient, but her jutting chin served to show Luke she didn't like it. Luke respected Isabel's protective attitude toward her patients. It showed how much she cared for the people in her hospital, most of whom she'd known all her life.

Luke rested his arm on the raised counter. "Tell me about Dr. McGill."

Isabel shot him a worried glance as she straightened her white uniform over her rounded hips. "That poor woman was awake all night. It was a good thing we didn't have too many really sick people because Dr. McGill kept ringing her bell. She was so agitated – something about a dream she'd had. The night nurse couldn't get her to settle down."

"I wonder why…"

"If you ask me, I think Dr. McGill's in some kind of trouble."

"Oh?"

"She told my night nurse she thinks she may have killed someone."

Interesting. Certainly, if she had killed someone, revenge could be a motive for the shootings… But what would make a doctor whose job it was to save lives, do or say such a thing?

"Are you sure she wasn't simply mixed up? Maybe the effects of something you'd given her?"

"Don't know. Anything's possible, I guess," Isabel offered, her gaze locked on Luke.

"Did she say anything else?"

"Nothing much that the nurse could make out, but she was some anxious."

"You never know," he muttered to himself, wondering just what kind of person this Dr. McGill was. A doctor who thought they killed someone was new in his experience – unless there'd been an accident during an operation or someone was given the wrong prescription – but Luke had learned a long time ago never to discount any possibility where human beings were concerned.

"Ten minutes, officer. Ten minutes, tops."

Luke started down the corridor to the last room on the left. He hated hospitals, every damned part of them from the Emergency Room to the Morgue. He'd seen far too many during his career.

Taking a deep breath, he opened the door and glanced into the room. Bright sunlight streamed across the narrow bed where his witness lay with her arm in a sling. Whether it was the small space Dr. McGill took up in the bed or the way she curled in on herself, Luke felt an overriding need to help her. Lots of women made him feel that way – one of his character flaws, he supposed.

Knowing how easily most people were intimidated by police questioning, and that the woman lying on the bed had been through a terrifying experience, he started gently, but firmly.

"Good morning, Dr. McGill. I'm Officer Carlisle, and I'm investigating the shooting last night."

She had been facing the window with her back to him when he'd entered the room. At the sound of his voice, she turned and faced him.

He stared in surprise. She was the same woman who'd

bumped into him on the ferry, only now her dark, curly hair was matted and clinging to her forehead and her face was drawn tight with anxiety. The pain and anguish on her face cut straight through him. He sensed something was terribly wrong in this woman's life, beyond any wound. Years of investigative work had led Luke to trust his gut – the litmus test that matched his experience with his instincts.

He had liked Dr. McGill's spunk when she challenged him on the ferry, even though her challenge had come with an evasive attitude. At the time he'd wondered what she was hiding, and maybe he was about to find out.

Raising herself up with her good arm, she leaned dangerously close to the side of the bed, her wrinkled hospital gown slipping off her shoulder. "Is Lisa all right?"

Keeping in mind what Isabel had said, he decided to proceed slowly. "Dr. McGill, please lie back. Why don't I raise the head of your bed, so you'll be more comfortable while we talk?" He saw the distrust in her eyes as he moved to the bed controls.

The bed hummed as the head of it tilted upward. "There. That should make it easier to talk...unless you'd like to sit in the chair?"

Dr. McGill leaned back against the pillows, the lines on her face tight with worry – an expression Luke had seen on many witnesses. "To answer your question, Lisa Wade was air lifted back to the mainland. She's in stable condition."

"Thank heavens. I've been so worried."

"Dr. McGill, can you describe to me everything you saw and heard those moments leading up to the shooting?"

"I don't know. It all happened so fast. I couldn't believe what I was seeing. It seemed like hours passed after the moment I realized something was wrong..."

Basically the same story the others had given him. "Dr. McGill, why were you and Ms. Wade on Grand Island?"

"A bird-watching trip."

"A bird-watching trip? Had you done this before?"

"Years ago. When my brother was alive, I used to come here a lot. Peter was a wildlife biologist working for the government. He spent his life on conservation projects all over the world," she said, her voice barely a whisper.

"What made you suddenly decide to take up bird watching again?"

"I didn't decide to take it up. I've always been involved in bird watching. But I've been so busy lately." She spread her fingers across the sheet covering her, flexing each finger as if to relax them. "I had a chance to come with a group of friends, and thought it would be a nice break from my normal routine and to catch up with old friends."

"And what about Ms. Wade? Did she often come here?"

"This was her first trip."

"I don't understand. You're telling me that neither of you came here on a regular basis, but on the one trip you make together, someone shoots both of you?"

Dr. McGill shifted in the bed, a frown deepening the line between her eyes. "What do you mean by that question?"

Dismay rippled through Robyn, momentarily knocking out the pain in her arm. *Why would the officer suggest that she and Lisa had some other motive for coming to Grand Island? What could he be thinking, and why?*

"I'm trying to get to the facts, Dr. McGill. You can see how this looks. Two women who seem to have no reason for anyone to shoot them, take a trip to an isolated island and are suddenly the victims of a professional hit man."

Robyn leaned back in the bed, his words of skepticism rolling over her. All morning, she'd been fighting terrible flashbacks to the accident three years ago. Some part of her mind recognized the flashbacks as a normal response to yesterday. But she couldn't forget how the police had questioned her three years ago, their disbelief evident in the way they spoke to her, just as this officer was now.

She'd been too grief-stricken and too trusting back then to stand up for herself against their persistent questioning. *Not this time.* "I don't care what you believe, or don't believe. I'm telling you the truth. We were here to go bird watching. That's all."

"How long did you plan to be here?"

"A few days."

"Who knew you were coming here?"

She wanted to tell him to take a hike, but past experience told her that would do no good. "The usual. My mother, my nephew, people I work with."

"Nothing unusual happened? Anyone take a special interest in your plans?"

Brad's sudden appearance as the group leader crossed her mind, but she said nothing. Brad might be the number one nuisance in her life, but he was totally harmless.

"Dr. McGill? Do you want me to repeat the question?"

"No. I heard you. There was nothing unusual."

"Do you have any enemies, Dr. McGill? Anyone who would want to harm you?"

"Enemies?" Only the police, she wanted to say, but knew the futility of it all. Policemen like Officer Carlisle would continue to pry into her life until they exhausted all avenues of interest to their precious investigation, regardless of what it did to her.

She'd learned how pernicious the police could be in the months after the boating accident. All those times she feared for her sanity, because of the police and their suspicions. No power on earth would make her revisit what had happened back then.

"Yes, enemies...or someone who would want to harm you," he said, his voice low, controlled.

She couldn't answer him over a rush of guilt that left her speechless. When the bird-watching group decided to meet on the island to commemorate Peter's work, Robyn had called Lisa and insisted she come with her. Lisa was an investigative reporter. Even though she was covering some big stories, she had taken time to be here with her, and so, had made herself vulnerable. Someone had found out that Lisa would be here, someone connected to whatever investigation Lisa was working on.

If she had been more involved in her friend's life, if she had been aware of what sort of investigative work Lisa was doing, this might not have happened. Instead she'd led her friend onto a lonely island, making her an easy target for whoever was out there who wanted her dead.

How could she have been so stupid? Robyn swallowed against the tears, her gaze shifting to the window. "I have no enemies."

The officer's sigh radiated disbelief. "You have no enemies? How can you be so sure?"

"I'm a doctor. No one would have reason to harm me."

"I need your cooperation, and I'm not getting it."

As if playing back an old tape from three years ago, she heard herself say, "I can't tell you what I don't know."

Robyn stared at the ceiling. Last evening had brought back all the pain, the torment, the grief and the horror of those months after Peter and Nathan died, as if the intervening years had never been. Fragmented memories or fabrications tormented her all night.

None of them made sense. All of them terrified her.

Was history repeating itself? When Peter and Nathan died, she'd been helpless to do anything about it, incapable of offering any explanation as to how they died, or what she could have done to save them.

And now if Lisa died. . .

She and Lisa should be out with the rest of the group, searching for early fall warblers, laughing and enjoying the day. She hadn't had a chance to tell Lisa her plans for a cruise of the Greek Islands, her plan to take Jason with her and to invite Lisa to come along with them. Jason had talked of nothing else over the past few weeks.

Exhaustion warred with remorse as she watched the officer move closer to her bed.

"Dr. McGill, I need something to go on – anything you might remember."

Robyn suddenly recognized the officer as the one she'd run into on the ferry. She hadn't paid much attention at the time. Now, she saw his hair was wavy and black, his dark eyes framed by equally dark eyebrows. There were laugh lines around his mouth, but the warm smile of yesterday had vanished. His lips were now a hard line that matched the determination in his eyes.

She might not like the way the officer questioned her but she had to try...if only for Lisa's sake. "I can't think of anything. There was nothing unusual. As I said, it happened so fast."

"I understand you were looking through your scope at the time of the incident. Did you see him? Did he look familiar at all?"

Robyn took a deep breath and closed her eyes. "I don't think so..."

Just like the accident three years ago, she couldn't recall anything about what happened on the marsh. Just like the night on the sailboat, when she'd lost the two people she'd loved most in the world, without one credible memory to explain what had happened. And now Lisa was in danger. Tears driven by loss and guilt welled up in her eyes. She blinked them back thinking how she was the common denominator here.

Something didn't ring true where this woman was concerned. Call it a colossal hunch, but his suspicion grew with each passing moment.

Something had provoked this incident. No one hired a professional hit man without a reason. It seemed Dr. McGill or Ms. Wade, or both of them, were mixed up in something, and someone wanted one or both dead. In his experience, that involvement was likely something illegal. Dr. McGill and Lisa Wade – a very public figure in the news industry – risked a lot if they were involved in criminal activity. And if they *were* involved, experience told him there would be big returns to compensate for the risks.

Only one illegal industry met that criteria.

"In your opinion, Dr. McGill, what happened out there? If the marksman wasn't after you or your friend, who was he after?"

Her movements were awkward, her glance evasive. "I don't know."

"Dr. McGill, this isn't getting us anywhere."

She met his gaze, her eyes welling with tears. "I know. And I'm sorry… I feel responsible for what happened out there."

Finally. "In what way?"

"I'm afraid for Lisa," Dr. McGill said, barely above a whisper, beads of perspiration shining on her forehead.

"Can you explain a little more? We're concentrating our investigation on Ms. Wade as the primary victim, because she sustained the gravest injuries."

With her fingers clasped in her lap, Robyn bit down on her lower lip. "I...I think I know why Lisa was shot."

Now they were getting somewhere. "Why?"

"Because of me."

You? "I'm not sure I understand." The doctor had been uncooperative up until now. *Why the sudden shift?* "How are you involved in what happened to Lisa Wade?"

Robyn worked the fingers of her free hand under the cotton neckline of her hospital gown as she stared at him. "If I had known what was going on in her life, I would never have asked her to come here with me."

He waited for her to continue. The room filled with silence. Somewhere outside, someone started a car. A lawn mower hummed in the distance. "Dr. McGill, why did Lisa Wade come here?"

"He had to be firing at Lisa. He had to be. If only I'd known she was in danger..."

"In danger?"

"Yes, Lisa was working on a story dealing with drugs--"

The door swooshed open. Isabel walked in, and took one look at her patient's tear- stained face. "Shame on you Luke Carlisle! She's been upset all morning, and now you do this." Isabel barked the words at him as she handed a pill cup and glass of water to her patient.

Luke wanted to question Dr. McGill further about what Lisa Wade was working on, but he knew that the police in Portland were interviewing her coworkers at the TV station. They were also checking her files. They would know what Ms. Wade was working on, and follow up. He hadn't gotten what he'd come for, but that didn't mean he planned to leave. Not just yet.

"There. You rest," Isabel said, tucking the sheet around her patient as she aimed a warning glance at Luke on the way out of the room.

. . .

Exhausted by the policeman's tactics, Robyn made herself as comfortable as she could in the lumpy hospital bed while she waited for him to leave. She felt embarrassed that she'd lost her composure in front of the police officer. He probably saw that as proof of her guilt.

She was so mixed up, and her arm pained so much, she could hardly remember what she'd told him. But it didn't really matter. In a few hours, she'd be able to go home, away from the memories, away from the horror of the past twenty-four hours. There was nothing she could do about any of this, nothing at all. Jason and her mother were waiting for her at home in Portland. Lisa would need her support and care as she recovered.

The door opened and Brad breezed in. "Robyn, you're all right," he said, his voice filled with relief as his gaze shifted to the officer, then back to Robyn.

"I'm going to be fine as soon as I get out of here. Thanks for everything you did last night. I mean it." Brad had stayed with her during the entire time in the Emergency Room, helping her, being a good friend. She regretted all the negative thoughts she'd had about him, the way she behaved at the inn.

"Seeing you look so much better is all the thanks I need. Has the doctor signed you out yet?"

"This afternoon. I can't wait. Where's the rest of the group?"

"They're at the inn. They sent me to spring you," Brad said, a grin lighting his face.

"I'm not finished interviewing Dr. McGill," the officer interjected, glancing at Brad. "Mr. Allen, now that you're here, I'd like to arrange to meet with each member of your group."

Brad scowled. "We told you everything last night."

"I just want to be sure. Do you mind?"

"Do we have a choice?"

The officer gave Brad a look that silenced him.

Brad shrugged. "Okay, when?"

Luke glanced at his watch. "How about fifteen minutes from now?"

"Sure. I'll meet you at the inn, and I'll tell the rest of the group to be there." Brad glanced at Robyn, his smile returning. "I'll be back for you a little later."

"I'll be waiting," she said, wishing he would stay to act as a buffer between her and the crusading policeman.

Luke watched Brad leave before he spoke. "How are you feeling, Dr. McGill?"

Was that genuine concern in the policeman's eyes?

It couldn't be. "I'm okay."

"Glad to hear that." He rested his powerful hands on the over-bed table, his gaze surrounding her, forcing her to look at him. "Is it true you told the night nurse you thought you killed someone?"

Shock pounded through Robyn, snapping her breath away. *Had she said that to the night nurse?* She couldn't have. It was all a bad dream; in the early months after the boating accident, her psychiatrist had called it survivor guilt. She blamed herself for Nathan's and Peter's deaths. But she could never harm them. Never. "Killed someone? I was so upset last night I could have said almost anything."

What else had she said to the night nurse? "Would you mind if we talked a little later? The nurse gave me something to help the pain."

He hesitated.

Robyn mentally crossed her fingers.

"Dr. McGill, I'll be back in a little while. In the meantime, I want you to try to remember everything, the ferry ride, your arrival at the inn, the incident on the marsh. Everything, including the fear you expressed to the nurse."

After all her efforts to keep the officer out of her life, she'd betrayed herself with the half memories that had nothing to do with the present. What a mess! There wasn't a chance that this man would leave her alone when she'd given him reason to be suspicious of her. With a heavy heart, she nodded agreement.

When Officer Carlisle handed her his card, his fingers touched hers. Her skin tingled traitorously where his heat warmed her. "If you remember anything more, no matter how trivial, call me." She watched him move away, his tall, angular form at ease in his uniform.

He turned at the door. "I understand you're discharged as of this afternoon. I'd like you to go to your room at the inn and stay there until I get in touch with you."

"What about Lisa? I need to get back home."

His face took on a cool, detached look. "Lisa is being looked after. It's your safety I'm concerned about." The door slid closed behind him, leaving her alone with her thoughts.

Beyond any doubt, he meant what he said. There was no uncertainty in his eyes, or in the way he moved. She also knew his concern for her safety was only the cover story for what he really wanted. He would question her until he was sure she had told him everything.

A cold shiver of dread wrapped around her heart. She had been the only witness to what had happened three years ago, and she remembered nothing. But if real memories were returning – memories shrouded in guilt about that night…

The kind of guilt that would destroy her and her belief in herself as a physician, sworn to uphold the sanctity of life.

CHAPTER FOUR

Something was wrong...out of kilter.

Luke's gut gave a nasty twist. The investigating officers from the Crime Unit were leaning toward the obvious conclusion. A well-known TV anchorwoman, known for her investigative skills, was nearly killed by a sniper and the shooting was probably related to one of her stories. The investigation into her work and who might be involved would continue in Portland, well away from Grand Island.

Everything made too much sense, fell too easily into place.

Luke knew in his heart that there was something not right about the police department's conclusion. Even if his instincts were wrong, it was way too early to draw conclusions. He believed Dr. McGill was in danger, and she wasn't telling him the truth – a lethal combination.

Luke had asked Alice Seymour, one of the other officers working on the island, to come in early for her afternoon shift. She had found nothing suspicious among the passengers or their vehicles at the ferry terminal this morning, and the locals had reported nothing suspicious. Alice was a rookie with drive and determination. She'd made it clear she wanted his job when he retired, and she could have it. Retirement was looking better every day.

"There you go." Alice placed a mug of tea on Luke's desk and sat down in the chair opposite him.

Luke had learned to accept the expression of guarded concern on Alice's face. He figured she was like everyone else – she wanted to know how an officer in the drug squad could have lived with a woman who trafficked in drugs and she must wonder why he hadn't known what was going on. There had to have been signs. And there had been. He simply hadn't connected the dots. That's what love had done to him – made him stupid.

Feeling the tension build, he rotated his shoulders. "I've been on the phone with the Crime Unit."

"And?" Alice plunked her cup on the corner of his desk, her expression eager.

"They're treating this as an attack against Lisa Wade. They're looking into her work, to see if there might be something contentious there."

"That's a real good plan. Anything from the lab?"

"Nothing we didn't already know."

Alice leaned forward. "I wish we had a little more physical evidence to go on."

Luke saw the clear signs of impatience in her movements, and figured now was as good a time as any for him to tell her his suspicions. If things unfolded the way he suspected, he'd need her help. "Alice, what if Lisa Wade wasn't the intended victim?"

Alice raised one eyebrow. "What makes you say that?" she asked, skepticism framing her question.

Could he trust his flimsy theory to a disbelieving young officer? More importantly, did he have a choice? He cleared his throat as he organized his thoughts. "I have a gut feeling about this case."

"Gut feeling?" she asked, her tone one of surprise.

He held up his hand to stop her response. Now that he had committed himself to revealing his concerns, he wanted to get them all out in the open. "Just hear me through on this. Two women are hit by a single bullet on a lonely marsh at sunset. On the surface, neither woman seems to have anything in her life that would suggest a motive for the shooting. But we know it was a professional hit, so that rules out a random accident. All the police efforts are being directed at the one most seriously injured."

"I have to agree that it makes sense to consider Lisa Wade as the target."

Luke didn't like the accommodating tone in Alice's voice. Alice was a by-the-book police officer, just the way he'd once been...

"I'm saying that we may be concentrating on only one plausible scenario, when an entirely different one is possible." Luke rested his hands on the scarred wood of the desk and leaned forward. "What if the intended victim was Dr. McGill?"

"We need motive." Alice's eyebrows arched. "Do we have one?"

Luke wasn't willing to mention his other theory, the one about drugs. With his past firmly behind him, he didn't want to go down that path unless he had good reason. "A doctor could have a whacko patient."

"Then, we have the question of opportunity." Alice tilted her head. "Her life is probably very predictable. Why not shoot her as she entered her office? Why wait for a lonely marsh on a small island off the coast?"

"Maybe the gunman made a snap decision. Maybe Dr. McGill cancelled his appointment to make this trip, and he was angry. You never know what can trigger a disturbed person."

"But isn't that a little far out, even for you? Professional hit men are seldom classified as disturbed in that sense." Alice hid her skepticism behind a grin as she picked up her cup.

"Maybe the disturbed person hired the hit man. It's just that...there's something too pat about this. If someone was after Lisa Wade, they'd have lots of opportunities as well..."

"You're right. But a professional gunman would have been certain who he was firing at. He wouldn't have made such a mistake."

"For the sake of argument, what if the killer meant to shoot Dr. McGill? The shot grazed her arm before hitting Lisa Wade. He missed on the first try. He's still out there. And if he's determined to try again, what then?"

"Then Dr. McGill is still in danger, especially vulnerable because all our attention is focused on Lisa Wade." Alice rested her elbows on the arms of the chair. "You really think Dr. McGill could be the intended victim?"

Luke met Alice's questioning glance. "I hope not. But until I have evidence, other than the severity of injuries...."

"I see," Alice said, but her expression said she didn't see at all. Next, she'd be asking him if he needed a vacation.

"Alice, look at what we know. Forensics believes the hit was professional. The shooter hit both women, probably because they were standing together, plus the shooter's spot was on pretty uneven terrain. His feet could have slipped as he fired. The rifle used was powerful enough to penetrate the soft tissue of Robyn's arm and strike Lisa's chest. He had to have a powerful scope, given the distance. Which would mean he should have had a clear sight on his intended victim."

"Yeah, and the Questar birder scope the women were

using was powerful enough for Dr. McGill to see the man who fired the rifle. It would make sense that he saw his victim, unless it went off by accident," Alice mused.

"Professional hit men don't make mistakes like that."

"God, I wouldn't want to see the face of the man about to shoot me, not like that. I read your notes. I noticed she didn't give any physical description, but who could under the circumstances? Poor woman."

"I contacted Dr. McGill's office and got the doctor that shares office space with her. It seems Dr. McGill has had some pretty serious problems in recent years."

"Serious problems... Of what sort?"

"She sought professional help after her brother and fiancé were killed in a boating accident three years ago. It seems she was the only one found onboard the boat when the Coast Guard arrived. There had been two others aboard the boat, her brother and her fiancée, but neither was found, dead or alive. The events preceding the accident are still unclear."

"So, this would make the second serious incident in which Dr. McGill was involved. Beyond that, I don't see the connection."

Alice wasn't on board with the idea. Luke sighed. "And I'm not sure there is one."

"This accident three years ago, did it have anything to do with drugs?" Alice asked.

"I'm looking into that, but it seems the investigation was a long one, and the case is still open. I'm tracking down the investigating officer. He might have something to offer." Luke shuffled the faxes on his desk and stood up. "If I had one shred of solid evidence...."

Alice scuffed the floor with her toe. It was obvious she didn't agree with the direction he was taking.

He prayed his gut was wrong. "I think it's time I had another heart-to-heart talk with Dr. McGill."

. . .

Robyn sat in the window seat at the end of the upstairs corridor of the inn, and stared out through the rain-misted glass. She'd made a call to the hospital in Portland. All Lisa's vital signs were normal, and the surgery had gone well. Her surgeon was optimistic about the outcome.

Packing her duffel bag had made her arm hurt, but had helped to block the mental image of the man who had fired the gun. Robyn pulled the air into her lungs, trying to tamp down the fright that bubbled up at the memory.

There was nothing wrong with her that getting back home wouldn't cure. She took another cleansing breath. When she got home to Portland she'd go to the hospital and see Lisa She'd be on her way as soon as Brad came back with the van.

She shifted in the narrow seat, trying to make her arm more comfortable. Brad and Sandy were driving her to the ferry terminal when they got back from their early morning birding expedition. She glanced at her watch impatiently.

"Dr. McGill?"

She knew the voice without looking his way. He had obviously tiptoed up the back way, ready to twist what she'd said into something sinister. Officer Carlisle had made it clear in the hospital he didn't trust her.

She waited, listening to the soft chimes of the clock in the reception room downstairs – its elegant notes in direct contrast to the apprehension tightening her throat.

There was nothing more she could tell him. All the signed statements in the world couldn't alter what had happened. "Yes." She supported her injured arm as she turned to face him.

He moved closer, towering over her, his presence filling the space. "I've got a few more questions about the shooting."

She eased her legs off the window seat and looked up at him. Under different circumstances, she would have liked his tentative smile and the solidness of him. "What can I do to help you?"

"How long have you been friends with Lisa?"

She sighed in resignation. "Years. We went to school together."

"What do you know about her personal life?"

Guilt niggled at her. She and Lisa had not been very close the past year. Blame it on their separate careers, and on Robyn's preoccupation with Jason and his problems. "I know she had a condo, she traveled in her job, and she is good at what she does. Everybody knows who she is."

"Lisa had a popular street drug in her possession. Did you know anything about her drug use?"

"Drug use? Lisa didn't use drugs, and I resent the implication." Were the police going to do to Lisa what they'd done to her? If the officer pursued this line of questioning, she would call Lisa's lawyer and alert him to what was going on.

"You were her friend and her physician, you must have known about the Dilaudid she was taking."

"She had a prescription from her surgeon after surgery last year, that's all."

"That's not all. Lisa Wade had a new prescription for Dilaudid, and thirty pills were found among her personal belongings."

Robyn remembered that moment in the bathroom. *Why hadn't she asked Lisa about it?* "People are allowed to get a prescription for pain. Obviously that's what she did in this case. Are you suggesting that she had a drug problem?"

"I'm not suggesting anything. I'm asking you because your name was on the prescription at the pharmacy."

Surprise followed shock as Robyn brought her gaze to meet his. Had she been so careless as to sign for a prescription without knowing the cause of Lisa's pain? It couldn't be. "I didn't prescribe any such medication. I didn't have any reason to."

"Then, how do you explain the prescription?"

"I can't, only to say that Lisa hasn't been in my office for over six months, and then, only to refill a prescription for birth control pills--"

Robyn stopped as the realization hit her. "It's not what you're thinking. Lisa would never forge my signature to get a prescription—"

"I'm afraid she did, unless you have another explanation."

"Lisa was working on a story about drugs. I don't know the details."

"The police in Portland are checking into that at the moment. But you're saying you did not prescribe Dilaudid for her?"

"I didn't write the prescription." And she knew where he was going with this but she knew Lisa would never forge a signature, not in a million years. There had to be some other explanation.

Robyn waited as he scribbled something in his notebook. The silence of the inn surrounded her, making her feel completely alone and vulnerable.

"Do you know any reason why someone would try to kill Lisa Wade?"

As much as she'd expected this line of questioning, his words came at her with all the force of a physical blow. Robyn held her injured arm close to her body. "Unless it had something to do with her work." She would go straight to Lisa's hospital room when she got back to the mainland. "Someone is watching her, right?"

"She's being protected around the clock." He gave a dismissive shrug. "It's not Lisa I'm worried about. It's you."

Her heart jumped in her chest. "Me? I hardly qualify. I'm a

doctor in a small practice. There's nothing remarkable about my life."

"Dr. McGill, you told the nurse at the hospital you were afraid."

"And I told you I don't remember saying that. They gave me medication--"

"Let me remind you; you told the night nurse that you were afraid you'd killed someone. Were you referring to the shooting on the marsh?"

Robyn felt the sting of tears. "I probably was. I'd just been injured. Who knows what I was thinking or what I meant?"

"Again, I ask you to clarify, if you can. You told the nurse you thought you killed someone. Can you explain?"

How could she explain to him? To anyone? She didn't understand it herself. "I don't know. I don't remember."

The officer scribbled quickly then returned his attention to her. "Have you ever had this experience before?"

She gave him a quizzical glance.

"Have you ever had reason to believe you killed anyone?"

"No! Of course not! Why would you ask such a thing?"

His eyes watched her with genuine concern and she had an odd feeling of comfort in the midst of her anguish. That surprised her more than she thought possible. A police officer was the last person she'd accept comfort from.

He eased onto the window seat beside her, forcing Robyn to move deeper into the corner. His gaze was thoughtful as he spoke. "Have you had any crank calls? Any unexplained incidents in your life recently?"

His words sent a sick feeling swarming through her, followed by the old feelings of guilt. "No calls, nothing unusual. No one has any reason whatsoever to want to hurt me."

"Do you have any patients in your practice who have a history of psychiatric problems?"

"Of course, every doctor has patients that have those kinds of problems, but I can't imagine any of my patients wanting to kill me."

There was a long pause as she waited to see if her answer satisfied him.

"Please understand. This investigation involves both you and Ms. Wade. We're looking into Ms. Wade's associates as well as yours. With your cooperation, I'm sure we'll have something soon."

There it was again, the implication that she was not cooperating, not being open. "I'll help you any way I can."

"Glad to hear that, Dr. McGill. You're feeling better?"

Not knowing how to respond to his sudden interest in her health, Robyn simply nodded.

The officer continued to watch her, to take in everything about her.

Was her life to be laid open to scrutiny again? Was there anything she could do to stop the inevitable?

Lisa's involvement in the story about drugs had to be behind all this. If they looked into that she was sure the investigation would lead the police straight to the person responsible.

Then she remembered the feeling she'd had on the ferry. Had someone been watching her because she was connected to Lisa? What if someone *had* been stalking her friend? Should she tell this policeman about the man on the ferry? Surely the officer would remember him? He had been standing beside the strange man on the deck. Would he remember?

"I want to help you find whoever shot Lisa."

"Then, you won't mind a couple of questions. It's about a boating accident three years ago. Can you tell me what happened?"

What was wrong with this man? There was no connection,

and there was no way she was going to let him dig up her past. "How would an accident three years ago help to find Lisa's attacker today?"

"It might eliminate you as the intended victim in this case, and make it easier to be sure we're on the right track," he said, his assessing gaze holding her captive.

If answering his questions would make him see how important it was that he find Lisa's attacker, she was willing to make the effort. "My brother died." She eased the words past her lips. "My fiancé died."

He leaned closer to her, leaving no space for her to avoid his intense gaze. "You were there when it happened?"

Robyn felt the beginning of a sob deep in her body, and forced it back. "Yes."

"It must have been frightening for you, and I'm sorry to have to bring it up again but I can't ignore the possibility that you were the intended victim of this attack."

Robyn felt her resolve crack into a myriad of tiny hairline fractures. "It can't be me. There's no reason for anyone to want to kill me." She reached out with her good arm, determined to grasp some part of him, to make him understand. "There's no reason whatsoever, for anyone to want to hurt me."

He pulled her outstretched hand into his. His warm strength more threatening to Robyn's resolve than any confrontation. "But you were on the boat when they died, a crime which remains unsolved. It must have been a horrible experience."

"Yes, it was. We were on my brother's sailboat, just off Brier Island." She held the memory in an iron grip.

"Just the three of you?"

She felt the pressure of his fingers. His encouraging gaze helped contain her fear as her anguish welled up in her chest. "Yes, the three of us."

"What happened?"

Robyn recoiled from the blank shimmering space in her mind. "I don't remember.... Everyone on the boat died except me." No force could hold back the tears as they slid down her cheeks now, unbidden salty tracks clouding her thinking.

"I know this is extremely painful for you."

He continued to hold her hand and his strength steadied her, leaving her vulnerable to him. She edged her fingers from the protective space of his hand. "Officer Carlisle. This has gone far enough. What's over is over."

Robyn placed her good hand over the fingers of her injured arm. "I've had to learn to cope with the loss of the two most important people in my life. It hasn't been easy."

"I understand."

"Do you?" She looked into his eyes. Genuine sympathy, like a physical force, flowed from him.

"Dr. McGill, as you know, there's still a great deal of information missing about what happened to you and Lisa."

"Yes, and I hope you find out who did this to Lisa as soon as possible." She squared her shoulders, and felt a stinging ache in her wounded arm. "You must realize I have to leave the island and return to work. I'll give you my private number. You can call me if I can be of any further help to you."

Luke leaned toward her, his expression solemn. "At the moment, we don't have enough information to be certain of your safety. I know you want to leave, but I can't allow it."

"What do you mean?"

"Because you don't remember what happened, and because we have so little to go on, I can't let you leave until I have more information. You may still be in danger."

"That's not possible. You have no reason to believe that the gunman fired at me. Besides, I'll be safe at home."

The stern set to his jaw, and the cynical glint in his eyes gave her his answer. He didn't believe her or trust her.

Robyn gritted her teeth. "I've had enough. I'm going home."

"Dr. McGill, you are my main witness and possibly the intended victim of a gunman's attack." His eyes never left her face and the determination in his voice didn't waiver.

"Officer Carlisle, I'm sure the people of this island like and respect you. I'm sure you do a great job, and your intentions are good."

"And your point is, Dr. McGill?"

"You may run this island any way you like. But you're not running me." Robyn tilted her head at him in angry defiance and was rewarded with searing white-hot pain shooting down her injured arm. "I will leave when I wish."

"What you wish has little or nothing to do with it."

Robyn waited until the officer had gone down the stairs to the lobby, waited for the rain outside the window to stop pounding, and then she moved. She wasn't through with this officer, not by a long shot. A plan was already developing in her mind. She would enlist the help of Sandy Fowler and Brad Allen. They would understand her need to get home.

She heard the birders return to the inn as she walked back to her room. The torrential downpour must have put an end to the outing. She waited for Sandy and Brad at the top of the stairs.

When Brad reached her, he stopped. The other birders bustled past him, intent on putting their gear away and changing into dry clothes. "I'm ready to take you to the ferry terminal, whenever you're ready," he declared.

Brad touched her shoulder, and for a few seconds Robyn considered changing her plan. He might see her need for his help as something more than what it was and try to take advantage of the situation.

Remembering the determination in Officer Carlisle's eyes made her decision for her. "I need to talk to you and Sandy. I need your help."

Brad's eyes narrowed. "What's wrong?"

"Please, just find Sandy and come to my room. I'm heading there now."

Robyn settled on the sofa in her room and waited. If the police officer had left her any other choice, Robyn would not have chosen Brad or Sandy to help her. She didn't want to encourage Brad's interest in her. Admittedly, she didn't know Sandy all that well, but the woman had always been very friendly toward her. Sandy had told Robyn on several occasions how lonely she was, and as a result Robyn had encouraged her to join the birding group, despite her physical limitations.

She planted a determined smile on her face as Sandy and Brad entered her room.

Sandy stood next to the door as if unsure of her role. "Robyn, I'm sorry––"

"What she means is we're here to help." Brad walked past Sandy and sat down beside Robyn on the sofa. "Tell us what's going on," Brad said, snaking his arm around Robyn's shoulders.

Robyn moved out of Brad's reach and beckoned for Sandy to sit down between them. "Officer Carlisle refuses to let me leave the island."

"Good heavens! Why?" Sandy peered at Robyn.

Brad got up and sat on the coffee table across from Robyn. "Go on."

"He thinks I may be in danger."

Brad leaned forward, a scowl on his face. "That's ridiculous."

"Of course it is, but he's determined to investigate the possibility. In the meantime, I have to stay here, at the inn, until he says I can leave."

"Why would he think you're in danger?" Sandy's voice was barely audible.

"The police believe that it was a professional hit. Lisa has police protection in the ICU, in case someone tries again."

"The local police are going to botch this whole thing," Brad said as his expression darkened.

"Robyn, why does the police officer think you're in danger?" Sandy spoke slowly as if she were trying to grasp the idea.

Robyn leaned back in the sofa. "He believes the gunman meant to kill either Lisa or me. But because the police on the mainland are watching Lisa around the clock, I could be vulnerable to another attack, especially since they haven't identified the gunman. They don't know the motive, or have any major leads at the moment. At least that's what I understand."

"What can we do to help?" Brad's gaze followed Robyn's every movement.

"I need you to convince the officer that I have to get home."

"You believe he'll listen to me?" Brad asked.

"It's worth a try."

"You can count on me," Sandy said. "What's the plan?"

Brad scowled at Sandy, his eyes darting around the room and back to Robyn. "He must have a good reason for wanting you here."

She wasn't going to mention Officer Carlisle's interest in the boating accident. "He wants to protect me." Robyn rolled her eyes. "As if I can't look after myself."

Brad reached across the narrow space that separated them and touched her hands, caressing her fingers in an intimate, circular pattern. "This probably isn't what you want to hear, but if the gunman is after you and not Lisa, you need to be protected."

Robyn shot him a look, and yanked her fingers free of his grip. "You don't believe that, do you?"

"I don't believe anyone would hurt you. But if you are in danger, there are too many opportunities in Portland for someone to go after you again. On a small island, with the police and myself looking out for you, you'll be safe."

"You?" Robyn didn't try to keep the disbelief out of her voice. Brad was the very last person on earth she wanted looking out for her.

"I told you a long time ago I won't let anyone harm you ever again. The police can count on my help, and so can you."

Aghast at this turn of events, Robyn searched her tired mind for an argument against having Brad get involved in her situation. "Brad, you need to get back to work. I can look after myself. I'll keep my cell phone on."

He shook his head. "Robyn, the policeman is right. We can't take any chances with your safety. I won't leave the island until you do."

CHAPTER FIVE

The smell of stale coffee and yesterday's donuts filled the air of the filing-cabinet-lined office belonging to Officer Carlisle. Above the filing cabinets the wall was covered with award plaques and framed commendations. Robyn took note of the fact that the officer's full name was Luke Garfield Landry Carlisle. Named for more than one cat with an attitude. Somehow it fit.

It was just after lunch, and Robyn had come here to state her case to the crusading policeman before leaving on the afternoon ferry. She'd spent fifteen minutes trying to break through his granite façade, but to no avail. The arrogant SOB had kept his silence while she rattled on, trying to reason with him.

Robyn could feel anger rising from her stomach, and stifled it with a show of calm. "I refuse to be closeted away while someone is out there threatening Lisa's life."

"Or threatening your life," he said with infuriating persistence.

"No one is threatening me."

"And if they were?"

She wanted to bang the desk with her fist. "You're not listening."

"Dr. McGill, it's for your safety—"

"My safety, be damned! My friend's safety is all that matters here. She's the one the killer went after. Lisa doesn't deserve this…" Her voice slid toward silence. She'd never forgive herself for putting Lisa in harm's way and she wouldn't do it again. But if Luke Carlisle was right. If the killer were after her and not Lisa…oh hell…

No, that couldn't be right. There was no one in her life that would harm her. No one.

If Robyn were the crying kind, this would be the time. But having Luke Garfield Landry Carlisle think she was a weepy female wouldn't do. Why it mattered what he thought escaped her, but that was immaterial….

"I have responsibilities, a busy medical practice, I am Lisa's best friend and her doctor. I can help the surgeon care for her." Lisa's surgeon was among the best. Her argument sounded a little weak, even to her. But if Luke Carlisle could be swayed to see things her way…

Officer Carlisle continued to watch in much the same way a parent would watch an errant child throw a tantrum.

His control irritated her, goaded her to continue. "Have you no compassion? What can I possibly do to help Lisa while I'm stuck on this island with you?"

He leaned forward in his chair and tapped the desk with his pen as he seemed to consider her argument. Robyn couldn't help but notice the powerful bulge of his shoulder muscles against the cotton of his shirt, the way his strong fingers held the pen, the way he frowned when he concentrated. He came around to the front of the desk and rested one hip on the edge.

Crossing his arms over his chest, he frowned down at her. The few inches that separated her from him were scant protection from his overpowering maleness. She leaned well back in her chair, putting as much distance between them as possible. When she tucked her hand into the pocket of her jacket, the sudden effort jolted her arm, sending an immediate rumble of pain down her and reinforcing her sense of vulnerability.

"Dr. McGill, are you all right?"

She shrugged and stared him down.

"We've been over this before. I have a responsibility to protect you," he explained.

"You said the man had a gun with a scope. You said he was a professional and a professional hit man wouldn't miss. He didn't, as far as I'm concerned. Lisa's investigations must have made some people angry. One of them decided to do something about it." Feeling trapped, Robyn rose and walked to the filing cabinet.

He followed her. "Arrangements have been made to protect her in the hospital. I have no doubt that Lisa will be kept from harm. But you—"

"We've been through all of this before. You have no reason to believe that anyone intended to kill me. I'm a doctor. It's my job to help others. I've told you all I know." When she turned to face him, her nose met his chest.

"Don't sneak up on me," she said to the wall of muscle at the end of her nose.

"I didn't." His words were punctuated by something that sounded suspiciously like a chuckle.

Trying to gain the upper hand in this circular argument, Robyn pulled her head back and planted her words firmly in the air between them as she glared up at him. "You have no right to keep me here."

There was an intimate quality to his gaze as they stood facing one another, but Robyn knew better than to mistake what looked like intimacy for what it really was – an officer of the law determined to get at the truth he believed she harbored.

Afraid he might press his advantage if he sensed her confusion, Robyn turned her back to him and studied the filing cabinet. She was running out of options.

Robyn had tried to reason with the officer by adding Jason's need for her to bolster her case. Her mother had lived with Jason and her since Peter's death. But the officer had answered that argument with one of his own. He made her see she could actually threaten Jason's safety by going home to him, and Robyn wouldn't do anything to jeopardize Jason's safety. Robyn had to admit the officer had a point, if – and it was a big if – she truly was in danger.

"Dr. McGill, just listen to me for one minute."

Reluctantly, she turned to face him. There he stood, his feet spread wide, his arms crossed over his chest, a stance that added even more substance to the man who stood firm for what he believed. An unbidden thought crossed her mind – he would be someone she could count on if she ever needed him.

The truth was, she would never need him. Win, lose or draw, she was leaving the island tonight. There was one last ferry to the mainland and she would be on it.

Knowing she needed distance to say what she planned to say, she stepped away from him. "I'm listening," she said.

He countered her move, by edging closer, close enough for her to smell the clean, scrubbed scent of his skin. "I'm going to level with you, Dr. McGill. I don't know why anyone would shoot either of you. I need you here to help me piece together what happened, and I need to keep you safe. The gunman may try again."

"The gunman is probably long gone. Besides, why should I go along with your hunch?"

"What if I'm right? What have you got to lose by

humoring me for a couple of days? If I'm wrong, you can push your I-told-you-so button to your heart's content. I'm sure you'd enjoy the chance to remind me of this conversation."

That and his grin of encouragement weakened her argument. He had a good point, for once.

"Dr. McGill, agree to help me for a few days. Stay in the inn as much as you can. If you want to go out somewhere, take someone with you or call me and I'll find someone to accompany you."

The depth of concern she saw in his eyes, the sensitivity on the part of someone she hardly knew, weakened her determination.

He took her fingers in his, a gesture that promised safety. "Please do this for me. If I have no proof to support my theory in the next couple of days, I'll take you back to the mainland myself."

He made sense for all the wrong reasons. If she could only make him understand how guilty she felt over what happened to Lisa.... "Could we come up with a compromise?"

"And that would be?"

"I'll go back home long enough to see Lisa."

"And your attacker will politely sit on his hands while you travel alone for a few hundred miles? I doubt that."

"You could come with me." What was she saying? The last thing she wanted was more up-close-and-personal exposure to this man.

"Thanks for the offer of your company. As much as it appeals to me, I have too much to do here. If I did let you leave, what assurance do I have that you would return?" He gave her a look that said how little he trusted her on that one.

But why should she be surprised? When was the last time a police officer trusted her?

She stiffened her spine and stepped out of the circle of his physical influence. "You will have to arrest me to keep me on this island."

Steel glinted in his eyes. "Anything's possible."

Luke Carlisle had had enough for one day. It was five o'clock in the afternoon and he had been staring at a pile of papers that lay tidied and lifeless on his desk.

Though his eyes were fixed on the pile of paper, his mind was on Dr. McGill. She was hiding something, something important. At the same time, he couldn't shake the suspicion that she was in danger. Damn it all to hell! Why couldn't she see that he was trying to help her?

Luke heard the door open in the outer office.

"Anyone home?" Alice Seymour called out.

"In here."

"Where's Dr. McGill?" Alice looked around with a grin on her face as she dropped into the chair across from him. "Did you lock her up?"

A sound at the door to his office announced Robyn McGill's return. She dropped her duffel bag on the floor and crossed the room to stand in front of his desk. "Either you arrest me, or I'm going home."

Luke gripped the edge of the desk, and tried to lock his expression into one of authority.

Dr. McGill stood before him, righteous indignation showing on her face, softened only by the gentle waves of hair falling around her cheeks. He was reminded again of how much the demanding doctor looked like his ex-wife.

Yet there were subtle differences. Dr. Robyn McGill didn't have any hardness in her eyes. He couldn't help but notice the way her Tilley pants hugged the soft curve of her hips, the way her cotton shirt strained across her perfectly rounded breasts. Just in the nick of time, he stopped his gaze from hovering over the hint of cleavage at the open neck of her shirt. She also had the sexiest mouth he'd seen in a long time. All proof that he needed a sex life.

And if he didn't gain control of this situation, he'd look like an idiot in front of the doctor *and* Alice.

"Dr. McGill, I'm sorry about your difficulties." Alice Seymour moved to one side. "Would you like to sit down?"

"No, thank you. I won't be here very long." She rested her good hand on her hip and gave Luke a penetrating stare. "I'm waiting to know if I'm going to jail."

His male pride danced around his endangered ego as he mulled over his options. If Robyn McGill stood her ground, would he lock her up? Not in this lifetime."Dr. McGill, you told me you'd do whatever you could to help find Lisa's assailant, and finding her attacker would prove which of you he was after. Finding Lisa's attacker starts on this island. Your help just might make the difference."

"And how do you intend to start looking for her attacker? Or are we to rely on your famous instincts?"

Luke heard her anger, but there was precious little he could, or would do about it. He fought back the crazy urge to reach for her hand. No more mistakes where this lady was concerned, and he knew touching her would be a major mistake. "Everything's being done to determine if the gunman was after Lisa. We're not sure if the shooter is still on the island, but it's possible. Meanwhile there's precious little effort being put into protecting you." He hadn't planned to be so blunt, but the good doctor had a way of getting to him.

"I can take care of myself."

Luke didn't answer right away because every retort he could come up with would be considered sexist by the woman standing in front of him, and he didn't need any more accusing remarks hurled at him. As much as he hated to admit it, Robyn McGill offered an exciting challenge. For the first time in a long while he realized just how bored, lonely and isolated he'd been feeling.

"I'm waiting," she said, and Luke could have sworn she was tapping her sneaker.

What the hell? He might as well go for broke. "I hate to ruin your day, but you're here until I say you can go. If you insist on leaving, I'm sure I can come up with some sort of legal reason to keep you here. How does hampering an investigation sound?"

"You wouldn't do that," she said.

He nodded. "I want you to keep your cell phone with you, and be sure you don't go out alone while you're here on the island. In the meantime, I'm sure you'll enjoy Raven's Nest Inn. It's better than a jail cell."

Back at the inn, Robyn yanked her clothes out of her duffel bag, and stuffed them back into the drawers. The officer was wrong, totally wrong. Lisa was the victim of this terrible shooting. Her friend was in mortal danger while Robyn whiled away the hours trying to convince a stubborn cop to use his head, instead of his gut.

As much as Robyn wanted to leave, she had no intention of telling the officer about her phone call to her office. The clinic staff had confirmed her calendar was cleared for two weeks and also what Robyn already knew; Lisa's last prescription signed for by Robyn was for birth control pills, nothing else. She wanted to get back to Portland so she could check into the situation.

"Here, let me help you." Brad strode through the open door into her room.

"Thanks, but I'm finished." Robyn flopped down on the edge of the bed. "You and the police have won."

"This isn't about winning. It's about your safety."

Robyn didn't like the patronizing tone in his voice, but there was precious little she could do about it. She had enough problems to deal with at the moment.

Brad placed his sweaty hands on hers. "What if you are in danger? At least if you're here, you have friends to protect you and a policeman who believes you're in danger. If you go home, there will be no one to look out for you."

Robyn didn't see how Brad could believe she was better off here than home, but she didn't argue. Frustrated and sleep deprived, she wanted to be left alone. "I can't take any more today." She lifted her fingers free of his. "I think I'll lie down for a while."

Thankful when Brad took the hint and left, Robyn stretched out on the bed. Her head swam with fatigue and worry. The shooting had forced some frightening memories to the surface. Some horrible, out-of-focus images she thought were gone from her life had returned. The same half-memories she'd experienced three years ago.

Luke Carlisle must never find out what she suspected happened that night in her past. If he did, there was no limit to the amount of damage he could cause in her life. But if she stayed on the island, she might be able to convince him that her past had nothing to do with this shooting. She'd make a call in the morning to her office and to Jason and her mother so she could arrange to stay a couple more days – until Officer Luke Carlisle found something else to worry about other than her.

Robyn closed her eyes.

.　.　.

Tangled in the sheets, sweat sticking to her skin, she awoke to a pitch-black room, except for a slash of light coming from under the door beyond the foot of the bed. Dread mixed with anxiety greeted her, and for a moment Robyn couldn't remember where she was. But the same old feelings of guilt and anxiety were with her. She must have been having the nightmare again.

She made her way to the window and opened it. The cool air shocked her heated skin. The backyard of the inn was ghost quiet and dappled in moonlight. The sudden chiming of a clock one floor below shook the silence.

Breakfast wouldn't be served for another four hours, and she was suddenly starving. The inn provided an after-hours snack on the sideboard in the dining room.

Quietly, she opened the door and tiptoed along the hall. The undulating snores of the man in the room two doors from hers kept her company as she made her way around the turn in the corridor leading toward the back stairs.

The door at the bottom of the stairs squeaked as Robyn unhooked the old-fashioned latch and stepped into the butler's pantry between the kitchen and dining room. A silver tea service glowed in the muted light of the full moon spilling in through the tall Georgian windows of the dining room. She welcomed the cool breeze swirling around her ankles as she closed the door behind her. Probably someone left the window open in the kitchen to compensate for the lack of air conditioning.

A muffled thud echoed from somewhere over Robyn's head. She glanced up to see the huge pewter chandelier tremble from the impact. *Had someone fallen out of bed?* Or did this have something to do with the murder mystery weekend? How she wished she'd taken Lisa up on her suggestion and joined the fun, searching for clues, rather than birds.

She turned her attention to the sideboard in the dining

room, gathering what she needed to make a peanut butter sandwich. The moonlight was lovely, but why was she making her sandwich in the dark? Smiling to herself, she went back to the butler's pantry and slid her fingers along the wall, looking for the light switch. Some instinct made her glance toward the kitchen.

A dark figure loomed in the space near the back door.

Her pulse pinged. Air froze in her lungs as the figure moved toward her, a ski mask covering his face.

She opened her mouth to scream.

His hands claimed her throat as he slammed her into the wall, knocking the air from her lungs. "You're dead," he hissed in her ear.

Two dark eyes glittered from behind the slits in the mask. Robyn pulled at his hands that squeezed her throat.

He tightened his grip, lifting her off the floor.

Bright starbursts mingled with the blackness forming before her eyes. Her aching lungs demanded air they had no hope of—

"Is anyone here?" a man asked, his voice hoarse with sleep.

A loud growling sound came from the man holding her. "I'll be back."

His hands released her, sending her tumbling to the floor. Gulping air, she crawled to her knees in time to see the man go out through the kitchen window.

CHAPTER SIX

M*idmorning the next day*

Robyn eased her weary body into the hammock on the screened porch of the inn. Ernest Coyne, the guest who had appeared in time to save her, had insisted on calling the police. Robyn was relieved when Alice Seymour showed up. Alice had been gentle in her questioning, but it didn't change the fear that clung to every breath Robyn took.

Her hands shook as she smoothed her hair back from her face. Bruises had formed on her neck, and her throat pained. She had refused to go to the hospital or to see a doctor. What was wrong with her was more emotional than physical.

Feeling totally alone, she'd called her mother. She'd been happy to hear from her, and to know she was safe. Robyn missed her mom and her nephew very much, and wished she could simply pack her bags and go home. Because of her concern for them Robyn chose to keep her thoughts about her safety to herself. It was beginning to look as though the officer was right. She could be in danger.

Her mother said the police stopped by to tell her that they'd check in regularly to see how she was doing. This news left Robyn a little concerned that the police might only add to her mother's natural inclination to worry. But her mother seemed to be happy to have someone stopping by, and Robyn was relieved to know that Jason and her mother were being watched.

Robyn was also relieved to know that her mother and Jason believed her story that she was bird watching every day. Robyn explained she was also helping the Grand Island Police with the investigation. She couldn't tell her mother her fear that going home might mean the sniper would follow her. Until last night, she'd honestly believed she wasn't in danger. But everything had changed. She would never expose her mother and Jason to that kind of danger.

After breakfast she'd called the hospital and was told by the surgeon that Lisa was out of danger and he was pleased with her progress. He expected to be able to move her from the Intensive Care Unit the next day. The fact that she had to stay on the island was less difficult to accept once she knew that Lisa's condition had improved. But she had a more immediate problem: After what happened last night, it was pointless to try and convince Garfield's namesake that she was not in danger.

There had to be some other explanation for last night. Whoever attacked her had meant to harm someone, not necessarily her. There was no way the attacker could have known she had left her room...unless he'd been watching... from the upstairs hall. Or maybe he was also a guest here at the inn?

No! She couldn't accept that idea. There had to be something else going on. For someone to be waiting and watching her inside the inn was ludicrous. She remembered the cool air she'd felt just before the attack. It could have been an attempted robbery, and she had simply been in the way.

What happened during the night brought back her guilt

around the boating accident that had killed Nathan and Peter, a feeling of guilt so strong she called her psychiatrist, Dr. Stanley, early in the morning. The phone call had been difficult because he seemed determined to get her to tell him more about where she was, and what was going on, than in helping her with the sudden reappearance of her intense feelings of guilt. But once she told him everything that happened, he'd been very reassuring. He wanted to set up an appointment for her as soon as she got back. He even volunteered to come to the island. She'd nixed that idea in a hurry. She needed more time before facing one of his intense therapy sessions.

The hammock swung slowly.... She closed her eyes and let her mind drift. The effect was hypnotic. The scent of wild roses surrounded her as the warm air nestled against her skin. Out here in the warmth and quiet, Robyn could almost believe that her life might someday be normal.

The hammock slowed to a stop. Opening her eyes, she met the policeman's assessing gaze. "Oh, it's you. Why aren't you out chasing a speeder, or something?"

Luke smiled down at her. "No speeders on Grand Island today. They've been banned. I have to find other ways to amuse myself. Were you asleep?"

"No," she sighed. "Just seeking refuge from the local policeman's inquisition."

"I came to see how you were feeling after last night."

"I'm fine, and right where you told me to be," she responded feeling trapped by his scrutiny.

Pulling his aviator sunglasses off his forehead, and tucking them into his shirt pocket, Luke looked down at her, his glance more analytical than familiar.

She knew the look. As a physician she had employed it many times to determine the emotional state of a patient. Being on the receiving end of such a careful scan was different, somehow invasive. "What can I do for you this morning?"

"I want to hear what you can remember about the person who tried to hurt you last night."

"Again?"

"Humor me. Your attacker went out the window that led to the verandah. The investigators may be able to find something, a print, maybe. In the meantime, I don't want you to go near your room. We're checking it as well."

"What has my room got to do with it?"

"If your attacker was looking for you, he would have found your room first, to be certain he knew where you were. So, your room, the doorknob, all the flat surfaces will need to be dusted for prints. The inn management have provided you with a new room," he said as if he were talking to a child.

His attitude pissed her off. She wasn't a child, and she wouldn't be treated as one. "That man appeared out of nowhere. Just before he attacked me, I felt a cool breeze, which makes me think he hadn't been waiting for me or anyone else. He was trying to rob the place, and I got in the way."

"And maybe pigs fly." He sat down on the edge of the verandah railing, one eyebrow hitched up under a curl that had dropped over part of his forehead. "One last time. Stick close to people you know. I realize that you feel confined and I also realize that you want to get out of here for a bit. But please don't leave here alone," he said, his words gentle as his gaze went to her throat.

Something stirred in the depths of his eyes as he looked at her bruises, something deeply personal. It occurred to her that Luke Carlisle might be a man with secrets of his own.

There was that feeling again; the feeling of safety she felt when he was close. Was she drawn to him because she was vulnerable after the shooting, and then the attempted strangling? Or was this man different from the other police she'd met?

She was certainly more at ease with him than the others, but the circumstances were also different. Officer Carlisle hadn't accused her of anything – at least not yet. "So, how can I help you?" she asked.

"First, how are you feeling?" His gaze never left hers, but his expression softened.

"A little bruising and a tightness when I swallow. Nothing that time won't heal," she said, touching her neck.

Why isn't he butt-ugly, overweight, cross-eyed, with a wart on his nose?

Instead, he was sexy, strong and obviously concerned for her; in a world where few people showed concern for the doctor they depended upon. She was beginning to like him.

But it had been the same way with Officer Russell Black, the lead investigator after the accident. He'd been so supportive, caring and professional...at first. And when his investigation went nowhere, he turned on her, making her the prime suspect.

As sweet as Luke Carlisle seemed at the moment, he was behaving just like Russell Black did.

Luke watched her with professional detachment as she got up from the hammock and sat down in one of the wicker chairs well away from him. "Lisa hasn't been able to help the police with an identification of the gunman. I have four photos of possible suspects in the shooting. I'd like you to look at them, if you're up to it."

He couldn't tell her that these suspects were picked from a group of known felons who had been released from prison in the past six months. Men who had committed similar crimes and had nothing to lose. Men who probably had no connection to the attack, but after last night he had to try something, anything that might provide a clue. He was grasping at straws and he knew it, but as long as there was a chance....

Luke watched as the uncertainty on her face gave way to determination. She held out her hand. "Let me see what you have."

Keeping his expression neutral, Luke passed her the four photos.

Robyn placed them on her lap and slowly lifted the first one. Passing it back to him, she shook her head. The second and third one produced the same result. As she reached for the fourth one, she bit her lip. "This one might be the gunman." Holding the photo up to the light, she squinted at it. "It's so hard to know for sure. The cap hid so much of his face."

Concealing his disappointment, Luke gathered the photos into an envelope. He hadn't expected her to identify any one of them, but he'd hoped. The Crime Unit would not be happy either. With so little physical evidence they'd drawn a blank.

The only hope they had was that Dr. McGill would remember something more substantial, anything that would provide a clue to the identity of this man. He sat down in the wicker chair across from her. "Robyn, I'd like to talk to you about our arrangement."

Her glance met his. A smile tinged her lips. "You mean, 'me Jane, you jailer'?"

"Your sense of humor's back, I see."

"It's nice to know you think I have one." She tucked her legs under her and flicked a strand of hair off her forehead.

"A sense of humor is the most attractive quality a woman can have."

"Ditto for a man."

"You're feeling a lot better. I admire your courage, especially after last night."

He had decided to take it slow, to let her lead the conversation. Alice Seymour didn't seem to think that there was much more to be learned about what happened the night before, but he felt compelled to talk with her about it anyway.

"Courage is overrated." She glanced at him, a rueful smile on her face.

"Whatever it is, you seem in remarkable spirits after what you've been through."

"I decided this morning that I needed something positive out of this trip. I've heard there's a riding stable on the island that teaches children to ride. I'm going to bring Jason here and enroll him when this is all over."

Luke saw the love and longing for Jason in Robyn's eyes and knew in that instant how strong the bond was between her and her nephew. "He'll enjoy learning to ride. I did."

This time, she gave him a strong, in-your-face smile that softened the longer she held his gaze. He could like this woman – her strength, and her caring – all of it.

Keeping his professional distance was essential, if he had any hope of finding the gunman. Yet, he was drawn to her this morning in a way he hadn't been before this.

The gentle breeze stirred the climbing rose bush that draped its green leaves around the post behind Robyn's head.

"It's a beautiful day. If you like, we can talk while we walk in the garden."

It would seem the officer was full of surprises today. First, he didn't grill her about what happened the night before, and now he wanted to go for a walk. Keeping her expression neutral, Robyn got up and went down the steps leading to the herb garden. The mingled scent of lavender and lemon balm comforted her as surely as the look of determination in Luke's eyes disturbed her.

What more was he looking for this morning? After showing her the photos, she assumed he would have other questions for her. His sudden change in demeanor confused her. Was his plan to keep her off balance? Luke Carlisle was too smart not to be piecing together some sort of scenario, and if that scenario included her life three years ago when her brother and her fiancé died...

She had loved Nathan completely. She had most of her wedding plans made before the accident. Cancelling them was a lonely job that added to the sense of loss she thought she would never overcome. Somehow she had managed to get this far in her grieving process. Nothing would make her go back to those memories, the loss as well as the horror of being a suspect.

The police had not recovered either Nathan or Peter's body, but whatever else they had discovered had been kept from her. She had always assumed they'd found something on which to base their suspicions of her. She'd been the only one who hadn't died that night, and there was no explanation as to why she survived. But what scared her most was that her memory loss might be covering up something horrible she'd done that night. Something that would hurt her family and her if it came to light.

Had they been attacked that night? Had the sailboat been boarded and had Nathan and Peter died trying to protect her? Or had her brother and fiancé died because she didn't have the courage to act?

Blocking the destructive thoughts, Robyn stepped into the garden with the warm sunlight pouring over her, acutely aware that her life had come full circle. She was again facing an officer of the law who might, sooner or later, believe that she was involved in what happened to Lisa. Without turning toward him, she asked, "So, what new evidence have you found?"

"Nothing, except you've been on this island less than a week, and have been attacked twice. We still don't have all the information we need to be sure about any of this. In the meantime I'm not prepared to accept that you aren't in danger."

"That's the best you can do? Try harder. And don't drag my past into it," she warned.

He shoved his free hand farther in his pocket and toyed with the cell phone he held in the other. "You were very lucky last night. I have this feeling that your attacker made a mistake in judgment, one he won't repeat."

She stopped near a rosemary bush. "A feeling. How do you expect to help me if you have no concrete information?"

He didn't answer.

"Okay, let me ask you something."

"What?"

"If someone is after me, how are you going to protect me on an island with only a couple of other police officers?"

"And if last night had happened at home? With your family?"

Jason and her mother could have been hurt. Or worse. "Oh God."

Trying to keep her thoughts away from the implication of Luke's words, she glanced around. Danger seemed so far removed from where they stood, surrounded by gently swaying plants and the rustle of the wind in the pines.

"Robyn, we can resolve all this if we work together."

She took note of the fact that he was calling her by her first name. "As long as you stop picking at my past."

"I can't promise."

At least he was consistent, she thought ruefully. They

walked through the herb garden and out along an old road behind the inn. She kicked a pebble ahead of her on the dirt road. "You must have checked into my life. What did you find?"

"You're loved and admired by your friends and your patients."

"Then, what more do you need?"

Luke held out his hand to stop her. "Wait right there." He knelt and examined the dirt in front of them. Turning slowly on his heels, he looked back toward the inn.

"What is it?"

"Someone parked a vehicle here in line with the inn. By the length between the tire tracks it was mostly likely a van or a SUV. Where's your room?"

She pointed to a window half hidden by the old apple tree, and just above the herb garden.

A frown creased his forehead. "This old track is blocked off at the road, but there are fresh tire tracks. Who would have been parked up here and why?" He spotted a couple of cigarette butts near the tire imprints. "We may have found something."

He stood up and opened his phone. "Yeah, it's Luke Carlisle."

He put his hand over the cellular phone. "Don't step any further." He pointed to the tire marks imbedded in the sandy loam. "It could be that the man who attacked you watched from this spot. The killer may very well have known every move you made in the past few days."

Luke and Robyn stood in the screened porch of the inn, inches from one another, but Luke could tell by her expression that much more than a few inches separated them. "As I said before, you need to be very careful where you go and with whom. If someone waited and watched the inn it suggests premeditation. And in all likelihood, that means the man who attacked you was on his way to your room last night."

Luke glanced around the grounds, wondering if the man was still hidden somewhere close by, waiting for his next chance. "Robyn, where did your group go that day after you left here? Was Simmons Marsh your first stop?"

For a few minutes she didn't answer, her shoulders hunched, her eyes brimmed with tears. "Luke, the man's finger. I remember, now." She held up her right hand. "He was missing the right middle finger, just above the first knuckle. I remember because it stuck out, kind of funny, when he squeezed the trigger...."

He wanted to shield her from the memory, but knew he was too late. He settled for putting the information away in his mind and touching her shoulder as he opened his cell phone to make a call.

"Are you okay?" he asked.

She drew a deep breath and met his glance. "Yeah."

He felt a strange desire do or say something to wipe the uncertainty from her face, and tell her everything would be all right – to offer a lie to soothe away the haunted look in her eyes.

He punched in the numbers and left a message for Andrew Webb to get back to the island as fast as he could. He would meet him at the inn when he got here. Within seconds, Andrew called back and Luke filled him in on what had happened and what they'd found. Andrew said he'd run it on the computer to see if any known gunmen were missing a middle finger, but the search could take a while.

Luke put yellow police tape around the tire tracks while Alice questioned the locals looking for anyone who might have seen the van behind the inn.

Meanwhile, he turned his full attention to Robyn and asked her again, "On the day of the shooting, where did you go when you left here?"

With a shuddering sigh, she murmured, "We-we went to Bear Harbor. A rare gull had been sighted."

Her trembling shook Luke's professional resolve to remain at a distance. The woman standing before him was in emotional pain, and no wonder, after what she'd been through these past few days. "Is there anything else you can tell me?" he ventured.

Her only answer was the lost expression on her face. Seeing her struggling with her anxiety drew him to her. He couldn't leave her under the circumstances. "I want to go to Bear Harbor. Will you come with me?" he asked trying to prolong his time with her.

"No. I'm going upstairs to lie down. I need time to think...about all this." She cradled her arm as she gave him a distracted smile. "Don't worry. I'll go straight to my new room."

Meeting her glance and seeing the defiant tears swimming in her eyes, once again, he admired her ability to maintain control. Women with less emotional strength would have been sobbing and crying by now. As he watched her turn and walk back inside the inn, he felt his connection to her grow stronger.

When Andrew Webb arrived, he went straight to work. "No information on the gunman with the missing finger, but we're still working on it."

"Okay. If you don't need me, I'm heading over to Bear Harbor to see what I can find. The birding group went there before going to Simmons Marsh. I want to see if there's anything there."

Andrew and Luke agreed to meet on the cliff road leading down to Bear Harbor as soon as Andrew was finished.

Despite everything going on Luke couldn't seem to keep his thoughts away from Robyn McGill during the drive to Bear Harbor. Somehow she had managed to get behind his defenses in a way that astounded and frightened him. He'd been keeping his emotional distance from women ever since his disastrous divorce. And now, out of the blue, a woman he'd first viewed as uncooperative and difficult, who bore a distinct resemblance to his ex-wife, had begun to claim his thoughts. Worst of all, he seemed powerless to stop it.

He supposed he could blame his preoccupation with Dr. McGill on his job, at least part of it, but the rest…

He pulled his police cruiser to a stop on the high point of the road leading into Bear Harbor. Climbing out of the car, Luke scanned the panoramic view spread before him; the deep blue-green water framed the deep green of the forest sweeping along the desolate shoreline. Bear Harbor was a place where dulse was harvested from the ocean floor at low tide, but most of the time the area was abandoned.

The stark loneliness of the scene gathered around him. Chickadees chimed in the stillness. The popular birding area down below him on the beach was in clear view from where he stood, perfect for a gunman with a rifle and a high-powered scope.

Luke assumed the gunman had watched the birders after they arrived on the island and that he might have followed them here, hoping for a shot. Luke moved off to the side of the road where the gunman would have had the best vantage point. A tall pine's branches whispered over his head, while its roots lay exposed at his feet. The hard packed clay around the spot, unmarked and dull in the flat light, held no signs of human contact.

Luke looked out toward the horizon to where a large,

white-hulled yacht had anchored just a few days ago. The water, spreading out toward the Maine coast, shimmered like glass – smooth and uninterrupted.

Luke remembered the first time he'd driven the road to Bear Harbor. It had been a miserably wet day. The fog completely obliterated the coastline. It was his first week on the job; a week filled with doubt as to whether his decision was the right one. At the time, he had little choice if he wanted to remain a police officer. That was so unfair as far as he was concerned. His wife, Charlene, had been sent to prison, and he was left to put his life back together.

All the wasted time and energy spent to get her into therapy had proved pointless when she was found guilty of trafficking in cocaine. After realizing her deceit and all she'd put him through, he couldn't find it in his heart to forgive her. She'd been defended by a high-priced lawyer from Boston, and never even attempted to get in touch with him after she'd been arraigned on charges.

Luke walked back toward the cruiser, remembering his first conversation with Amos Potter in Bear Harbor. The old man had been picking up beer bottles, dressed in an old wool jacket with the elbows worn through. They'd chatted for a while until Amos announced that he believed in the occult and that Grand Island was the secret rendezvous spot for the Prince of Evil.

He wondered what made him remember that. He shook his head in disbelief.

Luke walked around the area a little more, searching for any sign that someone had stood on this promontory and watched the scene below. He glanced around the ground and saw two cigarette butts sticking up out of the gravel a few feet ahead of his cruiser. If they were the same kind as those found near the tire tracks behind the inn...

As he moved closer to take a look he heard the gravely crunch of another vehicle approaching the area.

It was the Crime Unit van. Moving around to the back of his cruiser, Luke flagged the van into position behind him.

"Not another spot," Andrew said as he leaned his head out of the window of the van.

"You'd better check." Luke pointed. "There don't seem to be any tire marks, but there are cigarette butts."

"Right. I'll have a look." Andrew moved the van closer and cut the engine.

"The birders were here before they went to Simmons Marsh and the gunman would have had a clear shot of the birding area below from up here."

Andrew got out of the van and came toward Luke, his expression one of concern. "Luke, I hear you've decided to keep Dr. McGill on the island, even though she wants to leave. Do you think that's a good idea?"

So, the news had reached Portland. Luke averted his gaze. "I'm just not one hundred percent sure that Lisa Wade was the intended victim."

"I'll give you that, but should you get this personally involved?"

"I'm not getting personally involved. You know me better than that." He hoped his little white lie sounded close to the truth.

"And even though we have no idea who did this, or where they are, you're willing to risk keeping her here on the island? And if you're wrong, how will you defend yourself if she lodges a complaint against you?"

Andrew was avoiding the real issue, and that was one Luke had struggled with ever since Charlene had ended up in prison. Some people, especially those inside law enforcement, found it hard to believe that he was oblivious to what his wife was involved in. Some people were watching and waiting for what they referred to as his next misstep. He understood his friend's concern for him, but there was nothing going on here that was illegal or immoral. Instead of answering, Luke filled Andrew in on what happened at the inn the night before.

"So you feel this supports your theory that the police in Portland are watching the wrong victim?"

"Well, the attack on her last night increases the likelihood, doesn't it?"

"Could be. Or she could have interrupted a break-in." Andrew shrugged. "But you need to know how other people might view your position. That you might not be paying attention to what is so obvious to others, that your judgment could be called into question."

Luke recognized his friend's attempt to quietly point out the potential dangers. He also knew that he couldn't let Robyn leave the island, not when she could be in danger. Call it overcompensation for things in his past.... "Andrew, I promise – as soon as you guys can convince me Dr. McGill wasn't the intended victim – I'll send her packing back to the mainland."

"I understand where you're coming from, but you can't risk your career on this woman."

His job meant less to him with each passing day. And he was beginning to wish he'd quit after the incident with Charlene. "What if I'm right? What if she is in danger?"

"Then, get the proof – after you send her back where they have the resources to look out for her."

"The proof depends on you and what the lab finds. Meanwhile, whoever did this is still out there."

Andrew walked to the side door of the van and started to work gathering what they hoped would be evidence to lead them to a suspect.

Luke watched him do his job, but his thoughts were with

Robyn. Had he made a mistake by insisting she stay on the island? Was Andrew right? Was he letting his past interfere with his judgment? Was he trying, yet again, to help a woman who didn't want his help? Another woman who wouldn't tell him the truth, even when it might save her life?

CHAPTER SEVEN

As darkness seeped toward the island Brad peeked at Robyn who glanced out the van window. She'd agreed to go for a drive with him to one of the favorite birding spots on the island.

"Brad, I really appreciate your concern for me since the shooting. All of this has brought back memories for me, and I know you understand because you're the one who found me on Peter's sailboat. I often wonder what would have happened if you hadn't shown up with the Coast Guard when you did."

"Put it out of your mind. I was glad to help. We were all friends, and if I hadn't had to work that weekend I would have been with you, remember? Besides I promised Luke Carlisle that I'd look after you and I have to agree with the policeman. If someone *is* after you, between him and me, we'll keep you safe."

"I haven't been out to the Anchorage since the day Peter and I came here to look for Night Herons. It was one of his favorite birding spots on the island." The rutted road made the van bounce from side to side.

"I thought you'd enjoy a walk along the beach." He gave her another quick glance as he spoke.

"I would. After listening to Officer Carlisle's preposterous theories I need to get out and enjoy the island."

Brad could hear the tension ease from Robyn's voice. Despite all his preparations he was a little worried about the next hour or so. Not exactly worried – he knew how it would turn out when Robyn learned the truth – but he was still just a little anxious, wanting the meeting planned for that evening to go off without a hitch.

Last week he'd received a call from an old friend, someone from his past, someone who would change everything. All Brad had to do was give Robyn a chance to see how different her life would be when she confronted 'Roberto' – that was his friend's undercover name now. He hadn't known he was an undercover agent until he confided his secret to Brad five years earlier. After that Brad was pleased to help out in any way he could. But his friend had disappeared and Brad hadn't heard from him again until last week. When Roberto asked for his help Brad was pleased to support someone who led such an exciting life. He was looking forward to what would be expected of him. He loved the intrigue and the secrecy surrounding what Roberto did.

But what was most intriguing was that his friend had asked to meet Robyn in person. That was the last thing Brad expected but who was he to argue? He didn't carry the weight of clandestine operations and government secrets on his shoulders.

At first, Brad toyed with the idea of not taking Robyn to the Anchorage. He loved Robyn and didn't want anything to happen to her, but when Roberto said he only wanted to talk to Robyn, Brad couldn't refuse. Once Robyn heard the truth about that night on the boat, about how she'd been betrayed, she would be free to go on with her life. And he would be there for her. "I thought you could use a break from all the tension and the terrible stuff that's been happening to you."

"When you first suggested coming out here this evening, I wasn't sure if I should. Now that we're almost there, I'm looking forward to it."

He glanced across at her and saw the frown line forming between her eyes. "Glad to hear it. And you won't be disappointed."

"Thanks. This is my first birding trip since Nathan and Peter died...."

"We're going to have a nice drive and walk the beach in the moonlight. If you're afraid, don't be. I wouldn't let anything happen to you."

"I didn't get a chance to tell Officer Carlisle where I was going."

Thank the Lord for small mercies. "Don't worry. We'll be back before the officer has time to miss us." Brad pulled into the winding dirt road leading to the water.

"We should have brought Sandy Fowler with us this evening. I saw her sitting in the lobby of the inn earlier. I thought she went out birding with the group, but she hadn't. She seemed pretty keyed up about something. I worry sometimes that maybe I encouraged her to join an activity that's too stressful on her physically, given her hip problems although she seems to love it."

"I asked her to come along this evening." He shot Robyn a glance, not wanting to take his eyes off the narrow track for fear he'd drive into the ditch. "She said she had to rest. She has a lot of pain sometimes when she climbs over rough terrain, like we did today."

He hadn't really asked Sandy, but that was his little secret. He had several secrets where Robyn was concerned, not the least being her brother Peter.

Trying to keep Robyn from asking too many questions,

questions he might not be able to answer, Brad continued, "I'm sorry you couldn't join us today. The fall warblers were everywhere."

"Now that Luke has discovered tire tracks that might prove the shooter watched the inn, it may all be over by the time we get back this evening. Or if they find the man with the missing finger."

"Missing finger?"

"Yeah, I remembered something this morning. When I saw him through the scope I saw the shooter was missing the end of his middle finger. Luke thinks they will find the killer with that bit of description, something so unique should be easy to find in their police data bases, wouldn't you think?"

The police officer and Robyn were on first name basis. Tiny rivulets of jealousy trickled through him. Was the police officer using the situation to his advantage? Robyn was a beautiful woman and lots of men would. Was the cop using the shooting incident to promote his own personal agenda where Robyn was concerned?

There was no room for any other men in Robyn's life. Brad accepted her devotion to Jason, but another man? That was out of the question. "I imagine they have the name and address of the man by now. It will all be over before tomorrow. All the more reason for us to enjoy a walk in the moonlight. I know how much you love a moonlit night."

Robyn really looked at him...for the first time since they'd started out. "Brad, I hope you haven't read something more than you should into what has happened over the past few days."

"Like what?" he asked, annoyed that she was so oblivious to his feelings for her.

"You and I work in the same hospital, but that's all––"

"Hey! We're out to have a fire on the beach in the moonlight, not a date," he scoffed, trying to make light of her comment. Robyn hadn't spent any time alone with him for months, but tonight would change everything. He was counting on it. He slowed for the parking lot entrance he'd scouted out earlier. He pulled the van into the part of the parking lot that fronted on the beach.

Robyn seemed preoccupied about something, or maybe it was the memory of the last time she'd come here. Or maybe the busybody police officer was the reason. Lots of women loved a uniform, and maybe Robyn was one of them. Brad decided he'd have to keep a closer eye on the officer's activities where Robyn was concerned. No man was going to sweet talk his way into her life the way Nathan Green had, not if he had anything to say about it.

"Let's get out and go down to the beach." Brad opened his door, and was relieved to see Robyn unfasten her seat belt. If she had refused to get out of the van, he would have a problem.

Brad zippered his jacket against the chilling breeze blowing in off the bay. The moon formed a large white globe just above where water met the darkening sky. Brad walked around the vehicle and opened Robyn's door. As he did, he saw a vehicle hidden in the alder bushes off to the left.

If anyone else was out there, other than Roberto, the meeting would not happen. He knew Roberto wouldn't risk it.

Brad gritted his teeth. He wanted this meeting to happen.

Leo felt the thrill of excitement course through him. He was on the hunt and he was ready to kill. The rifle nestled against his side caressed his thigh with a lover's touch. The semi-automatic handgun snuggled under his left armpit was his insurance against any change of plans.

The bitch would be with someone he didn't know, and he

didn't give a damn. He only had eyes for her. The long grass near the stand of pines hid him completely. His friend had told him where to be and when, and he'd gotten in place and was ready to fire without raising suspicion.

He'd thought of every contingency. His van was parked back against the trees along the far side of the parking lot. If anyone asked, he was out with his cameras getting black and white shots.

He had used spruce branches to wipe out his tracks from the van to his hiding place, and he planned to use the same technique on his way back to the van. He'd had a little trouble out on the marsh, but tonight he wouldn't fail. He placed his feet firmly on the ground, checked his rifle and waited for the target to come into view along the water's edge.

As he snuggled the gun against his cheek, Leo felt the hairs on his neck rise against his collar, warning him that someone else was close by. Fear as hard as steel made him turn, his eyes searching – his mind on fire. A glint of moonlight on metal, the appearance through the scraggly pines of the one person who held the ultimate power over his life was the last image his retina would ever send to his brain. The short pop of sound was lost on the rising wind.

"Brad, I'm freezing." Robyn pulled her jacket tighter and huddled on the sand next to the rock outcropping where they sat. "The fire isn't putting off any heat. Why don't we go back to the inn?"

"Not much of a boy scout, am I?" he asked, his eyes dark pools in the firelight. Robyn had never seen Brad act so strangely. She'd been relieved and happy to come out here, anything to escape her horrible day and the confines of the inn. And Luke had said that she had to have someone with her when she went out, and she did. She loved this part of the island, but it wasn't the same without her brother, Peter. She felt a tightness in her chest. She missed him so much.

"Don't you like the view?" Brad put his arm around her.

"I love the view. That's the problem, too many memories. I guess I wasn't quite ready for this. I should have stayed at the inn." She got up and began to walk toward the water's edge.

"Look, a loon just ahead of you." He pointed, getting up and going to stand beside her.

Half-heartedly, she glanced along the shore. "I see it. They'll soon be migrating."

Robyn watched the shoreline, checking for other loons. Their long lonesome call brought a flush of memories. She and Peter had spent hours watching the loons on Cassidy Lake when they were kids. A movement at the edge of the pine trees caught her eye. Was it the flickering firelight playing tricks on her vision? "Brad, is there someone out there?"

Brad glanced toward where she pointed along the line of trees that led down to the water's edge, an expectant look on his face. "I don't see anyone." He took her arm and pulled her along with him. "Let's get closer so you can show me what you see."

Robyn suddenly sensed that something or someone was definitely out there watching them. The same feeling she'd had on the ferry. "Brad, this doesn't feel right. I'm sure I saw something."

"Let me look," he stood close to her, gazing in the direction she had pointed.

"Okay, enough, let's go. We can come back another time," she said, a chill running down her spine. "This was a mistake. I want to go back."

"On a beautiful night like this? Come on, Robyn, relax a little."

"I can't." Robyn twisted out of his grip.

"Come on now, you didn't really see anything; it's your nerves." He gave an excited laugh.

What was going on with Brad? She cursed her stupidity for coming here with him. She came, partly out of guilt, and partly out of the need to escape the inn for a few hours. Now, with the feeling of being watched riding her shoulders, and his strange behavior, none of that mattered.

"Brad, I've had enough for one night. I want to go back to the van."

"Let's walk down the beach for a bit first."

Robyn studied his face in the muted light. His eyes searched the woods as he stood next to her. "Brad, you stay if you want."

Robyn started across the sand away from him. He wasn't following her, but she really didn't care. She'd walk until someone came along and gave her a lift. There were always tourists drifting around the island this time of year. Maybe a birder would come by and pick her up.

"Wait for me," Brad called out to her, his voice sounding frustrated in the cool air.

Relieved that Brad had decided to follow her back, Robyn turned and waited for him.

"Robyn, it's a lovely night," he said pleading with her. "Why don't we—?"

The sound of gunfire screamed around her, tearing the night open.

CHAPTER EIGHT

Robyn fell and rolled across the sand to the water's edge, the sound of her own screams careening through her head. Paralyzing fear held her stiff in its grip as the chilled water lapped against her trembling body.

With her eyes closed against the fear, a memory flashed.

She clung to the rail of a boat as it bobbed in the water. A man leaned over the stern of the boat, his back to her. Someone groaned in pain.

"Robyn! Oh my God!" Warm arms wrapped around her, and someone sobbed into her hair, yet the image of the boat remained, drenching her in fear.

"I never meant for this to happen," Brad sobbed.

She was being gathered up like a child and cradled – just the way her brother had done so many times when they were young. She snuggled closer, drawing warmth and strength from the arms encircling her.

A man's face came into view. "Robyn, are you hurt?" It was Brad's face, and his arms shook as he held her.

"No, I fell——"

"What a relief! Someone fired a gun and I thought you'd

been hit." His arms tightened around her as he stroked her hair.

"I'm wet...." Robyn pulled away from the shelter of his arms and sat up, trying to sort out the reality of the deserted beach from the memory on the boat.

She had heard gunfire. Trying to clear the confusion in her mind, she stared around her at the dying light of the fire. There was no boat, only the sound of the dark water lapping on the shore.

"Please say you're all right." Brad's voice was nearly a sob.

"I'm fine. I want to get out of here, though. Now."

"We're getting out of here and going to the police." Brad stood and pulled her up with him, his arm tight along her shoulders.

She felt her knees shake as her legs took her weight. Anxiety mixed with anger in her stomach. "Brad, what happened? Who fired the gun?"

"I don't know, but we're not waiting around to find out." Half carrying her, Brad started toward the van, his breath coming in short gasps. "Robyn, I shouldn't have brought you out here. I'm sorry."

Robyn struggled to keep pace with Brad as he pulled her along. "You couldn't have known that some lunatic would be out here with a gun."

"I shouldn't have risked your safety. After what's happened to you, I should have used my head and kept you at the inn. The officer warned us all to keep you safe from harm."

Brad gathered her up in his arms, and ran the remaining distance to the van.

"What are you doing? Put me down."

He eased her onto her feet again, and held her with one arm as he took the keys from his pocket with the other.

Robyn heard the scrape of metal on metal just before he swung the door open.

"Climb in and get down."

The panic in Brad's voice struck a chord in Robyn. The urge to move as quickly as possible overpowered her need for reason. She scrambled across the driver's seat and into her own seat as fast as her shaking legs allowed.

Brad started the van and spun out of the beach area without a word. Robyn sat low in the seat and stared in horror as Brad gunned the van, narrowly missing an oncoming car. Alder bushes brushed Robyn's side of the van as the lurching vehicle skirted the edge of the ditch.

"Brad!"

Brad checked the rearview mirror before he spoke. "We're going to the police station. Get down on the floor!" He reached across, and placed a hand on her back, pushing her down and out of the seat.

Torn between shock and surprise at Brad's behavior, Robyn crouched on the floor of the van as it swayed and bumped through the night.

She watched Brad as he drove. His face was a mask of fear – not his usual calm, collected expression. She braced against the rocking motion of the vehicle, sorting through what had happened. *Why was Brad so frightened? Had someone intentionally fired at them?*

She summoned all the common sense she could muster, and took a deep breath. There had to be an explanation for the gunfire that had nothing to do with them. She and Brad were overreacting because of everything that had happened. "Brad, we need to let the police know, to warn people away from the area. Whoever fired that gun is dangerous. Someone could get hurt."

Brad punched numbers into the cell phone the van

carried for emergencies. "Officer Carlisle." Brad's eyes checked both side view mirrors as he waited.

"What do you mean? Where is he?" He listened, one hand on the phone and the other on the wheel as the vehicle rocked along the dirt road, gravel pinging along the sides of the van.

"Get him to call me. There's been another shooting. This time at the Anchorage." Brad slammed the phone closed and sucked air through his clenched teeth, his face an inscrutable mask.

"What in heaven's name is wrong with you?" she asked, Brad's fear spreading to her as they careened along the narrow road.

"I need to think," Brad muttered, his intense gaze never leaving the road ahead.

Robyn climbed into the seat and snapped on her seat belt. "Well, do your thinking out loud – for my benefit."

"What are you doing?" Brad yelled at her as she settled into the seat beside him.

"I'm behaving like a rational person." Robyn frowned at him. "I know you're frightened. We both are, we're miles from the beach now, and I'm not hiding on the floor, and you need to calm down. No one's after us."

"We can't be sure," Brad said.

Exasperated, she turned to him. "This is insane. No one is after us. Stop this right now," Robyn said as Brad swung the van up onto the highway and accelerated.

"I'm not taking any chances with your safety. We'll let Officer Carlisle investigate, if we ever find the stupid bastard." Brad roared down the road, taking the narrow turn leading down into Pier Point with such speed the van's tires squealed.

Without slowing, Brad slammed on the brakes at the entrance to the driveway, the rear of the van fishtailing.

"We're almost there." The relief in Brad's voice was palpable.

Robyn suppressed the anxiety gnawing at her throat as she searched the yard for the police cruiser. She needed Luke's steady approach, his calmness.

"There he is." Brad swung the van in beside the cruiser, nearly knocking into Luke. "It's about time," he shouted through the window.

A half hour later, Luke stood over the dead body of a man bathed in the light from the high-powered flood lamps blanketing the crime scene. In other circumstances, he would have cursed the futility of it all.

Not this time.

The man sprawled on the ground before him was missing the end of his right middle finger. Someone had killed the man who threatened Robyn's life. But Luke knew only too well, that there was likely another more dangerous scenario. If someone else had taken his place, the police would now have to start over to identify the latest shooter. Time that would leave Robyn vulnerable to another attack. Luke struggled with the dread seeping through him.

"The gunman had been armed with two weapons, a handgun and a high-powered hunting rifle. He'd been prepared to fire when he was killed. The gun must have gone off as a reflex action when he was shot in the back."

"I'll agree with you on that one." Andrew stood next to Luke for a few minutes, his eyes scanning the spectacle before him. The moon stood high in the sky as if overseeing the activities taking place inside the police cordoned-off area. The temperature had dropped a couple of degrees since sunset, making the air nippy, but no one seemed to notice.

Luke watched the men work, laying out their equipment, taking measurements.

"Did we find a vehicle, the one this man used?"

"No vehicles. We did find tire tracks along the dirt road near here. We're taking imprints to check against the tracks we found outside the inn."

"Do you suppose that the two people traveled together to this spot, then one shot Leo and left in the vehicle?"

"That's very possible." Andrea Webb glanced around the area. "You're thinking they knew each other? That the gunman was killed by his accomplice?"

"Anything's possible." Something niggled at the back of his mind…. "Can we turn him over? I need to get a better look."

"In a minute," Andrew said as he and his assistant finished their collection near the corpse's right side.

As he turned the body over, Luke stared in surprise. "Leo Lord."

"You know him?" Andrew asked.

"I'd met him once. A photographer. According to the locals, he came here a few years ago after retiring from the Coast Guard. I didn't know he was missing a finger."

"Something doesn't add up. If this is the man who fired at the women, he's a professional hit man. How could he have been taken out so easily?"

"He *must* have known whoever killed him…." Luke and Andrew glanced around the soft, sandy loam, searching for anything that might indicate where the killer stood.

"There, over by that tree." Luke said, moving as carefully as possible. "It looks like a footprint."

"And fresh as well." Andrew slid his cap back on his forehead as he stared down at the footprints in the damp sand.

"The person standing here had a clear shot." Luke gestured toward the body lying just a few feet away.

"My take on it is we're pretty safe assuming that this is the man who shot the two women. We'll comb this area carefully. Whoever did this deserves a medal," Andrew muttered.

"After we put her or him in prison."

Andrew stopped his careful observation of the area, and stared at Luke. "What made you say that?"

A stiff breeze lifted the gaudy yellow tape marking the crime area. "What if the killer was a woman?"

"We don't have anything to suggest that. Another one of your famous hunches?"

Luke pointed at the footprints at the base of the pine. "The foot prints are small, and should be deeper given the sandy soil. They aren't, suggesting a person who didn't weigh very much...either a woman or a very thin man."

"What's this?" Andrew pointed at a narrow hole near the footprint. "What would make an imprint like that? A stick?"

"Maybe" Luke rubbed his jaw. "Or a sand crab hole? Sand crabs leave this sort of mark. Or maybe a cane? Or maybe not related to the crime scene? Take your pick."

Andrew continued to stare at the odd imprint as he spoke. "Didn't you say Dr. McGill and a friend were out here?"

"Yeah. Brad Allen."

"What were they doing out here in so late in the day?"

"Good question."

"Luke, maybe we've been looking in the wrong direction. Maybe the killer is a lot closer than we think."

Luke felt the thought sink into his mind, leaving an open wound of dread. Why hadn't he considered the possibility before? "You don't really think Brad Allen brought her out here--?"

"Anything's possible."

Luke's gut contracted against the idea. He'd been the one to encourage her friends to stick near her as much as possible. When he'd learned that Brad had taken her for a drive he hadn't been suspicious… Was it possible that someone Robyn trusted put her in this kind of danger? Or even worse, acted in concert with the killer to get her alone where she could die without much chance anyone would come to her aid?

Exhaustion was making him edgy and paranoid. He turned his attention to Andrew Webb who had started his slow, methodical work on the crime scene.

"How many more trips to the island do I have to make?" Andrew joked.

"With any luck at all, this will be your last one."

"My wife's beginning to think I have a woman over here. You call. I leave in a rush to catch the ferry," Andrew kidded.

Luke appreciated Andrew's attempt at humor. It had been a grim night, starting with the call from Brad Allen. "Don't take it personally, Andrew, but I hope I don't see you again for a very long time."

Her sleepless night had changed nothing. A man had died. Robyn felt the grittiness under her lids. Every time she closed her eyes the beach rose in her mind in horrifying detail – the gunfire, the danger, but most of all the memory of a boat.

Both the incident on the marsh and the one on the beach had thrown up memory fragments for her that didn't make any sense. After hours of thrashing around in her bed, Robyn had finally given up. The innkeeper was still asleep when she crept downstairs to the kitchen and made herself a pot of coffee.

Now, as the wisps of fog cleared away from the garden, she sat in the screened porch, her hands wrapped around the blessed warmth of the steaming cup, waiting for Luke. He'd told her he'd come to her as soon as he could this morning, and she'd sought comfort in his words during the long hours of darkness.

Last night Brad had been wild with fear at the thought that someone had fired a gun near her. He had stayed by her side late into the night, his concern genuine. One of the other reasons she'd been awake last night had been the guilt she felt because she had distrusted him when they first arrived on the island. Her suspicions of Brad now seemed unfounded, especially in light of how kindly he had treated her after she'd been shot, and every day since. Only someone who genuinely cared would have been so kind and considerate.

At the crunching sound of tires on gravel, Robyn walked over to the screen door. A police cruiser pulled into the parking lot beside the inn.

A sudden rush of warmth, mingled with relief, flowed through Robyn. Somehow her world seemed safer each time Luke entered it. He didn't see her at first, but she saw him glance expectantly at the entrance of the inn, his expression solemn.

Robyn had learned something about Luke Carlisle last night when he took charge of the investigation, and did a thorough yet gentle interview with her. She'd expected the same attitude he'd exhibited when he interviewed her after the first shooting but the change in his approach left her both thankful and curious. And because he'd been kind to her, she'd warmed to him, and felt she was beginning to understand him a little better. Like her grandmother used to say: 'Every bad thing that happens has a seed of good planted in it.' Maybe her grandmother was right.

Robyn smiled and beckoned to him.

Luke moved toward her, his shoulders appearing to sag under his navy blue jacket, and there were gray circles under his eyes. She held the screen door of the porch open for him. "You've been up all night, too."

His weary smile filled her with unexpected pleasure as he walked to the steps and stopped. "Is that a diagnosis, Doctor?"

His voice eased the loneliness she'd lived with all night. A loneliness that all Brad's caring and overtures of affection hadn't alleviated. "No. You look the way I feel."

He stood on the porch step, his glance kind, yet assessing. What she saw in his face was more than tiredness. There was something else in his careful scrutiny. Did he need to reassure himself that she was okay? It occurred to Robyn that the people Luke Carlisle loved would always feel protected and cared for, and to think she might be someone he cared for added a bright spot to her otherwise dreary day.

This wasn't love between them, for sure… Far from it, but that didn't really matter at the moment. Still, a tingling sense of awareness bubbled through her, wiping away the long hours. She tilted her head up to meet his gaze. "Come in. You look like you could use a break."

His fingers enfolded hers, sealing the two of them off from the rest of the world and a long-buried feeling of being truly connected to someone began to stir near Robyn's heart. She wanted him to take her in his arms, to hold her close and reassure her that everything would be all right. It didn't matter whether that was true; she simply needed Luke to say the words.

Robyn wanted to tell him how glad she was to see him. But telling him something like that would reveal too much. And maybe, just maybe, her take on what was happening between them was a fantasy. A fantasy borne of shared circumstances. "Can I get you a cup of coffee?"

"No thanks. Maybe later. Robyn, I have something to tell you."

"I hope it's good news," was all she could think of to say.
"Let's sit down."

Luke's voice was so comforting Robyn wanted to forget why he was here this morning and just talk about ordinary things with him. Find out about the man Luke was.

"By all means," she said. Reluctantly, Robyn led the way to the wicker couch.

Luke continued to hold her hand when they reached the seat. Her flesh, under his fingers, was warmed by his touch. Whether the reason was exhaustion or worry, Robyn knew she wanted Luke to stay with her and spend time with her – even just talking or sharing a joke.

Not daring to let him see the need in her eyes, she stared at the rose print pillows.

"I've finished my preliminary investigation of the crime scene. Leo Lord, the man who fired at you and Lisa, is the victim of last night's shooting," he said, settling into the seat.

Robyn sat beside him, her mind struggling to grasp what Luke had just said. *Could it be that easy? That simple?* "Just like that? The man's dead?"

Luke nodded. "Leo Lord lived in a secluded part of the island. He worked as a freelance photographer after he retired from the Coast Guard. We're digging into his background to see what else he might have been involved in."

The nightmare had ended. She was finally free to leave…. The relief she felt made her light-headed.

"You're sure?"

His smiled, but it was an uneasy smile. "Yes."

So she was free. The threat was over. Without thinking she wrapped her arms around his neck and hugged him close.

"Oh, Luke, I can hardly believe it."

Luke's body stiffened, then his hands patted her shoulders.

"Sorry, I got carried away," she muttered. *Was he embarrassed?*

Disappointed that he didn't return her affection, Robyn eased away from him.

How stupid could she be? Coming on to the officer investigating a murder that involved her. What was she thinking? Had he made any move toward her, shown her anything but professional kindness? No.

"Don't be sorry," Luke said in a tone that sent Robyn's pulse bounding wildly in the chest.

Slowly Luke's arms tightened around her, pulling her into his circle of strength. She basked in the scent of him; the pressure of his muscled arms, the way his breath brushed her cheek. Her lips trembled just inches from his. He bent his head to hers, his eyes searching her face, silently asking... And then he moved his mouth close to hers. She breathed in, her whole body ready, her lips parted.

The first touch of his lips sent her senses whirling upward. She answered his kiss with her own, her lips tasting his, her arms inching upward toward his neck.

Luke groaned as his fingers traced a line of hot points across her shoulders. Locking his fingers in her hair, he pulled her closer, kissed her deeply. Her hands wove their way over the fabric of his shirt, brushing the hardened muscle beneath. Slipping her fingers under the loosened knot of his tie, she touched his warm skin. Her fingers feathered across the pulse bounding in his neck. Crazy, unreasonable happiness filled Robyn. Her heart soared as she kissed him back and knew the thrill of being desired by a man again. Need burned through her. Coaxing words were on the tip of her tongue...

Just as suddenly, his hands closed around her shoulders and he pulled back, his gaze piercing hers. "Whoa. This shouldn't be happening." The words coming from deep within Luke's chest pulled Robyn back to earth. He let go of her. "I.... We need to talk."

Hurt, she leaned back into the cushions and held her hands steady in her lap. She wanted to touch him, be touched by him. But pride held her in check.

Luke sat up straight and rested his open palms on his knees, his eyes meeting hers. "I-I came here to talk to you about something very important."

"If you say so," she said, struggling to recover from what they'd just shared. Searching for her normal composure, Robyn returned to the situation at hand. With an effort, she said, "You found the body of the man who tried to kill Lisa and me."

"We did." Luke stared at his hands.

Robyn felt as if they were reviewing the facts of some case other than her own. "What makes you so sure?"

"The man who died last night was missing the middle finger on his right hand."

"And what's the likelihood of two people--?"

"With the same missing digit? On this small island? Pretty slim."

Robyn's eyes stung with unshed tears. The anxiety of the past few days began to fade away. "I can't believe it. This means Lisa's safe, doesn't it?"

Luke sighed. "Lisa's safe."

"I can leave the inn and go for a walk. I've wanted to do that since I got up this morning. You don't know how much I've wanted to just go out for a walk without worrying that someone might be out there waiting for me."

"So, you did believe me after all?"

"Did I have a choice?" she asked, and gentled her tone when she saw the unease in his eyes. "I just didn't want to think that anyone would hurt me." She couldn't tell him that buried in her denial that she was in any danger, was the feeling that somehow, somewhere, she would pay for that night on the sailboat. Abandoning those you loved carried a price. And she had to have abandoned them. She was the only one the coast guard had found anywhere near the boat or in the vicinity. Robyn drew in a deep breath and held it.

But the gunman's death meant she was free to leave the island, go back to her life, to her job, her mother and her nephew…and to leave Luke. A strange feeling of loss attached itself to her relief when she realized she wanted to stay near the man sitting on the edge of the sofa. How had he become so important to her in such a short time?

She ignored the trembling in her hands, and the dull thud of her heart. "Do you know what Leo Lord was doing out there on the beach? Could he have been taking pictures?"

Luke shook his head. "He was armed, and waiting for someone."

"Why wait there? It's the last place on the island anyone would go."

"That's the whole point. He chose an isolated place where there would be no witnesses."

"To think that Brad and I were there; and very nearly witnessed another shooting. That's scary."

Luke took Robyn's hand in his, a move that surprised and delighted her. "The victim may have been waiting for you."

Robyn heard the words and instantly denied them. It couldn't be possible. "Waiting *for me?*" She heard her voice as if from a distance.

Luke moved closer to her. "He was armed with a rifle and a hand gun. He definitely planned to shoot someone."

Her tears blurred Luke's face, but it didn't blur the raw emotion she saw in his eyes. "I-I don't know…. You think the killer was waiting for me?" Unable to hold herself steady, she eased nearer to him, and found him waiting.

"I wish I were wrong," he said as eased her gently into the crook of his arm.

Warmth and sense of security enveloped Robyn, drawing her to him. Three long years had passed since Robyn had felt the way she was feeling at this moment. Three years in which she had convinced herself that she would never find anyone to share her life with, to feel safe around. She prayed this moment would last.... "Luke, if he's dead...." She spoke into his chest. "It's over, right?"

When he didn't answer, Robyn lifted her face to his. Their eyes met and the anxious lines around his eyes seemed more acute. "I'm right, aren't I?" she asked a second time.

Luke held her at arm's length, his expression one of resignation. "I can't be sure."

"What do you mean?" The man was dead. She and Lisa could get on with their lives. The stress of the past few days had stretched her endurance to the limit. "I am safe. I can go home, right?"

"Robyn, let me explain."

Robyn ignored the caution in Luke's eyes, caution that suddenly had a suffocating quality to it. She needed air and space and her freedom to breathe in the certainty that her life would soon be normal. "I've had enough, more than enough. If you can't simply say the words, and let me get back home––"

She looked into his eyes, and her heart sank at the concern she saw there.

"I know how hard this has been on you. I know I've asked more of you than I had any right to ask. I've been trying to keep you safe."

"And now you don't have to."

"Let me explain, will you please?"

"No. I've had all the explanations I can handle. As far as I'm concerned whoever killed Leo Lord isn't after me. If he were, all he had to do was wait for Leo to do his job, and then kill him. He didn't, which means he was after Leo, not me. They were out there at the Anchorage for reasons that had nothing to do with me."

"That's not the only possible scenario, Robyn."

"But it's the most likely. The man who killed the shooter isn't after me or Lisa or anybody else. The man wanted this Leo Lord person dead and he succeeded." She shot off the sofa and strode toward the lobby of the inn. "I'm going for a walk, a nice long walk before I pack to go home. The fall asters and the goldenrod are blooming along the roads, so beautiful this time of year. I need to have a pleasant memory of this place before I leave."

"Nice going, nimrod," Luke muttered to himself as he watched Robyn disappear. He should go after her, bring her back and make her see the danger that still existed. But he couldn't do that, at least not right now. The look in her eyes told him that she needed time to herself, to absorb the change, and he could hardly blame her. He'd go for a run to clear his head if he wasn't on duty.

In the meantime, he had to face a few things himself – like his attraction to her. The last thing he needed was to complicate the situation with feelings for a woman, a woman who resembled a woman he'd once loved, and who had betrayed him in the worst way.

Who was he kidding? What he felt for Robyn McGill *was* very personal. He'd stepped over the line. He'd let his heart rule his head, and he'd actually kissed her. Only sheer force of will had prevented him from crossing over the line completely. Andrew had cautioned him, and now he'd allowed his feelings to get in the way of his professional judgment.

Each time they were together, they grew closer. If someone had suggested that he would find a woman who looked so much like his ex-wife attractive, he would have vehemently denied it. And yet it was true. Robyn looked like his ex-wife but beyond the physical resemblance there seemed to be little in common between them.

Dr. Robyn McGill wouldn't be the kind of woman, or the kind of professional for that matter, who would use drugs of any kind.

He smiled to himself at the memory of the other day in his office when she insisted he lock her up, her feistiness. Dr. McGill was everything he liked in a woman. She had so much strength, and yet, he remembered how she looked the first day he had seen her in the hospital. Her vulnerability had awakened a need in him to protect her, to ease her pain.

Somehow, he had to fulfill his professional duty as if nothing had changed between them. He now knew his responsibility to help Robyn came ahead of his personal needs. He'd been wise not to act on his feelings beyond the kiss. But being wise obviously had a short shelf life where Robyn McGill was concerned.

He shook off his thoughts. Before anything else happened, he needed to speak to Brad Allen. He hadn't wanted to add to Robyn's worries by telling her about his suspicions. Yet if he was right, Robyn would have to be told sooner rather than later.

As if Luke had willed it to happen, Brad strolled into the porch. "Well, officer, there you are. I've been looking for you." Brad's frown punctuated his words. "Any more information on what happened last night?"

Cocky bastard.

"Just the person I was looking for." Luke jumped up from the sofa and strode toward Brad, his shoulders squared, his jaw set. "If you had anything to do with purposely exposing Robyn to the danger last night, I will see you in jail."

"Jail! Hey, wait just a minute. I had nothing to do with any of that. We were innocent bystanders."

Luke wanted to grab the man by the neck. "You? An *innocent* bystander? I doubt it." Luke grabbed the back of a wicker rocker instead of Brad's neck.

"Come with me. Someone led Robyn into a very dangerous situation and she tells me it was you."

Robyn hadn't felt this mixed up in a very long time. She felt a deep attraction to Luke Carlisle, and at the same time she resented the control he exerted over her life. He had every reason to be concerned, and she agreed with him...to a point. An island she and her brother had loved, that had offered a refuge from their busy lives, had become a hunting ground for a killer who was now dead. She hadn't felt this threatened since the night on the boat, and that threat which made her feel vulnerable and afraid.

Luke Carlisle still wanted to protect her, but his protection and the attraction she felt for him stifled her, clouded her thinking. She needed a chance to clear her head, to use her analytical skills to sort through what had happened to her life since she'd come to the island – something that couldn't happen at the inn.

Robyn needed to get away – to clear her head and her heart. A long walk was the perfect answer.

She tightened the laces on her sneakers, and double knotted them. She pulled a fleece sweater over her head, and pulled her curls through with her hand. Bundled up in sweat pants and fleece top, Robyn knew she looked like she was headed for the North Pole.

Not quite, but she would need to be warm where she was going, and by the time she returned it might be foggy.

The driveway of the inn opened onto the main road, leading to Harper's Cove. Positive feelings rang through her as she stretched her stride and settled into a blood-pounding pace. For the first time in days, she felt free. Free to go where she wanted, and to do what she wanted to do.

She couldn't let herself think about what had happened at the Anchorage. Someone had died, and solving the crime was the responsibility of the police. She had no role in it, and with a new crime to solve Luke would not have the time to involve himself in her life.

The upward climb of the road, as it wound its way out of the village of Pier Point, gave her a stitch in her right side, but even pain couldn't dull her pleasure.

Feeling the tension ebb as her level of activity increased, Robyn pondered her future. One good thing had come out of the past few days. She felt more confident and had less fear of water than she had when she arrived by ferry. She was actually looking forward to the crossing back to the mainland. She hadn't decided when she'd leave, but she needed to get home to her mother and Jason, and to check on Lisa...*and* see if she and Luke would miss each other.

What the future held for them would not be decided quickly, because she needed to sort out the flashes of memories she'd experienced. If she and Luke ended up having a relationship, she didn't want her past troubles to influence her future happiness. She would get in touch with her psychiatrist, Dr. Stanley, and start working on her dreams again. Robyn broke into a run.

She ran along the road as it wound down the other side of the hill and into the tiny village of Harper's Cove. Sweat trickled down her neck, and under her cotton bra, and still she raced. Several people stopped what they were doing and stared at her as she jogged past.

The breeze freshened as she followed the narrow road around a turn that led to the center of the village. To her left, she saw herring smokehouses painted bright colors – red, blue, and yellow – part of their facelift when they were converted from fish processing plants to tourist shops.

Brilliantly colored flags whipped in the breeze as tourists milled about the spaces tastefully set up with picnic tables and barbecue pits. The bright colors gave Robyn back her sense of emotional balance and she felt almost euphoric.

She would stop on her way back and buy something for Jason and her mother. They'd appreciate all the stories she'd have to tell them when she got home. On the phone, Robyn had intentionally played down the danger she'd been in, but now she'd be able to tell them everything about her stay on the island. She'd call them as soon as she got back to the inn.

Almost skipping with delight, Robyn slowed to a walk and crossed the tiny footbridge leading from the shore to the shops.

The low-tide odor of salt water and tar gave her senses a jolt. She had forgotten how strong the smell could be, and how much she missed the calming effect of a sunny day by the water. A small shop caught her eye, and she strolled over to examine the interesting window display, giving her heart time to slow to normal after the demanding run.

The storefront window was a blaze of colorful flags, draped in all directions.

Thankful to be alive and looking forward to heading back home, Robyn stood in front of the glass, and let the riot of color assault her senses.

The crystal-clear glass of the shop window reflected the scudding clouds behind her. A seagull glided to a halt on top of a post along the edge of the pier. Somewhere, a fishing boat roared to life, and people scrambled past her, headed toward the wharf and the chance for a boat ride around the harbor.

A man moved into view, tentatively at first....

A garden flag would make a great gift for her mother. The flags displayed in the window had numerous themes from gardening to sailing. Which one would she buy? Maybe the one with the humming bird, or the frog? The open sign in the bottom corner of the window beckoned..

Trying to make up her mind, Robyn glanced around the display window one more time. Reflected in the glass was the face of a man she thought she knew. A patient, perhaps? Should she speak to him? He had his baseball cap tilted down, his longish hair hid his features, and the collar of his jacket was pulled up over his chin.

She watched him, their gazes locked, and the skin on the back of her neck began to tingle.

Where had she seen him before? There was something so familiar about him…

He looked away, and his profile pulled at her memory. A sudden chill swept through her and she grabbed the cedar-shingled wall of the shop for support, her stomach rolling dangerously.

A man shouts an order she can't understand. She can hardly keep her balance because the boat is rocking so hard in the rough water. Someone is floating face down.... An angry face looms in front of her, blocking out everything.

A scream caught in her throat. Robyn staggered up the steps of the shop and pulled open the door.

"What is it?" a kindly voice asked.

Struggling to clear her mind of the memory, Robyn glanced around the shop, letting her mind focus on the beautiful flags and kites draped in every conceivable angle.

Breathe slowly, she cautioned herself, pulling the musty air of the shop into her lungs.

Instantly she knew what she had to do. "Please call Luke Carlisle for me," Robyn gasped.

The woman stared at Robyn as if she had just stepped from a spacecraft. "Just a moment. Who shall I say wants him?"

"Dr. McGill." Robyn forced the words through the rushing sound in her ears.

It seemed like a lifetime before the woman behind the counter put down the crossword puzzle she was working on, and dialed the number.

The woman put the phone back, suspicion shining in her eyes. "Officer Carlisle isn't in at the moment. They said for you to wait here."

The memory had been so vivid. And the man....

Robyn moved slowly to the window and concentrated her attention on the street outside the shop. There was no one out there. Moving to the other window Robyn glanced through the narrow panes. Nothing. *Had she imagined him?* Feeling like a complete fool, Robyn skirted a large barrel of children's kites and headed for the door.

In a sudden show of concern, the woman came out from behind the counter. "Would you like something to drink? A glass of water, perhaps?"

"No, thank you," Robyn murmured. A few moments ago, she'd been happily making plans. Then the sight of a man she couldn't identify had frightened her beyond all reason.

Everything now had a surreal quality to it, as if she were walking through a dream. Robyn clasped her hands together to slow their shaking. Her hair hung damp against her forehead. "Please, Luke, please hurry," she whispered as she stared anxiously outside.

CHAPTER NINE

When Luke picked Robyn up in Harper's Cove at the little tourist shop, she was so distraught, he was tempted to hire a plane and get her the hell off the island. He hadn't acted on that impulse for a whole bunch of reasons, starting with his own misgivings about what had happened.

He closed the double doors separating the den from the lobby of the inn. What he wanted to say to Robyn had to be said in private. On the way back from Harper's Cove, he had seen, first hand, just how devastating her flashbacks could be to her state of mind. From the way she'd behaved, he knew beyond any doubt, that his probing would hurt her – but still the cop in him had to know.

His gut told him that her flashbacks were part of the puzzle, but his gut wasn't good enough. Would he be able to get Robyn the protection she needed?

Andrew had given him another lecture when they'd been at the Anchorage the night before, about becoming personally involved, and Luke had ignored him, or pretended to. But Andrew Webber was nobody's fool, and Luke figured he should take the advice Andrew offered – if he could. Problem was, as of this morning, he couldn't.

Nor could he let anything distract him from the knowledge that Robyn was the victim of a deadly attack. He'd already compromised her safety by not making her understand that although the gunman was dead, she could still be in danger. He should have told her what he suspected after the incident at the Anchorage.

The flashback she had described had frightened her. If the fear generated by the memory had its basis in real experiences, his instincts told him understanding that might lead to whoever wanted her dead.

Luke watched Robyn open the door and walk into the room, skirting the periphery as if she were picking a safe spot where she could defend herself. The rush of emotion he felt at the sight of her so defensive, resurrected the dilemma he'd been struggling with all day. Leo Lord had been waiting for someone at the Anchorage, either Robyn or Brad. He believed it was Robyn. But whoever killed Leo was still out there, and no one knew what the latest killer's intentions were.

The charcoal smudge of exhaustion beneath her eyes didn't help his state of mind. He wanted to wipe away the strain he saw in her face, and put a smile back on her lips. Even as they'd left the shop he'd fought the urge to take her in his arms, to let her know that he cared, that he only wanted to ease the confusion he saw in her eyes.

Needing to be near her to shield her, Luke moved across the den and stood next to her. "Robyn, please tell me exactly what you saw outside the shop."

Robyn pulled an unruly mass of curls from her face and turned toward the window. "I saw a man."

"Go on."

"He was standing across the street from me. I saw his reflection in the window of the store."

"And then what?"

Without looking at Luke, Robyn moved to a straight-backed chair and lowered herself into it. "I saw water. Dark, cold, water...and, someone in trouble."

Luke knelt down by the chair and spoke gently. "Who was it, do you know?"

He saw hesitation in her face before she answered. "I don't know."

Luke put his hands on hers and felt her fingers tremble beneath his touch. "Try to remember."

Robyn bit her lower lip, and studied her hands.

"Robyn, I want to help." His hands found their way up over her arms.

"Oh, Luke," she moaned, moving into the space his arms had created.

His anxiety for her held his emotions in check, but it was a close call. She needed him. He needed her. It was as simple and as complicated as that.

The choice was his to make. Easing to a standing position, Luke nestled her against him.

"The flashbacks. I thought I was free of them. I'm not. I can't go on like this. It has to be over." She whispered the words into the cotton of his shirt, and he hugged her to him, desperate to ease the confusion he heard in her voice.

Luke let his fingers slide over her shoulders and down her back. Breathing in her flowery scent, he turned her face up to his, searching for an answering need in her eyes.

Arousal radiated from her body, igniting his. Ignoring everything except the woman he held in his arms, he answered her need with his own. The warmth of her lips on his, exploded through him.

Her answering moan, and the way her fingers knit their

way through his hair, pulled him closer to the edge. He brushed his fingers across her breasts. Her body arched toward his.

But he couldn't go down that road, not when postponing his questions could result in another incident. Forcing his hands down and away from her welcoming body, Luke slowly lifted his lips from hers. "Robyn, I can't."

Her fingers held his hair; her lips were open, waiting. "Please Luke. I need––"

"I know." Oh God how he knew! But he also knew he had a duty to her, less urgent but more important. And a job to do, one that had rules about this kind of thing. Gently, he slid away from her, his arousal a reminder of how much he wanted to act on his desire.

Moving across the large open space to the edge of the sofa, he tried to organize his thoughts. "Robyn, your memories may have some bearing on this case; if you could give me every detail, no matter how small or seemingly pointless."

"My memories? You want to know about my memories?" Surprise laced every word as she joined him on the sofa, her wary gaze never leaving his face.

He nodded.

"I'm confused and exhausted." She swiped at the dark strand of hair falling in her face. "Can we let this alone for now, and just be...together?"

"Robyn, as long as I'm the investigating officer in this case, I have to keep my relationship with you on a professional level."

"If that kiss had any professional meaning, I'd like you to enlighten me," she said, settling on the sofa next to him.

Out of the corner of his eye, he saw her tilt her head, ready to ask a question. He edged away from her and came up against a huge decorator pillow on the end of the sofa. He pulled it out, and placed it on the floor near his feet. He felt like a gangly, lovesick teenager.

Luke wanted to toss his responsibility out the window, grab the woman sitting beside him and do what they both wanted. But there was so much he needed to find out and that meant asking questions that only Robyn could answer. "Robyn, can we try to work together on solving this case? The sooner we do, the sooner it will be over."

"I want to help," she said, her sigh of resignation cutting deep.

A part of Luke was disappointed at how quickly she'd recovered from the kiss of a few moments ago. He wanted her to ache for him the way he ached. "How long have you been having these flash backs?"

"I lived with them for a year after Nathan and Peter died. I hadn't had any for a couple of years."

"And now?"

"They're back."

"Anything other than the flashbacks?"

"A nightmare I think. I wake up sweating, terrified and afraid."

"Have you had it recently?"

"Yes, a few nights before I came to Grand Island."

"Any particular reason it recurred then that you can think of?"

"I've been afraid of water, ever since that accident. I assumed it had to do with the fact that I was going on a ferry. I haven't been on any boat of any kind since...since the accident."

"What happened today?"

"Today I saw someone who must be part of a memory, or something. I don't know for sure. Since the shooting on Simmons Marsh, I've experienced pieces of a memory––"

"Go on."

"Someone is badly injured...and I'm there." She rubbed the palm of her hand and glanced around the room.

"Does the memory take place on the sailboat?"

"Yes. Or at least I think so."

"Tell me about the accident. I'm sorry you have to go through this right now, but I need to know."

"They found me sitting in the cockpit of the boat. My fiancé Nathan and my brother Peter were missing. I couldn't remember anything. They told me they believed Nathan and Peter had drowned."

"Who found you?"

"The Coast Guard. With Brad's help."

"Brad was there?" Surprise dumped adrenaline into his system.

"No. But, he knew we were out on the boat that day. When we didn't return, he called the Coast Guard."

Luke felt a dagger of anger stir his gut. *Funny how this creep keeps popping up in Robyn's life.* "Did Brad tell you why he wanted to go to the Anchorage last night?"

A flicker of annoyance skirted Robyn's brow. "He wanted to take me for a walk. He built a fire on the beach."

Luke knew he risked her anger by pressing further. "Why there?"

"Why not there? It's a wonderful spot." Defensiveness slid into Robyn's tone.

Why would a male friend take a beautiful woman to a deserted beach on a moonlit night? Jealousy flickered to life as he pressed her for more information. "It's an isolated place at the best of times, but even more so at night."

"Look, I don't know any more than what I've told you. What is this? You're talking as if you think Brad was involved in that shooting."

Until he could tell her something definitive, he'd keep his suspicions to himself. "There's always the possibility that the gunman was waiting for Brad," he offered with little enthusiasm.

Robyn gripped the arm of the sofa, her voice rising. "You don't believe that. You think Brad took me out there intentionally, don't you? You're going to do to Brad what was done to me when Peter and Nathan died, aren't you? You're going to make his life miserable to satisfy your own need to find a suspect."

Her stare chilled the air between them. "You can't believe that he intentionally placed me in danger out there at the Anchorage last night? The person I owe my life to? If he hadn't alerted the Coast Guard I might have died along with Nathan and Peter, and you think--?"

Robyn took a deep breath and exhaled with deliberate slowness. She closed her eyes. "Do you have any idea what you're putting me through?"

Luke knew too well and wished to God he didn't.

She opened her eyes and glared at him. "Do you have any idea what it's like to live with this?" She pointed at her head. "Do you think I haven't told my psychiatrist every detail?"

Luke said nothing. There was nothing he could say.

"For what? He couldn't help me, and you can't help me." She stopped and inhaled deeply, a second time. "I can't and I won't go through this again, not for anyone."

Luke watched anger and betrayal play out on her face. He felt an ominous tug on his feelings while he struggled to maintain his professional distance. "I wish I didn't need to do this, but I had to know what happened after the accident. The police in Portland gave me a quick rundown."

"What do you mean? You've been checking up on me? On what happened back then? Why?"

"It's my job."

"So if your job is so important, and clearly you don't trust me to know my friend's motives, why are you wasting time talking to me?"

"I've explained that."

"You can't help me one little bit by forcing me to go back over what happened three years ago. Every aspect of the accident was examined. Everyone close to me was scrutinized. I was forced to answer the same questions over and over – all because the police didn't believe a word I said. My career was nearly destroyed by the accusations hurled at me. The police didn't find Nathan and Peter. They didn't find any evidence with which to charge me. They simply made my life a living hell – all because I couldn't remember."

What could he say that wouldn't sound trite?

The tug-of-war raged on inside him. A very troubled woman sat before him and he could offer nothing. Except that if he didn't soon find a clue about who was after her, she could die and he would have to live with the knowledge that he might have prevented it.

But for him there was more to this than the possibility of a professional failure. Robyn was different from any woman he'd ever known, had eased her way into his life the way no other woman ever had. Her passion for those she cared about had also left its mark on him. There was no turning back.

With a determination brought on by the urgency of the situation, he stood up and turned toward her. "Robyn, the gunman who died at the Anchorage was killed by someone else. That someone else is still out there. We have no way of knowing what he plans to do next, but whatever it is I believe you're still in danger."

Her head snapped back, revealing angry eyes. "That's your theory, like it's your theory that Brad could be involved in what happened at the Anchorage. The gunman is dead, killed for reasons that have nothing to do with me. I am no longer a target…if I ever was one."

With complete calm resonating through her voice, she went to the door and turned back to face him. "I'm not taking any more of this. Whatever is going on in your life is no business of mine. It's obvious that you have a problem, and I suggest you do something about it. Neither your constant suspicion that someone wants me dead, nor your notion that Brad is involved, can be true. I won't listen to your unfounded accusations."

Robyn didn't know where she was going and she didn't care. Any place that would put distance between her and Luke Carlisle would do. Her heart pounded in rhythm with her shattered feelings as she rushed down the hall leading to the back of the inn.

Searing rejection came face-to-face with the anger of betrayal.

The gate leading to the herb garden was open, and feeling the need for the relief the herbal scents gave her, Robyn strode out onto the cobbled stone patio. Awash in the fragrance offered by the billowing lavender, Robyn sat down on the wrought-iron bench at the edge of the path.

She remembered the last time she'd been through here. It had been with Luke, just before he found the tire marks of the gunman. How things had changed since that moment, for better *and* for worse.

Intellectually, Robyn knew Luke was simply doing his job. But it felt as if he was putting his needs ahead of hers, and that hurt. She rubbed her face with her hands.

It hurts because you care.

She had forgotten the heady feeling of attraction, the excitement of awareness. She wanted to feel the way she had when he kissed her – and hold nothing back. When this mess was over...

If only Luke didn't believe the worst about Brad. Did Luke know something about her friend that he couldn't tell her? Brad had stood by her through it all and she cared what happened to him.

Robyn leaned back on the bench and breathed in the mixture of roses and bayberry that clung to the air. Luke had a job to do, and maybe that explained his behavior where Brad was concerned – and his belief that she was still in danger. Three years ago she'd spent months denying accusations of the police. Now she was driven to deny that she was still in danger. Was she right, or was she simply falling back on her old pattern, denying what she didn't understand or couldn't comprehend? Were her nightmares trying to tell her something? Were they more than nightmares, in fact could they be flashbacks based on real memories?

What if she had made a terrible mistake that night – one that had cost Nathan and Peter their lives? The open Atlantic had been choppy and cold, the wind hard out of the west. That much she could remember. The sails had been reefed down against the strengthening winds.

The air in the garden stilled around her at the memory. Robyn pulled her sweater tighter and got off the bench. A walk would warm her. The path meandered along the side of the garden, under the old crabapple tree that reached up past her window. The fog was coming in and wispy tendrils of gray mist moved forward from the raspberry patch that separated the garden from the sea. A typical day for Grand Island: One minute the sun shone and the next, fog blanketed everything.

Robyn sensed rather than saw something move just at the edge of her vision. A scraping sound behind her, bounced her pulse like a rubber ball. Someone else had entered the garden.

She turned and faced the gathering mist. "Who's there?"

Her voice sounded hollow in her ears, and she felt a little foolish.

Quelling the urge to make a dash for the open door of the sun porch, Robyn peered around her. Lanky maple trees stood guard along the far side of the garden, the encroaching fog clouding their upper branches. Just to her left, a mocking bird did a good imitation of a song sparrow, its trilling song sending sharp notes of loneliness trickling through Robyn.

Sudden memories of Peter followed in quick succession – his love of a bird's song, the way his whistles matched them note for note, his excitement the first time he'd successfully guided his sailboat into Bar Harbor and his many trips abroad to do conservation work. Remembering Peter brought a kind of peace to her troubled mind.

A rapid movement near the sage bush to her far right told her someone was definitely in the garden. "Who's there?"

"'God sees the little sparrow fall, he meets his tender view. If God so loves the little birds, I know he loves me too.'"

The voice was shrill, reverberating against the side of the inn. Shock waves of fear rang through Robyn as she heard the keening voice.

It was the hymn she and Peter had sung in church, a hymn that used to strike terror in her as a child.

Luke could have kicked himself for letting his feelings get in the way of what had to be done. To make up for his lapse, he called Brad's room and asked him to come to the den. Brad reluctantly complied and stood near the closed door of the den, his head cocked to one side.

"Give it a rest. Our trip to the Anchorage was completely innocent. I just wanted to help a friend." Brad lifted his shoulders in an indifferent shrug, and went to the same window where Robyn had stood earlier. "Do you have a problem with that?"

Growing dislike nibbled at Luke as he watched the studied arrogance of the man. Luke had no interest in having a verbal sparring match with Brad. He just wanted honest answers to his questions. So far, he hadn't gotten anything remotely satisfying. "Brad, I strongly suggest you help me with this investigation--"

"I *am* trying to help you." Brad moved away from the window, his cool appraising glance replaced by open hostility. "If you're so sure we were out there for some clandestine reason, why don't you just come out and say what's on your mind?"

"I'm not buying the idea of a casual drive in the country, so try again."

Where in hell have your interrogations skills gone? His instincts were dull, and had been since his talk with Robyn. As much as he knew he needed to interview Brad, he should have picked a time when his mind was on the job.

Luke tightened his resolve and concentrated on the situation. He was sure of one thing. Brad's whole demeanor displayed secretiveness and evasion. Brad was hiding something, and it was personal. "Are you having an affair with Robyn?"

"Are you kidding?" Brad snorted.

The resentment in Brad's voice was just a little overdone to Luke's ear. *Did Brad want Robyn?* If he did, it would have made more sense for Brad to take her out for a quiet dinner or to a movie. Not to a lonely beach at night. Still...how long had Brad harbored feelings for her? And had these feelings played a part in what happened that night three years ago? Had Brad known something would happen to her fiancé and brother on that sailboat? Had he been waiting to rescue Robyn?

Brad paced off the distance between the window and the fireplace. Toying with a small bronze statue resting on the mantel, he took a deep breath, and glared at Luke. "Robyn loved one person. Nathan."

Luke saw the truth in Brad's eyes. Brad wanted Robyn, but knew he couldn't have her while Nathan was alive: the perfect motive for murdering Nathan on his boat that night. But if so, what had happened to Peter McGill? He called Portland and see if Brad had been considered a suspect three years ago, and he hadn't been. "Did you know Nathan?"

Brad shot Luke an unguarded glance. "Yes, I knew him. We were all friends, sort of."

"What does that mean?"

"Nathan was the leader of the group. Everyone looked to him to organize the fun, you know, the parties, the boat trips. Women fell all over him."

"And?"

"Robyn and Nathan were together."

Luke didn't like the twinge of envy he felt for the unknown man who had held such sway in Robyn's life.

"It wasn't always Nathan and Robyn." Brad shoved his hands into the pockets of his pants. "Nathan and Lisa had been an item before that."

Luke let the information sink in. "And the women remained friends after Nathan and Robyn got together?"

"Hardly. Nathan broke Lisa's heart. When Nathan started dating Robyn, Lisa figured Robyn had betrayed her by taking Nathan away from her. They had a terrible fight and were bitter enemies – for a while."

Luke was beginning to see an entirely different picture, one that would require investigation. "What changed?"

"Lisa's sister died in a car crash about a year before the boating accident. Robyn was the doctor on call that night, and never left Lisa's side. That was when they patched up their differences."

Luke wondered if they were truly friends, or had Lisa held onto feelings of anger over Nathan along with her sister's death? Gruesome as it sounded, the human mind could do almost anything when emotions were involved. The loss of a lover to a best friend had been the cause of many homicides. But why would Lisa wait until now to attack Robyn, and nearly get herself killed in the process?

If Lisa harbored anger toward Robyn, she might have hired someone to act on her feelings. The fact that the gunman hit Lisa by mistake would have been a shock, but it had kept the police from seeing the well-known news anchorwoman as a suspect. He'd look into that once he sorted out Brad's role in all this.

Both men jumped as the doors to the den flew open, and Robyn stumbled into the room.

CHAPTER TEN

"Somebody's in the garden." Robyn's words spilled over her lips as she stood clutching the edge of the door, the words of the hymn still humming through her.

Brad strode across the room. "You don't have to worry. I'll take care of you. Wait here." He brushed his hands possessively across her shoulders.

She stepped away from him.

A look of chagrin crossed his face. "I'll check the garden." With that pronouncement, he was gone.

The sight of Luke standing in the middle of the room, concern evident on his face, left Robyn weak with relief. Gulping air into her lungs, she stared at him.

In two strides, he crossed the room and folded her into his arms. "Robyn, I should never have let you leave this room without me." His fingers smoothed her hair; his words blanketed her fear.

She clung to him, her need for his strength overruling all else. She was safe and secure in his arms. The cradling sensation warmed and soothed her while exciting all her senses.

"After I left here I went out in the herb garden. It was

foggy and I heard someone in the garden with me. I couldn't see him and he didn't answer when I called." Robyn rested her hands on Luke's chest, a moment's reprieve before she continued her story.

"It was probably one of the other guests." Luke spoke the words close to her face, setting up a tiny space of intimacy between them.

The whispering warmth of Luke's nearness clung to her as she glanced up at him. "I'm glad you're here."

"I wouldn't want it any other way." His eyes revealed much more than concern.

Robyn fought the urge to lose herself in his closeness, to let her newfound feelings for him soothe away her fear. It would be so much easier, so much more pleasant than the malevolent sensations that floated in the garden and on the periphery of her mind....

"Luke, I need to sit down."

"Sure." Luke led her to the sofa, his hand resting protectively on her shoulder. "Tell me what frightened you." Luke sat down on the couch, draping his arm around her, over the sofa, in a way that felt anything but casual.

"It wasn't what I saw, so much as what I heard." Robyn turned to Luke. "I know this sounds silly, but someone was out there singing a hymn."

Luke, a wide grin wreathing his face, tapped Robyn's shoulder with his fingertips. "That's not silly at all. You probably heard our resident loonie."

"Resident loonie?"

"You don't have to worry about him. He's lived here all summer in a fishing shack near Whale Cove. His name's Amos Potter." The relief on Luke's face was palpable. "Which hymn did he choose this time?"

A sense of dread knotted Robyn's shoulders. *Was it possible to have such a coincidence? Was it possible for life to play such a cruel joke on her?* To have someone sing a hymn that brought back such powerful memories of her brother in the midst of all the horrifying events of the past few days...?

"The song he sang has special meaning for me. It was a hymn Peter and I learned in Sunday School."

At that moment, Brad rushed into the room, an expression of concern on his face. "Whoever was in the garden is gone." His gaze moved to Luke, a scowl forming on his forehead. "Looks like I missed something. What were you two up to while I was gone?"

Ignoring Brad, Luke smiled reassuringly at Robyn. "Amos Potter is quite strange, but harmless. No one seems to know where he came from."

She knew Luke meant to lessen her stress about the frightening experience. To him, what had happened probably seemed pretty minor, but to her, it wasn't minor. She wanted to escape. She needed somewhere safe to go, away from the fear.

Forcing her hands to be still under Luke's, Robyn tucked her elbows close to her body to control her shivering. Her professional mind knew she was responding to the sudden relief she felt after believing she was in imminent danger – a normal response.

"Robyn, there's nothing to worry about. Amos Potter's recitation frightened you because you had just been through a terrible experience." Luke's voice was low, his tone a gentle caress.

His argument made sense. More than that, she wanted to believe him.

Exhaustion from the previous day and the fear that someone was still out there looking for her had made the incident in the garden into something it wasn't. Robyn let the air out of her lungs in a long, slow sigh. If everyone on the island knew about the old gentleman and his strange behavior, that was probably who it was and she could feel safe. "What I need is a long soak in the tub."

Relief showed in Luke's voice. "You do that. In the meantime, Brad and I will finish our discussion." He held her at arm's length – his eyes clear and focused on her. "I'll call you this evening."

Luke's closeness as he walked with her to the bottom of the stairs, comforted her. "Thanks for everything, she said."

"You're welcome."

His engaging smile tugged her up onto to her toes. She touched his cheeks, feeling the faint stubble along his jaw. "You're a very kind man, I believe we might have a future together," she murmured as his lips closed on hers, filling her senses.

Could this really be her? This woman who was going after what she wanted? She had always hung back and let the man take the lead – too shy to speak up.

She had turned the corner into a foreign place. A place she liked.

"No need to rush this," she whispered against his lips.

"Are you telling me there's some place else I need to be?"

"Not sure. Mostly I'm telling you I need to rest. I'll call you when I wake up." She wanted to savor every moment, to feel every feeling.

With exquisite gentleness, Luke touched her cheekbone. "I'll hold you to that, Doctor."

Robyn felt his gaze follow her as she climbed the stairs, and she luxuriated in every second of it. What was happening between them made her heart sing.

She wanted him more every time she looked at him. Funny how something so perfect could happen in the midst of such horror.

Opening her bedroom door, she looked around her room.

Even the fog outside couldn't alter the quiet elegance of the space. Its peacefulness reached out to her.

The inn didn't seem as lonely as it had after Lisa had been sent to hospital on the mainland. Yet, it now held a different kind of loneliness. Any space without Luke felt lonely. Seeing a burgundy book on her pillow, she moved to the bed. *What's this?*

As her fingers touched the roughened leather of the book, she knew exactly what it was and what it contained. The tattered pages rustled like silk as she flipped through them, searching for the page. She didn't have to look far. The only page completely intact was the page she sought.

"Luke!" Racing to the door with the book clutched in her fingers, she leaned over the banister, her shaking hands holding the book aloft.

She skidded down the stairs and bumped into Luke at the bottom. Robyn dumped the book into his hands. "Someone left this in my room."

Luke took the book from her shaking fingers and turned it over. "It's a hymnal. All eleven churches on the island have these."

"Look inside. Someone destroyed all the pages but the one with the hymn, *God Sees the Little Sparrow Fall.* It's the song I heard in the garden." Her voice quavered. "Someone was in the garden singing this and I just found this in my room. Oh My God Luke, someone's been in my room. Who would do this?"

"Who's doing what?" Brad asked, coming toward them. "Robyn, are you all right?" He came toward her, his arm outstretched.

Overwhelmed by fear, she didn't respond to his concern.

"Whoever did this is in need of a psychiatrist, if you ask

me." Ignoring Brad Luke led Robyn back up to her room, each step on the way up the stairs a crushing reminder that someone had been in her private space and left something that only she would understand.

Luke, his face a professional mask, led Robyn to the sofa in the corner of the room. "Robyn, tell me about this hymn."

"It's a hymn my brother Peter and I liked as kids. Then one day when we were home alone someone broke into the house. Peter and I were terrified. We hid in the attic, in the back of an old armoire. The intruder was singing that hymn. We were so afraid. I've never been able to listen to it without being reminded of that awful day.

"Luke, you convinced me that hearing that song was just a coincidence – the ramblings of a crazy old man. But I don't know anyone by the name of Amos Potter. The robber that entered our home and sung that hymn died. He is dead. Peter is dead."

Robyn sat down on the sofa, her mind racing frantically over the events of the past few minutes. "Why would someone be doing this?"

"Someone wants to scare you, frighten you off the island, possibly, or let you know who they are." He ran his fingers over the spine of the book. "Someone from your past is trying to tell you something. Robyn, who in your life would know how this would affect you?"

"My mom, Lisa, but she's in the hospital, Brad, maybe, and of course Dr. Stanley, my psychiatrist."

"Anyone else?"

"I can't think of anyone else. Someone who knew might have inadvertently told someone. What would be the point of scaring me like this?"

"Robyn, there is a whole world of weird people out there." His eyes took on a dark cast, an ominous coolness. "As a professional, you know what people are capable of."

"This is crazy." She fixed her eyes on a point on the ceiling to keep the tears from slipping down her cheeks. She had cried enough tears after Peter and Nathan's deaths. "There's no reason for this to happen to me."

Luke frowned at her response. "There has to be. Robyn, you know it's not normal for anyone to live with the sort of flashbacks you've told me about. They have to be rooted in your past."

"I'm only having them now because of the shooting." She glanced at Luke and saw anxiety tighten his lips. "The flashbacks will go away again."

"*Go away again?* How much longer can you live with those flashbacks and not know what caused them?"

Robyn wanted to fight him, to argue with him, to make him see she could handle the nightmares and the flashbacks.

His voice softened. "You need to face whatever is in your past. The events surrounding the boating accident might have something to do with what happened to you in the last few days. Or there could be someone or something else in your past. A patient maybe?"

"No. At least I don't think so."

"Well, something's going on. First there were the attacks that involved you, and now this incident in the garden and the hymnal on your bed."

Robyn felt cold to the bone. She hadn't wanted the conversation to go in that direction. Not yet. She needed time to think; to grapple with what she was feeling, her fear that her life was completely out of her control. "No, I don't think the boating accident had anything to do with this. There has to be another explanation."

Out of nowhere, an unwelcome sensation enveloped her. Someone was listening. *Was it Brad?* She glanced at the open door of her room and back at Luke.

He didn't seem aware of anything. She relaxed a little.

"Who would want to remind me of Peter by doing something like this?"

"Someone with a cruel, sadistic need to hurt you."

Luke stretched his legs out in front of him. A sharp worry-line cut the space between his eyes. "It's time we had a discussion about your living arrangements."

"Living arrangements?"

"You need protection."

"I thought I had it."

"Until we figure out what's going on and who's behind this, you need a hiding place, a place where the gunman would never think to look for you."

She had to admit he was right. She needed to be safe, if only to gather her strength to plan what she would do. Someone sick enough to try to kill her, and then to play games like this, would stop at nothing. The incident in her room proved the inn didn't provide adequate protection. "And where would that be?"

Luke looked her. "I should never have let you out of my sight, knowing there was a good chance someone else was following you. I should have acted sooner. I just didn't know what we were up against. With this..." He flicked a glance at the book resting on the table beside the sofa. "The picture's a little clearer now."

Fear shot through her as she saw the serious expression on his face. Facing each other across the narrow space, the meaning of his words hit her, dealing a blow to the slim grip she had on her sense of security. "Where, in heavens' name would I be safe? We're not talking about jail again. Are we?" she asked, trying for a little humor.

He chuckled. "Close. Very close." Luke closed the gap between them. His eyes were warm. "I want you to move into my house with me."

"What? Away from everyone?" *Except him. She would be close to him in the most intimate setting possible.*

"Yes. It's the safest place on the island. No one would ever suspect. And no one must know you're there." He gave her the kind of grin designed to win her over. "I have a house-keeper who comes two mornings a week. And two spare bedrooms. You can have your pick."

Being close to Luke twenty-four hours a day would guar-antee her safety, and put her close to the one man she wanted in her life. Hope, excitement and the clear sense that despite the difficulties in her life she was about to take part in an adventure. "Do I have a choice?"

CHAPTER ELEVEN

"Well, would you look at that?" Alice Seymour muttered to herself as she peeked out the window of the police station. "My esteemed boss has Dr. McGill with him, only this time, she has her overnight bag. It looks like Luke may be planning to break a few rules."

Luke closed the door behind Robyn, and used the moment to organize his defense. By the look of disbelief on Alice's face, he would need some professional reasons to support what he was doing. He offered the only explanation he planned to give. "Dr. McGill is going to stay in my house under our protection. There was another incident this afternoon, leaving me no choice but to bring her back here. I want you to keep this quiet. I don't want people to know she's here. If we're lucky, the person trying to get to Robyn will assume she's left the island."

"We'll do our best to leave a false trail." Alice grinned at Robyn. "Welcome aboard."

"Thank you."

Turning to Luke, Alice asked, "Anything else we should do right away?"

"We're fine at the moment. Dr. McGill has checked out of the inn. They think she's coming here to give her statement before she leaves."

"Sounds good to me. Do you suppose anyone will check?" Alice asked.

"That's where you come in. I want you to spread the word that Dr. McGill has left the island. I want you to arrange to have Robyn's private number placed on call forwarding to the extra line in my house. Robyn will put a message on the voice mail, and we'll use Caller ID to check to see who calls. No one will know she's not in Portland, and we'll know who's trying to reach her."

"Are you all right with that, Robyn?" Alice asked.

"Anything to get my life back. I still have a few days off work, so I don't need to explain my absence. If it takes longer than that...." She shrugged.

Luke watched Robyn's face as she spoke and the sheer determination he saw there impressed him. The woman who had seemed defensive and hesitant about her situation a while ago had changed to someone willing to take the situation in hand. With this change in Robyn he could concentrate his efforts on finding out who was after her. He'd get her settled, and then he and Officer Seymour would get to work checking and following up on potential suspects.

The first suspect was still Brad Allen. The man was arrogant, and clearly felt he had a special place in Robyn's life. As a guest at the inn, he certainly had the opportunity to do whatever he wanted. Although Brad had been with him in the den when Robyn had been frightened in the garden, he could have rigged a recording. That would explain why he rushed out to the garden after Robyn came in. He could have placed the hymnal on her bed earlier. Thankfully he hadn't been there when he decided to bring Robyn to his house.

To ease Robyn's fear, Luke told her he suspected that the person in the garden was Amos. He had no intention of making that assumption where the investigation was concerned. Amos didn't look the type to be able to move fast enough.... Still, there were a whole lot of things Luke didn't know about Amos, starting with why he'd picked this particular island to spend his summer.

He wasted no time ushering her through the adjoining door connecting the office with the house. They were greeted by a howl of pure feline disgust as a cat sailed onto his shoulders. "Down, Passion!" Luke grabbed the cat by the scruff of the neck and placed it gently on the floor.

"Passion? That's your cat's name?" Robyn looked from the cat to Luke.

He shrugged. "He's not mine. I inherited him." Luke cringed inwardly as he watched Passion sit down, stretch his hind leg up in the air, and proceed to clean his crotch. Or whatever that part of a cat's anatomy was called.

Robyn tucked her lips into a grin. "His owner must have had an interesting slant on life."

"He was named in honor of his night time activities."

"Named for his love life?"

"Yeah, for a thousand and one nights when my sister would have to get up and let the cat out, after going to bed. I took Passion for her when she moved in with her boyfriend who's allergic to cats."

"So, you're a cat lover?"

As they bantered back and forth he had this irrational need to touch her, to feel her body close to his. "I wouldn't go that far."

"I have a dog, a huge shedding monster of a dog."

"Dogs are nice." He tried to ignore the flare of awareness mixed with unease he saw in her eyes.

"They are…"

The only sound was Passion eating from his bowl in the kitchen. "Can I show you your room?"

Robyn slipped off her coat and went to the kitchen. "Who does the cooking?"

Luke followed her, thankful she had decided to change the subject. "I have a housekeeper who makes the occasional stew." He waved his hands in the general direction of the cupboards. "I have all the cooking utensils needed to cook. I just don't have any interest." He shrugged.

She smiled back, the first real smile he'd seen in the last few hours. Hell, he liked making her smile. "If you want to cook, be my guest."

Opening several cupboards, she peeked inside. "I'll need some ingredients."

"I'll get them for you later if you jot down a list. Right now, I have to talk to someone. Will you be all right?"

She leaned against the counter, the warmth of her gaze reaching out to him across the room. "I'll be fine."

Luke heard the clock chime on the stairs. He tried not to show his impatience, but he did have something he needed to do right away. Would she take him up on his offer to show her to her room?

"Luke, I want to be involved in finding out who's after me. I want to work on this with you."

Air slipped unbidden from Luke's lips; a knot at the back of his neck eased. If she continued to think like that, they might be able to delve further into her past. If he could get her to remember everything she could, it would assist in the investigation. "You will be, but not right now."

"Why not?" She moved to the kitchen table and pulled out a chair. "The killer at the Anchorage was killed by someone else, another killer – we know that. We have no description, no idea why he shot Leo Lord or whether that person is still on the island." She eased into the chair. "After today, it's pretty obvious someone is still out there. I thought you'd be happy to know that I want to help."

Happy wasn't the word he'd use. If she really wanted to help, he had a lot of questions for her, but that would have to come later. "Robyn, do me a favor."

"Yes." She lifted her chin and the gray-blue circles under her eyes hit Luke in the solar plexus. She was tough, but the day had taken its toll on her.

"I want you to take it easy for a while. Go upstairs, choose your bedroom and have a rest." He edged toward the door, knowing full well if he stayed he would want to take her upstairs and make love to her before she fell asleep. His body flushed warm at the thought.

Living in the same space with her would be a tightrope walk. The blurred line between his duty and his feelings for her had almost disappeared as it was. What occurred next between them would change their lives.

"Will I know which one is your bedroom?" she asked, her eyes alight with humor.

He wanted to keep the easy repartee between them. With all she'd been through, she needed it. And he needed to feel her eyes on him, her attention focused on him. "You'll know. Believe me, you'll know."

"Okay, so it's my turn to play Goldilocks?"

He would do well to escape before he gave in to his need for companionship and banter that Robyn offered. "Goldilocks sounds good. No Baby Bear bed, I'm afraid."

"Is that some kind of kinky offer?" she asked, openly flirting with him now.

He was getting out of here, pronto. "I'll be back as soon as I can. Don't worry about dinner. I'll pick something up for us."

She gave him a quick wave. "Stop being a cop. I'm a big girl," she said a teasing tone in her voice.

"Lock up and don't let anyone in," he warned.

"You don't have to worry about me. I'm through trusting anyone on this island." She crossed the room and stood near him. "How will I know it's you when you return?"

"I'll call first and leave a message. Don't answer the phone, whatever you do."

"Mum's the word," she said, giving him a jaunty salute.

Scowling to cover the answering grin spreading over his face, Luke stepped out into the corridor between the house and the police station. "Lock the door."

Robyn gave him a smile that went straight to his heart.

Luke waited until he heard the deadbolt click closed before he went into the office.

The fading light of day left long fingers of shadow on the blue carpet in Luke's living room. When he left he'd taken her upbeat mood with him. She sat alone on the sofa. Her life had been thrown in the air and smashed at her feet, and she seemed incapable of putting it back together or making sense of it.

Everything she believed in had been overshadowed by doubt, with the return of the confusing memories and the ugly events of the past few days. People she cared for had been questioned by the police over a shooting that made no sense. And her friend Lisa was in hospital.

Robyn tucked her legs up under her and waited for the tightness in her throat to ease.

Someone held the power to destroy her life.

The blunt truth burrowed through Robyn's mind. If she didn't do something to help herself, this faceless person would win, and she would never feel safe again. She rubbed her neck as thoughts raced through her mind. Luke seemed convinced that the person responsible was someone from her past – and Brad was at the top of that list.

Luke had to be wrong, but in the meantime…

Rummaging through the end table by the sofa, she found a pen and a pad of paper. Point by point, she listed everything she had done since she left home. The list was pretty mundane. She did remember feeling someone was watching her while they waited in line for the ferry. But more than likely it was Lisa they were watching.

What if her nightmare and the memory bits were *trying to tell her something?*

She would do what she should have done days ago. Luke had told her not to answer the phone, but he hadn't said she couldn't call out.

She got off the sofa and strode to the phone mounted on the wall near the kitchen door. She put on caller ID block and dialed the familiar number and waited for Dr. Stanley's receptionist to answer. Her fingers drummed a tattoo on the wall as she counted the rings. Dr. Stanley worked evenings as it suited his patients and his temperament. *Why then was there no one in the office? Where could he be?*

After a few more rings, Dr. Stanley answered.

"Robyn, I'm so glad to hear from you. Is everything okay?"

The familiar counselor tone that once had soothed her now irritated her. Things had changed, and she needed answers. His skills as a therapist, over the past few years, had helped her gain insight into her phobia, but not its root cause. She had not been afraid of water before the accident. After months of therapy Dr. Stanley had agreed to the ferry trip to Grand Island. Although the doctor agreed, Robyn was pretty certain he hadn't believed it was the best route for her. Robyn had insisted upon it – a decision she now regretted.

It didn't matter. For now she was more interested in her patient record than in any therapy. She needed access to the information her record held. "I'm okay. Dr. Stanley. Have you got a minute?"

"Sure. It's so good to hear from you again. How's it going? Is there anything I can do to help?"

"As one professional to another I need to know what's in my file about the first few times I came to you. I don't mean my condition. I want to know if I told you my dream about someone in trouble."

After a long pause, he said, "You know those are my private notes."

Was he stalling? And if so, why? She waited, trying to keep her anxiety and impatience under control.

"Robyn, I explained to you when we started your therapy that after what you'd been through, it would not be unusual for you to have nightmares about what happened." He hesitated before continuing. "That doesn't make them real," he said as if she thought they were reality and he had to convince her otherwise.

Why was he acting this way? Her nightmares had been the focus of her life. She hadn't mentioned them to him recently, but that changed nothing. "Isn't it a little unusual, after so long, for me to have no memory of what happened on that sailboat before I was found adrift?"

"Memories are difficult to evaluate sometimes, and often wreak havoc on the unconscious mind." His soothing tone did nothing but annoy her now. With the shooting on the marsh, she had to see if learning about her nightmares could help her sort out what was going on in her life. After the incident of the hymnal she was sure her memories and her dreams held the key to the chaos around her. And regardless of what was discovered, she had to know what they meant. "Dr. Stanley, the first memory I told you about was how I thought I had been involved in what happened to Nathan and Peter, that I had been negligent somehow, right?"

"Robyn, this is *not* the kind of discussion I want to have over the phone. Do you want me to make an appointment for you? I'd be more than willing——"

"No. I want you to get out my file and check your notes on my first visit to you, and see if I mentioned anything about killing someone."

"Robyn, are you sure this will help? Reliving these sorts of memories would be better done in my office, under my care."

Robyn refused to believe that Dr. Stanley didn't have answers for her. She'd spent enough time in therapy, and the man knew everything there was to know about her. "Please, Dr. Stanley, just do as I ask."

"I'll have to call you back," he said. "Where can I reach you?"

"Dr. Stanley, I'm calling on someone else's phone and I cannot give out their number." She tried to get control of her rising anger. "Please do as I ask, now."

There was a pause, and she heard him put the phone down. After so many visits to his pristine office, she could visualize him going to his confidential files. They were in the corner, behind the door, next to the table that held his collection of gilded cigarette lighters and the mahogany humidor where he kept a collection of expensive cigars. She couldn't hear the familiar squeak of the filing cabinet, but she knew where he'd gone for the information. There seemed to be an extra long pause as she waited for him to return to the phone.

"On your first visit, we talked about your sleepless nights and loss of weight, general fatigue...."

Robyn listened as he read down the page.

"Ah, yes you did talk about a dream. Something about a gun.... You thought you had a gun in your hand or near you when the water opened up around you. You saw a face...."

There was a long pause before he spoke again. "Robyn, the dream is back, isn't it?"

A hard lump blocked her throat, making speech impossible. There were no words to express the feeling of dread eating a hole in her stomach. *If she was somehow involved in what happened, if the police had been right to investigate her....*

"Robyn, are you there?"

She heard what sounded like papers being shuffled.

"Robyn, if that dream is back, I need to see you as soon as possible. It's not safe for you to be going through this without my professional help. You know I care what happens to you, and you've been through so much. Can I arrange an appointment for you? Or I can meet you at the inn? I can take the next ferry to Grand Island."

He knew she was on the island but had she told him she was going to be at an inn?

You're sounding paranoid. Watch it. Of course Dr. Stanley was only doing his job. She shook her head, forgetting he couldn't see her. "It was so kind of you to offer to meet me, but that won't be necessary. I'm all right."

"No, dammit it! You're not all right. I want you to tell me how and when we can meet. I want to know where you are."

What was going on with him? Had he tried to call her at the inn, and was told she'd checked out? He'd always been the picture of calm – never yelling like this.

"Dr. Stanley, I'll be in touch with you, I promise." A yelling psychiatrist was the last thing she needed in her life at the moment. Robyn didn't want a confrontation with the man either.

"Sorry Robyn for sounding off, but it's been a difficult

week. Look, if you need me any hour of the day or night, just call." He gave her his latest unlisted cell phone number.

Robyn hung up and moved to the safety of the sofa, her head spinning. All her worst fears swam anew in her mind. Dr. Stanley's notes from her first visit confirmed the nightmare about the gun and her belief she had witnessed something – or been part of something sinister and dangerous. Except for her bad dreams a few days before she came here, she'd somehow managed to put that out of her conscious mind...until the shooting.

Fingers of fear tapped up her spine. A cold-blooded killer had attacked her and Lisa that day on Simmons Marsh. That event had sparked Robyn's memory of a gun in her hands and someone dead.

Why would the shooting cause the memory to resurface? Was she somehow involved in what happened that night her brother and fiancé disappeared? Had she done something that had put Peter or Nathan in harm's way? Had she hurt them?

What had she done that night on the boat? Had she tried to save Nathan and Peter from their attacker, or had she left them to face whatever had happened? Or had she managed somehow to escape and now a killer was looking for her?

Darkness swirled around her as she hugged her knees to her chest, seeking protection from the thoughts slashing through her mind. *Was her denial hiding the vicious truth of her actions? Had she let them die? Was the gunman someone who knew what she'd done, and wanted her dead?*

Luke slowed the cruiser and turned into Amos Potter's yard in Whale Cove. Darkness crept across the planks of the pier. The piles supporting the pier created sentinels of shadow stretching over the mirror-calm water.

The man lived in a shanty on the end of an abandoned pier; a pier that had once played host to the largest cod fishing fleet on the eastern seaboard. Today, it was reduced to a temporary resting place for the occasional pleasure yacht or sailing boat.

In short, no one disturbed Amos Potter's makeshift home. The location wasn't the only reason no one bothered the old man. Amos was strange. Even the school bullies didn't make fun of Amos. They feared his uncanny abilities, his look-through-you stare and his ability to almost fade from sight as you watched.

Ever since Amos had appeared on the island, he had been a source of wry amusement to Luke.

The garden episode with Robyn changed all that. Luke grimaced. The old goat better have an explanation for frightening Robyn. If he wasn't the one in the herb garden, it meant the killer had decided to make the whole deadly issue more personal. Or the killer liked to toy with his victims, frighten them even more than they were already. Caught between the two possibilities, he almost wanted it to be Amos and his strange ways.

Luke called in his location and climbed out of his cruiser. The flat calm of a tide at full height, gave the pier an eerie quietness. Although the sun was below the horizon, the after light still allowed Luke to see as he approached the door. The *thunk* of his boots on the wooden pier was the only sound, except for the cooing of pigeons on the peak of a smoke house nearby.

With just the slightest whisper, a blue heron lifted off the shallows near the shore and careened over Luke's head, probably on a flight path toward its night roost. Luke's knocking on the wooden door reverberated through the cooling air.

No answer. He waited, giving the hut a careful once-over

as he did so. There was nothing out of the ordinary about the grayed clapboard and tar-paper structure. Full garbage bags were braced against the wall near the door.

Knocking again, Luke eased onto the balls of his feet. He turned the knob, but it held fast. The old bastard should be home. If not, Luke would have to wait until the next day to find him. One thing was certain – calling him was out of the question. Luke had unsuccessfully tried to call when one of the local residents had complained about him. Amos Potter didn't have a phone.

The power lines to the pier provided the power needed for the navigational warning light at the end where it jutted out into the water. Anxious to have a discussion with Amos, Luke did a quick circuit of the hut. Rounding the corner, he saw that the back of the hut looked a lot like the front, with one exception. There was a high-powered antenna mounted at the back, out of sight of the main road.

What use would a derelict like Amos have for a sophisticated transmitter? With as little sound as possible, and his right hand hovering over his sidearm, Luke approached the only window on the back of the hut. He scanned the room in the failing light. He couldn't see the radio he knew would go with the antenna, but a smart man would hide a radio, the way he'd hidden the antenna. There were a few books on a shelf on the back wall near the bed. Amos didn't strike Luke as a reader. A sliver of light caught Luke's attention near the wall just inside the window. Craning his neck, he struggled for a better look. A cylinder-shaped object with gauges.

Air tanks.

Why would someone, passing himself off as a derelict for four months, have a set of scuba tanks? Surely Amos was too old to get certification as a diver. Luke backed away from the window, his mind running through the possibilities. He reached the car without drawing a breath, and grabbed his radio. He let dispatch know he had not located Amos Potter.

When he did locate Mr. Potter, he would have a lot of explaining to do.

Darkness, like a cloud, crept into all the tiny spaces that surrounded Robyn on the sofa as she sat hugging her legs. What if she had been involved in the death of someone...if she'd done something on the sailboat that night that could never be forgiven?

She needed to talk to a friend. She couldn't call Lisa, but maybe Brad would be helpful. But she couldn't let Brad know where she was. Luke had warned her to keep her location a secret.

She couldn't talk to Luke either. Her admission to him that she had dreams about a gun and that she might have killed someone would force him to investigate the possibility. And if he did and discovered that she was somehow involved in Peter's and Nathan's deaths, it would be over between them. She knew how awful it sounded to be more concerned with a relationship than with the investigation into another person's death, but she couldn't help how she felt. The police had investigated the accident and hadn't found either body, and yet they'd tried to make the case that she was involved.

Out of the corner of her eye, she saw a flicker of light in the window. *What if someone was watching her from the street right this very minute?* She'd been certain that someone had been outside her room at the inn while she and Luke were talking about the hymnal. *What if?* Robyn unwound her legs and rose from the sofa. Passion, who had been curled by Robyn's legs, protested loudly.

"Sorry old fella." Robyn gave the cat a gentle massage

behind the ears and was rewarded with a loud purr. "I'll be back," she whispered.

Nothing moved outside the window, and only the humming and clanking of the fridge, broke the silence of the house. She snapped the living room drapes closed and spotted the open drapes in the dining room. She fumbled for the pull chord as she glanced out into the backyard. A large pole-mounted light spread a yellow tint over the police van parked near the garage.

A shadow moved near the vehicle. *Or was it the light mingled with the shadow of the trees playing across the glass?* Yanking on the chord, she closed the drapes.

Get a grip! You're safe. No one knows you're here.

The sofa offered a welcome haven as she scooped up the cat and sat down again. There were spots on the wooden arms where the shiny stain had given way to the lighter, dull underlying wood color. The fabric was worn in all the right places.

Robyn imagined Luke sitting there, watching a game on television, or reading the newspaper. She wondered if he liked baseball, or maybe soccer. She wondered about a lot of things where he was concerned.

The kitchen light fanned into the living room, leaving a bright trail along the carpet. Funny how fear could make you notice everyday things, things that linked you to reality. Taking a deep cleansing breath, she rested her head against the back of the sofa.

She couldn't let her fears get the better of her. If she were ever to find out who was after her she would have to put a leash on her imagination. She listened to the familiar sounds, the fridge clicking off, a car passing on the street, and directed her mind away from her worries.

Luke wanted her to get some rest, and it wasn't bad advice, given the day's events.

First she would call and see how Lisa was doing. Lisa had been moved from surgical intensive care to one of the surgical nursing units. She dialed the familiar hospital number and her call was transferred to Lisa's room.

"Hi kid!" Lisa's voice sounded tired, but pleased.

Robyn fought back a flood of emotion and steadied her voice before she spoke. "It's so good to hear your voice. How are you feeling?"

"Much better. I can hardly wait to see you. Are you home?"

"No, I'm still on the island. The police haven't finished the investigation."

"So, what's that got to do with you coming home?"

Robyn didn't want to worry her friend, but at the same time, she knew Lisa had a nose for the truth. "He wants me to stay here where I'll be safe."

"Who are you talking about? Safe? You'd be safe at home. Robyn, what's going on?"

"I'm not sure. Luke's theory is that the shooting had something to do with the boating accident."

"You're kidding!" A bout of coughing interrupted Lisa. "Damn tubes."

"Do you still have a chest tube?"

"Yeah, it's coming out tomorrow. Never mind changing the subject. What's the story?"

"He wants to investigate the events around the boating accident."

As Robyn waited for Lisa to respond, guilt overwhelmed her. What a selfish thing to do. Calling Lisa to dump on her when Lisa was ill. "Let's talk about something more cheerful. We've had our quota of doom and gloom."

"How about having you back here, safe and sound? That's a cheerful thought."

"Yeah."

"I got an even better one. Let's try getting to the bottom of what's bothering you, Robyn. I know you too well. Something has you scared."

Caught between her need for Lisa's advice and concern for her friend, Robyn hesitated.

"Come, on. I'm bored silly in this hospital. Give me something to focus on," Lisa urged.

Aside from Luke, she hadn't told anyone but Dr. Stanley about her nightmare. "After the shooting, I had this dream, or something. In the dream, I had a gun."

"A gun. That's not possible. You're the last person I know who would ever have anything to do with a gun. It has to be just a bad dream."

Robyn couldn't tell Lisa she had had the dream several times since the accident. Only one person knew that, and his professional advice hadn't helped her.

Lisa's voice was low and muffled. "Robyn, let the officer do what he needs to do." Her voice cleared as she continued. "I never really believed the police got to the facts of that accident. I still believe that something wasn't quite right about the way Nathan and Peter died. They were both good sailors; both of them knew how to handle a boat whatever the conditions."

Robyn trusted Lisa. "Go on."

"Robyn, you're the strongest person I know. You have always been clear headed and willing to face whatever came along. In all the years I've known you, you've never shied away from anything. When you get back home, I want to show you something I've been working on. In the meantime, you need to concentrate on one thing."

"What's that?"

"It's been over three years since the accident. If I were you, I'd start investigating that psychiatrist you've been going to."

"What do you mean?"

"Just this. Why can't you remember what happened on that sailboat? Why are you riddled with guilt about what happened that night? If that psychiatrist was as good as he claims, he would have gotten to the bottom of all this by now. Instead, you're living with all sorts of emotional baggage that won't go away."

Robyn and Lisa talked for a while longer, but all Robyn could remember was Lisa's questions. They kept rolling through her mind as she sat on the sofa after the call. Lisa's question about Dr. Stanley stemmed from her friend's general distrust of psychologists and psychiatrists. But Lisa had raised several good questions. *Why didn't she remember what happened on that sailboat?*

Robyn had to trust Luke to find her a way out of this particular mess, even though it might lead to something else. Luke's help might reveal she had been hiding something all these years, something that might incriminate her. Luke believed her past could have something to do with her present situation. Her flashbacks held the key. And around it went.

Needing something to do, she gathered up the cat again and eased off the sofa. In protest, Passion leaped from her arms and returned to his position, paws curled inward, eyes narrowed to slits. The cat watched Robyn gather up her bag and move toward the stairs. The wooden stairs took a turn about halfway up, creating a narrow landing which held a droopy Boston fern, over which hung a painting of Mallard ducks. The stairs ended just outside the bathroom door. She flicked the switch, bathing the hall in warm light. Curiosity propelled her along the hall and into the first bedroom.

The room was all male, with green area rugs atop a shiny

dark wooden floor and dark wainscoting on the walls. The king-sized mahogany bed, with a green duvet, dominated the room. The far wall held a series of family photographs. Somehow, entering Luke's bedroom felt like an invasion of his privacy. At the same time, being in such close contact with his personal things made her want to know more about him.

The windows at the foot of the bed looked out on the back deck and garage. Everything in the room was neat except for the small bookcase near the window. Avoiding any contact with the window, she stepped closer to the over-flowing bookshelves. Many of the books pertained to boats and yachts of all descriptions. Most of the titles were familiar to Robyn – Peter had been an avid collector of books about boats. Strange, how her thoughts were on Peter this evening, and on how much fun they used to have. Peter had been her best friend in so many ways. And she missed him.

Her fingers played along the glossy finish of a book lying on the shelf. She had never questioned anyone involved in her rescue about what they had found, not even Brad. She had been too devastated by her loss. But she had also been afraid. After this was all over, she intended to find the people who rescued her and get some answers.

The soft chime of a glass-encased clock on the armoire reminded her she was trespassing and she reluctantly backed slowly out of the room.

There were qualities about Luke that Robyn admired. His rock solidness fascinated her. His ability to make her feel included and valued as a human being attracted her as well. But the thing she liked most of all was the feeling of being safe when he was around.

Never in her wildest dreams had she ever expected to be attracted to a police officer. And the fact that he shared her feelings was even weirder. Luke's eyes told her what his willpower wouldn't let his body prove. His need for her was as great as her need for him. After losing Nathan, Robyn had given up thinking she'd ever find someone else to love. The void left in her life could not be filled – or so she'd believed. There was something so special, in the knowledge that Luke had begun to fill that void, opening up a whole new world for her.

She made her way along the corridor and found herself in a tiny bedroom as completely feminine as the previous one had been masculine. There were white eyelet curtains held back by velvet ribbons and a matching white eyelet bedspread. What kind of man decorates a house like this? Maybe a sister had helped…. Or was there another woman?

Robyn had given little thought to Luke's personal life until now. What if he had a girlfriend? After all, a man like Luke wouldn't have any trouble finding a woman to share his life. The thought saddened her even as it piqued her interest.

Dropping her bag at the foot of the bed, she ran her fingers over the shimmering white eyelet on the bedspread as exhaustion and worry bubbled to the surface. It looked so right…so ordinary – in a good way.

Only once before had she experienced such a feeling of helplessness and that was three years ago. Except for her mother and her psychiatrist, she'd dealt with all of that alone. Lisa had tried to help, but Robyn couldn't trust anyone other than her therapist with her fears. At least now she had Luke's help. Yet, she couldn't quiet the little voice in her head that told her that Luke's help would mean she would also have to trust him with her secret – the one that now haunted her dreams again.

Wanting to block the outside world, Robyn closed the blind and kicked off her shoes. If she let him in on her secret, would his professionalism demand he diligently investigate her actions that night three years ago?

If he did, what would he find?

Robyn knew the answer even as her mind formed the question. Her life had changed forever that night. And in the aftermath she'd doubted herself and her ability to care for others.

CHAPTER TWELVE

Unanswered questions dogged Luke's drive home. He wanted to go into Amos's hut and find out what the old man was up to. The only thing stopping him was the fact that he didn't have a search warrant, and to get one he needed time and a prosecutor who would believe what he was saying. Pretty difficult given that the police on the mainland had decided that Lisa was the victim and the shooter was dead.

Luke called in and waited for Alice to answer. He told her what he'd found at Amos Potter's shack. "Luke, I've called everyone who might know where Amos Potter is and nobody has any idea. It seems he's disappeared from the island."

"How convenient for him."

"Yeah, I know how you feel. If that man had anything to do with this he has to have a motive. What could that be?"

After finding out that Amos wasn't who he seemed, Luke had a sudden urge to talk to Robyn; to be sure she was okay.

"Well, we'll know more by tomorrow. I'll be back in about

half an hour. Any other word?" Alice knew he was referring to Robyn.

"Not a sound, but I've been out on patrol most of the time. Do you want me to check on her?"

"No. I'll be there as soon as I can."

He had been surprised to find the high-tech equipment and the scuba gear in Amos's old shack, but it felt good to have a suspect to concentrate on after days of spinning his wheels on the investigation front.

So far, he had two possible suspects, Brad and Amos. Brad hadn't killed Leo Lord, but his interest in Robyn and his evasiveness were suspicious. Amos Potter might be old and rail thin, but that wouldn't stop him from firing a gun. Were the two men connected? Or were they working alone?

Luke was tempted to forget his promise to bring home dinner and simply head back to his house. He wanted to see Robyn. He blew the air out of his lungs. If he didn't follow through with dinner, she would be curious and he would feel compelled to explain where he'd been and why. He didn't want to frighten her any more than necessary until he knew what was going on with Amos.

He dialed his home number as he pulled into the local take-out. He let it ring until the answering machine came on then left a short message.

Excruciating dread seeped into Robyn's mind as she stood in the boat's cabin listening and waiting. Loud voices drummed through her head; anger and fear filled the night air.

With only a few feet separating her from them, she scrambled up the companionway onto the deck. Their voices grew louder as she moved closer.

Witnessing the struggle, she screamed out in panic. She stum-

bled, her knee hitting the steering wheel of the boat. The men advanced toward her, their bodies loomed over her.

Screaming, she threw herself sideways and fell.

"Robyn! Robyn, where are you?"

Her head hit something hard as Robyn landed on the soft white mat beside the bed. *Where was she? How did she get here?* The dream clung to her like plastic wrap, her fear leaving her body cold and clammy.

Luke rushed into the room, turning on the light as he did so. "I heard you scream," he said, his voice filled with urgency as he knelt down beside her, his hands reaching for hers.

Scrambling up onto the bed, Robyn blinked at him in the bright light. "I must have fallen asleep and fallen off the bed." She rubbed her eyes.

Luke sat beside her, his assessing gaze watching her every move.

She forced the dream to the back of her mind. There was no way in the world she could tell him about her dream at this moment. "I scared myself when I fell out of bed."

"You were screaming. Are you sure that's all?" Luke's eyes scanned her from her bare feet to her moist forehead.

Robyn tucked her feet under her and leaned back against the pillows. She needed to put space between her and Luke. Her conversations with Lisa and Dr. Stanley must have triggered the dream because this one had been different, less fragmented, more frightening. And she could still feel the anger and fear...and see the blurred faces of the two men.

She feigned an easy smile. "What did you bring back for supper?"

Luke rested one hand on the eyelet covering of the bed, his expression still one of concern. Yet his eyes were warm and thoughtful. "So, you're hungry? That's encouraging. I brought Chinese."

"I'm starved." Thankful for the change of topic, Robyn got up off the bed and walked to the door. "Let's eat while it's hot."

She walked ahead of him down the stairs, searching her mind for a topic of conversation that would allow her to put her dream behind her. "Does Passion like Chinese?"

"Passion is a pig. He eats everything except raw veggies."

"Oh, a cat with a passion for things other than night life." She smiled up at him as she made her way down the narrow stairs.

"You could say that." Luke caught up with her at the bottom of the steps, and they went to the kitchen.

Standing at the counter together, they opened packages and got plates out of the cupboard. There was something so comfortable about standing next to him. Once or twice their hands brushed, raising Robyn's awareness of him. When they sat down across the table from one another, it was as if they had eaten together many times before. For a fleeting moment, she imagined what it would be like to be married to Luke.

Robyn resisted the urge to let her mind play with ideas of home and hearth. There was too much at stake. Too many opportunities for things to go wrong. Too many things that had already gone wrong.

Luke opened the cupboard and took out soy sauce then reached into another cupboard and pulled out glasses. His body moved with the ease of an athlete, his hands drawing her attention as he placed things on the table. What would it be like to have those hands moving slowly over her? Her body warmed from her hair to the tips of her toes.

"Want me to put on some music?" When his gaze snagged hers the air between them sparked.

"Sure, what do you have?"

"Is there any chance you like Natalie McMaster?" Luke looked just a little sheepish.

"I went to a concert of hers in Portland a couple of years ago. Jason came with me. He wasn't that excited about it at first, but he got to meet her backstage and that settled it for him."

Luke disappeared into the living room, and came back accompanied by the lilting beat of fiddle music. "I always feel I'm home when I play one of her tunes."

Happy and content, Robyn smiled across the kitchen table at him. "This is great. I haven't been this hungry in ages." Everything felt so right, so perfect. And yet, neither of them had said anything of importance to each other – they behaved just like two ordinary people sharing Chinese food. Feeling more at ease than she had since she arrived on the island, she couldn't resist the chance to know more about Luke. And now seemed like a look time to ask. "The room I was sleeping in is so feminine."

"Are you asking me who has the female touch, given there are two guys – make that one guy and one neutered male cat – living here?"

"Yeah, sort of."

"The decorating in your room came from happier times when my wife and my sister decorated our house in Portland."

"You didn't want to change it?"

Sighing, he rose and brought the Chinese food cartons to the table. Opening one he dished more onto his plate and offered her more – she declined. "I suppose I should have. But there had been so many changes. Besides, you like it. So, it's served a good purpose."

"I'm sorry. I shouldn't pry." She toyed with the food on her plate, hoping that he'd forget her nosiness.

Luke looked at her, as if deciding on a course of action.

"It's all right. I met Charlene just after I got my first job with the police. I missed my family. I guess you could say I was at a low point in my life, and she was there when I needed someone to feel close to. My mistake."

"Mistake?"

"My wife, Charlene, was a cocaine user, a fact she forgot to mention during our marriage. She was very good at hiding things, yet she demanded to know everything going on in my life. Then when I was working on a case involving drug smuggling, and she started asking too many questions, I should have seen what was going on."

"You mean she was trying to get information from you?"

He nodded. "To pass on to her drug-smuggling friends."

"You've got to be kidding!"

"I wish I were."

"Where is she now?"

"In prison."

Robyn remembered a chance remark that Lisa had made about the officer who had turned his wife in to the authorities. "What did you do?"

He shrugged. "What could I do? When I caught her using drugs, I knew the trust had gone from our marriage. I began to watch her. Actually, I followed her to one of her meetings with a man I recognized – one of the suppliers we'd been watching. I verified my suspicions and turned her in to the authorities."

What would she have done if someone in her life had committed such a crime? A few days ago, she had no sympathy for a man who turned in his wife to the authorities. Now she understood perfectly. Some crimes cried out for punishment, regardless of who the perpetrator was. "It must have been a very difficult time for you."

His hands rested quietly on either side of his plate. "I took this posting to get away from it all. I considered getting out of police work, but I had too much time invested in it, and most days I like what I do for a living."

She could see the tension in his face and the loneliness in his eyes. Robyn couldn't imagine how it felt to face such a situation, but she had to admire his willingness to continue doing what he did.

"There hasn't been a day when I didn't wish I could have stopped Charlene from using drugs. If I had known what was going on, I might have prevented her from getting involved in the drug business. I blame myself for being so blind to what was going on in her life."

"You can't take responsibility for her actions. She was an adult. She may not have chosen her addiction, but she chose how she dealt with it."

"It doesn't matter anymore. Charlene divorced me when she found out who turned her in." Luke leaned back from the table, signaling the end of the conversation. They finished their meal in silence.

"I'll cleanup," Robyn said, scooping the plates up and taking them to the counter.

"There's no dishwasher, but I have my dishwashing badge," Luke said, pulling a cloth from the drawer as he watched her run hot, soapy water into the sink. "I'm glad you got some rest."

"I did. Thank you." Was it only because of all the time she had spent without a man in her life, or was Luke every bit as attractive as he seemed?

Luke leaned one hip on the counter as he waited for her to wash the dishes. "I had a busy afternoon, but not very productive, I'm afraid."

"Where did you go?"

Luke didn't speak for a few moments. His attention seemed centered on the task of wiping the dishes as she placed them on the draining tray.

Not wanting to lose him to his solitary thoughts, she continued, "I made a list of all the things I did from the time I left the house until the shooting. I came to the conclusion I lead a pretty dull life."

"Every little bit helps," Luke said with muted enthusiasm.

She liked it better when they were sharing their lives, not worrying about the present situation. "Care to tell me what's going on?"

"Robyn, I'm trying to track down the man who I'm sure is responsible for frightening you today. Whether or not he's responsible for anything more than that remains to be seen."

She saw the hard look in his eyes, and knew in that instant that he would be a dangerous enemy. The man standing so close to her in such an everyday setting would stop at nothing to get to the truth – including *her* truth.

"I need more than a list of what you did prior to coming here. It's important to do that, but I still think we need to go back farther into your past."

She closed her eyes, trying to silence his words. He wanted information, and she had to trust that he needed what little she could tell him. "Luke, I'll help you if I can."

His smile of relief gave her a sense of dread. She was going to be living in the same space, in such close contact that her secret could very easily slip out. She had been present at the scene of some sort of altercation aboard the sailboat; her dream this evening told her that much. Whatever else happened during that time on the boat was still hidden from her. But should information come to light proving that she'd hurt or killed someone she knew it would spell the end of her relationship with Luke.

"I just can't nail down a motive for this. I know of no reason why anyone would want to harm you. Brad mentioned that you and Lisa had a falling out over Nathan. Can you tell me about that?"

What else had Brad told him? "There's not much to tell. Nathan and Lisa went out together for a few months. It didn't work out. Lisa always wanted to have the upper hand in a relationship, be the one who made the decisions. That didn't work with Nathan, and she didn't see the breakup coming. She accused me of getting between them. It wasn't true."

"Was Lisa upset?"

"Lisa? Not really. She never wanted to be tied down to just one man."

"You're sure about that?"

"Absolutely."

"Then, you believe we need to look elsewhere for a motive?"

"I've been saying that all along. Is it possible that whoever's behind this had mistaken me for someone else?"

"Anything's possible."

She somehow felt better with the idea that it might just be a mistake. She slipped into the chair at the table. "If that's true, how can we find a way to stop them?"

"I said it's possible, but I don't believe it's a viable option."

Robyn held her breath as if her life depended on it. "What *are* you considering?"

"We have to go farther into your life and see if there is anything else. I keep coming back to the idea that someone very close to you wants you dead."

The air caught in Robyn's throat.

"Robyn, have you wondered why Brad took you to the Anchorage the other night at the exact time the killer was waiting, ready to kill?"

"No, of course not. Brad wouldn't do such a thing."

"Well, the evidence is pretty strong that he did." Luke moved to the table and sat down.

"I don't believe he did it intentionally. I think it was a coincidence," she said with finality.

Luke stared at her, his gaze moving over her face. "Leo Lord was waiting with his weapons loaded, for someone to come out on the beach. The person who killed him was hiding behind a tree not far from him. Leo's gun was ready to fire when he was killed. At least two people knew about some sort of meeting that night on the beach – Leo and his killer. The weapon Leo had in his hands at the time was the same one used on you and Lisa. Brad and you were the only two people on the beach at the time of the killing."

"You don't know that."

Luke stood up and came around the table toward her. "Robyn, why did Brad take you out to that God forsaken place?"

Robyn saw the anger in his eyes, and for a moment, she was frightened. "I don't know. He said he wanted me to see the moonlight on the beach, to have a chance to relax."

There was a long pause as Luke towered over her. She didn't dare look up and let him see her fear. She didn't believe that Brad would harm her. However, she did believe that Luke wouldn't give up on any suspect until he had the truth. His ex-wife's arrest was proof of that.

Luck settled his hands on his hips, his right hand brushing his holster. "From here on, stay away from him. I wouldn't believe a word Brad Allen said."

Luke watched with a heavy heart as Robyn sought the comfort of the sofa in the living room.

Wanting to be with her, to explain to her why he'd said what he had, Luke followed. "Robyn, I'm sorry to suggest this, but Brad's actions are very suspicious."

"What you're suggesting is out of the question. Brad would never hurt me."

Sinking into the sofa beside her, Luke took her hands in his. "Robyn, it's been very difficult for you to accept that someone who would seem to care for you could put you in danger. Denial is a way of protecting our inner selves when we are threatened. I know that better than most people. But you can't keep your head in the sand. You need to understand what has gone on here."

Robyn's gaze moved away from Luke. "It's just that Brad has been my friend for a long time. He's always been there for me."

"You and he have a relationship."

Robyn tried to pull her fingers from his. "Not a romantic one. We were close, mostly because of the boat accident."

Robyn ducked Luke's penetrating gaze, and he sensed that she felt some level of guilt where Brad was concerned. For the life of him, he couldn't imagine why. Not wanting to intimidate her any farther, Luke settled back into the corner of the sofa. "I gather that Brad wanted a relationship with you. Why didn't it happen?"

"It was my fault, I guess. I couldn't feel anything for anybody after Nathan died. It was just too soon after his death."

Robyn's face mirrored the fatigue Luke felt. They were both tired and stressed out. He didn't feel right about asking her sensitive questions when she was clearly tired. But he couldn't abandon the idea that Robyn knew more than she was willing to say. Or maybe she wasn't aware that she had information that could be important to her case.

Either way Brad Allen was a suspect. Robyn McGill was loyal to him.

"How does he feel about you now?" The question sent a look of shock flitting across Robyn's face.

She got up and went to the window. "He still thinks there's a chance for us."

Luke followed her, standing as close to Robyn as he dared.

"Is there?" He knew he had no business asking such a personal question. Worse than that, he wanted the answer for himself, not for the investigation.

Robyn put her hand out, as if to ward him off. "No. No, there isn't."

Luke felt the kind of relief he had no right to feel. This was a police investigation, not a contest between two men for the love of a woman. "Okay. I'll accept that you don't want a relationship with him, but that doesn't mean there isn't reason to watch out for him. It's possible that Brad may have been involved in the shooting at the Anchorage. For your own safety, I want your word that you will not let him know where you are."

Luke recognized the signs of shock in Robyn's eyes as he said the words, and for the second time in his career he wished he weren't a policeman.

Later that evening, he heard the shower shut off and knew Robyn would soon walk past his bedroom. Getting out of his chair, he closed the door. He didn't want to see her right now. The tiredness sapping his control could spell trouble for him and the investigation. He heard her soft footfall along the hallway, and in his mind he traced the fine line of moisture he imagined clinging to the hidden parts of her.

His body stirred, awakened by his thoughts and his need for her. The attraction he felt for Robyn added a whole new dimension to his life, a life he now realized had been lonely and unfulfilled until he met her.

But he had to concentrate on the investigation without

adding that complication. And too easily, Robyn would become a complication. Hell! Who was he kidding? She already was a complication, or he wouldn't be waiting until tomorrow to ask her the questions he needed answered.

He was sure the motive lay hidden in her past, and his instincts told him to look closely at Robyn and Brad. Their friendship had been a long one without a love affair to complicate it.

The undercurrent flowing between Brad and him, one man to another, told Luke that Brad had not given up the idea of having a relationship with Robyn. Brad was obviously a very patient man when something he wanted was in play.

The phone rang beside him. Because he seldom got off-duty phone calls, he grabbed it. He listened to Alice's apology for disturbing him then waited for her to continue.

"Luke, I have Amos Potter on the other line and he wants to speak to you. He says it's urgent."

Luke snorted in disgust. "You mean he's capable of a coherent sentence?"

"More than one it would seem." Alice's voice took on a sharper note. "He says he has to talk to you right away."

Luke drummed his fingers on the latest copy of *Sailing Magazine* resting in his lap, as he reviewed his options. He wanted to talk to Amos, but he needed to make it a formal interview, not have some clandestine meeting. Meeting tonight meant another night of lost sleep, but if it brought a conclusion to one part of the investigation, it would be worth it.

"Alice, tell him to come to the office in twenty minutes."

"You want me to go pick him up?"

"No, let him find his own way here. If what he has to say is so damned important that it can't wait, he can get here under his own steam." Luke reached for his clothes hanging over the end of the bed as he spoke. "I'll meet you downstairs in a few minutes."

Luke scrambled back into his uniform. As he entered the hallway, he considered telling Robyn where he was going, but changed his mind. It had been a long day and she was probably asleep. He closed his bedroom door and tiptoed down the stairs.

This had better be good. If Amos Potter could explain away his expensive radio and his scuba gear, without revealing something worth knowing, Luke would be surprised.

But, then again, it had been a day of surprises.

Alice sat shaking her head back and forth very slowly as she met Luke's glance over Amos Potter's head. Everything about the man sitting across the desk from Luke was offensive, including his body odor.

"I'm telling you I haven't done anything to Dr. McGill. I have no reason to bother her." Amos's voice had a raspy quality to it that irritated Luke even more. "It's for damned sure I didn't use the juvenile scare tactics you described. What could I hope to gain by scaring the nice doctor?"

"I'd suggest that it's in your best interests to give us a full statement of your activities for the last four days, especially your interest in the yacht moored off Bear Harbor. Besides, you're the one who wanted to see me." Luke raised one eyebrow and waited.

Amos sat up straighter in his chair. His usual blank gaze had disappeared.

"I know I've given you little reason to trust me, but I can explain my behavior." Amos looked over his shoulder at Alice and back at Luke. "I'm working undercover. I'm here waiting to see if there is any attempt to smuggle people through here.

Interpol seems convinced there is." Amos rubbed his head with the back of his dirty gray, open-fingered gloves, grinning apologetically. "I know I don't smell like a rose garden, but it's part of my cover."

"You mean we might be dealing with an international incident?" Alice asked, her expression one of disbelief. She met Luke's gaze, and he saw in her eyes that she was beginning to see the possibilities. Solving a case like this would give Alice a promotion...maybe to the mainland.

Luke remembered when he hoped every case he worked would lead to a promotion...another lifetime ago. Tonight, all he wanted was the truth that would finally settle this case. Then he'd seriously look at retirement. "Tell us what you came to tell us."

"We have reason to believe that two members of the biggest Mafia family in Russia will be smuggled into the United States. My job is to report any suspicious activities."

"And?" Luke and Alice spoke in unison.

"There has been a yacht under surveillance since it entered American waters a couple of days ago."

"So that explains the radio antenna I saw on the back of your hut."

A flash of anger flipped across Amos's face, and disappeared as he returned Luke's stare.

"Would you like to fill me in on what you're doing with the scuba tanks?"

"Nothing at the moment, but if I have to get aboard that boat, I'll need the gear."

Luke settled back in his chair and evaluated the man sitting across from him. International policing and surveillance wasn't part of his experience. He'd be on the phone to Portland first thing the next morning looking for verification of Amos's story.

Alice looked as if she needed fresh air. Luke reverted to a

tried-and-true stall tactic while he considered what action he could take concerning Amos Potter. "Would anyone like a cup of coffee?"

"Sure, I've been busy this evening. A cup of coffee would be great," Alice agreed.

Both men watched Alice leave the room. "She's enough to make me want to blow my cover," Amos said.

Amos's near-leering grin needled Luke's annoyance at the man. Luke ignored the remark. "Do you know anything about the attempted murder we're investigating?"

"Hardly. I do know there was a man staying at the Oracle Motel in Harper's Cove for a couple of days. I've sent a photo off for identification. Mean looking bugger, but he didn't do anything that I could label as criminal."

"I'd like a copy of that photo along with any ID you get."

"I'll have to see."

"There's no 'have to.' You'll give me what you get."

"You'll have it, but you'll have to go through my boss to get it." Amos Potter gave his version of a warm smile as he spoke.

Luke wouldn't believe a word this man said until he made the phone call in the morning. In the meantime... "You will keep me informed of anything you see that might be suspicious. I'll decide if it has anything to do with the murder of Leo Lord."

"I can do that much," Amos said.

A half-hour later Luke mulled the man's words over in his mind as he made his way back to the house through the connecting door. He had left Alice behind, spraying disinfectant throughout the office. The corridor connecting the house and the office gave a welcome blast of warm air after the chilled space created by all the open windows; fresh air being declared a necessity by Alice.

Without thinking, he checked the back door that led to the parking lot. It was unlocked. Someone had been careless. Probably his cleaning lady when she left earlier. He'd remind her to lock it the next time he saw her.

Pulling out his keys, he opened the door to the house. Closing the door quietly behind him, he reached for the light switch.

That was the last thing he remembered.

CHAPTER THIRTEEN

Robyn's arms ached from the force of the blow she had given the intruder. The clay flowerpot didn't have a dent, but the man lying flat out on the floor by the door leading to the office, hadn't fared so well. Still holding the pot aloft, Robyn tiptoed to the bottom of the stairs, and looked up, expecting Luke to appear from his bedroom. Strange that Luke hadn't heard anything. He must sleep like the dead. "*Woops!* Bad choice of words," she muttered into the uncertain darkness surrounding her.

Luke would be pleased with her when he saw how she'd handled the intruder. She called his name and heard her voice echo up the stairwell. Luke must be a real sound sleeper. Of course his door was closed. *Why hadn't she thought of that before?* She hadn't had time to alert Luke when she heard the sound of someone at the door. Lucky for both of them, she'd been in the kitchen getting a glass of water.

Frightened as she had been at having to deal with an intruder in the night, she realized she had put an end to the criminal's plan. This was her first attempt to take charge of her life since Nathan's death, and she'd done a real good job.

What had taken her so long to return to her old assertive self?

A sense of something approaching pleasure surged through her. Clutching the pot, she wished the intruder would stir, just a little, and give her reason to hit him again. Imagine the nerve – breaking into a police officer's house?

Where was Luke?

She called his name again and the man on the floor stirred. Robyn clutched the pot. If the intruder woke up before Luke pulled his bones out of bed, Robyn would hit him again.

To improve her aim, she needed more light. Edging closer, she reached across the man on the floor and flicked on the hall light. The man rolled over, rubbed the back of his head and squinted up at her.

"Luke!" The pot fell from her hands, sending a spray of loam and shards of broken pot cascading around them. Robyn crouched beside him. "Luke! Oh God, I'm sorry." As Luke turned his head, the light revealed the beginnings of a huge shiner beside his left temple.

"What have I done?"

"You nearly beheaded me." Luke eased forward on one elbow, moving his head slowly from side to side as he spoke.

"Stay there. Don't try to get up." Robyn moved closer so his head rested on her lap. "Look at me."

"Do I have to?"

"I'm a doctor, for heaven's sake! Do you have a pen light?"

"No."

Robyn stared into his eyes, intent on checking his pupils as much as she could in the muted light.

Luke lifted his head. "Let me up."

Robyn wrapped her arm around his shoulders and forced him back into her lap. "Stay where you are. You're hurt." *And you are gorgeous in your injured state, all those black lashes, pale skin and rumpled hair.*

"And you're crazy. What ever possessed you to hit me?"

Robyn felt her pulse quicken and stopped her sudden intake of breath just in the nick of time. Being aroused by an injured man was hardly appropriate behavior for a doctor. She chided herself even as she held him snugly against her. "I thought you were an intruder."

"Intruders don't come in through the entrance from the office."

"How was I supposed to know that?"

The dulled look in his eyes gave way to just a hint of pleasure as he smiled up at her. "So, Doc, is this the new you? Taking on all comers with my trusty flower pot?"

He had a good sense of humor – something else she liked about him. "You'd better hope not." Without thinking, she reached for his pulse under his chin. "I thought you were upstairs in your bedroom."

"Fast asleep?"

"Something like that." She felt his pulse pound against her fingers. Was the rapid pounding of his heart due to his injury, or something else? She lifted her fingers from his neck.

Robyn fidgeted with the strap of her silk pajamas as she tried to hide the fullness of her breast behind the flimsy fabric. Luke's head rested inches from her tightened nipple. "I didn't know you had gone out."

Luke drew a deep breath and settled closer. "I see."

"Does your head hurt?"

"Not too bad." He touched his temple. "I'm going to have a hell of a bump. We'd better get our story straight before I face Alice and the folks of Grand Island tomorrow morning." His gaze meandered over her breasts, up her neck, across her face to her eyes.

Robyn's heart tripped in her chest as his gaze trapped her with its intensity. "I'm sorry."

She touched the same spot – her fingers tangling with his. His closeness and her vulnerability charged the air between them. His lips were so inviting, her mouth ached to touch his in a kiss.

Warmth and caring washed over her in equal measure as she held his head. As much as the strong policeman appealed to her, the injured man in her arms held her heart. She watched in fascination as he studied her face, knowing he had to feel the pounding of her heart through the silk of her poor excuse for night wear she'd bought on impulse a few months ago.

"It didn't break the skin," she murmured.

He turned in her lap so that his head rested in the soft hollow between her legs. The movement sent spikes of heat charging through her.

"You mean, *you* didn't." His grin was pure pleasure, forcing Robyn to look away. "I have to give you full marks for effort. My temple will be a ravishing shade of purple by morning. Wonder how I'll explain that away."

She gave him a gentle push. "You'd better sit up so I can get a better look at your injury."

Luke eased himself to a sitting position and faced her. His lips looked warm and soft and were so near that his body heat warmed her exposed skin. Robyn swayed toward him.

Without warning Luke's lips were on hers, his hands holding her shoulders in a vice-like grip. She touched the crisp fabric of his shirt as her fingers sought to find a way to his skin beneath the fabric.

Her fingers followed the pounding of his heart like a blind person reading braille. All the pent-up passion she'd denied for so long flowed into the kiss she gave him.

Luke groaned and pulled her down onto the floor, his

tongue claiming her mouth as he angled her body beneath him. Robyn twined her fingers through his dark hair, his scent taking possession of her. She wanted him more than she had ever wanted anyone in her life....

She clung to him, her body molding to his. She loved the scent of him, the strength of his arms, the way he held her so tightly, so securely.

"No," he said, his voice harsh against her lips. He pulled himself away from her, leaving cool dampness where only seconds ago his body fused with hers.

"This isn't right." His voice held more than a note of desperation.

"What are you talking about?" Robyn watched as he sat up and held her away from him.

"I'm talking about *us*. There's too much at stake, here." In the light spilling around them, his eyes were distant, his breathing under control.

Flustered, Robyn silenced her pride with her need to understand. "Are you saying you don't want me?"

Luke got up, his movements slow, his face void of any expression. "If that's what it takes."

Feelings of betrayal chased feelings of anger. "I don't get it." Blood pounded in her head; her body craved release. She struggled for equilibrium as she saw him lean against the wall as if he needed the support it offered.

"I don't expect you to."

Suddenly aware of her near nakedness, Robyn whispered, "Well, the next time, tell me what the rules are, will you?"

Although his gaze never left her face, his eyes were brooding and dark. "You're my responsibility."

She heard the cool formality in his voice. "I can look after myself."

"As long as you live in my house, I'm responsible for your welfare." The finality in his tone sent cold shocks of reality through her mind. He saw her as someone he had to look after, not someone he cared about. So...she was a duty to him. Nothing more.

Embarrassment mingled with resentment as she stood up. "I was going to tell you I'm sorry I hit you."

"But you changed your mind."

"You could say that." She wanted to say more, to make him think how little his sudden change meant to her. But her body still surged with the heat of passion. The ache that stirred within her would have branded her words a lie.

Fighting off tears, Robyn turned and made her way up the stairs with as much dignity as her trembling body allowed.

Luke watched her walk calmly away, waited a little longer and then climbed the stairs to his room. He wanted to put a second shiner on the other side of his head for his dumb behavior. The bed was lumpy, the sheets crumpled and lonely.

Twice during what remained of the night, he got out of bed determined to go to her and do what he knew they both wanted. Yet, something held him back. He'd told her it was his responsibility to her that held his feelings in check. That was partly true but the real reason had more to do with what was going on in her life.

Despite what the police on the mainland believed, for him there was no doubt that Robyn had been the intended victim. He realized how little real evidence he had to back up his claim, but that didn't alter his suspicion. His only possible proof was the death of Leo Lord. Why would Leo have stayed on the island, ending up on a deserted beach ready to kill again, if his intended victim had been Lisa Wade?

Which brought him to the *other* reason why he'd kept her here with him. A part of him couldn't bear the thought of leaving Robyn or sending her away, and that was the most dangerous part of all. He wanted her safe with him, whether here or in Portland. He had no doubt that she would agree to go back home, especially after his dumb performance this evening.

Luke pounded the pillow into a defenseless lump and grimaced as his bruised temple touched down. Something in Robyn's past had to be part of the danger she faced. It had to be. But what?

She was a woman who appeared to have no enemies – until she arrived on Grand Island.

What was the connection? What was he missing?

Light crept into the room, like an unwanted cur, mangy and slinking. Luke unwound his body from the coiled position he'd held most of the night. A jumble of thoughts flooded his mind.

Mentally, he listed the points. He *really* cared about her. She needed his help to find out who was after her and why. She cared for him. He had recognized it in the way she'd held him after she attacked him and her vulnerable glance just before she went upstairs the night before.

Someone close to her was likely involved in the Anchorage incident. Robyn had tried to brush the episode with Brad off as an effort by Brad to be her friend – perhaps more. She had defended Brad when Luke tried to draw a logical connection between Brad and what was going on. The other birders he'd interviewed had told him that Robyn had been on the island before with her brother, but they couldn't remember Brad being on any recent birding trips over here. He was filling in for the regular leader of the group.

As his feet touched the floor, a chill swept through him.

All this time he had only looked at this from one perspective – Robyn's innocence.

What if she and Brad were in this together? What if they had intended to meet someone at the Anchorage and the meeting had gone wrong? When he called Portland about the boating accident three years ago, he'd been told that she had been a suspect. They had stopped investigating Robyn McGill when nothing turned up. Brad had been the one who got the Coast Guard to pick her up out on the ocean in her brother's sailboat. How had he known where she was, and what sordid set of events transpired before she was picked up?

As much as he hated himself for thinking this way, he couldn't ignore the possibility that Robyn and Brad were working together. Or maybe Brad made it *appear* they were working together.

But he couldn't believe that she had anything to do with the disappearance of her brother *and* her fiancée. Robyn was good and kind, and loved by too many people to be involved in such a horrific event. Still…when Leo Lord had been shot to death at the Anchorage, Brad and Robyn had been there.

What if Brad didn't tell the whole story? What if Robyn and Lisa's friendship had not been as strong as it seemed? Brad suggested they'd been in love with the same man. What if Robyn and Brad lured Lisa to the island? And the light footprints near the pine tree at the Anchorage? Could they have been Robyn's?

Robyn had kept insisting she be allowed to leave the island and go to Lisa. What if Robyn's demands to see Lisa had another purpose? A deadly one?

He prowled his bedroom, searching for relief from his ugly thoughts.

What if he'd made a mistake? What if he'd let another

woman play him for a fool? Was Robyn like his ex in more ways than simple appearance?

Having him believe that Robyn was the victim would be useful if she and Brad wanted to avoid suspicion. After arguing with him about everything, why had she been so quick to grab the chance to live in his house?

Did she have another motive for agreeing so easily? Being with him would mean that she'd have lots of opportunity to find out where his investigation was going.

If he had let himself be led down the proverbial garden path by another woman with a hidden agenda, he needed a slap to the head. Drugs may not be the motivating factor in this case, but that didn't eliminate the possibility of other motives and other sets of circumstances he hadn't considered.

God! He scrubbed his face with his hands, feeling the hard bristle along his chin. He had played the gallant knight to the hilt when he offered her the chance to stay in his house. What better way for Robyn to keep tabs on how the investigation was going? What better way to know if she and Brad were in danger of being discovered?

Somewhere on Grand Island.

A man scowled at the phone as he waited for his caller to finish. "Yes, I know Leo Lord is dead." The cigar clenched between his teeth tasted rancid. He hated phones, but this call had to be made. And he was talking to his boss in the organization, so he had to show respect.

"Leo doesn't matter. What's important is the completion of the project. We must get the cargo to port. The two Russians must reach safety as soon as possible. That's our priority," his boss clarified.

"I've made arrangements--"

"That goes without saying. If you feel this doctor is a danger to you, then do what you must. I understand that Amos Potter helped you. Nice to have friends. He claims his performance in some garden was pure Shakespeare. Amos feels pretty confidant that she left the island on the first available ferry after his little performance. He also had a some fun with the local cop, giving him a little misinformation."

Silence filled the phone. The cigar sent a fine trail of smoke drifting toward his nostrils as the man waited for his boss to be done.

"What's the matter? Don't you appreciate what Amos did for you?" his boss asked.

"Absolutely. But is he sure she's left the island? I need to know. With so much interest in Dr. McGill, it's impossible for me to get to her."

"Yeah, and losing Leo must have reduced your chances. Too bad the good doctor can identify you. My suggestion would be to get out as soon as you deliver the goods."

"That's probably a good idea." Never. He had his own agenda once he met his obligations to his boss. He was brokering a shipment of nuclear isotopes. He had a buyer for them, and was about to close the deal.

"I assume you plan to kill the doctor?" There was a pause. "Just get out before you're caught."

"They can't catch me. They never have."

"Overconfidence can be dangerous. Call me when you've done the job and you're well away from the island." A deadly pause filled the line. "Oh and by the way, I hear you may have other fish to fry."

The cigar teetered on the man's lips. "What are you talking about?"

"Nadia seems convinced you have plans to promote your own entrepreneurial efforts. She had better be wrong."

The line went dead. His boss was onto his plan all because of Nadia, a bitch whose ugliness repelled him, but whose usefulness had been essential to his plan. She'd done what he asked because he'd made her believe he loved her. He'd even gone in the van to the Anchorage with her and Leo just to please her. On the way back he'd been very generous in his praise of her until he learned that she'd killed Leo, leaving the good doctor alive and well. He'd forgiven her for not killing the doctor, but if she were using what she knew against him, he would be forced to end the relationship – permanently – something he planned to do further down the road anyway.

He traced the scar on his face, smoothed his neatly trimmed beard and swore. He had to move quickly. The isotopes were his ticket to a small island in the South Pacific. He had hidden them carefully on his yacht, and he would see that they got delivered to their new owners.

First, he needed to be free to move around Grand Island without fear of being identified by the woman who stood to ruin his plan. This time he wouldn't trust the job to anyone else. This time he would take care of it himself.

CHAPTER FOURTEEN

Robyn woke with a start with a headache pounding her skull. Her sleep had been fitful and frightening. A man's face drifted through her intermittent periods of sleep, changing back and forth between the stranger from Harper's Cove and Luke. Both faces had stared at her with absolute coldness. She sat up and looked around the room – the memory of last night flashed through her mind.

She didn't believe in violence of any form and couldn't believe she was capable of hitting anyone. That was before she had seen her friend shot and her life threatened by pointless, faceless violence. Last night she had intentionally struck someone, knowing she would hurt him, proving that she was capable of defending herself if she had to.

Now she wondered if it were possible that she hit someone that night on the boat? Or had she taken it further than that?

Don't go there. Not today.

She moved her thoughts away from violence, a guilty grin suffusing her face. *Talk about knocking a man out to get his attention!* Leaning back against the pillows, she touched her lips with the tips of her fingers and remembered their passionate kiss.

He had tasted so good, so sweet. Words she would not have applied to him before she hit him over the head. She had no doubt that he wanted her. And she wanted him. She wanted everything about him, the fire in his lips, the strength of his body, the warmth of his arms.

She listened for sounds of him in the house and wondered if he had gone to work. She wanted to find him asleep – to be able to crawl in beside him, and have him wake to her need for him. Grabbing her robe, she slid her feet into her slippers and tiptoed down the hall. The door to his room stood open, the space immaculate. Apparently what had happened the night before had not disturbed his sense of order.

Entering the bathroom, she turned on the shower. Routine had always been comforting to Robyn when she needed time to think. After the dream she had last night, she needed routine more than ever. One thing was certain: Helping Luke discover who the killer was would speed up the capture of the man, and perhaps allow them much needed time together.

Slipping out of her robe, she stepped into the shower. She inhaled the musky scent of the soap as she smoothed its fragrance over her skin. Ever since the day on Simmons Marsh her frightening dreams had increased in frequency and duration. The man she had seen in front of the shop in Harper's Cove had joined her dream last night. She had no idea why, yet something about him niggled at her. He seemed so familiar. Had he been in her dreams before? Did she know him?

Yes, the man at Harper's Cove was very definitely part of

her dream, but she was quite certain he had never been part of her life.

Unless...

The image rose like a ghost in her mind. The soap she was holding slid from her fingers.

She had to write everything down, while the memory still lingered. She grabbed a towel, slipped her feet into her slippers and opened the bathroom door. She ran smack into Luke. "Oh! I thought you'd left for work."

"Not yet. I need to talk to you."

"If it's about last night. I'm sorry." She resisted the urge to look at his lips. His eyes were equally dangerous, glinting steel and aimed at her.

She mustered a small grin. "I'm really only sorry for the whack I gave you with the flower pot. The rest––"

He didn't return her smile. "We'll talk about that later. I want you to come downstairs."

Robyn was acutely aware that a towel was the only thing standing between her and the man she had so unashamedly kissed just a few hours earlier.

"Can it wait while I get dressed? Oh, I have something to tell you. I know how my dreams may be linked to what has happened."

Luke's gaze skipped down her half-nude body. "Get dressed. I'll wait downstairs."

Luke must have found out something important for him to look so serious. Whatever it was, she'd deal with it. She suddenly felt as if she could handle anything.

Robyn scrambled into her clothes, her pulse dancing in her throat in tune with her feelings. Luke Carlisle was easily the most intriguing man she'd ever met. She saw her reflection in the mirror and noticed the high points of color in her cheeks.

In the midst of the worst time of her life, she wanted a

man whose stated purpose was to control her every move. Robyn leaned closer to the mirror. And here in his home, under his protection, she felt so safe, so cared for...and yet she had never been in greater danger.

A few minutes later, skipping down the stairs, she tried to put a lid on her eagerness. It would be much better to seem in control – if only for the sake of appearances.

Whatever Luke wanted had to be important. He was not the kind of man who would waste time. She slowed to a casual stroll as she entered the kitchen. The smell of fresh coffee warmed her, bringing a smile to her lips.

Luke was on the phone, his back to her. She grabbed the coffee pot, nearly tipping the contents on the floor as she poured a cup. The coffee tasted so good, such a lift to her senses. She waited for Luke. There was something so damned appealing about him as he stood there, a distant look of concentration on his face. While she watched him, she went over what she planned to say to Luke when he got off the phone. The fragment of memory gave her a sense she might eventually get back at those people who were making her life such a hell.

Luke hung up the phone, his expression tense. Where before his eyes had held the cool hues of determination, they now held concern. He fidgeted, his hands finally coming to rest on the kitchen counter behind him. "Robyn, I have bad news."

Somewhere a warning bell sounded. Robyn eased the cup onto the counter. Something deep inside her told her she didn't want to hear what he had to say. The feeling had surfaced only once before in her life – when Peter and Nathan had died.

Her fingers locked around the edge of the counter as she waited. "My mother? Jason? What is it?"

Luke put his arm around her, his strength offering solace. "No. They're fine... It's Lisa."

What did he mean? She felt his arm tighten around her. His face swam in front of her.

"Lisa?" she asked, not really wanting to know any more.

He nodded. "She died this morning."

CHAPTER FIFTEEN

S hock held Robyn in its grip. She didn't know how long she had been sitting on the sofa, nor did she know when Luke had put his arms around her. Terrible, mind-numbing loss washed over her, suffocating her heart and mind. It couldn't be true. Lisa had been so alive, so upbeat when they spoke.

Robyn's throat ached from tears she held back by sheer force of will. The sofa she sat on, that had once felt so comforting, now felt alien. She squeezed her eyes closed in a vain attempt to suppress the idea of Lisa's death. Robyn steadied one hand with the other. "What happened?"

Luke pulled her closer and pressed his chin against her forehead. "They're not sure, a blood clot, maybe."

Robyn could not imagine a world without Lisa. They had been through so much together, from grade school, straight through the trouble over Nathan and up to the present. There had never been a time when they didn't care for one another. There had been so many good times; so many moments shared together that kept them close, no matter what else happened around them. Now it was gone....

A flood of tears threatened to break through the wall, scattering her self-control. "I don't understand how it could have happened. I talked to her just a day ago."

It seemed like a lifetime, so much had changed. "She said she was feeling much better. They had transferred her out of intensive care."

The trembling started in Robyn's hands, and spread down her body. "I told her I would be there soon.…. I can't believe this. I can't."

"I'm so sorry."

Luke's arms were warm and supportive. Robyn wanted to let go of everything, let Luke take over for her, feel her pain, face the agony of knowing Lisa would never be with her again. A terrible weariness shunted through her. She felt weak, disoriented, as if this were a dream and she was sleep walking her way through it. "What am I going to do without her? She was my best friend."

Luke hugged her against him, his warmth waging a losing battle with the cold emptiness invading her body. "Hold on to the memories. All the things you shared."

"If only I can."

"You can." His hands wove their way up her back, smoothing away the knotted tension at the base of her neck. Momentarily distracted by the pleasure of his finger whispering along her neck, Robyn raised her gaze to meet his.

Luke's half-hearted attempt at a smile made the sadness in his eyes even more poignant. The steady, supportive way he met her gaze made Robyn feel less alone. "I'm glad you're here."

"I am too."

"I have to go to Portland. Do you understand? I have to be there for the funeral." She glanced at Luke's face, and saw his encouraging smile slip away.

"Robyn, I don't know if that's a good idea. It's not safe for you to be out there alone, especially since whoever is looking for you will assume you'll go to Lisa's funeral."

"But Lisa had protection and she still died. What if someone killed her while I sought the safety of your house?" Rage rose through her. She'd never felt this kind of hard anger, this need to lash out at the world, at the hopelessness of it all. Lisa should have been here with her enjoying a few days of relaxation and fun. They deserved that. They needed that. Now everything had changed, never to be the same again.

"Robyn, I understand how you must feel."

No one understood what she was feeling right now. She didn't understand it herself. She wanted revenge. She didn't know where to direct these horrible feelings coursing through her. She fought to control the anger tearing at her, making her eyes burn, her chest tight. "You may understand how I feel, but that doesn't change what I have to do. I've got to get to Portland to offer support to Lisa's family." She needed to be there for herself, to find something, anything she could do to answer the need for action on Lisa's behalf.

"I'll go with you."

"No. I want to do this alone." She couldn't tell him that she wanted to find out if there was any chance Lisa's death wasn't an accident. Luke would argue that investigating Lisa's death was a job for the police. But the police had accomplished little so far. And while they muddled through their investigation, her friend had died from her injuries. She would talk to Lisa's doctor to see if an autopsy was underway.

Robyn remembered the Dilaudid prescription, and how Lisa might have gotten it. That was her fault too. Robyn couldn't wait until a police investigation was completed to know if her friend's death had been the result of foul play. If

someone had gotten to Lisa while she lay ill and vulnerable…
while she was here protected by the police….

If it turned out that Lisa had been the intended victim all
along, Robyn would never forgive herself for hiding out on
Grand Island while her friend's life was in danger. "I should
have been there for her. She would have been there for me."
She waited for the tears that wouldn't come.

"Don't blame yourself."

Wanting to strike out at someone, anyone, she turned on
him. "Who else can I blame? What if her death wasn't an
accident? What if all this time you were wrong, and the killer
got to her?"

Robyn saw the shock in his eyes, and turned away. She
couldn't possibly expect him to understand the guilt she
harbored over her friend's death. Guilt had been a part of
Robyn's life for too long, and she was *so* sick of it.

She had let her father down when she stopped ferrying
between her parents and remained with her mother.
Emotionally torn between two people who had gone their
separate ways – who both claimed they were acting in her
best interests when they argued over custody – had nearly
destroyed her. Out of desperation, and a need to put some
stability in her life, Robyn had chosen her mother's family
and their roots, blaming her choice on her father's perfec-
tionism.

Her father had reacted by standing in judgment on everything Robyn did in her life. Robyn had withdrawn from him
because otherwise she'd be locked into a hopeless pattern of
never being good enough or smart enough to please him.

Then Robyn let her brother and fiancé down when she
couldn't remember what happened when they died. And
when her best friend was in danger and needed her, Robyn
hadn't been there for her, and instead, had guarded her own
safety above all.

"I'm not wrong about who the killer is after." Luke's voice radiated determination.

"You hope," she shot back.

"Robyn, you can't change the past, and you can't be held responsible for what happened to Lisa. You've just had a terrible shock, on top of everything else that happened to you in the past week."

"I can't change the past. But Lisa didn't need to die. It was my fault, my mistake to bring her along with me. Either way, I'm responsible for her death."

"Stop. Please don't do this to yourself, to us." The sincerity of his words only added to her guilt.

Later that day Robyn relaxed for the first time since she'd picked up her rental car at the ferry terminal. She was close to Portland, close to everything near and dear to her. She'd calmed down a little and the anger had subsided. The traffic approaching the city was relatively light, but Robyn kept her attention on the road ahead. She wanted to see her mother, Marie, and Jason before she went to the funeral service. Getting home was the only thing she wanted, and the one thing she needed to help her prepare emotionally for what lay ahead.

She'd called her mother, and told her she'd be there for the funeral. Robyn put off Marie's other questions until she got home where it would be easier to discuss the events of past days, face to face. She would have to be careful about what she said, as she didn't want Jason to hear too much, and she didn't want her mother to worry any more than was necessary.

When Peter died, Marie had moved in with Robyn and together they had made Robyn's house a home for Jason. Robyn had missed her mother and Jason while she was on

Grand Island, and had worried incessantly that something might happen to them.

She cruised along the highway that passed through the old part of the city. As Robyn turned off the highway onto the narrow road leading to her house, she realized that for the first time in years she wanted to look ahead to the future. Since Nathan's death, there hadn't seemed to be much reason to plan, and Jason's adjustment process had devoured Robyn's time and energy when she wasn't at work.

Once on the road leading to her home, Robyn slowed and swung into the long driveway leading to her house overlooking the river. From somewhere behind the house Sam, her dog, raced to greet her, his tail wagging furiously in welcome. Although he was part German Shepherd Sam would never make it as a guard dog. He loved people too much.

"Down, you crazy dog," Robyn said, struggling to open the door against the heavy paws resting on the car door. "Let me out, and I promise to get you a treat from your treat bag…"

As if the dog understood, he leaped down, wagging his tail so hard his body gyrated.

"Robyn!" yelled Jason, rounding the corner of the house at a full run. She opened her arms and the ten-year-old ran to her.

"I thought you were never coming home," he said, his voice catching.

Until that moment, she hadn't realized how it must have seemed to Jason when she stayed away longer than planned. His father had gone on a pleasure trip and never returned. His mother had gone off to Las Vegas without saying goodbye. Tears stung her eyes as she hugged his sturdy body to hers, so thankful to be home. "Where's Gram?"

"She's putting the coffee on. Where have you been? Why

didn't you come home sooner?" Jason fired the questions in rapid succession. Robyn answered them as truthfully as possible.

After being away from him for a few days, Robyn was surprised to see that Jason seemed to look more like his father than ever. Robyn loved Jason as much as if he'd been born her child. It had not been easy to take over as his parent, and sometimes she worried that she wouldn't be up to the job of raising a teenager when the time came. Yet looking into his eager face, none of her worries mattered. They would meet the challenges of his teen years together.

She loved Jason more every time she was near him – the kind of love she hadn't realized was possible.

For a fleeting second, she wondered if Jason would like Luke, but she squashed the thought. Luke and she were a long way from being part of each other's lives. "Let's go find Gram," she said, ruffling Jason's reddish-blond buzz cut.

The kitchen smelled of cinnamon buns and brown bread.

"Oh, Mum, who are you cooking for now?" Robyn asked, tossing her bag on the chair and throwing her arms around her mother.

"I'm cooking for you. Who else? Now that you're home I want to hear what's been going on. I've been very worried. And Lisa…I'm so sorry. How could this have happened?"

"Can I have a cup of coffee first?" she asked, hoping that would satisfy her mother until she had time to explain.

Marie McGill had been the best cook in Robyn's grade school class. All the kids wanted to sample what Robyn brought to any school event that required food. When she was in school in Chicago, and her father was becoming a famous plastic surgeon, her mother had continued cooking as she'd always done. The resulting pounds had been one of the major areas of contention between her parents as her father had always expected his wife to look perfect. After all, the pursuit of beauty was her father's stock-in-trade.

Marie had not been interested in looking like a twenty-year-old in a forty-year-old body, and that had started the downward slide in their marriage. Robyn hadn't faced what was happening. She tried to hold her parents together – to no avail. When they divorced her father was seen around town with a woman Robyn's age, and that had made a teenage Robyn furious.

"Here, sit down. I've got the coffee made." Marie placed a plate filled with home cooking in front of Robyn along with a cup of the best coffee anywhere.

"Thanks, Mom." Suddenly starving, she bit into a delicious cinnamon roll.

"I'm having one too, Gram." Jason eyed Robyn's plate as Marie placed a glass of milk at his elbow.

Robyn and her mother talked about what had been going on, Robyn keeping to her promise not to tell her mother any more than she had to. Jason sat quietly listening, his eager gaze never leaving Robyn's face.

Robyn checked her watch. She wouldn't have time to do what she needed to do if she didn't get going. What she had planned had to be her secret. No one else could know.

"I have to leave a little early for the service, Mom. Can you meet me there?"

"Sure, dear. But where do you have to go? You're not thinking about going to work, are you?"

"I need to stop by the hospital for a few minutes. I have some things to look after." If the police hadn't removed Lisa's home computer Robyn planned to find out what Lisa meant to tell her that day on the island. Lisa had been working on a story about illegal drugs being brought into the country through coastal areas. Just after she was shot, she'd told

Robyn she had something to tell her. Whatever it was, had to be on Lisa's computer, or in her safe.

She planned to go by Lisa's condo and see what she could find. The police had probably already been there looking for information, but just in case they missed something....

There was no way in the world Lisa could have been involved in anything illegal. She had to be researching for the documentary she'd mentioned that morning on the ferry.

"Robyn, you look so tired. I hope you're not putting too much strain on yourself. ."

Robyn gave her mother a warning glance. "I'm okay, Mom. Please don't worry."

Marie sighed in resignation. "If you say so. Still...try to get to bed early tonight."

Robyn didn't have the heart to tell her mother that she might not be coming home this evening, that she might be going back to Grand Island. "We'll talk later; I promise."

Her mother gave her an assessing look. "I'll meet you at the funeral service. I've already arranged for my bridge partner Sally Monroe to stay here with Jason."

"I don't need anyone to babysit me," Jason said, his chin up in the air and a scowl on his freckled face.

Robyn smiled at her mother over Jason's head. "We're all grown up, are we?"

A half-hour later, Robyn used the key left under the planter on Lisa's front step to let herself into the condo. As she closed the door behind her, she glanced around at what had been, at one time, very familiar rooms. It saddened Robyn to realize that she and Lisa had let their respective careers rob them of their time together. They had been good friends, and nothing should have interfered with that.

She dropped the keys onto the hall table as she closed the door behind her. Everything looked so familiar: the autographed photo of a Flamenco guitarist that Lisa had been given on a trip to Spain, the huge collection of copper pots visible through the open door leading to the kitchen, the random arrangement of plants in the bay window of the living room.

At that moment the space seemed like it was the only thing left of the best friend she'd ever had...

Holding her tears in check, Robyn pressed her fingers to her temples to ease the headache hovering in the back of her head. She had to stay strong. Today of all days.

"Think about something else – anything but the next few hours," she whispered into the stillness. She'd left Luke on Grand Island without one word from either side as to what was expected of the other. After she said she wanted to come alone, he didn't try to stop her. Robyn was a little hurt that he hadn't pressed her to let him come along. But at least Luke was finally respecting her wishes. After all, she was the one who turned down his offer.

Despite his apparent indifference, Robyn assumed that Luke wanted her to return to Grand Island after the service. And she was willing to return, mostly because she wanted to rest for a little while longer, to think through what she wanted to do with her life. She'd always been too busy for any real examination of her life and where it was heading. Lisa's death had forced her to think about her life, how she wanted to live the rest of it. Lisa had always done what she loved, had made a difference in how people saw the world around her. But Lisa would never be with her again.

Don't think about it. Do what you need to do. Try to get through the day as best you can..

Luke had said nothing to her about where she would fit in his life, leaving her too fearful of rejection to explore her feelings. Between his training as a police officer and his natural reticence when it came to letting his emotional guard down, Robyn had no idea where she stood with him. She didn't feel she had the right to ask any questions of a personal nature, and he had certainly kept his questions professional.

There had been that interlude when she'd knocked him out, when they'd nearly made love on the floor of his house – but he hadn't been in his right mind, so that didn't really count. Yet the memory brought a smile to her lips as she glanced around Lisa's living room.

Robyn made her way up the stairs, and opened the door to the spare bedroom that doubled as Lisa's home office. The air was stuffy and warm, what you'd expect in a house that had been unoccupied for nearly a week. There were books stacked in the corner with a huge Panda bear piled on top.

Robyn remembered the day Lisa got the stuffed bear she named 'Pepper.' As usual, a handsome gentleman had come along while she and Lisa waited for Jason at the fair grounds. He was carrying the Panda, and looking foolish. He spotted Lisa and immediately started up a conversation with her. The end result was a dinner invitation for Lisa, and she became the proud owner of 'Pepper,' the panda. Lisa had tried to convince Robyn to join them for dinner, but Robyn refused. Only months later, the man Lisa met through Pepper became Lisa's boss at the local TV station. Lisa's life had always been charmed that way. Lisa called it 'activating her aura.' Robyn called it luck.

Lisa's computer was gone, which must mean the police had it. But Lisa always kept a paper copy of anything she was working on in the safe at the back of her closet. Lisa had told Robyn of the safe and its contents years ago after swearing her to secrecy. Robyn knelt down in front of the cupboard door behind Lisa's pants rack. Opening it gently she stared at the round knob in frustration. She didn't know the combination.

She made a half a dozen attempts to get into the safe, but to no avail. "Use your head," she muttered to the empty closet. What were some of Lisa's interests? That might provide a clue to discovering the word to unlock her safe. She entered all the obvious number combinations, one after the other...

Robyn shifted in the cramped space. It had to be something of special interest to Lisa... Lisa had won an award for her investigation into the awarding of highway contracts. Robyn and Nathan, along with the manager of the TV station had been special guests at that occasion.

Robyn turned the knob stopping at the last two digits of the year, followed by the month and day of the award ceremony and the safe door popped open.

Robyn read as quickly as possible. The report was in draft form with a lot of notations typed in parentheses throughout the document. There was a long section concerning the possible entry points for illegal drugs along the Bay of Fundy and the coast of Maine.

There was also a short note concerning prescription-drug fraud, how she'd come across information and a reminder to follow up on it as a separate project. The majority of the file related to interviews with people about boat activity in and around the Coast of Maine – the informants' names were obviously in code. Robyn highly doubted there was a person named 'Toothie.'

Robyn recognized Lisa's writing style, and knew by the last dated entry that she had been working on this report two days before she left for Grand Island. Again there was a quick notation about keeping notes about prescriptions. Had Lisa managed to get an illegal prescription for Dilaudid as part of her story? She must have. The report was lengthy.

Near the bottom, Lisa had put in a short comment about an older man she'd interviewed in a small village on Brier Island off the coast of Nova Scotia.

There was a note that read, "Reminder: Ask Robyn what she knows about this man's story...." Maybe this was what Lisa meant that day on Simmons Marsh right after the shooting when Lisa said she had something to tell her. What was the connection between the man on Brier Island and her? Lisa obviously thought there was one. Robyn rubbed her forehead in thought. If Lisa's investigation was about to expose someone's criminal behavior, her friend could have been the gunman's target all along.

Robyn put in a call to the police, talked to one of the officers she knew from her work in Emergency, and told him what she'd found. He said they already had Lisa's computer, but promised to pass the information on to the investigating officers. She called Lisa's doctor and was told that they had done an autopsy but that the report wasn't finished. As she spoke to him she felt suspended somehow, as if she were asking about someone she didn't know. Whether it was denial setting in, or shock, she wasn't sure.

With a heavy heart Robyn drove to the cemetery. The only service Lisa had wanted was a quiet graveside memorial service, and true to her wishes, people had gathered, waiting for the Reverend Macaulay from the Episcopalian Church Lisa attended. The only sound was the soft rustling of pine branches overhead as the mourners filed along the perimeter of the burial site that was draped in green velvet. A huge mahogany casket rested on brass frames. Although dark clouds swathed the city in gray a few hours earlier, the hillside cemetery was now awash in bright sunshine.

Robyn and her mother were among the first to arrive.

Standing there, Robyn didn't know how she would get through the service without crying. It was as if whatever part of her mind that had given her the energy and determination to get through this had deserted her.

She would never see her friend again, but memories of Lisa were everywhere. They had played in the park next door to the cemetery when they were children, and Lisa's family had owned an elegant Victorian house a block beyond the entrance to the cemetery. They had written ghoulish stories in their eighth grade English class about the huge headstones just above where Lisa would be buried. Thinking they were very sophisticated and worldly in their choice of reading material at the tender age of thirteen, they had hidden their first romance novels in the hollow posts at the entrance to the cemetery.

Together, Lisa had Robyn had attended Lisa's grand-mother's funeral in this cemetery.

Robyn searched the solemn faces looking for Lisa's mother and father. At the corner, near the top of the grave, Robyn saw a group of the staff from Lisa's office. Among them was the distinguished-looking man, Edward Parsons, who had given Lisa the Panda bear. Robyn fought for composure as she met his gaze across the heads of several mourners.

Gradually the space around the site filled and overflowed down toward the gnarled apple tree at the base of the plot. Over the heads of several people Robyn knew only by sight, she saw Lisa's parents arrive. Lisa's mother clung to her father's arm, while with her other hand she clutched a white linen handkerchief as if terrified it would get away from her.

"I'm going over to speak to them," Robyn whispered to her mother.

"You go ahead, dear. I'll wait here."

Robyn made her way to where Lisa's parents stood, their

faces stiff and tear stained. When Lisa's father saw her, the tears coursed down his cheeks and he wrapped his free arm around her. "We're so glad to see you home safe and sound," he said, his voice breaking.

Robyn struggled to maintain her composure as she hugged the one person who had understood her anger over her parents' divorce, and one of the few people who had encouraged her to remain true to herself when her father had tried to belittle her decision to become a family medicine specialist rather than a plastic surgeon. "I am so glad to be here with you," Robyn whimpered, at last letting the tears flow.

Regret, like a vicious force, overcame her as she stood holding two of the people she loved most in the world, and the two she was least able to help at the moment. "I'm so sorry. I should never have encouraged Lisa to go with me to Grand Island. I don't know what to say, or how to say it. Please forgive me."

"There's nothing to forgive. Lisa wanted to be there. We're just glad that you were with her when she was injured. It made all the difference in the world to her."

Lisa's father had to see the truth when he looked at her. He had to. "I couldn't help her. I let her down. I should have come home with her." Instead, she'd stayed behind, hiding out like the coward she was while her friend suffered.

"You were in a lot of danger. We know that. Don't you ever regret what you had to do." Reginald Wade spoke softly but forcibly, and Robyn clung to the caring support knowing she would drown without it.

When neighbors approached to pay their respects, Robyn returned to stand next to her mother. When the graveside service started, she sat quietly while the minister told of Lisa's life, of her accomplishments and about how she would be missed by her family and friends.

Desperate to ease her grief, Robyn glanced around at the other mourners. A lot of their classmates from high school were there and a few of their university friends. Brad wasn't there, which surprised Robyn.

How could he not know about Lisa's death? It had been in all the papers.

During the service, Robyn watched the group of mourners, looking for anyone who might be watching her. *God! How sick was that?*

As she pulled her gaze back to the preacher, a thought suddenly occurred to her – she'd grown accustomed to Luke's constant attention and concern. She couldn't help wishing he was beside her now.

When the service ended, Robyn took her mother's arm as they started slowly toward the parking lot. Robyn walked her mother to her car. "See you at the house, Mom," she said.

"I'll be waiting for you," Marie replied, love and caring evident in her tear-soaked eyes..

Robyn hugged her mother close to her, desperate for the warmth and love of her mother's arms.

She was about to go to her own car when she saw him. Back near the border of maple trees that separated the cemetery from the park, a man stood. He was watching her with caring visible on his face. "Luke." The name escaped her lips before she was aware she'd said it.

He started toward her, his stride long and purposeful. She waited for him, the stress of the past hour washing away at the sight of him. He looked so handsome in a gray suit and soft blue tie. *Why hadn't he said he was coming to the service?* She would have waited for him.

"I'm sorry you had to go through this. I would have been here earlier, but it took awhile to get away," he said, his body leaning close, protectively.

She swayed at his nearness, and in that instant she knew

she had never needed anyone in her entire life the way she needed Luke Carlisle. "I'm so glad you're here," she said, completely aware of how utterly inadequate her words were in expressing her feelings.

"I am too, but you weren't alone, you know." He nodded to two men standing near the edge of a group of mourners.

"You sent the cavalry?" she asked, feeling a strange happiness settle over her.

"I couldn't risk anything happening to you."

Luke wanted to take Robyn in his arms and smooth away the terrible strained look on her face. She had left Grand Island so quickly he couldn't tell her what he'd needed to say. He'd wanted to tell her how important she'd become in his life, and how she'd helped him see what a lonely existence he'd been living.

At the moment, he couldn't tell her how he really felt, but he would see to it that she was protected and cared for. When he got past his own stupid hang-ups, she'd hear the words he'd rehearsed and left unsaid.

"Is there somewhere we can go? Somewhere we can sit and talk? You look exhausted." He wanted to touch her, wipe the tear stains off her cheek, but he couldn't trust himself to stop at that. He wanted so much more.

"Mom and I came in separate vehicles. She left a few minutes ago, and I have my rental car. I need to go home."

Luke wanted 'home' to mean something different to her than what it did now, but he had no right to interfere in her life. She'd offered him more, and he'd declined. He had no right to put pressure on her now, especially under the circumstances. "I'll drive you wherever you want to go. I'm not leaving you, Robyn. I can't."

The words had slipped out, uncensored. He wasn't ready

215

to commit to any woman, but something about Robyn tied him to her in a way he couldn't explain. He hadn't taken the time to delve into it, but somewhere deep in his gut he knew that this woman who cared so much, who hurt so deeply, would always be part of his life. She stared at him, uncertainty evident in the way she held her shoulders and the circling movements her fingers made along the brown leather of her shoulder bag. "I want to go to... I need to get away from here..."

"Anywhere you'd like. I mean it," he said.

She glanced around at the other mourners preparing to leave, her eyes red rimmed, her voluminous hair held in check by two silver combs.

He'd been holding his breath, and finally let the air slip from his lungs.

When Robyn hesitated, Luke saw an opportunity to do what he'd wanted to do since he'd made his way to the cemetery. He took the keys to her rental car from her hands. "Get in. I'll drive you."

"Thanks." Robyn slipped into the passenger seat and gave him directions to her house.

When they arrived Jason and her mother were waiting. Marie smiled in welcome when she was introduced to Luke. Jason wanted to know all about the job of being a policeman.

Anxious as he was to get Robyn alone, Luke patiently answered all Jason's questions. As Luke talked to Jason, he began to enjoy himself. Having no children in his family, not even nieces and nephews, Luke was unaware of how enthusiastic a child could be, how eager they were to ask questions.

Somewhere in the conversation, a sense of sadness slipped in. He had no children. There was no one to greet him when he got back to Grand Island other than the staff at the police station. A sudden ache in his throat signaled his need to concentrate on Jason.

The child had a quick mind, and a surprising ability to concentrate on detail. Maybe all kids were like that now. It didn't seem they were like that when Luke was that age, but things change.

Every once in a while Luke would catch Robyn watching him. Their gazes would lock, and one or the other would smile, and it all seemed so impossibly right. Luke was sure Marie had a lot of questions about him, and that pleased him in an odd way.

"Would you like to stay for dinner?" Marie offered.

Robyn exchanged glances with Luke. "Luke and I have things we need to discuss before he leaves."

"And the last ferry for Grand Island leaves in a couple of hours," Luke said.

Marie's expression was one of disappointment. "I wish you could stay here and talk." She sighed. "But if you have to go somewhere, please be careful."

"We will, Mom," Robyn said, hugging her mother close, soaking in the scent of her mother's perfume. "Mom, I promise that I'll be back as soon as I can, and then we will talk. I have so much to tell you."

Marie gave Luke a quick glance. "Will he be part of what you have to tell me?" She smiled gently.

"Maybe."

"Don't forget about me," Jason said, coming to Robyn and wrapping his arms around her.

"Who could forget about you?" Robyn asked, pressing a kiss to the top of his head.

He scowled and looked at Luke. "They're always kissing me," he said by way of explanation.

"I hear you, buddy," Luke said, giving him a high five.

They drove in his car along the tree-lined streets leading

from Robyn's house with no particular destination in mind. The brightness of the day was in direct contrast to the subdued atmosphere of the car as Luke followed the meandering streets into the old parts of the city. An occasional traffic light or pedestrian stopped them, but other than that they simply drove.

Neither one of them spoke a word. More than once, Luke glanced at Robyn.

They came to an intersection where a narrow road led toward the river. On impulse, he turned down the lane away from the city sights and sounds. They both needed a quiet spot, and this looked as good as any. He pulled to a halt on the edge of a grassy knoll overlooking the river.

He felt the warmth of the sun on his cheek and opened his window. The gentle tinkling of water as it eddied over the rocks along the river's edge was the only sound. The far shore, visible from where they parked, stretched for miles, a green carpet edged by the blue water.

"Beautiful, isn't it?"

After what seemed like a lifetime, she looked at him. "I can't go back to Grand Island with you. After the service today, I realize my place is here. I found some materials in Lisa's condos, and alerted the police. They may need to talk to me. I hope you understand."

He didn't understand at all. He wanted her with him, for his sake as much as hers, but he had no right to interfere. He'd been angry when she packed up and left – angry at himself mostly. But even angrier at the unending and dangerous situation Robyn seemed to be involved in.

"Robyn, I want you to be safe, and maybe it is safer here, but only until the man who's after you finds out where you are. You've been lucky, so far. He hasn't succeeded, but that doesn't mean he's given up." He glanced at her to see if what he said had any effect. He couldn't tell because Robyn had lowered her head so her face was hidden from him.

"Don't you see? I'm so tired of worrying, hiding, watching my back. Wondering who might be after me. I spent half my time at Lisa's funeral looking for any man who was taking a special interest in my being there. I was so preoccupied with my worries that most of the time I was unable to focus on what was important. When I should have been thinking of my friend, I was thinking about some sick asshole who might want me dead!"

"I promise you we will find this person. I promise you." What else could he say? Unable to stop himself, Luke gathered her in his arms and held her head against his chest.

The scent of her, the warmth of her skin filled him, blocking out the emptiness he'd grown accustomed to over the years. This was a woman who could be trusted to know how he felt, a woman who felt things every bit as much as he did – and who would be true to those feelings. He'd been holding back where Robyn was concerned, where his happiness was concerned. He had to take a chance. Otherwise he would never know what might have been if he'd been brave enough to try.

"I want you to come back with me to Grand Island. I know you would rather be here with your family, and I have no right to ask you to return there with me. But if you do, I promise you I will find the bastard behind this, if it's the last thing I do. Robyn, I need you with me. It's as simple as that."

There, he'd said it. The silence was beyond deafening as he waited for her response. As the moments dragged on, he mentally kicked himself up one side of the car and down the other. *What a stupid ass thing to do!* What did he expect the woman to say? That she wanted to put her head back inside the lion's mouth? That she would gladly leave her life and her medical practice at a moment's notice? He wanted to bang his head on the steering wheel in total disbelief at his stupidity.

"I'll go on one condition. I want you to tell me what's going on – and none of this police stuff about things being confidential, or only on a need-to-know basis. I am *not* going to hide out in your quarters while you run around the island doing your thing. I want to work with you on this. Is that understood?"

He wanted to whoop with joy, but he settled for holding Robyn tighter. "You won't regret this, I'll see to it."

"I may if you don't give me room to breathe," she said, from the folds of his shirt.

"Sorry." Luke eased her into the crook of his arm, tilting the steering wheel up out of the way as he did so.

"I've wanted to do this since the moment I saw you at the cemetery." He touched her cheek gently, very gently. He kissed her slowly, the tiny bow of her upper lip, the fullness of her bottom lip. He needed this moment to last.

Robyn kissed him back, as a chuckle started from somewhere deep inside her. "Is this a date, or are we simply parking like two teenagers?"

"Want to get into the back seat with me?" he asked, laughing, really laughing for the first time in days. God! It felt good.

CHAPTER SIXTEEN

Robyn had only been back in Luke's house for a couple of days, but it was beginning to feel like home. She'd driven her own car over to the island, and Luke had hidden it inside the police garage. He still didn't want anyone to know she was staying at his place. Somehow being with Luke made Lisa's death more bearable. He was very attentive, and only occasionally did he seem preoccupied after they returned from Portland.

Still, Robyn felt confined at times. She spent hours cleaning and sweeping and discovered that it helped to soothe her, the repetitive quality offering her a peaceful reprieve. . . With all the time she spent studying and all the long hours she'd worked, housework had disappeared from her list of priorities. Anything that was done around her house was done by her mother and the occasional crew brought in to clean the entire house..

Working around Luke's place felt so good, so natural, and they were getting along amazingly well for two people thrown together by circumstance. She'd grown to like the scent of cleaners she'd been using for the past few days, and took a certain pride in the fact that the cat prints were no longer creating an abstract pattern on the polished wood of the coffee table.

Funny, she'd never really thought about what it would be like to live with a man. Even though she and Nathan had planned to marry, they'd kept their separate houses because it made perfect sense at the time. Now, she wondered why they hadn't moved in together.

She glanced across the sun-filled room to where Luke worked on a stack of papers. "How's the paperwork going?" she asked, putting the broom back in the closet.

"Slow but necessary. My mother was the one who enjoyed paperwork and bookkeeping."

"What was she like?"

"Mom was a great mother even though she worked long hours. She valued everything because she had so little. I don't know how she managed to raise my sister and me on her salary as a school receptionist, but she did." Luke smiled at her as he continued to put paper into various file folders on the desk.

So Luke knew how it felt to be the child of a single parent. She wanted to ask him about his father, how Luke coped without a father. She already worried about Jason being without a father and how that would affect him. She wanted to ask Luke about his upbringing, yet something in Luke's demeanor didn't invite questions about his private life. "It sounds like you had to pitch in, do your share."

"We did. My sister was a good cook. I looked after all the outside chores, and looked after my room. In high school, we both had after-school jobs. It might sound like we missed out on things, but we didn't."

Robyn tried to imagine Luke as a young boy Jason's age. He would have been really cute with his dark, curly hair and brown eyes. "Did you play sports?"

"A little baseball in the summer. That was about it."

"You must have been very close as a family?"

"We were."

He continued with his work, while Robyn read the local paper over again, just to fill the time. There had been no word about the man who attacked her, nothing in the paper, and nothing from Luke though he continued to insist she not answer the phone.

For the past few days Robyn had not had any flashes of memory, and thought those might be over. As long as nothing else happened, Robyn held out the hope that her life might return to the way it was before the attack.

Even so, Robyn knew nothing would ever be the same. Without Lisa, Robyn's life would be so much different, so lacking in the spark that Lisa brought to her life.

"I have to take my turn out on patrol, but I'll be back as soon as I can. Will you be all right?"

Robyn glanced at him, and saw the warmth back in his eyes. He was only an arm's length away, and Robyn wanted him to reach for her, but knew he wouldn't. He simply wasn't ready to take their relationship any farther, and Robyn didn't know how to respond to him without seeming clingy and demanding.

She wanted Luke, more than her pride would let her admit, more than she'd ever wanted any man. She wanted to be a part of everything that involved him, from his job, his family, his interests, his likes, his dislikes – all of him. She knew all that would take time. Luke had been hurt badly by his ex-wife's criminal behavior, and would be a long while trusting a woman the way Robyn needed to be trusted. She saw the answering awareness in his eyes as she stared into his face, but he made no attempt to touch her. "Thanks for asking. I'm fine."

Dare she mention the man on the ferry? She had been

waiting for a chance to talk about it, and maybe this was the moment. "I remembered something that might help in your investigation."

"You did?"

"Just before you told me about Lisa, I was in the shower and I remembered that the man I saw at Harper's Cove."

"You mean the man that frightened you?"

"Yes. He looked like the man who was so rude on the ferry. At first I thought I was mistaken, and then Lisa's death left me little time to think about it. But in the past day or so, I'm convinced that I saw the same man twice – once on the ferry, and once outside the gift shop in Harper's Cove."

He moved closer. "Let me get this straight. The man on the ferry and the man at Harper's Cove are the same?"

"That's my impression…. It's hard to be sure."

"That would make sense, and would support the idea that you were being watched from the time you got on the ferry."

It was terrifying to think about. "But why?"

"Something must have occurred that day before you boarded the ferry." Luke's eyes were distant. "Is that all you remember?"

"Yes, I think so." Luke didn't seem very interested in what she had to say, and maybe that was a good sign.

"Nothing you need me to bring back?" His voice mirrored the preoccupation she saw in his eyes, and the way he rolled his shoulders as if to free himself told her how much he wanted to go.

"No," she answered. *Was that it? Wasn't there something else he wanted to say?*

"That's good. Then I'll call you later."

What had happened to all the intimacy between them after the funeral service?

Had she imagined that he cared for her? Or was she simply a lonely woman who mistook ordinary kindness for something else? No! He owed her an explanation of what was going on. What he was thinking. "Not so fast. I want to know what's happening with the investigation."

He picked up his keys from the hall table. "Not much at the moment," he said.

"I'd like to talk about what I found in Lisa's condo. She was investigating the drug trade along the coast. I'm sure that's how she had that prescription for Dilaudid. She was gathering information on who was trafficking and who was selling. As far as I'm concerned my first opinion was correct. Lisa was the target. She was getting too close to the truth, too many people stood to lose too much."

He didn't say anything, which really infuriated her.

"What do you think?" she demanded.

"I don't know, but I'll check with the Major Crime Unit and see what their investigation has uncovered."

"Is that all?" she asked, infuriated that he seemed to have so little to say to her about anything that mattered.

"I have to go."

Robyn watched him leave, realizing that a gulf had formed between them in the past few days and she'd been totally unaware of it happening. How could that be? Was it his job? Was it simply a case of two people who didn't share enough of their thoughts and feelings?

She yearned for a chance to see if their relationship could work. But she was stuck in nowhere land: Luke was totally preoccupied; he believed her killer was still out there; her friend was dead; she'd become a housecleaner; and she couldn't get in touch with her birding friends because Luke didn't want anyone to know she was staying here with him.

She knew they were still on the island because there'd been a very rare sighting of an albatross. It had been in the news. The bird had obviously been blown off path by the storm that had struck the open Atlantic the day before.

There would be even more birders coming from the mainland to catch a glimpse of the huge bird.

She heard the phone ring, but let it go to the answering machine. Her first thought was that Luke was calling her, but when the machine clicked on, she heard her mother's voice, frantic with worry. "Luke are you there? Robyn? Robyn, please call me. I need you, please."

Robyn grabbed the phone. "Mom, what is it?"

"Oh, thank God you're there! It's Jason. He's disappeared. Just like that. Gone. When he got up this morning he seemed preoccupied, anxious about something. I didn't think too much about it. When he asked to go to the mall with his friends, I agreed. He misses you, and I thought he needed time with his friends. He was supposed to meet them at the mall over two hours ago and he never showed up. I can't imagine where he could have gone."

"Did you call the police?"

"Yes, I did. They're on their way over here now."

"Mom, please don't worry. It's probably a misunderstanding. Have you called the friends he was supposed to be meeting?

"Yes. When Jason didn't show up at the mall, his friends waited for a while and then called here. That's how I found out he was missing."

Anyone watching her with Jason would know how much she loved him. On the day of the funeral they'd stood in the driveway of her house and hugged. What if the killer decided to take Jason to get to her? *No. No. That couldn't be.*

"Mom, I'll be there just as soon as I can. Don't leave the phone in case he calls. I'll get the next ferry, and I'll call you every ten minutes on my cell phone."

"Hurry, dear." The plea in her mother's voice ripped through her, shattering her control.

She had to find Luke, tell him what happened. She dialed

his cell phone and waited what seemed like forever before he answered. "Luke, Jason's missing."

"I'm on my way."

Robyn raced upstairs; her knees shook so badly she nearly lost her balance. She'd managed to hold it together when she was on the phone to her mother, but now her mind filled with horror at the thought of what might have happened.

Visions of Jason, bound and gagged, or worse...seriously injured, rolled through her mind. Jason would be terrified, and the thought filled her with fear. Was he alone in some dark place? In two hours they could have taken him anywhere, done anything to him.

Thinking of Jason brought memories of her brother, Peter, whistling back.

The last time she'd seen Peter alive was when she came up the companionway of the sailboat. Peter and Nathan were near the back of the boat. Peter looked angry, the way he'd be looking now, if he were still around to know that his son was missing and in danger.

Fear knifed through her, aided and abetted by the lack of sleep she'd been experiencing. She needed to be able to think clearly if she wanted to help find Jason. She had to find him...

Robyn struggled to keep her thoughts positive but the pain and shock over the situation nearly overwhelmed her. She would have to help her mother find a recent photo of Jason. They would need to help the police any way they could.

Suddenly her whole life came crashing down on her: being accused of involvement in Peter and Nathan's death, the pain of knowing that Lisa had been shot, the fear of remembering what happened so long ago, all came to a head with Lisa's death.

And now, Jason....

Robyn stood in the bathroom, tears choking the air from her lungs, her head pounding so hard she could hardly breathe. She yanked open the door to the medicine cabinet over the sink, and started pulling out the various bottles, looking for an aspirin to ease her headache. In her haste, she knocked over a container and pills spilled over the counter, and down onto the tiled floor. "Oh, shit!" she muttered, bending down to gather the pills into the bottle while fighting to see through the tears swimming in her eyes.

She swiped at her eyes. "For heaven's sake, calm down," she fumed to herself.

"What in hell are you doing?" Luke's angry voice filled the room.

CHAPTER SEVENTEEN

"I was getting an aspirin. My head is aching," she said, surprised at his tone.

"Are you sure that's all?"

"What do you mean?" she asked.

"What were you doing in my medicine cabinet?" he asked, his voice filled with suspicion.

"What in hell does it look like? I needed an aspirin and spilled a bottle of pills."

Luke knelt down, gathered the pills and put them in the container. "Know what these are?" he asked holding out the bottle showing the label.

"A narcotic pain killer. Your prescription. So what?"

"So, were you going to take them?"

"Are you out of your mind?"

He stared at her without saying a word.

"Look, I don't have time for this craziness. If you don't believe me, that's your problem. I have to catch the next ferry to the mainland."

"Whatever was going on in Luke's head didn't matter. It couldn't matter under the circumstances. He didn't trust her... End of story. She had to get home. Somehow, she had to make it to the ferry and make it home, where she belonged, not just for now, but for good. She couldn't live around someone who didn't trust her – regardless of her feelings for him. "I'll get my things," she said, turning her back on him and going to her bedroom.

With robotic movements, Robyn packed her belongings, walked downstairs and out to her car. She didn't see Luke, and she didn't want to. She tossed her things in the back seat, clicked on her cell phone and climbed into the driver's seat. She pulled out of the driveway without looking back. The drive to the ferry terminal was the longest ten minutes she'd spent in her life as the worry over Jason was nearly trumped by her feeling of loss.

With a heart weighed down by remorse, Robyn pulled into the ferry line and was relieved to see that they were starting to board. She dialed her home number, but the line was busy. She put the phone down on the seat beside her, holding tight to the idea that in a couple of hours she'd be there for Jason. She'd be where she belonged.

She couldn't let her thoughts dwell on leaving Luke behind. She couldn't concentrate on anything but getting home. That was all that mattered. Seeing the cars just ahead of her start to move, Robyn eased her foot onto the gas pedal.

The urgent wail of a siren cut through her misery. Ignoring it, she eased forward, concentrating on the bump created by the steel ramp on the downward approach. Suddenly, the police cruiser was beside her car, its light flashing. She glanced over. It was Luke, and he was waving her to a stop.

She stopped and watched as Luke made his way to her window. She had half a mind to ignore him, but he might have news about Jason. Rolling down her window she forced herself to be pleasant. "Did I forget something?"

He leaned in the open window and the scent of his spicy aftershave, carried by the warm breeze, assailed Robyn's senses. "I just got a call from your mother. She found Jason. He'd gone to another friend's house and hadn't told her. I gather Jason's under your mother's version of house arrest at the moment."

"Thank you, God," she murmured, feeling so much better than she had a few moments before.

"Yeah, just when you needed something to go right." His gaze wrapped around her.

"Thank you," she said, wanting to touch his cheek, a foolish notion, given what he'd said to her a few minutes earlier. "I'm so glad you caught up with me, but you could have called me on my cell phone."

"I want to talk to you about what happened back there." Luke rested his powerful forearms on the open window, inches from Robyn's cheek.

"What good will *that* do? Nothing's changed."

He gazed intently at her, his usually gray eyes now flecked with tiny shards of yellow. "I don't know. I just don't want you thinking that I am usually so cruel."

Deep in her heart she knew he was a very kind man. Nothing he'd done until this morning could ever be considered mean or cruel. "What did you have in mind?"

He smiled, and suddenly Robyn felt so much better.

"I'm going to go back to the office. And, if you'll follow me, I'm going to see if I can convince you that we should start the day over. I don't want you to leave."

"Is that your duty as a police officer talking?"

"No, it's me trying to make sense of why I behaved so badly back at the house..." He touched her hand where it rested on the steering wheel. Robyn suppressed a shiver of expectation.

231

"You could do that without me", she said, her eyes meeting his.

"Not as well, and certainly not when I have this powerful need to know how you'll feel about what I have to say." He offered a look of apology with his words. "What do you say? I will even scrounge up a bottle of wine if your headache's gone." His smile widened to a grin, and Robyn suddenly couldn't resist smiling back at him.

"Headache's gone. Why don't you see if you can drum up an apology?" she asked, her heart pounding.

"That's the least I can do," he said, and the air between them tingled with excitement.

"I'm ready to listen," Robyn said, a slow warmth sneaking up her body.

Robyn settled in on the sofa, waiting for Luke to return from making a call. She suspected that it had to do with finding her attacker, but for once she didn't care. All she could think about was Jason. Robyn had been happily surprised when Luke had taken her for a drive out to Shark Tail Lighthouse and apologized for not trusting her, promising never to behave that way again. They sat and talked, first about Jason, then Luke's heartbreak over Charlene's betrayal of their marriage. He'd seen Robyn on the floor scrambling for pills, but when Charlene was caught in the act it had been a different scenario. He saw her shake with need for her addiction and watched her take a handful of pills before she could talk rationally to him. And he admitted when he found Robyn on the floor trying to pick up the pills, it had made him crazy.

Robyn had felt so close to him when he confided in her. As she listened to him, she understood that Luke was a man who lived by the rules, who believed in the rule of law and who had been forced to face the pain and humiliation of his wife's criminal behavior. Taking her into his confidence about his wife helped her to understand his anger when he found her going through his medicine cabinet.

"A penny for your very ominous thoughts," Luke said, coming to sit next to her.

"How do you know they're ominous?"

"That cute little furrow you've etched between your eyes," he said, giving her that smile – the one designed to lift her spirits.

She was beginning to see Luke differently than she had a few hours earlier. He was still handsome, still able to make her heart trip in her chest, and her body to warm at his touch, but aside from those things, everything had changed now that he had crossed that line from sexy friend to intimate confidante. The line separating their lives had begun to fade when he talked to her, told her things she knew were painful for him to talk about.

Luke didn't trust people easily, maybe didn't even trust himself where people were concerned, especially those who could hurt him. Yet, he'd been honest with her, and she knew what it meant for him to take her into his confidence.

Could she be honest with him, totally honest about something that affected her personal life and her professional life? She had to try. "Luke, I want to explain something to you. Something we should have talked about earlier."

Luke poured two glasses of red wine, set them carefully on the coffee table, and then settled back on the sofa beside her. "I'm listening."

Mentally crossing her fingers Robyn faced him. "I want you to understand something that I haven't told very many people. When Nathan and Peter died, I wanted to die too. I couldn't cope with the idea that something so horrible had happened to the two people I loved most in this world. On top of that I couldn't even remember the incident, or my part in it. I did not know how painful, how utterly soul destroying, grief could be. Then, there were the senseless nightmares, the terrible feeling that I had done something wrong. Maybe, on some level I believed I must be involved. To think that I might have done something that resulted in their deaths forced me to seek professional help."

Luke gently placed his large hand over her shaking fingers, stilling them. "You have to stop tormenting yourself," he murmured.

"But I'm a doctor. My life is about curing people, saving them. I still can't shake the idea that whatever happened to Nathan and Peter was somehow my fault. I was there, and yet I can't remember anything about their disappearance or how I ended up on the sailboat alone. I started seeing a psychiatrist, and he tried to help me. I wasn't sleeping. Night after night, I'd lay awake, afraid that if I fell asleep, I'd dream and wake feeling even more upset. I would have done almost anything to blot out the agony of knowing that I was alive while Nathan and Peter had died – and no one knew why. I couldn't work. I took stress leave."

Luke put his arm around her, gently, encouragingly. "I'm so sorry you had to go through that. And Dr. Stanley still hasn't been able to help you retrieve your memories of the incident on the boat?"

"No. I spent hours in therapy, and still wake up at night with fragments of memories that are frightening. I feel guilty about that and don't know why." She relaxed into the shelter of his arms, thankful that she'd explained a little bit of what was going on with her. "Luke, what if I was involved somehow in Nathan and Peter's death?"

He hugged her close to him, his strong arms anchoring her to him. "Not a chance."

As she sat watching him, a thought occurred to her.

"Luke, you mentioned the illegal prescription drug trade. Among Lisa's notes I found information that said she had been looking into the prescription drug trade and how it's manipulated. Could she have gotten her prescription for Dilaudid as part of her investigation?"

"It's possible. You realize that Lisa's computer was turned over to the police?"

"Yes. I talked to a friend of mine at the police station in Portland."

"The Drug Investigation Unit is already working on it with Major Crime."

"Didn't you promise to share what you learned with me?" she asked.

"I did. I didn't mean to leave you out like that." His eyes met hers. "I'm not very good at this sharing thing, am I?"

Afraid that she might do something silly, like cry, Robyn concentrated on his throat, the way his Adam's apple moved when he spoke, the way the dark hair on his chest curled along the edges of his open shirt, the twitch of a muscle along his jaw. All the things she now knew she couldn't live without.

"Robyn," he said toying with her hair. "I let my feelings about my ex-wife get mixed up with how I responded to you and how I felt about you. Today and the pills was a good example. And it doesn't help that the two of you look so much alike." He ran his fingers along her hairline, stroking her skin, sending tiny tendrils of pleasure coursing through her.

"Just how much do we look like one another?" She managed to force the words through her lips.

"Just enough to confuse me sometimes, but the resemblance ends there – with appearance. You're not like her in any meaningful way."

Where was he going with this?

235

Robyn wanted him to kiss her; for him to make love to her. "I'm so relieved to hear that."

"I couldn't love a woman who abused her body with drugs, who lied and cheated. Charlene destroyed everything we had together when she got involved in using and selling drugs. I will always regret the fact that I didn't discover what was going on, until it was too late."

His lips followed his fingers along the sensitive skin of her face, taking her breath with his gentleness. At the same time, his hands were moving over her shoulders, down over her arms, spreading warmth, inviting.... She looked up at him and saw the heat in his eyes, a heat that matched her own. "Luke, I--"

"Shh..." His hands were in her hair, working their way along her neck. His mouth found hers. His lips touched hers, lightly at first.

Robyn's breath caught in her throat when Luke kissed her bottom lip then moved to the cupid's bow of her upper lip as he'd done before. All the pent-up emotion of the past few days found release in the flood of need rushing through her. It was as if the pain of losing Lisa could be eased by the strength of her desire. Reaching up, she tangled her fingers in his hair and pulled him to her.

With exquisite gentleness, his fingers traced the outline of her lips. His touch gave her a sense of belonging, of being alive, of him. Robyn groaned and opened her lips, eager to explore and be explored. The need to feel alive almost over-whelmed her. She wanted to reach out to him, to let him know how much she needed him. A sense of rightness, of knowing the moment had come, swept through her. "Please don't stop."

Luke's arms tightened around her, moving her back against the sofa. His hands started a slow roam down her body as his tongue explored the depths of her mouth. His fingers touched her nipple, erect and waiting for him. A flood of heat engulfed her as she pulled him closer. Her hands fumbled with the buttons on his shirt; her fingers wove their way down his chest and over the taut muscles of his abdomen.

His gasping intake of breath was all she needed to hear. He wanted her as much as she wanted him.

This time, she would not be denied.

She drank from his lips as if parched, taking his tongue deep inside her mouth. His body, warm and hard, strained against her. He drew his mouth from hers and slid his lips over her straining nipples, pressing against the fabric of her shirt. She moaned as he lifted the shirt over her head and cupped each breast in his powerful hands.

For Luke there was no turning back. He knew then she needed him and he was there in every sense of the word. The years of celibacy pushed him to take quickly what was so freely offered. He fondled her nipples and saw the answering desire in her eyes. He tasted her, sucked gently on each erect nipple, savoring the answering intake of breath through her lips.

He kissed the soft skin on top of the hollow between her full breasts, tasting the saltiness of her skin as his fingers sought the dampness between her thighs.

Robyn moaned, her pelvis straining toward him in open invitation. Her moan of pleasure engulfed him. He palmed her breasts, eager to remove the fabric restraining them. She threw her head back, peeled off her clothes and helped him get free of his.

She thrust her body against his. Her lips moved down his body arousing every inch of him. He groaned, rolled them over, and pulled her under him as he eased between her legs.

. . .

The pressure of his arousal against her damp heat started a drumbeat in her body. She strained to meet him, her body rocking into his. Her need answering his. His breath was hot against her neck, as his lips moved down her body, caressing each tender part – tormenting and arousing her. She clung to him, her fingers digging into his shoulders, her body melding with his. No matter what the future held for her, Robyn knew that this moment, this intimacy between them was more than a balm to her hurt and pain.

Rising above her, Luke eased himself into her and began the long slow strokes that drove Robyn to the edge. The rhythm of his movement picked up speed. His body tensed, his shoulder muscles glistened.

She felt the moment of his release and just as he went over, the ripple of orgasm surged through her.

For what seemed like hours, they lay entwined, with room to spare on the narrow sofa – their need tamped, but not extinguished. Lying so close to the man she loved, Robyn had time to think about what the future held, and where her life might be headed.

Luke hadn't said he loved her, nor had she said the words. But for the first time in a long time, Robyn felt secure in herself as a woman. She had found a safe place with Luke, and however it turned out she knew that without him, she wouldn't have made it through the past week. Robyn played her fingers along his chest, marveling at the tautness of his skin and the hard muscles just below the surface. He had been quiet, and she had been content to simply lie beside him on the sofa, the bottle of wine untouched on the table.

In the midst of her devastating loss, she had found a

happiness she never knew existed. She had found someone capable of real passion, of kindness. She planned to hang onto that.

"Luke, I have to tell you something."

Luke ran his fingers along her arm and across her shoulder, sending shivers of pleasure down her spine.

"Something pleasant, I hope."

She leaned away from him and regretted every inch of separation. Making love had cleared her mind – weird, but true. She suddenly had a glimpse of what her life could hold, and how much she needed to learn what had happened that night three years ago so that she could be happy moving forward. As much as she wanted to remain in the warmth of his arms, she had to tell him what she knew. With Lisa's death, the need for an answer increased. "I have remembered something else that might be important."

Luke shifted around on the sofa and sat up, pulling her against him. "What is it?"

"I want you to help me figure out what's going on with me."

Luke reached for his shirt and slid his arms into it. "You're sure you want to talk about this right now?"

Robyn knew Luke was giving her a chance to forget what she had been through the last few days, but she had to talk about this before her courage failed her. Two people she loved had died on that sailboat, something she would carry with her for the rest of her life. Could she trust Luke with her fear? "Luke, what if I am guilty?"

"Of what?"

"Of being involved in what happened on the yacht? What if someone believes that I killed Nathan and Peter? What if they want revenge?"

"Revenge for what? And why would they have waited three years?"

"I don't know, but two people died, and I lived. What if what I did out there caused someone to want me dead?"

"And you think that you deserve to die? Is that it?"

How had he known her thoughts already, or was it a lucky guess? "Maybe..."

"And maybe it's payback time; is that where you're going with this?"

She nodded.

He pulled her into his arms, his body hard against hers. "Whatever happened on the sailboat didn't include you hurting anyone."

"How do you know? How can anyone know what I did or didn't do that night?"

"You say you remember everything before that night on the sailboat. If you were involved in anything that included harming two people you loved, you'd remember what led up to it, wouldn't you?"

"Yes. I suppose... I didn't do anything to anybody, that I know of."

"Robyn, you may never know what went on that night, but you can't let the past stop you from being happy now. "

She clung to his words as she snuggled closer.

After a few quiet moments, she glanced up at Luke. He lay with his eyes closed, feigning sleep, but the half smile on his lips betrayed him. What she would give to wake up every day like this. To love someone and have them not only love her, but believe in her. His belief that she hadn't harmed anyone, his support and caring was enough for her to move forward, to change her attitude from blaming herself to really looking for answers. "I've made up my mind. I am not going to sit around and let the bastard get away with this."

Luke placed his hands over hers. He opened his eyes, his expression one of pleasure. "Whoa! Sounds like you mean business."

"Don't give me any of your head-patting routines. I'm serious. I want to find this animal. And you're going to help me."

Luke rose up on one elbow, pulling her closer as he did so. He looked down into her eyes. "I'd do anything in the world for you."

"You would?" Something deep inside her stirred to life, some indefinable sense of wholeness that spread delight through her.

Luke squeezed her to him. "I would."

"I want to go over everything I can remember. If I had had the courage to do this sooner...."

Leaning down, Robyn scooped her clothes off the floor. She dressed quickly, her mind working on the problem. "I owe it to Lisa to find out who's behind this."

He nodded.

"What if my unwillingness to believe I was the target delayed the investigation? I can't change what I've done, but I can do something to make amends."

"What do you have in mind?"

"What if it's me they're after because I know something or someone...?" Robyn went to the window, her back to Luke as she gazed out into the backyard.

Luke got dressed. "Tell you what. Why don't we go over to the office and get started on this. I'll get Alice to take over for me there, and you and I will go through everything you can remember, starting with the man you saw on the ferry."

Robyn turned. "I would feel better if we could do it here. I want to really concentrate on this."

"If staying here will help, I'm all for it."

"It will." Robyn rested her hands on her hips. "Something good has to come out of everything that's happened."

Relieved to see that Luke was willing to help her, Robyn walked around the room, taking in the now-familiar objects that were a part of Luke's world: the framed photos of his class at the police academy; the computer that was always on; the collection of books stuffed into crowded shelves near the desk...

Luke's living space reflected the man who put his job first at any price. He would be a staunch ally, but he would also be a policeman first and always, ready to act when circumstances dictated. Would she be able to see it through, especially if what they found pointed to her greatest fear?

Robyn's fingers gently massaged the spot on her arm where the bullet had grazed her skin. The dressing was gone, but not the memory of what had happened out there on the marsh. Now that she had made the commitment to follow her memories to their source, she felt the chill of fear deep in her stomach.

Whatever she found out would not bring Lisa back, but it might find the killer. The fear of finding out the details of that day had held Robyn from pushing too hard. Denial had also held her back. Having admitted to herself and to Luke that she wanted to know the truth, she had no choice but to follow through.

Somewhere off the coast of Maine.

"We got to do something." The unlit cigar wedged in his fingers snapped into two pieces. The luxurious surroundings of the yacht were wasted on him as he felt the iron grip of defeat.

"Why? What does it matter? Your work with us is nearly finished." The Russian spoke in accented English. "You have only to deliver us to the plane at this place you call Pier Point and your responsibilities are over."

The man caressed the faint scar running along his hairline. "It's not that simple. The woman who died was a reporter for the local TV station. On an island where nothing bad happens, the deaths of two people in a week, related to the same incident, will bring national television coverage. The press is already trying to suggest that the TV reporter's death was not an accident. That she was investigating drug smuggling, and was killed because of it. Moving you gentlemen ashore, getting you to a safe location before moving you to your new home may be hampered by all the publicity."

"That's your problem," the Russian growled. "Don't make it ours." The Russian rested his hand on the polished surface of the bar. "You did a beautiful job, arranging to give each of us a whole new identity. We thank you for that." The Russian glanced in the mirror behind the bar and touched his new nose and cheeks as if unable to accept that they were his.

"The arrangements are made?" The Russian emphasized the last syllable.

Envy curdled his blood as he eyed the two Russians sitting on *his* bar stools on *his* yacht as if they had not a care in the world. When they were gone he would be left to clean up the mess.

His vice-like grip on the Waterford crystal goblet marked his palm. He still hadn't figured out how to get his load of isotopes ashore. His crew knew nothing about what was stashed below deck. There was no one else on board other than the two Russians he'd picked up off Sable Island, Nova Scotia six hours earlier, during which they'd done nothing but brag to him about their plans when they reached the US.

Once he got these two ashore, he'd be free to contact the man in Boston who would look after the isotopes. Just a few feet below them, in a locked room, rested his retirement plan.

Careful to disguise his urgent need to be free of the two men who sat across from him he considered his options.

Could he risk moving his cargo without knowing whether Robyn was still on Grand Island? She had to have recognized him that day on the ferry. She'd stared at him twice, proof enough for him. And if she hadn't immediately recognized him, she'd figure it out sooner or later.

Both men were still watching him. Feigning indifference, he rotated his shoulders to relieve the tension. "Well, we might as well get this show on the road." He gathered the goblets and put them in the bar sink.

"We'll get our things." The two Russians crossed the salon and closed the door behind them.

He squeezed the bridge of his nose. He needed time and opportunity to get the isotopes to his contact. He needed the freedom to move around without being fingered by a woman. His contact in the birding group didn't seem to know where Robyn was at the moment.

He had to assume that Robyn had recognized him on the ferry that day, and that he hadn't died that night on the sail-boat. She had to have told the police everything by now. He could hope that no one had believed her. After all, she had sought professional help, and that might mean that people didn't believe her when she reported seeing a man believed to be dead.

But he couldn't take a chance on someone believing her story.

Robyn took the cup of coffee offered by Luke and hugged its warmth to her. It felt so good to finally feel safe and cared for, the way she'd never imagined possible.

But in her heart of hearts, she recognized the truth of something Lisa had said long ago: 'Only those who dared to risk exposure – dared the tiger of remorse that waited in every revelation of secrets – had a chance at complete happiness.' And Robyn wanted to be happy. So much.

"Okay, whenever you're ready. " Luke sat down on the sofa beside her, and she moved away a bit. It wasn't that she didn't want him close to her. She feared telling him about the memories mixed with dreams that had driven her almost to the point of madness. Whether dream or memory, the cold steel of a gun in her hand had been her secret burden, one she'd shared with no one but Dr. Stanley. There were days when she was convinced that she dreamed it all up. As far as she knew, there were no guns found on the boat, and no indication that any had been used, so she'd pushed the idea back each time it surfaced.

Robyn began slowly. "The dream is always about water. I'm terrified by the noise and confusion in the dream. I can't see any faces, but I know we're in danger." Folding her hands in her lap, Robyn decided not to look at Luke, but to just tell him what she knew.

"What kind of danger? Is there someone in the dream threatening you?"

"I don't know. It must have to do with confusion, the noise. Maybe I'm afraid that I'll be left alone. I feel loss and I want to feel safe. Always, there is this sense that I will never be safe again." Robyn rubbed her forehead. "Let me start at the beginning. The day of the accident was perfect for a sail. Peter, Nathan and I were on board the sailboat for one last sail before Peter left for Russia."

Luke touched her, but still she resisted the urge to look at him. "Why was Peter going to Russia?"

"He was to be a guest lecturer at a symposium held in Moscow on shorebird habitats."

"He was a biologist?"

"Yes. He worked at the University of Maine. His sailboat was his dream. We were so busy that week, getting ready for him to leave. Nathan owned an import business, sold coffee machines and cookware. He was interested in getting into the Russian market, and he and Peter talked for hours about what Peter would do while he was there. We were on the boat, celebrating, having fun. We had set a course for Brier Island. I had gone below to make dinner...."

She sighed and closed her eyes. "The next thing I remember is waking up and finding myself alone on the sailboat. The Coast Guard told me they had found the sailboat adrift off Yarmouth, Nova Scotia."

"The police told me they found me in the cockpit. I was cold, disoriented and dehydrated. The police could find no evidence of what happened to Peter and Nathan. They later assumed that Peter and Nathan had died on the sailboat that night, leaving me the only witness to something I still can't remember. I have no idea what physical evidence they found. The only explanation I can come up with is that there was a freak wave that washed them overboard."

Fear rose in her chest, stinging her eyes with unshed tears. The old feelings of guilt and loss swarmed her. She clutched his hand.

"Don't Robyn. We can do this later."

"No." Robyn forced the memory to the front of her mind and continued. "I must have passed out after they went overboard. That's when the dream takes over."

She saw the compassion in his eyes, and wanted to curl up in his arms. Tears pressed against her eyelids. "I've carried this so long. Too long." She cleared her throat. "Even when they showed me the empty boat, I still felt as if Peter and Nathan were there. My psychiatrist thinks I was just protecting myself from the shock of their deaths."

"No bodies were found," he said

"No."

"And you had trouble believing they were gone."

"Not finding their bodies made it so difficult. One minute they were there and the next minute––"

"Robyn, can you tell me more about the dreams?"

"I'm lying in a boat or on the floor of the cockpit and someone is screaming. It might be me. I'm not sure. I can't see anything around me, but I hear angry voices."

"Do you believe this is part of what really happened?"

Robyn looked at him in horror. "No! Of course not. How could it be? Peter and Nathan never argued. They were good friends. We went everywhere together."

"I'm just trying to understand where your dreams are coming from."

Robyn let out a long sigh. "I-I don't know. It was such a confusing time. When I came to, the Coast Guard was there, the sails were flapping…. I remember the sound."

"Flapping sails would suggest that the boat's auto pilot steering mechanism was disabled, leaving you to drift with the tide. And it was Brad who found you, right?"

"Yes, he brought the Coast Guard."

"How did he know where to look?"

"He knew we'd gone out for a sail, I suppose. Everyone knew that Peter liked to sail toward Brier Island. It's a birding area. He had all the latest navigational equipment on board. Maybe they picked up a signal or something…."

"With the auto pilot off, you were lucky that the boat didn't run aground."

"I guess so. All I could think of at the time was that I wasn't hurt. The possibility that I might not have been found didn't hit me until I was on the Coast Guard boat…."

Robyn bit down hard on her lip, welcoming the stinging pain it caused.

"Do you remember any other event besides the dream?"

"No. But I need to know what happened between the

three of us enjoying a sailing trip, and me waking up alone on the boat. I've been afraid of water ever since."

"Robyn, please try to understand. What happened to you may be perfectly straight forward, and you may be suffering the effects of a very traumatic experience. The shooting on Simmons Marsh may have brought those memories to the surface, blending the two frightening events as if they were one."

Robyn closed her eyes and focused her mind to follow his logic. What she could remember of that night and what she could remember of the dreams were similar in several ways... "You sound just like Dr. Stanley."

His hands enclosed hers, and she squeezed them with all her strength as she told him, "The man I saw in Harper's Cove is the man I saw on the ferry and he's the same man who is mixed up in my dream."

"That's possible. You're the only one who would know, and that's the danger – that you made the connection."

His words chilled her, but his closeness gave her courage. Determined to stay with it, she searched her mind for more fragments and clues.

"Robyn, try to recall what he looked like, how he moved."

Searching her memory for the features of the man in Harper's Cove, she closed her eyes. "I had stopped to catch my breath after running down into the village of Harper's Cove. I was looking at the window display of one of the shops when he appeared behind me. He was tall, thin, I think. I didn't actually see him move. On the ferry and in Harper's Cove, he was just standing there. When I saw him down on the car deck, the sun was in my eyes and I couldn't see his features. When I saw him on the passenger deck he had sunglasses on and a hood pulled over his head...and a thin beard I think."

"Can you remember anything else about him??

She shook her head. "Not really."

Luke's shoulder touched hers as he moved closer. "Have you had other memories or dreams since the accident?"

She opened her eyes. "Just that one." But there was more. Robyn recoiled from telling him about the gun...

"Robyn, are you all right with this? Do you need a break?"

Robyn faced the man sitting so close to her and saw the raw feelings of worry in his eyes. The realization curled around her heart in a warming sweep. "I don't have much more to tell you. I've been doing much better this past year. Lisa and I were on this trip as a break from all the pressures in our lives. She'd been there for me after the accident, and yet we'd spent so little time together the past few months--"

Robyn began to shake.

Luke wrapped her in his arms and pulled her toward him.

"There's something more, isn't there? You told the nurse at the hospital something. What was it, Robyn?"

Telling Luke what she had feared more than anything about that night could end everything between them, everything she wanted. Could she trust the life she wished for to the man she loved, if she confided her fear to him? Luke Carlisle would want to know the truth, one way or another.

Could she have a life with Luke if she couldn't trust him with everything that was a part of her? What chance for happiness would they have if she didn't tell him everything? Robyn knew first hand the kind of things that could stress a marriage. She'd watched her parents tear at one another with their distrust. She couldn't live that way, and she suspected that Luke couldn't either.

She leaned back and looked up at the ceiling, not daring to watch the impact of her words on a man sworn to uphold the law. "There is a gun mixed up in my dream. Somehow, I'm holding a gun. Why would I be holding a gun? They didn't find one on the boat. They didn't find any gun residue on my hands, even though they did the test."

At an airstrip on Grand Island.

Brad's hands shook as he waited for the van carrying the cargo he would fly to a remote landing strip in Maine. He'd learned to fly when he was in high school, never thinking that it might come in handy in this sort of situation. He thanked his lucky charms for good weather instead of a wall of fog. He had instructions to fly to a small, unused airstrip north of Bangor. A hearse would be there to pick up the cargo.

He checked his watch again. Nearly midnight.

The sky cascaded with stars, crisp and sparkling. Brad ticked off all the other reasons for being out on a night like this. The first one was Robyn. He smiled into the darkness. This birding trip had several bonuses he hadn't dared hope for. He would make good money for the flight tonight, and he and Robyn were now as close as they had been after the accident.

It was a good thing she didn't know what he knew. It would cause her pain and problems and she already had her share of problems. She didn't need anymore. But she did need his protection. The damned police officer thought he was smart, sneaking her into his house, thinking no one would know. Brad was smarter than that. He overheard their conversation at the inn during which Luke Carlisle had decided she should move in with him. Robyn was still there. Brad wasn't leaving Grand Island until Robyn did.

A movement caught his eye and Brad saw three figures moving toward him. *What the hell?* His first impulse was to run. There was no van, no cargo in sight. The three men kept moving closer. Brad stood his ground and steadied his knees.

"Oh, it's you." Brad let the trapped air out of his lungs.

"Who else were you expecting?"

"What are you doing here?" Brad clapped him on the back and shook his hand. "I didn't expect to see you." It was true. Roberto could have sent someone else to deliver the goods.

"I need to talk to you." The man put a restraining hand on Brad's arm. "Wait until we get these two on board."

"They're my cargo?"

"You got it."

"Are they political refugees?"

"You could say that." The man held the cabin door of the plane open for the two men.

Closing the door, he patted the side of the plane. "These two are worth a lot."

"To our side."

The man's eyes glinted in the half darkness. "Yeah, to our side."

Brad watched the man move toward him. He was suddenly very relieved that he towered a tidy four inches over him. His friend was a very intimidating man. The scar on his face, his wide shoulders and the way he studied everything around him, made him a man not to be ignored.

Brad never admitted to anyone just how romantic he thought his friend's work was. Sometimes he wondered if the man had a '00' rating and then felt silly for considering that.

"Brad, I'm going to have to impose on you one more time."

"Sure, you name it."

"I need to see Robyn."

"Oh, I'm sorry things went so badly at the beach that night. Thank God you got the killer. Robyn--"

"Where is Robyn?" The man held the lighter to the end of his cigar.

Surprised at the questions, Brad hesitated. "She's staying at the police officer's house."

The man coughed until he choked, creating a cloud of smoke around his head. "What the hell! How did that happen?"

"I don't know. I assume the police want to be sure she's safe." He didn't really believe that. No one would hurt Robyn. He figured Luke Carlisle was putting the moves on Robyn, and he planned to put a stop to that right after he moved the cargo for his friend.

"Maybe you should give up those cigars. Not good for your health."

"I want to see her."

"I'll see what I can do," Brad said, wishing he could tell someone about his role in helping an undercover agent of the US Government. He loved his country and would do anything he could to help their cause.

CHAPTER EIGHTEEN

Morning light streaked across the black-and-white tiles of the kitchen floor as Luke fumbled with the coffee pot. The edginess that made him drop things had its cause rooted in the spare bedroom, and the woman who slept there. He was more afraid for Robyn than he could ever admit to her, and the fear knotted his stomach.

If there was any chance that Robyn's belief about a gun could be substantiated, he had to follow up. The police reports hadn't mentioned any weapons being found, but he needed to check again. To do that, he would have to talk to the investigators on the mainland.

Face it, he scolded himself as he opened the fridge door and took out the cream. You have a bigger problem than the investigation. You've turned a professional relationship into a personal one. He was falling for her, but could he trust his feelings? Could he trust her? He had trusted in the past and then watched his feelings destroyed by the deceit and lies of his wife.

And there was the whole thing about Lisa Wade. If he had doubted Robyn for one minute where Lisa was concerned, those doubts disappeared last night. Now he was convinced that Robyn was not involved in any plot to harm Lisa. The woman he'd held in his arms was incapable of such a thing.

Luke was convinced that the whole fiasco on the beach at the Anchorage could be laid at Brad Allen's feet, and that Brad was also tied to the killer. The bigger question was whether or not Brad was the one calling the shots. Luke concentrated on putting bread in the toaster as his mind ranged over the possibilities. The more he thought about it, the more he wanted to get his breakfast over with and get to work.

"Good morning," Robyn said as she slid into a chair at the table.

"Good morning yourself. Want coffee?"

"Yeah, sure." She got up and moved to the counter beside him. "I'm a pretty good cook. Why don't you sit down?"

"No. I have toast started, and there's yogurt, fresh fruit, bagels."

"I know. I gave you the grocery list, remember?" She smiled, and suddenly he felt like a school kid.

"I bow to your superior knowledge of the inner workings of my kitchen."

"That's more like it. Get a move on out of my way." She gave him a gentle push.

"You're sure?" he asked, acutely aware of her hands on his back.

"I need something to keep me occupied."

Luke tried to coax his mind away from the gorgeous woman busily making breakfast in his kitchen. It didn't work.

Last night when Robyn had let him know, in no uncertain terms, that he was welcome to sleep with her, he couldn't make love to her without feeling that was committing to more than just a night in her bed. The closer he got to her the more he felt the need to go slow – for both their sakes. "How was your sleep?"

She toyed with the dishtowel as she leaned against the counter. "Not great. I was afraid all our talk last night would bring the nightmare back. I stayed awake, worrying."

"And did it?"

She turned her back to him and he saw the lift of her shoulders, and the slight tremor of her body. "No, but I'm so tired…."

The lonely tone he heard in Robyn's voice had him up and out of the chair and pulling her into his arms before he was aware he was doing that. "It's all right." He patted her shoulders, helpless to know what else to say. He felt the warmth of her body as she clung to him. He breathed in the scent of Robyn's hair as he held her, knowing that he was just one move away from taking her to bed. He wanted her, every part of her and to hell with anything else.

Without looking at him, Robyn stepped out of his embrace. Her sudden move away from him left a deep, unsatisfied ache inside him.

"I spent all night like this. I can't spend all day this way." Robyn smoothed her hair from her face, and stepped around him. "I need to do something, anything to find out who is out there waiting for me. I hate being cooped up here, not able to go anywhere. Not able to do anything outside of here. I'm beginning to think that Dr. Stanley was right."

"About what?"

"When I told him the dreams were back, he wanted me to come home and he said he would help me. Maybe I should."

Regret writhed in Luke's gut. She had spent a miserable night, and he could have helped her, comforted her. Why hadn't he thought about how she would be feeling? Why hadn't he put aside his own turmoil and gone to her last night? Instead, he let his own insecurities separate them.

Robyn pulled a frying pan out of the cupboard and took eggs out of the fridge. "We need a real breakfast." She behaved as if everything was fine, even though she'd just told him she thought she should go home and return to therapy. Her well of strength seemed bottomless, but he knew it wasn't. No one's could be.

He sat and watched her cook breakfast, bring the filled plates to the table and pour two cups of coffee. She slid into the chair, took a sip of her coffee. Luke tasted nothing as they ate in silence.

"Luke, when I finally fell asleep last night. I dreamed about the accident. The gun was as close to me as you are." Robyn put her cup down, but not before Luke saw the tremor in her fingers.

"I don't know what happened." She rubbed her forehead. "But there was a gun. I've worried that I might have shot someone...."

He couldn't imagine what it must feel like to be a doctor facing the possibility – however remote – that they might have used a gun. Robyn hadn't spoken aloud about it, but she had to be wondering if she was capable of turning a gun on another human being. And what connection did a gun have to someone wanting to kill her? "Robyn, I asked you this before. Have you had a patient who is capable of this attack on you?"

Robyn pushed the eggs around her plate before she answered. "No one comes to mind." She took another sip of her coffee. "I have one patient with serious mental difficulties, but he's in the psychiatric hospital."

"For how long?"

"Forever, as far as I know."

"Well, I'll check on that. Anyone else?"

"No, most of my patients suffer the usual illnesses for their age and general health. Nothing sinister or dangerous."

Luke saw the weariness in her eyes, but there was one more person he needed to ask her about. "Why did Brad come on this birding trip?"

"He loves birding." Robyn fiddled with her napkin.

"But?"

Robyn bit her bottom lip as she met his stare. "He wasn't supposed to come on this trip. The man who was supposed to lead the tour developed the flu. It was a last-minute change."

"Did you know that when you decided to come?"

"No, if I had known that Brad was the tour leader, I wouldn't have come."

"Why? And how did he end up leading the tour if he came last minute?"

"I wouldn't have come because I don't want to encourage Brad. I'm not sure how he came to lead the tour..."

Thank God Brad didn't know Robyn was living in his house. But it wouldn't be long before he found out. Brad had been in on everything that had happened to Robyn from the beginning, from the boating incident to the two shootings.

Luke had not followed up on his suspicions as thoroughly as he should have. It was time he did. If Brad learned where Robyn was staying, and he was involved in what was going on, Robyn wasn't safe.

He had to go to Portland, but he couldn't leave Robyn alone. He'd been meaning to get in touch with Russell Black, the officer in charge of the boating accident investigation three years ago, but with everything that had been going on he hadn't taken the time. Of course being the only one who thought there was a connection between the accident three years ago and the shooting, he didn't want to leave looking into the old case to anyone else. Now he had no choice but to go back to the mainland and go over the file. He called Russell Black and he agreed to meet Luke in Portland.

"Robyn, I want you to come to Portland with me. Today. I need to go over the police records on your accident. I want you with me."

Color drained from Robyn's face. "I'd rather not go there."

Thick chunks of fear sank to the pit of her stomach as Robyn stared at Luke. "I don't know why you want me to go with you."

"I told you. You'd be safer with me."

"Because of Brad?"

"Because of Brad and what we discussed last night."

She had to make him see reason. "You don't know if the boating accident has any bearing on this situation." If he went through the old records and found out that they had seriously investigated her role in the accident, he'd find out they considered her a prime suspect. It seemed the police were investigating her for more than the fact that she was the only one on the boat when it was found adrift, but what they knew or suspected hadn't been shared with her.

"Luke, I thought you and I were working together?"

Exasperation thickened his voice. "We are. Come with me. The investigating officer, Russell Black, has agreed to meet me and go over the case."

"Russell Black? I'm not going anywhere near that man." Russell Black had been the officer who had basically accused her of being involved in Nathan's and Peter's deaths. She'd had no defense at the time because she couldn't remember what happened, and the man had made her life a living hell for months after the accident.

"Why?"

She couldn't tell Luke the reason without tainting his perception of her. What officer, whose wife had been mixed up with the law, would not believe what Russell Black would say when he and Luke met to talk about the investigation? Russell Black had made no secret of the fact he thought she was involved in the deaths of Nathan and Peter. He'd worked tirelessly to prove his point. "I don't want to see Russell Black. We have nothing to say to each other…"

"Let me worry about Russell Black. I want you with me where you'll be safe."

"I feel safe here."

"Well, that's a switch. A few days ago you fought me like a tiger to let you leave. What changed?"

"I don't know what you mean." The lie made a paper cut across her conscience. She knew only too well why she didn't want to go with him. When Luke learned that she had once been the prime suspect in the disappearance of Peter and Nathan, something she'd never told him, she would lose him. He would not trust his love to another woman who deceived him.

In spite of Luke's support and encouragement, she could not shake the feeling that she could have killed someone. It would have been an accident, but that didn't matter. It was too late to uncover the truth, but digging into it further could permanently damage any hope Robyn would find happiness with Luke.

"Robyn, come with me and help me find out what happened. I won't let anyone hurt you. And I don't want you to continue to believe that you were involved in what took place on the sailboat. Nathan and Peter died, and somehow you were saved. I want to see firsthand what there is to know about the incident on the sailboat, but I want you to be with me when I do."

Robyn wanted to trust him with all her heart and soul, but she didn't trust herself the way he did – to believe that she was innocent. She had never been able to accept that she had survived by some stroke of luck. And now Luke's insistence forced her to a new realization.

She had always believed in her own guilt. That's why she woke up after a dream hating herself. "Please, leave it alone."

"No, I won't." His voice was emphatic, his expression hard. "Don't you want to know what the police learned?"

"Just because you want to go on a wild goose chase, you're insisting that I join you. I don't want to go. You're making me feel that somehow I'm letting *you* down when I refuse to go. What you're really doing is letting me down, making me relive one of the worst things that ever happened to me. "

Feelings of hopelessness filled her. *What chance did they have, if he persisted in digging up the past?*

If Luke could turn in his wife for trafficking in drugs, he would not hesitate to turn her in if he found evidence linking her to the deaths of Nathan and Peter. And maybe that would be for the best. If she killed her brother and her fiancé, she deserved to be punished.

"I think enough has been said," she whispered over the scratchiness in her throat. "I won't go with you."

"Robyn, don't do this to us. Don't make my job even more difficult. I need you with me so I have peace of mind. So I know you're okay…"

Seeing the remorse on his face made her wish she could do as he asked. But it was all too complicated, too painful for her to face now. Whatever he discovered when he searched the police file would force him to keep searching for the truth. She couldn't deal with the pain and agony she'd face while he did it – regardless of the outcome.

She would wait for him to leave and decide what she'd do next.

The silence between them spread through the room like ground fog as both waited for the other to speak and break the impasse. Finally, with a sigh of resignation, Luke said, "I'll wait for you at the ferry terminal. Ten o'clock. If you change your mind...." With that, he went upstairs.

The house felt so empty, so abandoned, just the way her life would feel when he walked out for good. Robyn gathered up the dishes and filled the sink with water – anything, any activity not to face the very real possibility that she would never see a smiling Luke again.

After the accident, everyone had been so kind – so unwilling to even hint at the possibility of foul play – especially when the only one to accuse was a respected doctor. She'd lived with their furtive glances, their polite whispers... and never once did she let anyone know just how much it hurt her that she couldn't defend herself. For weeks she waited and hoped that Peter or Nathan would be found. The need for closure was so strong, she thought of nothing else but the relief of finding out how they'd died.

Her mother had supported her through all of it, and now she might have to revisit the whole thing again if Luke found anything new that would reopen the case. She didn't want her mother to worry anymore. It wasn't fair.

And Jason. How would he feel if he thought she'd done anything wrong? Or worse, that she'd harmed his father? Even if Jason discovered that she had been negligent in Peter's death...

Her mind turned over the desperate scenarios that wouldn't let her alone as Robyn made her way upstairs to her room. She might as well pack her bag, and get ready to go back to the mainland. She picked up her keys from the bedside table, the glint of silver reminding her that Lisa had given her the key chain.

Just touching the cool metal brought back memories of her friend. The crazy things that once made them laugh. The

Halloween night they got caught soaping the neighbors' windows. The day the choir director called their mothers and asked that they leave the choir because of their naughtiness. The double date that turned into a disaster, leaving them to walk home in the dark. The plans they had for their lives, plans that had fallen prey to the demands of their busy careers. She wished there was another chance to make things right, to make amends.

"I'm sorry, Lisa. So sorry," she whispered into the silence. "For everything, especially this trip. "A warm breeze blew in the window and wrapped around her, and for just a few moments, it was as if Lisa were with her, telling her not to worry. That everything would be all right. Memories of Lisa whirled around her: Lisa's laughter, her smile, the way she brightened everyone's life with her joy. The warmth of the air around her was like a breath of freedom, of release. "Thanks," she murmured into the stillness.

Luke had been gone for only a few hours and she missed him more than she'd thought possible. He had to have been disappointed when she didn't meet him at the ferry. She imagined him making the drive to Portland, meeting with the people, his colleagues, gathering the files and sitting down to read them. After that, she didn't dare think about what he would know and how he would feel.

In desperation, she flicked on the television. The midday news was on with Barry Cox, the man who had shared the anchor spot with Lisa for several years. Curious, Robyn settled down to watch.

"Lisa Wade, a member of the staff of this station, is the subject on everyone's lips today. The autopsy report has not been made available as yet, but authorities say there is reason to suspect foul play. Lisa, a personal friend of Dr. Robyn

McGill, had been working on a story about drug smuggling. As you will remember, Dr. McGill was found adrift in her brother's sailboat after the disappearance of Nathan Green and Peter McGill. Lisa was with Dr. McGill on Grand Island when she was shot by a professional hit man."

Aghast, Robyn listened as Barry made insinuations that pointed to a possible connection between Lisa's death and what happened three years ago. Her mother had to be watching this. Her mother watched every news program all day long. She would be devastated. And Jason. To have these insinuations made public would force Jason to revisit his father's death, and to face the suggestion that someone he loved could be evil.

All because of someone's career greed, a child's life was about to be irreparably damaged. Clutching the phone in her hands, she dialed her home number.

Her mother picked up on the first ring. "She's not here," her mother said, her voice shaking with anger.

"Mom, it's me."

"Thank heavens! Have you seen the news? That darned Barry Cox is trying to say you're involved in something illegal. And dear Jason...Robyn, what are you going to do?"

"Mom, please don't worry. You know there's no truth in it. It's all rumor and innuendo. Barry's is trying to grab headlines."

"Well, he's got your father worked up."

"Dad? How did he hear about it?" Her father would be furious with her for bringing shame on the McGill name.

"I don't know. He called here this morning, wanting to know how he could reach you."

"I don't want to talk to him."

"I know, sweetie, but he's the least of your troubles. The press have been calling here all morning."

"Oh, Mom, I'm sorry. I wish I were there."

"No! You have to stay away from here. They have no right to be interviewing you. And don't worry about Jason. I'm keeping him home from school today. You know how kids can be. He hasn't seen the news and I won't let him. The little monkey is absolutely delighted to be able to spend the day on his computer."

"Will you call me every hour and let me know how you're doing, Mom?"

"I will, darling, but I don't want you worrying about us. I know how to handle things. I always have. Your father taught me to be tough."

"Thanks, Mom," Robyn said and hung up.

The phone blared again. It was probably her father with all sorts of I-told-you-so remarks and I-thought-I-taught-you-better-than-that comments.

"I might as well get it over with," Robyn muttered as she scooped up the phone.

"Yes, Dad?"

"Oh, good morning. I'm Jamie Patterson from the *Courier* and I'm looking for Dr. Robyn McGill. Would you be able to tell me where I could reach her?"

Robyn slammed the phone down.

As the hours dragged by, Robyn waited in dread for the arrival of some ambitious reporter looking for an interview. A doctor with possible involvement in drug trafficking would make a sensational story. With nothing left to do and nowhere to go, Robyn went from window to window, hoping for some distraction from her thoughts.

The living room windows looked out on the narrow front lawn. A man in blue coveralls was mowing the lawn, his plodding stride speaking volumes about his enthusiasm for the work.

Luke's L-shaped living room turned into a dining room with a long slim window at the end that offered a clear view of the backyard. The dining room window ledge held a model sailboat with cotton sails, a miniature replica of the tall ships. Robyn ran her fingers over the wooden hull of the boat, the smoothness of it soothing her. Pulling the drape aside, she peeked out at the backyard.

A Boston Whaler with the familiar police markings, rested on a trailer with a smaller trailer beside it. She wondered why they didn't keep these boats at a marina... with a sharp intake of breath, Robyn stared at the black rubber dinghy; *a Zodiac.*

On the day of the accident, the sailboat had been towing a Zodiac to ferry them between the mooring and the dock of the yacht club. She'd gone over what had happened that night, what she could remember, yet she hadn't remembered that until now. The Zodiac had been tied to the stern of the boat – ready, if it were needed.

She could almost smell the thick rubbery scent of the powerful craft. She'd ridden in one numerous times, and could pilot the snub-nosed dinghy around the moorings at the yacht club with the best of them. Peter said she was the best little Zodiac navigator in the business. The memory brought back other pleasant times they'd shared: Peter's first sailboat, his first race, all the times she'd crewed for him...

As she turned from the window, another fragment of memory broadsided her.

Darkness, and someone screaming. Someone reaching to pull the Zodiac in close to the boat. Sails flapping in the wind and the sound of gunfire....

Breathless and panicky, Robyn made her way to the sofa, the feelings released by the memory still floating ominously in her mind. *What had happened?* She sank into the cushions as the memory began to blur and fade, the sounds becoming a mere echo.

Yet the image of the Zodiac as it bobbed in the wake of the sailboat was as vivid to her as if it had happened only moments ago. What she had just experienced suggested that someone pulled the Zodiac in closer to the boat. Nothing unusual in that.

But the sound of gunfire? Could she have mistaken the sharp snapping sound of the metal sail cleats against the rigging as gunfire? The sound was similar. In fact, that could be the explanation for what she'd heard.

Was it possible she had made a mistake this simple?

If the metal cleats had made the sound, not a gun being fired, she was free. Finally free of the guilt that she might have shot and killed someone. Because she thought she heard shots perhaps she'd imagined she had a gun in her hand.... She paced around the dining room table, a smile forming on her lips. Wait until Luke learned about her theory.

Robyn jumped at the sound of knocking at the door leading to the backyard. No one knew she was there. She stayed still, trying to decide what to do. It might be the housekeeper, or the man she saw mowing the lawn. More likely it was a reporter.

Robyn tiptoed over to the steps leading down to the back door at the end of the hall that divided the police office and the house. From her vantage point, she could see through the glass of the small window. Someone stood outside the door.

"Robyn." A female voice rang through the wooden door.

Sandy Fowler? "Oh my God!" Robyn cried. Racing to the door, she twisted the knob on the deadbolt and yanked the door open. "Am I ever glad to see you!"

"Me too! I didn't know if you were here or not. I just took a chance." Sandy wrapped her arms around Robyn as laughter spilled from her lips. "We've been so worried about you."

"And I've missed you," Robyn said, hugging her back. "Come on in."

Sandy placed her cane by the door. They linked arms as they headed up the narrow steps and down the narrow hall to the door of the house. "Where have you people been? I thought I'd see you at Lisa's funeral."

"Lisa's funeral?" Shock filled Sandy's face. "What are you talking about?"

"I thought you knew. I assumed someone told you. It was in the paper."

"We've been camped out along the west coast of the island, waiting for a Barred Owl. No cell phone reception. No one heard anything about Lisa."

"I'm sorry you didn't hear. Lisa died in hospital. I went to her service."

"I would have been there if I'd known. Brad would have wanted to be there too. How are you doing? Are you here alone?"

"For the moment."

"Well, not anymore. I'm here."

Sandy's sympathy lifted Robyn's loneliness. Sandy needed a friend as much as she did.

"And I'm so glad to see you. Losing Lisa has been very difficult. There are times when I can't believe she's gone. Did you finally see a Barred Owl?"

Sandy followed Robyn into the kitchen, her limp clearly visible. "Yes. It was so exciting. What a rotten break! And Lisa was doing so well. I thought she was coming out of the hospital in a couple of weeks."

Talking about Lisa hurt. The kind of hurt that made her stomach pain and a lump grow in her throat. "That was the plan."

"After all the things you've done for me, I wish I could have been there for you," Sandy said, her voice catching, her eyes filling with tears.

Don't cry. Not now. "I'm glad you came. I've really missed you people. I suppose you'll be heading home tomorrow."

"Yes. Will you be able to come with us?"

"Oh, Sandy, I want to go back with you. I'm just not sure if I'll be able to leave."

"Are the police still investigating?"

"Yes."

"What are the police investigating?" Sandy asked, her tone cautious.

"They're trying to find the killer's connection to me." She didn't want to say more and hoped that Sandy would drop the subject.

"They believe the killer knew you? How? A patient?"

"Or someone hired by someone I knew in the past."

Sandy's face radiated shock. "You mean they still think someone wants to kill you?"

Robyn remembered that day in the inn when she talked to Brad and Sandy about the fact that Luke wanted her to stay on the island for her own safety.

"Yes. After an incident at the inn Luke Carlisle arranged for me to stay here where I'm safe. You're not to tell anyone you saw me here. Promise me," she insisted.

"I promise, but I don't believe this can be happening to you. There must be some mistake. No one would want to hurt you."

Robyn saw concern in Sandy's eyes, and was touched by it. "It's only a theory. I don't know anyone who would do that either. I told Luke he was wasting his time."

"But he's not listening." Sandy closed her eyes as if in thought. "A good cop with good instincts...."

"Sandy, can we talk about something else?" Robyn

glanced around the kitchen. "Sit down and I'll make a pot of coffee."

"No, really. I came here to check on you and to see if you wanted to go to Shark Tail Lighthouse. Brad spotted a huge flock of ducks early this morning. Everyone's going out there," Sandy said hastily.

"I'm not supposed to leave the house...."

"After what you've been through, you need to get some fresh air. I promise we won't be long."

Robyn waivered. Luke had been adamant that she remain hidden in the house. But she needed to get out for a while. She missed her friends so much... She'd given up hope that Luke would call, and she felt terrible every time she thought about how they parted that morning. She'd begun to pack when she remember the key ring Lisa had given her. Luke was gone and probably wouldn't be back for her anytime soon, if ever.

Her friends were waiting. If Luke came back with information connecting her to a shooting, she would need the support of her friends. And Sandy Fowler was a true friend, someone she could trust. She needed someone to talk to, to spend time with until Luke returned and she faced his disappointment with her. Sandy's offer brought into focus her sense that all of this felt so unreal. She couldn't get her head around the idea that someone was after her. Sure, she understood Luke's concern, but she was tired of being afraid and worried. She wanted to feel the excitement of rejoining the birding group if only for a couple of hours. "I'll get my jacket and binoculars"

Once out in the driveway, Robyn was surprised to see that there was no one in the van. "Where is everyone?"

Sandy stopped and stared at her, an anxious frown on her face. "They're out at the lighthouse. We're supposed to meet them there."

There was an edge to Sandy's voice that was a little unsettling. Robyn quelled her suspicious mind. *Who wasn't on edge these days?*

"Hurry up." Sandy opened the driver's door. "The birds won't wait."

Robyn climbed into the passenger's seat while Sandy climbed in the driver's side – her expression one of excited anticipation.

CHAPTER NINETEEN

The tall columns of rock that made up the jutting mass of Shark Tail Lighthouse, reached out into the ocean. Robyn looked down over the jagged rocks protruding through the foaming water smashing along the bottom of the cliff. Ahead of her stretched a narrow footbridge leading out over the gorge to the base of the lighthouse, which rose majestically above the rock, its light framed in red – the white shingled, four-sided shape of the building a reassuring spectacle.

The wind whipped her hair into a swirling mass that threatened to block Robyn's vision. Her grip on the railing tightened as she listened to the thunderous pounding of the surf a hundred feet below. Only birders would be out here on a day like this.

Sandy came up behind Robyn, her uneven gait punctuated by the gusting wind. "What a beautiful sight," she said as she grasped the railing next to Robyn.

Robyn had to agree, but wondered how the ducks would manage to find refuge in the rough water below. "The ducks must be on the lee side."

"Yeah," Sandy said.

"Where are the others?" Robyn barely heard her own words as they were yanked from her lips by the wind.

"Out there." Sandy pointed in the general direction of the lighthouse.

Dedicated birders were known for risking life and limb for a new bird sighting. "What did they find? A group of harlequin ducks?"

"No, a large grouping of eiders, I think," Sandy called against the force of the breeze.

Sandy hadn't brought her cane with her. How would she manage out there on the rough ground? "Are you sure?"

"Of course I am. Silly!" Sandy stepped past Robyn and moved out onto the narrow footbridge, making her way slowly along the swaying bridge.

Robyn looked out along the winding ribbon of bridge, undulating in the wind, debating what to do.

"Come on," yelled Sandy, her thin, mousy brown hair leaping and jumping around her narrow features as she gestured impatiently to Robyn.

Torn between needing friendly companionship and half-formed fear, Robyn stood still.

"What are you waiting for?" Sandy's voice bounced in the wind.

She put her case of nerves down to the past few hours, and followed Sandy. A lull in the wind made the walking easier, and they reached the end where the bridge hooked to a ledge of rock.

"Whew! I haven't been out here for a long time." Robyn, thankful to be on solid ground, pushed her hair out of her face and stared around. Ground-hugging junipers webbed their way over the rocks leading up the path, ending at the lighthouse. In the calm space created by the shelter of the lighthouse, Robyn looked around for the others. "Are you sure we were to meet them here?"

Sandy didn't answer. The sudden calm created by a lull in the wind only added to the eerie quality of the moment.

A gull swooped down, its legs extended in landing mode. It came to rest on a piece of granite peeping out from under the juniper. Robyn looked around for any signs that they were not alone on this narrow pillar of rock.

"Sandy--"

"Robyn. You're the best friend I've ever had. You know that. There isn't anything I wouldn't do for you." Sandy's smile was forced, her eyes wild, her breath coming in short gasps.

Where did that come from? Robyn hadn't a clue what was going on. Something about Sandy's expression made her fearful. She shouldn't have left Luke's house. Robyn stepped closer to the bridge, placing her hand on the railing for support.

Sandy straightened, her chin high and proud. "I've had a hard time making friends. No one wants a cripple. Everyone's nice, but--"

"Sandy, I was only too glad to help you when you needed it, but you have lots of friends." Robyn pulled the wind-whipped hair out of her eyes as she spoke.

"Not friends like yours." Sandy came toward Robyn, skidding on the rocky surface. For a few frantic seconds Robyn thought Sandy intended to push her.

Stepping onto the bridge, Robyn balanced as carefully as possible while the sound of the pounding water below her feet played havoc with her courage.

Oh God! Why had she agreed to come here?

Driven by fear, Robyn pleaded, "I don't know what you want. I--"

Sandy, her eyes squinting at Robyn, stood perfectly still

despite the wind frothing around her. "I don't want anything," she said, her voice loud.

A frightening thought blocked Robyn's mind. What would make Sandy want to climb along such a dangerous bridge in this weather? "If you wanted to talk to me, we could have done that back at the house. Sandy, please tell me what's going on."

"I needed privacy. I needed to know that no one could overhear our conversation."

In spite of the cold and the anxiety running through her, Robyn sensed that Sandy told the truth. Sandy had gone through a rough time after her leg surgery left her with a limp. It was testimony to Sandy's determination and willpower that she hadn't been left with a more serious disability.

Sandy's harsh laugh shattered her thoughts.

"Just because of this." Sandy tapped her shortened left leg. "You think there's something wrong with me here." She pointed to her head, and laughed louder.

The sound had a hysterical, frantic edge to it.

Robyn took stock of her situation, and what she saw didn't offer encouragement. They were standing at the base of a footbridge on the edge of a rock, from which there was only one exit.

The wind fell silent. Soothing words seemed the only solution.

"Look, I didn't mean to make light of your situation with your leg." She watched Sandy, hoping her words would have the desired effect. "It's just that you brought me out here with the understanding that the others would be here with us."

Sandy moved back, clutching the low-growing spruce trees to steady her as she made her way to a weathered bench near the base of the lighthouse. "I don't mean to frighten you, Robyn. I'm very worried about you."

"Worried about me? I don't understand."

Sandy sat down, beckoning Robyn to follow her. "I would be in real trouble if what I'm about to tell you fell into the wrong hands."

Shocked by what Sandy was saying, Robyn decided to stay right where she was. "Trouble from whom? How could you possibly get in trouble?"

"That shouldn't concern you. All my life I've wanted what everyone else had – someone who cared. And now I have it, and nothing's going to jeopardize that."

Who was Sandy involved with? Was it someone Robyn knew? Robyn had heard rumors about Sandy's mysterious lover, but hadn't paid much attention. Now she wished she had.

She watched with growing trepidation as the tears coursed down Sandy's cheeks. There seemed to be only one thing to do. Let Sandy say what she'd brought Robyn here to say. "Go on."

"Robyn, you are in real danger."

"I know that."

Sandy scowled. "I'm not just talking about your safety, right now." Her eyes had a strange glint to them. "I'm talking about the fact that if he isn't stopped, you will never be safe. God knows people have tried. But when he makes up his mind...."

"Who are you talking about?"

"I'm talking about the man who's after you. The one who wants you dead."

Robyn tightened her grip on the railing. "What do you know?"

"I can't tell you, or I'll lose him. I've loved him for so long, waited for him, promised him anything to have him with me, but it's too late, too late...."

Sandy seemed to be apologizing to someone.

"Sandy, please, you're not making sense−−"

"Get off this island, and leave the country." Her words hissed through her lips as she glared at Robyn. "He will not let you live. He has too much at stake. Do you understand me? Don't wait around. Go! Now!"

Unspeakable fear drowned out all but the crashing of the words in Robyn's head. The pounding surf below her feet became the sound of gunfire...*and then someone fell off the boat into the writhing water....*

She had to escape, to save herself from the horror.

Turning quickly, Robyn tripped and fell headlong onto the floor of the bridge. Pulling her knees up under her, she stood. Heedless of the jarring motion of the bridge and the thrashing water far below, she raced across the clattering wooden planks.

Fear ran free through every corner of Robyn's mind as she scrambled toward the land end of the bridge. She had to get back to the police station − to Alice Seymour for help. Her chest hurt from the effort to pull air into her lungs. Her throat burned when she reached the safety of the cliff edge where she threw herself down on the matted grass and wild roses that covered the ground bordering the entrance to the bridge.

She fought for every breath. Regaining some composure, Robyn looked back along the bridge through the gathering fog and failing light but Sandy had disappeared.

It couldn't be. Sandy had been sitting on the bench near the base of the lighthouse, in clear view. Yet, the bench was empty and the only movement around the lighthouse was the swaying of the lone pine caught in the force of the wind coming off the open water. *Had Sandy jumped?*

No. Sandy wouldn't do that. She must have gone around

the lighthouse to the other side where she wouldn't be seen by anyone on shore. Instinctively, she glanced around the rocky promontory. The sighing of the wind in the tall creaking cedars and the wisps of fog were her only companions. Robyn forced her legs under her and scrambled farther up the slope. Out of the trailing bits of fog, a figure emerged, running toward her.

"There you are." Brad slid to a stop in the gravel. "I went to the house and couldn't find you."

Relief, like warm honey, slid down through Robyn. She threw her arms around Brad and sobbed into his neck.

He held her against him, his arms crushing her into his body. "Robyn, how did you end up out here?" His lips were nestled against her ear.

Robyn could feel Brad's body moving slowly, suggestively against hers.

"Brad." She pulled away and looked into his eyes. The breeze slid his hair high above his forehead, his sharp features giving his face a sinister quality. "I came here with Sandy. She told me that the group was out at the light, looking for ducks. I should never have believed her, but she came to the house. She said that you told her how to find me."

Brad placed his hands on her shoulders, giving a gentle squeeze. "I didn't tell Sandy anything. I haven't seen her for the past two days. Where is she?"

Robyn eased out of his grip and stood just up the slope from him. "I don't know. She brought me out here. She said you had spotted a large flock of ducks, and that the whole group had gone out to the lighthouse. Was that all a lie?"

"Robyn, Sandy hasn't been doing very well lately. She's very emotional, very anxious. You must have known that."

Robyn was a medical doctor and she hadn't picked up on that. She hadn't known about the story Lisa was working on, either. "I should have realized that something wasn't right."

"Did she say anything else?"

"She talked a lot about some man, someone she cared for very much."

"I've heard parts of that story," Brad said, standing so that he blocked the wind from piercing Robyn's light jacket.

Robyn looked over her shoulder toward the footbridge, and back at Brad. "I left her out there. If she's having difficulty, she isn't safe out there alone. I've got to go back."

"You're not going anywhere, except back with me."

"But we can't leave her here."

Brad zippered his jacket and hunched his shoulders against the rising wind. "Listen to me. The birding group just got back from White's Island. Sandy didn't go. She told them she was returning to Portland. Instead, she's out here frightening you." Brad's glance was fearful.

Robyn began to shiver.

"You're going to catch a cold. Here, let me help you." Brad pulled the hood of her jacket over her head and lifted her face to his.

"What ever made you come out here with Sandy?"

What could she say? That she was fed up and wanted to escape the mess her life had become? That she was afraid that Luke would return with the evidence that would destroy their relationship? "I wanted a break."

"Why didn't you call me? I would have taken you anywhere you wanted to go. I've been worried about you."

"There's been so much going on. I've been so sad about Lisa."

"What about Lisa?"

Brad didn't know. "Lisa died."

"She what?" He grabbed Robyn's shoulders, forcing her to face him. "You're kidding!"

His sudden movement startled her, but after what she'd been through in the past little while she didn't have the energy to respond. "Her funeral was two days ago. I assumed you knew. How could you *not* know?"

Brad tried to pull her closer, but she blocked him.

"Robyn, I'm sorry."

"It was in all the papers. Where were you?"

Brad didn't answer right away. Robyn was about to walk away when he said, "I had a problem. I couldn't be there with you, and I'm sorry. Please understand."

Under normal circumstances, she might have understood, but today had turned out to be a long way from normal. "What kind of problem keeps you from reading the newspaper, or watching TV?"

"Robyn, don't push me on this. I'm sorry I messed up. I should have been with you, taken you to the funeral. You have to believe me. I wouldn't let you go through something like that alone if I knew," he said, a contrite tone in his voice.

"It's all right. I went to the funeral," Robyn said, hunching her shoulders against the rain that had suddenly started to spit at them.

A dark gleam showed in his eyes. "I suppose Luke Carlisle went with you."

"No, he didn't."

"Why do I not believe you?" he said accusingly, all caring gone from his voice.

Brad's condemnation annoyed Robyn. He always seemed to assume he had the right to control her, to pass judgment on her. "Right now, I don't care what you believe. I want to get out of here."

"I'm sorry, Robyn. I can't seem to do anything right today. I didn't mean to accuse you of anything. I'm just worried about you."

"Brad, I told you. I was out here with Sandy. All I want is

to go home. If you want to help me, take me home." Robyn pulled the hood of her jacket closer around her head and started toward the small parking lot that ran along the ridge above them.

Brad caught up with her. "I'll take you back so you can pack your things and get out of here."

CHAPTER TWENTY

The warmth of the van provided a welcome respite from the chill of the wind as Brad drove out along the narrow track. Robyn shivered in her jacket and rubbed her palms together. The whirling warmth of the van's heater gradually spread across Robyn, pushing away the harsh images of the scene at the lighthouse.

All she wanted was to get safely back to the house and into dry clothes. Once there she'd deal with the potential problem of the press, a problem that now seemed trivial after her experience with Sandy. *Why had she gone with Sandy? And why had she gone with Brad that day down to the Anchorage?* She realized she had acted out of sympathy and guilt, rather than using common sense. She glanced over at Brad and felt guilty about everything in her life. *How had she gotten to this place where guilt drove her to act irrationally?*

Everything would be so much easier if Luke were with her. But her chances of having Luke in her life seemed less with every hour he spent on the mainland. He was a man driven by a need to protect those he loved, and yet he was a police officer who played by the rules, no matter what the personal cost. Hadn't he proven his law-abiding beliefs by sending his wife to prison?

Brad checked the rearview mirror. "Does anyone know where you are?"

Robyn gave him a distracted glance. "I didn't have time to tell anyone."

"You should never have left the house. You should have stayed right there. I'm sure Luke would have advised against you leaving without him."

A thought suddenly blindsided Robyn: She hadn't questioned how it was that Brad knew where she was staying. It was a secret known by very few people, all sworn to keep their silence. *How had Brad found out?* It couldn't have been Alice. It couldn't have been Luke.

It was on the tip of her tongue to ask Brad how he knew where she was staying, but she wanted to get back and away from him a lot more than she needed to know something that he probably wouldn't tell her anyway. Besides, engaging in conversation with Brad could easily end up with him talking longer than it took to drive back to the house and delay her further. All she wanted at that moment was to escape back to the place where she felt safe.

"Brad, I don't want to talk about it."

"So, I screwed up and didn't take you to Lisa's funeral. I've done so much for you, proven time and time again how much you mean to me." Brad pounded his fist into the steering wheel. "Ever since Nathan died, I've been there for you, helping you, waiting——"

"For what? Brad, what are you waiting for?"

Brad roared the van around the sharp turn leading down to the road. The van swung, spitting gravel out behind it. "You can't pretend not to know." He ground the words out.

Brad rolled to a stop in an abandoned driveway and reached for Robyn. "You have to understand."

"Don't do this," Robyn said, her voice warning him off. Determined to keep his advances at bay, Robyn slid toward her door.

"Robyn, what is it? Why are you suddenly so angry at *me?*"

She didn't want a fight, and she sure as hell did not want to be left on the roadside in this weather. "Brad, I've had a bad day. I think we need to cool it."

"Are you coming back with me to the mainland?"

"I have a lot on my plate at the moment. They're still investigating Lisa's death and what really happened. Now, I have Sandy acting weird. I don't need anything else." She planned to go over to the police station office and tell them about Sandy as soon as she got back.

"What has Sandy done?" Brad suddenly became solicitous, his tone one of caring. Robyn began to wonder if bringing up Sandy had been a good idea.

"Get me back to the house, and I'll tell you."

The relief flowed through Robyn as they pulled into the parking lot behind the police office. As she grabbed for the door handle to escape inside, she realized she'd have to satisfy Brad's curiosity or he'd follow her.

"Sandy wanted to warn me. She told me someone wanted to kill me and she said I needed to get out of the country."

"I don't believe it. How would she know anything about what you should or should not do?"

Robyn looked out the window at the smooth blanket of grass running to a line of spruce trees at the back of the police office. "I don't know. That's why I was wondering if she's crazy."

Brad was silent for so long that Robyn finally turned to face him. "Say something."

"I don't think she's crazy. I just can't figure out where she's coming from. A woman who works in a library and seems to have little contact with the rest of the world tells you she knows you're in danger. Maybe she reads too many mystery novels."

"Or, she really does know something. If she doesn't, she's crazy. Why take me out to such a lonely spot?" The stress of the last few hours hit her with the force of a moving train. Because of her blind faith in a friend she'd had a terrifying experience. Whether Sandy was crazy or really trying to warn her, she'd had enough. In future, she would think very carefully before she did anything where her friends were concerned. Tears welled, but she didn't want to cry, not in front of Brad. She wanted the solace of her room in Luke's home.

"Robyn. I should have been there for you today. I should have been at the funeral. You can't imagine how bad I feel."

Robyn heard the ardor in his voice, a warning bell that cleared her thoughts. She moved as far as she could toward the door on her side of the van. "I told you, I don't want to talk about that."

"Talk about what? That you don't care about me? You're overwrought, tired and scared. Nothing is going to look right to you."

"How I feel right now will not change."

"Robyn, don't say that. Not right now. We're more than just friends, and soon I'll be able to show you."

"Show me what?"

"Never mind. You'll understand soon."

What was he talking about? Weariness dogged Robyn's thoughts. "Brad, for the last time, you and I are friends, that's all. I need to go in. I'm expecting to hear from Luke."

Anger glistened in Brad's eyes. "I suppose you think your cop friend will save you?"

Robyn studied Brad for a moment. His stiffened jaw and the anger simmering in his eyes hid little of how he felt. She knew there was no room in her life for what he wanted.

There never had been, never would be. "Brad, I do not plan to die on this island. Luke cares for me and he is doing his best to find out who could be behind all this."

"And you believe him, that he's looking out for you?" he said, his brows arching skeptically.

"Yes."

"I don't want to frighten you, Robyn. God knows, you've been through enough. But what if Officer Carlisle is in on this? He's in the perfect position to control what is investigated, and what's not. Why didn't he find out who fired at you before the gunman was killed? It would have been a hell of a lot easier to catch *him* than it will ever be to get whoever is after you now."

"That's not true."

"Think Robyn. Your trouble didn't start until you came to this island. Remember the night at the Anchorage? We had a hell of a time finding Officer Carlisle when we needed him. Maybe, he had to cover his tracks? Who would know better than a cop how to do that? He might be keeping you from making contact with the authorities, rather than keeping you safe. What if he's the man who's trying to kill you?"

"You're wrong. Luke would never do anything to harm me. I'm not listening to any more of this." She opened the door.

Brad grabbed her arm with a grip that burned. "Harm you?" He snorted. "He's using you." Brad yanked on her arm, pulling her closer to him, anger spilling out with every word. "Your precious police officer may have something to hide."

He tapped her arm, emphasizing his words. "Wake up, Robyn, before you're dead."

The working day was nearly over, and the staff in the Portland office were getting ready to go home. Luke had met with Russell Black. The man explained that he had suspected Robyn of being involved in the disappearance of Nathan Green and Peter McGill. When pressed he didn't have any evidence, a fact that had frustrated him. Russell offered to go over the file with him, but Luke had refused his offer. He wanted to go through it thoroughly and if he had questions he'd call him.

Luke had nearly finished reading the report from the boating accident three years ago. There had been a lot of police hours put into the investigation, including interviews with people along the coastline who might have seen something. Nothing was found to clearly link a suspect to any of it. Russell Black had repeatedly interviewed Robyn, and each time she told the same story. Checks were done on her story, along with an interview with Brad Allen. It was documented that he'd alerted the Coast Guard when they didn't return. The bodies of the two men were never found, and it was assumed they'd been taken out with the tide.

It was very clear that Russell Black suspected Robyn was involved in something illegal, but had no evidence to support his suspicions except that she was the only one found alive, or dead, on the boat. It would seem that Russell Black's suspicions were based on the fact that she couldn't remember anything, and the investigating team didn't believe her.

In Robyn's statement, she said she believed she had been drifting in the sailboat for some time when the Coast Guard found her. The Coast Guard said she'd been incoherent and unable to remember anything. She had been hospitalized for a period, then sent home under a psychiatrist's care.

Luke scanned the list of items found on the boat, and he was relieved to find that no guns were on the list. He knew only too well that it didn't mean there hadn't been any. Other than that, the list seemed pretty typical of equipment and gear found on any sailboat.

He scanned the list one last time... Something *was* missing from the list. A fifty-foot sailboat would need some type of small craft for getting back and forth between the shore and the sailboat. No dinghy was listed on the inventory. It could have been lost during the time Robyn drifted alone on the boat, and the time the coast guard showed up. *Or...*

Luke made a note, and kept reading.

What had a naturalist, a doctor, and a businessman been doing on that boat that resulted in the death of two of them? Or had they fallen overboard in a freak wave? Doubtful, because Peter McGill had been an experienced sailor.

He read on, looking for the explanation the police investigator had come up with. There didn't seem to be one. No weapon was found. The yacht was pristine except for the torn mattress in the main cabin.

Luke's stomach lurched as a thought took shape in his mind. So far, Robyn had told him the truth. What if her flashback of the sound of gunfire and the person lying face down in the water was also true? What if someone fired a gun and killed someone on that boat, and then escaped in the dinghy? But how had the gun gotten into her hands and why was there no residue when they tested her?

Or had someone boarded the boat, killed the two men and – not realizing she was aboard – left the boat to drift out with the tide? Robyn could have witnessed whatever happened...

But why would they try to track her down now? If she had witnessed something criminal or illegal, why wait three years before going after her?

It didn't make sense and that made Luke's gut churn. "Better to be safe than sorry," he muttered, dialing his number. He left a message on the machine for her to call him back and he left the number in the office where he sat, growing more agitated with each passing minute.

Robyn should be at the house. The last time he'd checked with Alice, everything was going well. He called again, and still no answer. He called the office.

Filled with foreboding, he hit redial on his cell phone as he ran from the office into the corridor, narrowly missing Andrew Webb.

"Luke, I checked. No undercover agent on Grand Island. No Amos Potter. We'll get Officer Seymour to pick up the man for questioning."

Bile burned Luke's stomach. "Andrew, I need your help."

"Anything, you know that."

Cursing himself for being such a fool, and for leaving Robyn alone, Luke told Andrew his suspicions.

"I hope you're wrong, but you'd better get back there and see what you can do. I'll get one of the small surveillance planes up."

With his heart beating a tattoo against his chest, Luke made one more attempt to reach Robyn.

"Thanks for the ride." Robyn grabbed the door handle, anxious to escape. She desperately needed to speak to Luke, to tell him what she'd discovered. He would know what to do.

"Not so fast." Brad shut off the engine. "I'm going in with you." His expression was open, without the hardness she had seen earlier. "I want to make sure you're safe."

"I'll be fine."

"I'll be the judge of that." Brad opened his door and got out.

He was driving her nuts with his strange over-protective

behavior, but Robyn didn't worry too much now that he'd brought her to Luke's home. Alice was just next door in the police station.

Sandy's words kept repeating in Robyn's head as she climbed out of the van and walked toward the back entrance of the house. Sandy had to know the gunman. She had taken Robyn to a place that was completely private. *But why would Sandy go to all that trouble and not tell her the killer's name?*

They were approaching the house when Alice ran out through the back door. "Robyn, you're wanted on the phone. It's Luke," she said, tossing an assessing glance in Brad's direction.

Eager to hear his voice, Robyn raced forward, grabbing the phone from Alice. "Luke? Did you find anything?"

"Robyn, are you all right?"

"Sure."

His voice relaxed a little. "I needed to know you're safe."

Robyn needed him so badly her only thought was to keep him on the phone. Any contact to steady her nerves. "Luke, I'm so glad you called. I remembered something."

"Tell me."

Robyn took a deep breath and hoped that what she said would make sense. "We always towed a Zodiac on the back of Peter's sailboat so we could get back and forth from the marina to the boat."

"Yes, I assumed that." There was a guarded quality to his voice.

"I remembered someone trying to pull the Zodiac close to the boat...."

"The report doesn't mention anything about a Zodiac, or any type of dinghy."

"Luke, I don't understand. It would have been there when the Coast Guard brought the boat into the marina."

A long pause stretched across the lines and for a few moments, Robyn feared the connection had broken.

"I don't think there was one attached, honey."

"Well then what happened?"

"I'm checking on that. I'll be back as soon as I can. In the meantime, just do as I ask and stay out of sight. Promise me."

"I promise. Brad's here and he—"

"Brad! What's he doing there?"

"He gave me a drive home. He's—"

"A drive home? Robyn, where did you go?"

"It's a long story. Sandy Fowler invited me out to the lighthouse."

With Luke's protest ringing in her ear, Robyn told him the story, and as carefully as she could, she told him about the warning Sandy had given her.

"Robyn, I can't emphasize this enough. Tell Brad to leave. Get in the house and lock the doors. Talk to no one but Alice. Your life may depend on your behavior in the next few hours. I'll be there as soon as I can."

"Luke, this can't be happening. I'm scared. I'm really scared. How could Sandy have gotten involved in something this awful?"

"I don't know, but I intend to find out. It's going to take a little time, but I'll be there as fast as I can. In the meantime, do exactly what Alice tells you to do."

"I will Luke, I will," she murmured, wishing with all her heart that he was there with her in that moment.

"Good girl," he said, his tone softening for the first time in the conversation.

A terrible loneliness, followed by raw fear, washed over Robyn. "Luke, please hurry."

"I'm on my way. Just remember to stay out of sight. Put Alice back on, will you?" His question was an order and Luke was back to sounding like a cop.

Robyn passed the phone back.

Robyn and Brad stood at the back door of the police station. His hard stare never left her face as he continued the argument he had started several minutes ago. Brad was determined to come in with her. She was equally determined that he leave.

"Please go." Robyn stood with her back to the door, ready to do battle with Brad. "Luke will be here soon. He says I'm to stay in the house alone and wait for him."

A ripple of dread slid through her. She had forgotten to ask what Luke had found.

"Robyn." Brad rested his hand on the doorframe just above her shoulder. "You and I have to talk. So, if I can't come in with you, we'll do it out here."

The intensity of his stare forced Robyn to break eye contact. "Whoever is after me is not going to get away with it. Luke found something." Her words sounded steadier than the emotion driving them.

"What? Did he say what he'd found?"

"No, he didn't."

"Robyn, do you believe I'm involved?"

"No!"

"Well, you're sure as hell acting as if you do."

Robyn searched his face, the set of his jaw. *Was he involved?* She had never asked him. She'd only ever been thankful that he'd told the Coast Guard where to search.... "Brad, why did you take me to the Anchorage?"

It was his turn to drop eye contact. Robyn had her answer. "Luke was right. You took me out there, knowing the killer waited--"

"Get inside, now!" Alice demanded as she ended the call with Luke.

Thankful for the interruption, Robyn pushed the door open.

Alice stepped in front of Brad. "Leave. Now."

Brad stepped around Alice. "Robyn, that's not true. It would never be true. I took you there to settle something between us, so we could get on with our lives."

"Settle something. I could have been killed!"

"No! Robyn, do you remember when you were found on the boat?"

"It's all I've thought about in the last few days."

"Something happened out there, something we know you don't remember."

"Brad!" At the limits of her endurance, she pushed him away from her. "You know how hard it's been for me. If you know something, tell me!"

"I can't tell you anything, right now." He lowered his voice. "I promise you, if you will just be patient, I'll soon be able to put your mind at ease about a whole lot of things."

"Like what? Tell me."

"I meant what I said before. Luke may not be who he seems." Brad took a deep breath and rifled his fingers through his hair. "It's the only explanation. Think about it, Robyn. Why is this happening? I did a little checking. Luke worked on the special drug squad before he was dumped into this job. He may have gone over--"

Alice moved in on Brad. "Leave now, or I'll arrest you."

Brad's eyes switched from Alice to Robyn. "You've lost your objectivity on this."

She had let people like Brad push her around all her life, starting with her father. "Get lost! Get out of my life. Your theory about Luke is crazy. And you're crazy!"

"Robyn!"

"I mean it. I've wanted to say this for so long. Years of you haunting my every step, interfering in everything I did.

Always wanting to know what was going on in my life. I must have been out of my mind to let you get away with it. I don't want you in my life anymore. Do you understand?"

Alice's voice was deadly calm. "Move away. Get in your vehicle and leave."

Brad's expression was one of shocked disbelief as he stepped away from her.

The old guilt of thinking she'd hurt someone swarmed around her, but she forced it back. She'd finally said what she really thought. And it felt so good.

"Robyn, you can't mean it. We've been friends for years. I've done everything I could to make you happy. And I have so many plans for us."

"Get it through your head. *There is no us.* And I don't believe you anymore when you say you wouldn't hurt me. Luke believes you took me to the Anchorage so that the killer could get another opportunity to shoot me. And like a fool I defended you when Luke tried to accuse you of being involved in the attacks against me."

Brad's angry glance swept her from head to foot. "You're falling for the bastard." His words rang with accusation.

Robyn knew the complete truth of his words. She did love Luke. Brad's voice slipped to a whisper, his gaze sweeping the space around them. "Robyn, we need to get away from here and back home where you'll be safe."

She backed toward the door as a flash of insight quieted her mind. For the first time, Robyn knew without a moment's doubt what home meant to her. It meant being with Luke. That realization gave her heart permission to believe in the impossible.

"Brad, I *am* home."

. . .

Exhaustion gnawed at Robyn as she climbed the steps to her bedroom, one step at a time. The hem of her silk nightdress snagged on her foot, nearly knocking her forward. The glass of milk she held in her hand sloshed dangerously near the rim. She'd checked every window and door. Alice had checked around the outside, and was sitting in the corridor between the house and the office, her gun on her lap. And Luke would arrive soon.

Still, Sandy's words hung in her mind. *Was the gunman someone from her past, someone she had known? Why had Sandy warned her to get as far away as possible?*

Or, was Sandy as crazy as she'd seemed? Robyn's thoughts matched the back and forth movement of the milk in her glass. At the top of the stairs, she turned toward her room. She'd taken a bath to help her relax, and a glass of milk to help her sleep. But what she really needed was to have Luke's arms around her.

Passing Luke's bedroom, she peeked in. Everything was in order, so soothing to the jumbled state of her mind. She felt drawn to the calmness the room offered, and again felt the longing that had been with her so vividly these past hours. *Why not fall asleep in his bed?*

She entered his room, put the glass down on his night table and lay back on the bed. His scent was on the pillow and an overwhelming sense of his presence surrounded her. It was as if he were in the room.

Needing to feel close to him, she pulled back the covers and crawled between the crisp cotton sheets. The residual scent of Luke's aftershave clung to the cotton fibers as she hugged Luke's pillow to her. Luke would come home to her, and when he did, she would be waiting in his bed. A feeling of contentment settled over her, easing her toward sleep....

. . .

A little later the muffled squishing of sneakers on hardwood drifted toward her. Somewhere the floor creaked. Robyn nestled into the pillow, was content that Luke would soon enter the room. Her body stirred, lighting the slow fire of anticipation.

Another muffled sound, this time just outside the bedroom. Groggy with sleep, Robyn opened her eyes, but saw no one. The LCD display on the clock read 9:15 pm. The rest of the room huddled in darkness, except for the filtered light of the window that faced the backyard.

Robyn stretched and moved to the other side of the bed, expecting Luke to ease down on the side of the bed, and wrap his arms around her. "Hi," she whispered into the darkness. "I've missed you." She pulled back the covers.

The sound of shattering glass echoed through the upstairs hall.

CHAPTER TWENTY-ONE

Terror rode Robyn's spine like a charging buffalo. Something had smashed against the wall in the bedroom across the hall. *Her bedroom.* Robyn's fingers trembled on the keypad of the phone as she punched in the police station number. The ringing beep of the phone continued as she listened for the intruder. The answering machine came on, giving instructions on how to reach the officer on duty. The mechanical voice gave a number. With her mind focused on reaching Alice, she dialed the cell number, her hands trembling so much she could hardly be sure she'd hit the right keys.

No answer. *Where was Alice?*

Easing the phone back onto its cradle, Robyn held her breath and listened. The house stood deathly still.

An overpowering urge to scream filled her mind as Robyn tried to control her panic long enough to come up with a way to escape. If she could make it out of Luke's bedroom and down the stairs without being spotted by the intruder....

Forcing her fear to the back of her mind, she eased out of

the bed, praying that she made no sound as she tiptoed out of the room. Without looking back, she crept toward the stairs.

Clinging to the railing, she slithered downstairs toward the door that connected the house to the police station. Weak with relief, she reached to pull the locks, but they were already undone.

She stopped, listening for the intruder. *Had she made a mistake? Had it been Luke she heard coming up the stairs? Was he in her bedroom now, looking for her?*

But Luke would never have left the connecting door unlocked.

With her heart pounding in her ears, she opened the door and stepped out into the corridor. Her feet bumped up against something soft.

She reached down. Her hands came in contact with someone's head. She jerked her hand back.

Overcome with fear she fell to her knees. In the dim light of the back corridor, she could make out the silent form of Alice Seymour. Instinctively, she checked the officer's carotid for a pulse. Nothing.

Oh God! She glanced around frantically, trying to think of an option, any option that would get her to safety. There was a police suburban parked near the boat trailer. If she could find the keys and get to it, she might be able to run.

Keys. The keys had to be somewhere easy to find. Cautiously, she stepped over the body and moved toward the office. Scanning the wall behind the desk, she saw two sets of keys. She grabbed both.

Out the back way was the fastest, but it meant going past the dead body of Alice Seymour. Swallowing against the terror and fear welling up in her, Robyn made her way back past the body, past the door and was about to unlock the door to the backyard when she heard it.

The soft tread of someone moving behind her, coming along the hall, coming closer to her with every footfall.

Crushing the keys in her fist, she eased open the door. With one quick glance over her shoulder, Robyn stepped into the darkness. Edging along the building, she saw the Suburban only feet away from her. Moving as quickly as she dared, she crossed the paved drive with seconds to go before she reached the big SUV. She glanced toward the back of the house.

Two men were standing together, their yellow rain slickers fastened tightly against the rain. She watched as the glow of a cigar lit a spot near the man's face. In slow motion, he raised his head and looked straight at her.

The face swam before her eyes, weaving the fabric of her memory into a nightmare.

Safe arms held her close as the world rocked around her. Peter's arms. Slowly the wave of consciousness reached her mind, and she lifted her head from the comforting chest on which it rested. "Peter?"

The arms holding her tightened. "Robyn, lie still. You're safe with me." Brad's voice wafted down to her as her stomach threatened to rise into her throat.

The bone-chilling air and the sound of water rushing over the hull of a boat cleared her mind. She was on a boat with Brad, headed God knew where. Yet she'd been in Luke's room, hadn't she? Her mind fought for control of the memory fragments floating freely in her mind.

She'd made it out of the house, out past the dead body of the police officer.

Robyn forced her way out of Brad's arms, and sat up. "Brad, where are we going?" The speed of the boat drove the wind into her face.

"We're on the way to the yacht."

"What yacht?"

"You'll see."

Fear hung in the air like icicles. "How did I get here?"

The last thing she remembered was seeing someone's face, and she had been outside dressed only in her nightie. Her fingers skirted her body. She had a jacket on over her jeans, a turtle neck sweater. Her feet were in her...*sneakers?*

Someone had dressed her while she was unconscious.

"Stay still. You fainted." Brad reached to restrain her.

Had she? She wasn't sure. "What are we doing?" She pushed forward off the seat and stood up.

Brad reached for her, but she stepped away from him and clutched the railing.

"I have to go back to the house. I have to talk to the police." She steadied herself against the undulating movement of the boat, searching her mind for what it was she had to tell the police.

"Robyn, sit down before you fall down."

A memory flashed. A face. "We have to get out of here."

"Sit down, Robyn."

Frantically, she clung to the rail of the open powerboat as it slammed across the dark waves. "Brad, help me, please."

"I'm taking you where you'll be safe. We can't trust Luke." Brad glanced toward the cabin of the boat, as if he expected someone to appear.

Luke filled her mind, warmed her, gave her courage to think past the fear tearing at her soul, the dark, nameless horror that possessed her. Luke would be on his way to her. He'd said so. She could trust him – with her life.

"That's not true."

Brad stood up and put his hand on Robyn's arm. "Come back and sit down with me. You don't have to worry. Everything is going to be just fine. You'll see. Remember, I said I wanted to help you settle something in your life? So you can move on?" His words whistled past her, caught in the rush of air created by the fast moving boat.

"Help me settle something? Brad, what are you talking about?"

For a fleeting moment, Robyn considered trying to enlist the help of the stranger driving the powerful boat. As quickly as the idea formed, she dropped it. The stiff set of his shoulders told Robyn to look elsewhere.

"Brad, we have to get back to shore. Please," she begged, fighting back the fear pressing hard against her chest.

As she waited for Brad to speak, she offered a silent prayer that Luke had returned and discovered her missing. "You won't get away with this. Luke's on his way home."

"What the officer wants is not the issue. I've waited much longer, so has someone else. We're leaving tonight. Everything had been done to make your disappearance seem normal... Expected."

The triumphant gleam in Brad's eyes confirmed her worst fears. All trace of her disappearance had been wiped away; some story would be told to cover her absence. No one would check until it was too late.

"Who are we going to see?" Her words bounced from her lips as the boat abruptly lost speed. She braced her feet against the slowing of the boat and looked up at the large white yacht coming toward her.

"You'll know soon enough." Brad took her arm, holding her against him. The boat moved into position beside a set of stairs leading up the side of a yacht.

Without a word, he pushed her ahead of him. Robyn moved as slowly as she could up the narrow steps as her mind raced over the possibilities. Someone was waiting for her, someone Brad knew well. The boat below was her only chance of escape, but the crewman was still at the controls, preventing any chance to get away.

Jumping was out of the question because the yacht was in the way, and Brad would simply come into the water after her. If she could convince Brad they had to go back, that he was in danger as well... One quick look at his face told her that Brad was intent on getting up the stairs.

With defeat nagging at her, Robyn moved up the stairs and onto the open deck of a yacht. Without breaking stride, Brad walked her over to an open door leading into a large room redolent with deep gold carpeting, mahogany paneling and crystal fixtures.

The lilting harmony of a piano concerto filled the air. Subdued lighting created a sense of warmth and intimacy. The opulence of the boat's salon did nothing to ease Robyn's fear as she entered the room and glanced around.

"I hope you like what you see."

The familiar voice slid over her raw nerves with bladelike accuracy, nicking and tearing at her heart as it went. She swung around, her eyes searching for its owner.

Except for longer hair, the carefully trimmed beard and a scar running down the side of his face, the man looked the same. "Nathan."

"Hi honey. It's nice to see you again." His clear gaze and snake-cold eyes made his endearment a lie.

Robyn gripped the arm of the nearest chair as she slid down into its cool leather cushions. "Nathan, I don't understand--"

Her eyes sought Brad's face for confirmation of what was happening.

Brad smiled at her, as if he found some pleasure in her disbelief.

As he watched her, Nathan's long fingers wrapped

around his silver lighter. "It's quite simple. I'm here and you're here."

Robyn struggled to connect the man before her with her memories from the past – of the man she had planned to marry. She glanced at Brad but his expression was one of smug approval. Luke had been right all along. Brad was in this up to his rotten neck.

The shaking started in the pit of her stomach and rapidly made its way up into her chest and arms. With iron determination, Robyn bit down on her lower lip and buried her fists in her lap to control their trembling. "What is going on?" she asked them.

This time when Nathan spoke he came and stood in front of her, his arrogance spewing from every part of him. "Let's just say you and I have a little unfinished business."

"You didn't die...."

She groped to find meaning in what her mind could barely comprehend. "But, you and Peter both died––"

"Peter died, that's true. I, on the other hand, did not." He gave her another one of his glib smiles. "But, Robyn, let's not dwell on the past, shall we? You know the old saying: What's over is over."

In a dreamlike state, Robyn followed the movement of Nathan's hands as he touched the lighter to the tip of the cigar he held between his fingers. In that second she saw another man with a beard and a cap pulled down low over his face. "You were in Harper's Cove."

"Yes, I watched you. I had no choice after the debacle on the marsh. Stupid man! And I paid good money for his services."

Was he saying he sent that animal after her? That couldn't be right. Nathan might have changed into someone she didn't know, but a murderer? No....

Robyn stared at him, trying to find some hint of the

loving Nathan she had known behind the cunning smile, the smooth façade. She saw only a man with cruelty inscribed on all his features.

For years she had waited and prayed that this man – standing so arrogantly in front of her – was alive. She had grieved for him, held his memory close to her heart. She had believed that she was responsible for that night on the sail-boat, that night that had altered her life forever.

How could she have loved him? Why hadn't she seen his arro-gance, or any hint of what lay hidden under his smoothness? Why had she not seen him for what he was? What had made her so naïve? There had to be an explanation.

"Nathan, what happened to Peter?"

"Your beloved brother found out what I do for a living. He had the nerve to tell me to stop, as if I'd listen to a geek like him! He threatened to tell you. I could handle you, if he tried to tell you anything – you always were such a gullible woman, so easily led by all those noble notions of yours. But what really got Peter in trouble was when he threatened to go to the police. I had no choice but to stop him."

Her brother and Nathan had been friends. "Stop him?"

"Who else do you think did it?"

She couldn't get her mind around what Nathan was saying. "*You* killed Peter?"

"Yes, we were standing in the cockpit of his cherished sailboat. He was yelling at me, telling me I had no right to you. That I was a common criminal."

"You shot him," Robyn said, as if in a trance as a chunk of memory floated menacingly close. She had heard them argue in the aft cabin, had seen them tearing into one another, stumbling up the companionway, each scrambling to get a stronger grip on the other.

She had screamed at them to stop.

"I saw you go up the stairs together. I watched you slam

my brother's head against the steering wheel, pull a gun from somewhere behind you." The nightmare of blood on her hands bloomed in her mind. She glanced up at him, at his confident stance, while she remained pinned by the memory of what this evil man had done, the man she had once loved.

Then, she remembered waking up in the boat, going down the steps, finding the cabin torn to pieces...

And here they were on the water again. Nathan was alive and well, while Peter had died a horrible death at the hands of a man he thought was a friend. Despite her fear and loathing for Nathan, Robyn asked, "How did you get off the boat?"

"The Zodiac, of course," said Nathan, contempt in his voice. "You see, my little accident allowed me to start a whole new life. A life you have the power to ruin if you recognized me."

The man standing before her gave a laugh filled with loathing, shaking Robyn to the core. "Ruin you? I didn't know you were alive," she said.

Nathan's stare was cold, heartless. "You saw me on the ferry, the car deck. Remember?"

A sinking feeling spread through Robyn. "I saw a man, but the light blocked me from seeing his face."

"Don't lie to me! I saw you meet the police officer at the top of the steps. You told him what you'd seen on the car deck."

"I did not. Meeting the police officer was a complete accident."

Anger twisted the scar on Nathan's face. "You mean to tell me you had no idea who I was? You didn't recognize me at all?"

Robyn stared at him. "No, I didn't expect to ever see you again. I never saw your face. It was hidden.... I thought you were dead."

Nathan stared at her, a shocked look on his face. "I went through all this, risked my neck for nothing. Well, for God's sake. All this for--" He shrugged, and exchanged glances with Brad. "I can't change the past. Sooner or later, you would have remembered."

Brad stepped forward, his hand moving protectively to Robyn's shoulders. "It's going to be all right, Robyn. You'll see."

Brad was involved in this plot to kill her, just as Luke had suspected. Her pent-up anger suddenly found an outlet. "Don't touch me! Don't ever come near me again. Was this the surprise you were talking about? So you alerted the Coast Guard because you're the one who knew what Nathan was up to. You wanted the yacht found because you knew I was on it. You miserable excuse for a human being!"

"Nathan." Brad's voice carried uncertainty tinged with disbelief. "Tell her about Peter. How Peter was a member of the Russian Mafia. How you killed him in self-defense--"

"That's a lie, Brad! How stupid can you be?"

Pleasure highlighted Nathan's face. "Oh, Robyn. Showing righteous indignation, are we? Defending your wimp brother?" He laughed as he took another drag on the cigar. "Brad, I have to agree with Robyn. You are stupid."

Brad stuttered. "I-I don't understand. You told me—"

Nathan stopped in mid-exhale, his eye boring into Brad's face. "Stay out of this."

Nathan turned his attention back to Robyn. "As I said, my accident was my creation, a way to disappear for a while. The depth of the Bay of Fundy provided the perfect cover story – body presumed lost at sea and all that. On the other hand, your disappearance will be real."

Brad sat down in the chair across from Robyn. "Nathan, don't do this. You don't mean it. You said you wanted to see Robyn, to explain--"

"If you interrupt me one more time, you'll be gone. Understand?"

Robyn watched the two men, her mind flying from one option to another. The man she'd loved was gone; the man standing before her was a killer. She couldn't waste time on the reasons, or the consequences. Brad was part of Nathan's plan, whether he liked it or not.

Nathan intended to kill her, just as he'd killed Peter. If she didn't think of something soon, she'd be dead. She wanted to run, and to do that she had to be standing. "I need a drink."

She got up and moved rapidly to the bar, noting that her sudden movement caught Nathan off guard. She picked up a crystal glass and slopped what smelled like brandy into its glistening depths. Clutching the bar for support, Robyn tried to organize her fear-clogged thoughts. To make her rush to the bar look legitimate, she took a sip. The burn of the brandy seared her throat. Her grip tightened on the honed edges of the crystal. What a fool she had been. She had once loved Nathan, had planned to marry him…and now he was going to kill her.

"It's hard liquor, now, is it?" Nathan slid his fingers down her back, teasing the sensitive skin along her spine, the same way he'd once done when she'd thought they were in love.

She tensed, suppressing a gag. His revolting behavior gave her the strength to develop her plan. Whether it worked would be a matter of luck. Robyn clutched the edge of the bar as if she were about to faint. "Nathan, I need air. I'm going to be sick." She didn't have to fake the queasiness.

"Not now. We have business to discuss." He reached for the decanter of brandy.

While he was busy pouring himself a drink, she decided she might have time to escape. Seizing the moment, she dashed to the door.

Nathan moved behind her with snakelike speed, his iron

grip closing over her injured arm. A sickening wave of pain rose from her arm to her shoulder. She smothered a scream.

"Nathan, take your hands off her, right this minute. What the hell is wrong with you?" Brad's voice rose in anger. "Whatever undercover work you're doing for the government doesn't include hurting Robyn. Let go of her."

Nathan glared at Brad. "You were as easy to fool as Robyn." Nathan's glare swerved back to Robyn. His eyes bored into hers, his hot cigar-drenched breath cascaded over her face.

In that moment, she felt an overpowering urge to wrap her hands around his throat and squeeze. She hated him with every ounce of her being. Yet she never let her eyes shift away as she matched his stare.

He had killed Peter. He deserved to die.

Without loosening his grip on her arm, Nathan turned away from her and faced Brad. "I guess it's over between us. You were a big help Brad, and I want to thank you for getting Robyn to come to the Anchorage to meet me. You had no idea that Nadia was there, waiting to stop Leo. Letting Nadia in on what was happening was my mistake. Let's just say that her days as a librarian are over."

Brad ignored Nathan, his pleading gaze locked on Robyn. "I'm sorry. Oh God, I'm sorry. I had no idea. I'll make it up to you, Robyn. I promise--"

Nathan pulled a long slender gun from his pocket and aimed it at Brad's chest.

His movement was so fast, so unexpected, Robyn had no time to react. *"No! Nathan, don't!"*

Robyn heard a sound like corn popping, and Brad fell to the carpet, blood oozing from his throat.

"Oh no!" Robyn cried in horror. Heedless of Nathan, the gun he held, or the damage he could inflict, Robyn wrenched her arm free and knelt beside Brad.

Even as she searched for a pulse, she knew he was dead.

Shock jackknifed through her, taking all feeling with it. She had no time to mourn the loss of Brad. The bastard standing over her, waiting for her to stand up, had killed both men in cold blood. She had no defense against the sure knowledge that she was next on his list. She could identify him. That's why the gunman had been hired to kill her. Nathan's orders.

Robyn bought a little time by keeping her head down and her fingers resting gently on Brad's neck as she frantically searched for options. She was trapped on Nathan's yacht with no one to help her. She might gain a little time if she could hide somewhere onboard, but it wouldn't be enough, unless there was someone to help her.

Luke seemed a lifetime away.

Her only chance of survival rested with the faint possibility she could get out on deck. What she would do when she got there, if she did, wasn't clear. The one clear thought she had was that she would rather attempt to escape than die as Brad had.

Inhaling all the air her lungs could hold, Robyn eased to a standing position. When she focused on Nathan, it was as if nothing had happened. His lips held his smile in an eerie grimace. His eyes were cold. The gun had vanished. "Robyn, I'm sorry about Brad. I really am. He--"

"Nathan, I'm going to be sick." Racing for the open door of the cabin, she made it to the railing of the yacht before he grabbed her.

"You get back here," Nathan hissed in her ear. "I'm not finished with you."

He was too late to stop the deluge of bile and brandy that flushed past her lips.

"For God's sake!" Nathan let go of her and moved out of range.

Robyn leaned over the rail and let the sickness come. Sick for Peter, for Lisa and for Brad. Sick for all the time she had grieved for a monster. Sick for all the time she had spent feeling guilty about not being able to remember; for all the time she'd believed she might have killed someone. As she stood there, clinging to the rail, some part of her mind took note of the fact that Nathan had backed away from her, maybe even far enough for her to climb over the rail and fall into the sea....

As the retching eased, Robyn assessed her chances; a leap into the dark water – the one thing she feared more than anything...other than certain death.

The choice was surprisingly easy. Clutching the rail beneath her body, she moved her weight forward onto the balls of her feet.

The pointed roundness of something cold and unyielding, rammed into her back. "Don't even think about it." Nathan laughed as he nudged the nose of the gun harder into her ribs. "You'd be dead before you hit the water."

While time stood suspended, they faced each other. The speculative grin on Nathan's face made Robyn's thoughts spiral out of control as her life unraveled before her.

Desperate thoughts plunged through her mind, wrestling with the dying hope that she might be able to reason with the man she had once loved. Nathan had deceived her and used her for his own ends – ends she still didn't understand – and she had been too blind to see. Had been too easily swayed by a man who appeared to be so attentive to her for all those months she'd been engaged to him. Seeing him now as he really was seemed almost beyond belief.

"Step over here." Nathan's words formed shards of ice in the air between them.

Robyn walked toward him, her mind focusing on the ember of an idea....

"I don't have time for your worthless attempts to get away. I want you back in the salon."

"Nathan, I feel better out here. I might be sick again." She prayed the uncertain light would prevent a close examination of her face. Until now, Robyn had blocked out the pain and the horror of the memory that had been buried inside her mind. Suddenly, everything came crashing in on top of her; every lousy, horror-filled memory swirled in kaleidoscope formation, slashing her mind and heart.

"You sick bastard. You shot my brother." Her voice rose from her stomach, bringing all the agony of the memory with it.

"I had to. Your brother overheard me making a call."

"You pulled out a gun." She held her hand toward him, the memory pulling her forward. "You pushed Peter off the boat and then you shot him while he was helpless in the water." The horror of those last moments of Peter's life bubbled up in her. Her head ached, her vision faltered.

"So, my lovely, you do remember. Tell me what happened next?"

"You grabbed me by the shoulder." She reached upward to touch the spot. Her glance swerved to his face. "You forced the gun into my hands. I fell backward."

"I wanted to see if you'd dare to use it on me." He watched her with a look of inquisitiveness on his face. "You didn't. You passed out. The gun joined your brother in the water. I left on the Zodiac. Twenty minutes later I was a free man."

All the months of agony she'd suffered over the loss of Peter, over her fear that she was responsible for what had happened, collided with the sure knowledge that the man standing before her had committed an unspeakable act – and he was without remorse.

Out of her fear and loathing came the urgent need to show him she wasn't going to give in to his intimidation. She squared her shoulders and matched his stare. "You disgusting, worthless excuse for a man."

Nathan raised his arm to strike.

A form moved behind him.

CHAPTER TWENTY-TWO

Sandy Fowler stepped out of the shadows. "Nathan, what are you doing?"

Nathan's shoulders lifted as he turned to face her. "Nadia, honey, go back to the cabin. I won't be long."

"Don't order me around. I'm not your servant, not anymore." Sandy limped slightly as she moved forward.

"Nadia, do as I say. Now."

"You said you loved me. You said if I helped you, changed my name, took a job as librarian, waited for you, we could go away together."

"Nadia, not now. You hear me?"

Sandy laughed, and the sound beat a tattoo of hope along Robyn's shoulders.

"Nathan, I've loved you for so long," the woman Nathan called Nadia, said. "I'd do anything for you."

"Nadia, can't you see I'm busy?"

"Really? Does our boss know what you're busy with? Isotopes? Making a profit and not sharing it?"

A muscle jumped under the scar on Nathan's cheek. "How did you find out about that?"

"Up until the instant I learned you'd brought her here...." She nodded in Robyn's direction, "I was even willing to help you with your little side deal. Not anymore." Sandy pulled a gun from her pocket and pointed it at Nathan. "You told me not to trust anyone. You'll be pleased to know I'm finally listening."

For an instant, fear chased panic across Nathan's face. And for one fleeting moment the hardness in his eyes gave way to something gentler as his gaze locked on Robyn.

For one long second, something resembling regret slid across his features before being replaced with a hard stare that made his scar stand out in stark relief against his pale skin. He turned to face Sandy. "Nadia, what do you want?"

"Have you forgotten that you moved our boss and his bodyguard onto the island a couple of nights ago?"

"No, of course I haven't."

"I'm awaiting confirmation that they arrived in Milwaukee. I'm going to join them. Are you coming with me?"

"There's been a change in plans."

Sandy's voice was low and soothing. "You'd prefer someone else, is that it? Someone without an obvious disability? Someone beautiful."

He nodded.

Sandy's eyes snapped with anger, her hand tightened on the gun. "You're not going to make a fool of me anymore."

"It doesn't matter now," Nathan said.

"It does too. I won't let you harm Robyn. I saved her from Leo." She glanced at Robyn. "I overheard you and the police officer talking about you remembering the missing finger, and I knew it was Leo who tried to kill you. I would never have let Leo Lord hurt you that night at the Anchorage. You were a good friend. He was an awful man."

Robyn felt her panic subside a little as an idea took hold

in her mind. "Thank you, Sandy. I really appreciate you helping me, and warning me."

"Warning her? What the hell is that about?" Nathan glared at Sandy.

"You were going to hurt her. I couldn't let you do that. You promised me that when this was all over, when your cargo was safely delivered, you and I would go away."

"Yeah, I did say that," Nathan said, his voice low, his words spoken with quiet force.

A suspicious frown formed on Sandy's face. "Well, I'm staying right here with you, until I know what it is you want with Robyn."

Robyn saw Nathan's hand slither up the edge of his jacket as he coolly observed Sandy, his voice holding a vicious threat. "Nadia, for the last time, go below."

"No. I love you, Nathan. I'm staying right here. Say what you have to say to Robyn, then let her go."

What was Sandy trying to do? Nathan would kill them both.

"You heard what I said. I'm not going to repeat myself." Nathan stepped one step closer to Sandy, making him one step farther away from Robyn.

Robyn blocked their heated words from her mind. Things were escalating to an argument that would end in at least one more death.

Glancing sideways, Robyn measured off the distance to the railing. It was her only hope. If she waited until they were deeply entrenched in their fight, she might have a chance. But once she started for the railing, she would be committed. Hesitation would mean certain death.

Her body tensed as her mind raced through the moves she would have to make to clear the railing and fall. Heart-numbing fear mushroomed in her like the impending threat of a twister headed in her direction.

A low rumbling sound filled the silence of the night.

"What's that?" Nathan focused his sharp gaze toward the source.

"It's a power boat and it's moving this way," Sandy said, disinterest in her voice.

As Nathan moved to the rail, Robyn stood transfixed, unable to grasp the idea that she might have been given a chance to live. Maybe Luke had come home and found her missing. *If he started a search, would it have led him here? What would Nathan do if he thought the boat closing on the yacht was a police boat?*

Nathan wouldn't give up without a fight. A fight he could rig in his favor – if he had a hostage.

As if he read her thoughts, Nathan turned to her, a deadly smile on his face. "Did you do this? Did you send someone looking for you?"

"No, how could I?" she offered, watching as a new surge of fear wrapped around her heart. The erratic movement of a light on the approaching vessel indicated how quickly it was closing the distance on the rough water.

Could she do it? Could she bring herself to fall straight down into the deep, dark water?

Her fear of water rose in her throat like the tide, hampering her ability to breathe. The old feeling of suffocation clutched her chest. The thought of water closing over her, a body sinking....

Peter had died that way. Peter, her only brother, and Jason's father, had died because he'd tried to save her from Nathan.

It was now or never. Closing her mind to the danger, she raced to the railing and scrambled over it.

"Stop her!" Nathan yelled.

With heart-stopping slowness, Robyn clung to the rail. Sucking in all the air her lungs could hold, she let go. The night-blackened water reached up to welcome her.

A shot rang out. Robyn waited for the sting of the bullet.

The image of Alice Seymour's dead body made Luke push the throttle full forward. The answering roar of the twin outboards as the Zodiac crashed over the waves added to the anger coursing through his body. Someone had killed Alice in cold blood, and taken Robyn.

He hadn't waited for the other police boat or the Coast Guard. They'd found Amos Potter, and he'd offered up the location of the yacht and the fact that Nathan Green was on it. But getting the information had taken time they couldn't afford. He had to reach the yacht, or everything he ever wanted in his life would be gone.

Either Robyn was on the yacht at anchor about a mile off White's Point, or he was out of options. Amos had disclosed Nathan's alias – Roberto Costello was the owner of the yacht.

Andrew and he had learned the identity of the yacht owner only minutes before they'd reached Grand Island. The son of a bitch was an international smuggler who had used several aliases to disguise his activities.

Seeing Nathan stand trial would be one event Luke wouldn't want to miss.

Luke knew that if Robyn were on the yacht, she had to know by now that Nathan was alive. His chest tightened, thinking about how much of a shock Nathan's sudden appearance would have caused her.

His mind went back over the past few hours when he arrived at the house to find Alice dead. He'd never forget the sight of his partner's lifeless body, but finding Robyn's torn nightgown in the corner of her room had been the worst moment of his life. He had to fight hard not to give in to the fear that she'd met the same fate as Alice. The only hope he had was that if Nathan had her, he would not kill her, at least not until he'd gotten what he'd wanted from her. The question was this: What exactly did Nathan want from Robyn?

Once again cursing his stupidity at not taking Robyn with him when he went to the mainland, he'd taken the Zodiac and headed out from Harper's Cove. And now he was only minutes away from discovering if his hunch was right. The lights of the yacht drew nearer as he accelerated across the choppy water.

He considered boarding the yacht if backup didn't arrive. What if they were about to pull anchor and get under way? Without a search warrant there would be little or nothing he could do if the owner refused to allow him on board.

Luke slowed the Zodiac as he neared the yacht and switched off the lights. A sudden movement focused his attention. Someone stood near the rail. He saw the slim silhouette of a woman....

As quickly as possible, he angled the Zodiac closer to the yacht. There was a sudden movement on the deck above them. He cut the engine.

Why in hell hadn't he gotten here sooner? If anything happened to Robyn....

Helpless to do anything but wait, Luke watched in stunned silence as the woman moved to the outside edge of the railing; she leaned down toward him. It had to be Robyn. "Jump. You can do it," he said, his words punctuated by the smack of water along the side of the Zodiac. Grabbing a paddle, he angled the boat sideways and yanked off his jacket, ready to dive in after her. His heart slammed into his throat as he watched the woman he loved drop off the side of the yacht, her body speeding toward the roiling water.

Robyn fell straight down, her body receding into the depths, leaving only a small break in a choppy wave.

Luke dove and swam to the spot where Robyn had gone

under. Grabbing air, he dived straight down. With no light to guide him, he swam deeper, searching the murky water with his hands, swinging his arms in wide arcs, hoping to touch her.

Aware that the impact of the water would have knocked the air from her lungs, he swung his arms through a wider arc as he angled deeper. The quiet of the water stood in direct contrast to the raging fear in his heart. His lungs were bursting when wispy strands of hair touched his fingers. Swimming faster, he reached for her, his fingers making contact with her face.

Luke, his lungs screaming now, pulled her to him then, kicking the water to gain momentum, he shot upward.

The two of them broke the surface of the water just as the Coast Guard patrol unit rounded the end of the yacht. Gasping for air, he and Robyn bobbed together, holding each other, completely unaware of the rush of armed men headed for the stairs leading up to the yacht and the people on board.

Luke held her face in his hands, his heart banging against his chest wall at the look of stark terror in her eyes. "Robyn, you're safe."

He held her gently, with a steadiness that disguised his own fear. The woman he loved had come close to death. Without her, his life held little meaning. Never again would he go through this type of situation. He wanted a life for the two of them, away from the vagaries of police work and criminals. Whatever it took, he would find a way to have a life that allowed them both to be happy.

The rumble of an engine, the sound of Andrew Webber's voice, made Luke glance up. "Let's get her on board," Andrew yelled over the roar of the of the twin outboards.

"Wrap your arms around my neck," Luke said as he felt the frantic beat of her heart against his hands. Resisting the urge to crush her to him, he swam with her to the police boat.

With infinite tenderness, Luke helped her up the ladder. Once on board, he carried her in his arms to the front of the boat.

"Robyn, it's all over," he said, nodding his relief to the helmsman.

"Luke," she choked the word out. "I've been shot." Robyn huddled in the circle of his arms, her teeth chattering against the cold, her eyes wide with shock.

The reality of her words cut through him. "Where?"

"I'm not sure. Nathan fired at me as I went over the side of the boat."

Luke rocked her gently in his arms. He couldn't ask her anything about Nathan without hurting her, and he would never hurt her again. To reassure himself that she wasn't injured, Luke scanned her shaking body, looking for traces of blood. "I don't see anything." He wrapped a couple of police-issue blankets around Robyn.

Luke wanted to believe what he saw, that she was safe with him and there was no injury – no visible injury at least. But he knew Robyn had to be suffering terribly after the shock of the past few hours. But none of that mattered at that moment. She was here with him. "You don't know how afraid I was when I saw you jump."

Robyn huddled closer to Luke, wanting to hide from the horror of the past few hours, trying to block out the pain of knowing what happened to Peter. She could only imagine the agony her brother must have lived through when he realized that Nathan was going to kill him.

The rest of that night came flooding back to her. Peter and Nathan had been having a beer while she'd been cooking

319

supper for the three of them. She hadn't heard the beginning of the argument, but knew it was escalating by the harsh tones in their voices.

Minutes later they'd come through the companionway door, and into the aft cabin where she heard them shouting and things breaking. Despite her pleas for them to stop, they'd climbed back up the stairs to the deck, Peter calling Nathan a liar, Nathan swearing and threatening Peter.

She'd been terrified, and had gone out on deck to stop them when....

Her body shook as the memories played across her mind like some macabre video.

"Robyn, darling. Hang on, we'll soon be ashore." She clung to Luke's words – her lifeline in her world of fear and confusion.

Unshed tears burned her throat. Peter was killed at the hands of a mad man, and she had stood by, unable to help her brother in any way. What she wouldn't give to see her brother, to say good-bye, to have him realize how much she missed him, and how much she would always miss him. To tell him what a great kid Jason was, how proud she was of both of them, all the things she hadn't had the time to say.

She loved her brother, and she would miss him for the rest of her life. Strangled sobs shook her body.

"Robyn, honey, I'm here." Luke held her tightly in his lap, smoothing her hair.

She clung to him, absorbing Luke's strength, the depth of his caring, and knew she could never willingly be apart from him again. Their closeness was complete, as if where one ended and the other started.

"Don't let go of me, will you?" she murmured into the softness of his neck.

"Never, ever, again will I let you out of my sight," he said, kissing her cheeks, her lips, warming her shaking body.

"I love you, Luke Carlisle."

"Not nearly as much as I love you," he said, his smile going straight to her heart.

"How and when did I get so lucky?"

"Luck has nothing to do with it."

Memories of the yacht leaped in her mind. "Luke, Sandy is on the yacht with Nathan," she said through chattering teeth.

"Yeah. Andrew has been in touch with the Coast Guard. They have the situation under control. Nathan is in custody. They found Brad's body."

"I know. Nathan shot him right in front of me. Brad tried to defend me, and Nathan shot him." Robyn couldn't cry for him, not now – not because she didn't care, but because she couldn't cry anymore.

Luke saw the anguish in her eyes. "Hey, it's going to be all right. Brad was a good friend in the end."

Luke couldn't bring himself to tell her that had Brad lived he would have been charged with smuggling illegal immi-grants. The plane he piloted to the airstrip in the wilds of Northern Maine had been impounded, the illegal immi-grants arrested, and Brad had only been allowed to return to Grand Island so that he could be watched to discover his contacts.

"It's all over."

Robyn buried her face in his chest. "It will never be over. Nathan killed Peter."

He wasn't sure he heard her correctly. "Say that again."

She repeated her words, her shaking intensifying as she slipped closer into shock.

"Hang on. Don't think about anything, only you and me,

and how we're going to be together." He hugged her to his body, warding off the pain in the only way he knew how.

Nathan killing Peter made sense in a bizarre way, given what he'd been told about the man's criminal operations. He could only imagine the motive, and he wasn't about to ask Robyn to explain.

A part of him wanted to climb onboard the yacht and kick the living shit out of the bastard, but that would be too easy. Luke forced the rage from his mind. Robyn needed him to help her deal with the trauma of what she had seen and heard. The officers who had come with him and the Coast Guard would look after the rest.

The professional in him knew he had a duty to perform, but his love for Robyn kept him with her. He belonged with her. He always would. Even if it meant giving up his career as a police officer, he would never again allow his professional life to distance him from his personal life. "What happened is over. It's not part of your life anymore. Concentrate instead on the fact that you're safe, and I plan to see to it that you're always safe."

There would be a time for all of the unpleasantness when the official investigation was underway.... For now, only one thing mattered.

Luke needed to say something he should have said days ago. Until a few hours ago, it didn't seem so urgent. Now, it was all he could think about.

"Robyn, I love you. I want you to marry me," he said, holding her tenderly.

At first she didn't answer.

"Anyone home?" he asked, kidding her a little.

Slowly, she lifted her head and looked into his face. Wet, exhausted and shivering, she had never looked more beautiful.

"I love you too." The depth of the feeling in her eyes made him want to leap with joy.

"I'm getting you out of here, now." Luke grinned as he kissed her chilled lips, and was immensely relieved when she kissed him back. He cuddled her closer to him, sheltering her from the cool wind created by the speeding patrol boat. "I want the love of my life to be warm and dry when I make my formal proposal of marriage."

"Marry you?" Robyn's lips moved over the skin along his neck. "Now?"

"Like I said, I'll present the proposal when you're safely tucked away in my house with a glass of wine."

Robyn eased her arms around his neck, and the kiss she gave him sent heat surging through him. She lifted her mouth from his, and peered into his eyes. "You're serious."

"Never more." He kissed her nose playfully.

Robyn snuggled closer. "Let's go home."

THE END

I am so happy to know that you read Desperate Memories. This story came to me while I was vacationing on Grand Manan Island, a lovely remote island off the coast of Canada. Many months later, I finished writing this story. If you enjoyed reading Desperate Memories I would love you to write a review for me by visiting my book page on Amazon.

This book is part of my Women in Danger series, each book written about women who find themselves threatened and in danger of losing their lives.

My next book, Desperate Acts is about a woman whose perfect life is destroyed by an unthinkable act of revenge. Here is a short excerpt;

Chapter One

Terra Cameron would remember this moment for the rest of her life.

The soft light of the moon spread over their naked bodies as she snuggled next to her husband, Sean. Happy didn't begin to describe how she felt. "Honey, what are you thinking about?" she asked, trailing her fingers over his jaw, feeling the beginning of light stubble growing there. "That the sooner you're pregnant the better. I want a house full of kids." "Sean!" She pretended to be shocked. "We've been married all of eight months."

"So?" he asked, his mouth caressing the soft skin between her breasts.

"So does this mean you don't want dessert?" she asked, her body melting under his touch.

"You *are* dessert," he said, his voice a husky whisper as he kissed her neck. "Not that the dinner you made wasn't spectacular. It was." He smoothed her hair away from her face, his eyes dark and impenetrable in the soft light of the bedroom.

She loved Sean Cameron with every fiber of her being. He was her life, her future, and now with a baby on the way, they had a whole new experience to look forward to. She had made dinner, planned every part of it down to the last bite, all to make the night ahead the most wonderful night of their lives. She couldn't wait to see the happiness on his face when she told him she was pregnant. "If we're going to spend the rest of the evening in bed, I'd better close up the house." "I'm here, ready to make love to you, and you're worried about locking up?" he asked, his dark blue eyes focused solely on her. "I already checked. Every door in this house is locked."

"But did you put the alarm system on? I need to have the alarm on, you know that." Taking her hand in his, he kissed each finger, slowly and deliberately. "Some day I'm going to cure you of your fears...all of them," he whispered.

She'd like to simply curl up next to him, lose herself and for just one whole night, not think about anything, including the past. "I'll be right back," she said, pulling her hand away from his lips and reaching for her white robe.

"Just you remember what's waiting for you right here," he called as she headed down the hall toward the door to the garage and the security system keypad.

She passed the living room and dining room where the high ceiling reflected the shimmering light from the back garden fountain. She imagined this space filled to over-flowing with baby things, lots of baby things... In the kitchen the dishes from the evening meal were scattered over the counters, the cluttered stovetop stood quietly in the semi-darkness. "I'll clean this in the morning," she whispered into the silence.

Reaching the back entrance, she punched the 'stay' button

on the pad. 'System failure. Door ajar' displayed on the screen.

"Shoot! One of us must have left the door to the lower deck open," she muttered, smoothing her tangled hair off her face as she went down the stairs leading to the lower level. She was sure she'd closed the door after they came in from the deck...so sure... And Sean had said he'd locked all the doors.

Reaching the bottom of the stairs, she hit the switch and the room was bathed in soft light from the ceiling pot lights.

This was Sean's favorite room in the house, one he'd spent hours planning and designing. He called it his man cave— and it was, with its home theatre and general all round space for her husband. As she made her way around the corner, past the wall-mounted television and the wet bar she saw the French doors that led to the stone patio.

They were open. The motion detector light cast a hard blaze of light on the outdoor space. Her heart tripping wildly against her ribs, she closed the door and locked it before moving back toward the stairs.

Just then someone moved out from the shadowy space beside the bookcase next to the French doors.

Gasping in surprise, she stumbled back, nearly falling.

Another man appeared beside her, his face covered in a black mask.

"Don't move," he said.

A scream started in her throat, extinguished immediately by a large hand covering her mouth. Powerful arms pulled her backwards, crushing her chest. "What have we here?" Terrified she struggled against him. His grip tightened.

"You utter one sound and I'll kill you," the intruder said, his voice soft and sure. "Where's your husband?" he demanded, yanking her back against him, lifting her feet off the floor.

Panic clouded her vision, trapping her mind, her body trembling. "Bedroom," she choked out the word, pointing toward the ceiling.

"Nice, real nice. That's where we're going." He dragged her across the floor. His fingers squeezed her left breast— her yelp of pain was muffled by his hand.

"Like I said, shut up. We're not here to hurt you. We're looking for that bastard you married. He's going to die for what he did."

You can purchase this next book on Amazon

To learn more about Stella and her books visit her website:
www.stellamaclean.com

While visiting her website, join her newsletter group for all the latest news and quick previews of upcoming books and events.

ABOUT THE AUTHOR

Stella MacLean is a story teller. Simple as that.

An author of books, both fiction and nonfiction, she has served as Writer in Residence at Vancouver Public Library in Vancouver, British Columbia. She loves to travel, spend time with friends and family, along with her husband and her fur babies in her home near the Bay of Fundy in Atlantic Canada.

Stella relishes the hours she spends hiding out in her office making up stories about the lives of imaginary people. Having found love again in the third act of her life, Stella enjoys telling stories about people who find love elusive and complicated, but still try with all their hearts.

Stella's past includes being a registered nurse, from which she has drawn story ideas for several of her books. She went back to university when her children were older and was granted a Commerce Degree, majoring in Accounting, from Mount Allison University in Sackville, New Brunswick, Canada.

OTHER BOOKS FOR YOUR KINDLE BY STELLA MACLEAN

THE RIGHT GUY SERIES

Finding Mr. Wrong

Finding Mr. Gorgeous

Finding Mr. Valentine

Finding Mr. Fixit

Finding Mr. Amazing

LOVE ALWAYS SERIES

Remembering You

The Good Daughter

LOVE IS ETERNAL

Young Love

Of Love and Life

WOMEN IN DANGER

Unimaginable

Desperate Memories

Desperate Acts

Falling Prey

HARLEQUIN BOOKS

Unexpected Attraction

Bringing Emma Home

NON-FICTION

Living Successfully With Chronic Pain

* 9 7 8 0 9 8 7 8 2 9 5 4 2 *